DUTY CALLS

ON PERIREMUNDA THE populace are rioting. With local forces unable to contain the widespread civil disorder, Commissar Cain and his regiment of Valhallans are called in to help. However, it seems there is more to the rebellion than first appeared and Cain suspects sinister forces at work behind the scenes. When the commissar is reunited with Inquisitor Amberley Vail his fears are realised as he is thrown into a deadly conspiracy that even he might not be able to emerge from alive.

For Hester: Chaos incarnate.

A BLACK LIBRARY PUBLICATION

First published in Great Britain in 2007 by
BL Publishing,
Games Workshop Ltd.,
Willow Road, Nottingham,
NG7 2WS, UK.

10 9 8 7 6 5 4 3 2 1

Cover illustration by Clint Langley.

A CIP record for this book is available from the British Library.

ISBN 13: 978 1 84416 465 3
ISBN 10: 1 84416 465 9

Distributed in the US by Simon & Schuster
1230 Avenue of the Americas, New York, NY 10020, US.

This is a work of fiction. All the characters and events portrayed in this
book are fictional, and any resemblance to real people or incidents is
purely coincidental.

See the Black Library on the Internet at
www.blacklibrary.com

Find out more about Games Workshop
and the world of Warhammer 40,000 at
www.games-workshop.com

IT IS THE 41st millennium. For more than a hundred centuries the Emperor has sat immobile on the Golden Throne of Earth. He is the master of mankind by the will of the gods, and master of a million worlds by the might of his inexhaustible armies. He is a rotting carcass writhing invisibly with power from the Dark Age of Technology. He is the Carrion Lord of the Imperium for whom a thousand souls are sacrificed every day, so that he may never truly die.

YET EVEN IN his deathless state, the Emperor continues his eternal vigilance. Mighty battlefleets cross the daemon-infested miasma of the warp, the only route between distant stars, their way lit by the Astronomican, the psychic manifestation of the Emperor's will. Vast armies give battle in His name on uncounted worlds. Greatest amongst his soldiers are the Adeptus Astartes, the Space Marines, bio-engineered super-warriors. Their comrades in arms are legion: the Imperial Guard and countless planetary defence forces, the ever-vigilant Inquisition and the tech-priests of the Adeptus Mechanicus to name only a few. But for all their multitudes, they are barely enough to hold off the ever-present threat from aliens, heretics, mutants – and worse.

TO BE A man in such times is to be one amongst untold billions. It is to live in the cruellest and most bloody regime imaginable. These are the tales of those times. Forget the power of technology and science, for so much has been forgotten, never to be re-learned. Forget the promise of progress and understanding, for in the grim dark future there is only war. There is no peace amongst the stars, only an eternity of carnage and slaughter, and the laughter of thirsting gods.

Editorial Note:

Cain has alluded on many occasions, in the portions of his memoirs that I have so far had time to edit and disseminate, to the fact that from time to time he became embroiled in Inquisitorial matters, usually at my behest. Not unnaturally the circumstances under which he became an active, albeit invariably reluctant, agent of His Majesty's most holy Inquisition have become a matter of some speculation among my fellow inquisitors, and it is with this in mind that I chose the following extract from the Cain Archive to circulate next. Here, in his own words, is his account of the first occasion on which I was able to make use of his somewhat dubious talents following our initial meeting on Gravalax a couple of years before.

Astute readers will realise that some elements of this present narrative were foreshadowed in my previous selection, Cain's account of his activities during the First Siege of Perlia. This

extract, however, deals with events that occurred a dozen years later than that, early in his period of service with the Valhallan 597th; when Cain refers back to his previous experiences, it should be remembered that he's doing so with a considerable degree of hindsight (though not as much as he was to acquire later, during the Second Siege of 999 M41, at the height of the Thirteenth Black Crusade).

As always, Cain's account of events tends to concentrate on his own part in them to the virtual exclusion of any other considerations, and, as always, I've attempted to redress this by interpolating material from other sources whenever it seems appropriate. Unfortunately one of the most reliable, and least readable, eyewitnesses from this period of his career continues to be Jenit Sulla, whose redoubtable martial skills are once more unleashed on the defenceless Gothic language. Readers possessing any more than the most rudimentary appreciation for literature may wish to omit these passages, feeling that the additional clarity they provide is scant recompense for the ordeal of wading through them.

Despite my own involvement in much of what follows I have resisted the temptation to comment directly at any great length, confining myself as usual to such footnotes and occasional other interjections as seemed appropriate, and breaking the original unstructured account into chapters for easier reading. The bulk of the narrative, as always, remains unadulterated Cain.

Amberley Vail, Ordo Xenos

CHAPTER ONE

IF I'D HAD any hopes of a quiet life once we got to Periremunda, they didn't last for very long. Mind you, these things are relative. By the time we arrived the regiment had spent almost half a year in the warp, with only a few days spent in real space on Simia Orichalcae and a rather longer period being comprehensively debriefed by Amberley and her Inquisition lackeys on Coronus Prime after our unexpected return there,[1] so even the fact that the entire planet seemed on the verge of imploding into anarchy wasn't able to diminish the troopers' enthusiasm at finding themselves back on terra firma for the foreseeable future. In fact the prospect of getting stuck into a flesh and blood enemy,

---

1. *Cain and the 597th had stumbled across a necron tomb on the ice world they'd been sent to defend from an orkish incursion. It's a testament to Cain's considerable resourcefulness that so many of them survived the experience.*

instead of the blank-faced metal horrors we'd faced on
their frozen tomb world, was a positive bonus so far as
most of them were concerned.

'At least these bastards can bleed,' Major Broklaw
said, summing up the mood of the regiment in his
typically forthright manner.

Colonel Kasteen, commanding officer of the
597th, nodded judiciously, concurring with her exec-
utive officer's assessment. 'Anyone know what they're
revolting about?' she asked.

I shrugged. 'Haven't a clue,' I admitted. As usual I
hadn't bothered reading the background briefing
provided by the Munitorum, and, as usual, it
seemed, I hadn't missed much. I knew that Broklaw
was punctilious about such things, if only to save
Kasteen the bother of wading through the verbiage
herself by providing her with a cogent summary, and
if neither of them was aware of the reason that half
the planet seemed on the verge of erupting into
armed rebellion the answer clearly wasn't to be
found among the data files. 'These situations are so
fluid that all the news we had when we left Coronus
will be completely out of date by now anyway.'

Both officers nodded in agreement, and as so often
before I was struck by the contrast between them;
Kasteen's red hair and blue eyes stood out vividly
against her pale complexion and the muted tones of
her uniform, while Broklaw's slate-grey irises almost
matched the colours of his clothing, combining with
his dark hair and equally pale features[1] to make him
appear to merge with the shadows surrounding him.

---

1. *A common characteristic of iceworlders, who, in the nature of things,
tend not to get out much, at least if they can avoid it.*

We were standing in the quietest corner we could find of what was in the process of becoming our command centre, leaning on the railing of a metal gantry overlooking the wide rockrete floor. Below us troopers lugged boxes and equipment around, arguing heatedly with one other over where they were supposed to go, and our enginseers connected cables with what seemed to me to be an almost wilful disregard of potential trip hazards or accidental electrocution. (Since most of them were at least as much metal as flesh, I don't suppose the odd jolt of electricity would have bothered them too much in any case. Some of them even seemed to like it.)

In other words our deployment was proceeding as efficiently as it ever did, and as usual I was content to stand back and let the lower orders get on with the grunt work while I considered the wider issues, like how to ensure that my own stay on this peculiar world remained as comfortable as possible. In this I had the inestimable assistance of Jurgen, my aide, whose degree of indispensability was matched only by the power of his body odour. Secure in the knowledge that even now he was sequestering the most desirable quarters for my own use, and was setting up my office in a suitably inaccessible location, so that I need only be bothered with the most pressing of duties, I returned my attention to the conversation.

'Why do the peasants ever revolt?' Broklaw asked rhetorically. It can hardly be denied that uprisings occur right across the Imperium with monotonous regularity, only to be put down with commendable vigour by the appropriate authorities, to the extent that in themselves they're hardly a remarkable event.

In general they tend to be spontaneous and barely organised, sparked by a particular grievance or sense of injustice, and easily contained by the local law enforcement agencies or Planetary Defence Forces. But the insurrection on Periremunda was different.

For one thing, it was rare for a co-ordinated campaign of violence to break out across the entire surface of a planet almost simultaneously, without any of the usual warning signs like riots, protests, or the burning of the governor in effigy[1] cropping up beforehand. It was even more rare where the planet in question was, for the most part, quietly prosperous, with an unimaginative and Emperor-fearing population, and a governor who actually appeared to care about the welfare of his citizens. And for almost a dozen Imperial Guard regiments to be deployed in response was almost unprecedented. That implied that someone high up in the subsector command staff thought the PDF couldn't be relied on to contain the situation if it continued to deteriorate, which implied in turn that their loyalty was suspect. And that, you may be sure, was enough to set the palms of my hands itching, in the uncomfortable fashion that they tended to do when my subconscious was joining dots and coming up with a picture that my forebrain really wouldn't like at all if it had been able to bring it into focus.

'There's bound to be a briefing,' Kasteen said, following the swearing, sweating troopers lugging her desk into the office that she'd earmarked for her personal use almost as soon as we'd taken possession of

---

1. Or *occasionally in person.*

the jumble of warehouses that had been allocated to us as a staging area and makeshift garrison, on the periphery of the starport landing field. On the one hand that suited me very nicely; I always like to feel I'm close to a line of retreat if things turn out badly, and a pad full of orbit-capable shuttles within easy running distance is about as good as it gets. On the other, though, it meant we were nicely situated for rapid deployment by dropship to anywhere trouble might flare up, and if my itching palms were anything to go by, it wasn't likely to take too long to materialise.

Another gaggle of troopers scurried in and out of Kasteen's cubbyhole with chairs to go along with the desk, and we all sat, looking out over the floor of the warehouse again. She'd chosen well, I thought, one of a line of glass-fronted cubicles on a mezzanine gallery roughly halfway up the wall facing the big doors fronting the loading docks. From here she'd have a commanding view of everything going on in the main body of the building.

And outside it, too, at the moment; the doors were open, admitting a steady stream of laden troopers, lugging boxes from the backs of the trucks backed up to the loading bays, and a flurry of snowflakes from the open expanse of rockrete outside where our Chimeras were snarling their way through a thin film of freezing slush. By Valhallan standards, of course, it was warm enough, most of the men and women I could see still in their shirtsleeves, some of which were even rolled up. It was chilly for me, though, and I was as grateful as ever for my commissarial greatcoat, into which I huddled, trying to ignore the

draught punching its way in through the open door. Abruptly the chill breeze became imbued with the odour of month-old socks left to marinate in compost, and my aide appeared in the gap.

'Tanna, sir?' he asked, depositing a tray on the newly installed slab of wood between us.

'Thank you, Jurgen,' I said, accepting the fragrant beverage gratefully, while he handed tea bowls to Kasteen and Broklaw, who held their breath almost by reflex as he moved closer. They sipped their drinks thoughtfully, and I tried to restrain the impulse to gulp mine, feeling the warmth spreading gradually through my body as I swallowed. Jurgen refilled my bowl.

'You're welcome sir.' He handed me a message slate. 'This came in for you a few minutes ago.' I took and scanned it, and glanced up at the two officers.

'Well,' I said, trying to restrain my sudden flare of enthusiasm at the prospect of being able to skive off to somewhere a bit warmer for a while. 'This might give us a few answers, I suppose.'

'Who's it from?' Kasteen asked, her surprise showing in her voice. We'd only been dirtside for a few hours, hardly long enough for anyone on Periremunda to be aware of our presence yet, let alone send us messages.

'The local arbitrator,'[1] I said. I skimmed the slate across the desk, so she could read it. 'He wants to discuss jurisdictional protocols, in case our boys and girls get a little over-exuberant in their off-time.' This

---

1. Like many provincial worlds, Periremunda had only one resident representative of the Adeptus Arbites, charged with overseeing the work of the local law enforcement agencies.

was a common enough request when a Guard regiment or two pitched up on a planet somewhere, so that when the troopers started getting into mischief (which they invariably did, or my job would have been pretty pointless) everyone involved knew whether they should be handed over to the local courts, the military provosts, or directly to the Commissariat.

Of course you'd probably get as many different answers to that as there were commissars on the planet, but in my case I always asked for any of our troopers who got into trouble to be remanded directly into my custody, a habit I'd got into right at the beginning of my career with the 12th Field Artillery, and seen no reason to break in the years since. For one thing it fostered the impression among the troopers that I cared about their welfare, and would always go out of my way to take care of one of our own, which was good for morale generally, and for another it gave me a good excuse to leave the regiment in search of more congenial activities on a fairly regular basis. On the occasions I couldn't be bothered, or was genuinely too busy, I could always rely on Jurgen to take care of the paperwork. I shrugged. 'I suppose I could just call him back, but...'

'You're thinking of going in person?' Kasteen asked.

I nodded. 'I'm sure he'd appreciate the courtesy, and it never hurts to make a good impression.' Not to mention the fact that the planetary capital was a good couple of thousand metres lower, and a damn sight warmer, than Hoarfell, where we were currently stationed.

Broklaw looked concerned. 'Get some rest first, at least,' he counselled. 'You've been on your feet since we made orbit.'

'No longer than anyone else,' I said, contriving to look as if I was stifling a yawn. In truth I wasn't all that tired, having managed to catch a short nap on the shuttle trip down, which had not only refreshed me a little but had conferred the added bonus of avoiding Jurgen's inevitable discomfiture at being airborne in an atmosphere. I'd never known him to actually be sick, such a thing being beneath the dignity he fondly imagined was conferred on him by his exalted position as a commissar's personal aide, but his anxiety about the possibility tended to combine with the physical nausea to make him sweat like an ork, which in turn would ripen his habitual bouquet to quite an astonishing degree. I shrugged. 'Besides, it's too good a chance to miss. If anyone can tell us what's really going on here, it's the local arbitrator.'

'Good point,' Kasteen said. 'If you think you're up to it.' She looked at me narrowly. 'Anything you can get out of him is bound to be more reliable than the pap we get through the usual channels.'

'My thought exactly,' I said, 'and the more we know about what we're facing here, the better we'll be able to deal with it.' Words that were to have something of a hollow ring, in retrospect, but at that point I had no idea just how little anyone really knew about the true state of affairs on Periremunda, apart from a handful of people who knew altogether too much for comfort.

Editorial Note:

Although Cain is reasonably explicit about the topographical peculiarities of Periremunda, he only bothers to be so when they impinge in some manner on his own experience; something which is, of course, entirely consistent with his attitude throughout the archive. I have therefore interpolated the following extract, which I hope will make much of what follows a little more readily comprehensible.

From *Interesting Places and Tedious People: A Wanderer's Waybook* by Jerval Sekara, 145 M39

LIKE MANY WORLDS with unusual characteristics, the early history of Periremunda is shrouded in conjecture and legend. One can be reasonably certain that it was originally discovered some time around the

middle of M24 by the explorator Acer Alba, only to be promptly forgotten again due to his untimely demise, probably in an affair of honour over the affections of a courtesan. Following the rediscovery of Alba's notes by Magos Provocare, a tireless challenger of the unknown whose unorthodox views frequently attracted the opprobrium of his peers, the planet was eventually colonised in the early years of the 27th millennium.

What makes it worthy of the discriminating wayfarer's attention, at least for a short while, is the fact that by any reasonable definition of the phrase the world as a whole is uninhabitable. The equatorial regions are not so much hot as literally molten, the rock itself bubbling from below the ground in a constantly shifting sea of liquid magma, while the rest of the surface is a desiccated desert in which nothing seems able to live. There are, however, scattered pockets of habitability, no less comfortable than other, more Emperor-favoured worlds. Vast plateaux, too many to count, soar upwards from this arid foundation to heights sufficient to take them into the cooler air where life itself is possible, and hundreds of the larger ones, which can stretch for tens of kilometres across, boast cities, farms, and manufactoria equal to those of the fairer globes most of us are pleased to call home.

Climate and temperature are more a matter of altitude than geography here, enabling the jaded traveller to experience a wide variety of environments with little more effort than that required to hire an aircar and

chauffeur, although, as is so often the case with back-water planets, some caution is advised when attempting to find accommodation, as even the most prestigious local establishments can, on closer inspection, turn out to be somewhat basic in the facilities they offer.

CHAPTER TWO

IN THE EVENT, the arbitrator was suitably flattered by my request to discuss our business in person, not least, it seemed, because my reputation had preceded me as it so often does, and scarcely another hour had passed before I found the ground dropping away beneath me once again. Jurgen had managed to secure us seats on a courier shuttle with urgent business in Principia Mons[1], his manifest pride in being able to find us transport so quickly only partially mitigated by the realisation that having done so meant having to get airborne again for the second time in one day. Nevertheless he bore this travail with the phlegmatic

---

1. *The planetary capital. Technically the somewhat unimaginative name referred to the plateau on which the city was built, but since the equally dully named Principia Urbi had sprawled out to encompass most of it, the two had become virtually synonymous. If Cain was ever aware of the distinction, he makes no mention of the fact.*

stoicism with which he accepted everything else, only the thickening of the air around him and the whitening of his knuckles mute testament to the discomfort he felt even before we'd left the pad. (Although, being Jurgen, I suppose it would be a little more accurate to say that his knuckles went a paler shade of grime.) It would probably have suited both of us better if I'd left him behind, but protocol demanded that my aide accompany me on an official visit to an Imperial official of such exalted rank, so we'd both have to make the best of it, Jurgen trying to ignore the discomfort of his rebellious stomach, and me trying not to picture the reaction of the arbitrator when I turned up with him in tow.

Perhaps it was for that reason that I turned my attention to the landscape falling away beneath us, getting my first real glimpse of the planet that we'd come so far to protect. I knew intellectually that we were perched on the highest and most desolate plateau of this patchwork world, but seeing the reality from the air brought the strangeness of our position home to me in a manner that no amount of background briefing would ever have been able to do. Hoarfell was huge, so many kloms[1] across that disembarking from the dropship had felt like stepping out onto any other planet in the Imperium. Now, as our shuttle banked away to the south-east, I found myself able to appreciate the sheer scale of it for the first time.

The first thing to attract my attention was the field at which we'd landed, and which, like most of the

---

1. *Kilometres; a common Valhallan colloquialism that Cain had picked up, among others, from his prolonged association with the natives of that world.*

other dirtside facilities scattered across the face of the planet, combined the functions of a starport with those of an aerodrome for the local traffic. This was, of course, considerable, given the peculiar topography of the place. With very few exceptions, where adjacent inhabited plateaux were both close enough and sufficiently similar in height to allow the construction of viaducts between them, taking to the skies was the only way to shift anything from one tiny island of life to another. As a result the amount of air traffic criss-crossing the globe was truly staggering, given its relatively modest population of a mere billion or so. Even on the short trip to Principia Mons, which took less than an hour, I caught sight of innumerable other aircraft, ranging from two-seater skycars to wallowing cargo dirigibles the size of warehouses, around which swarms of smaller planes buzzed like insects.

As we rose above the city of Darien, the densest concentration of citizens on Hoarfell, I found myself being put in mind of the firewasp nest I'd stumbled across on Calcifrie (which had turned out to be remarkably useful in deterring the party of eldar reavers pursuing me at the time, but I digress), a never-ending swarm of bright metal insects swirling about the landing pads as they receded into the distance. Though the densest concentration of aircraft was hovering above the aerodrome there were plenty of others buzzing around the rest of the city, private skimmers and aircars for the most part. I made a mental note to suggest to Kasteen that we get our Hydras deployed as soon as possible; rather too many pilots were crossing the space above our garrison for

my liking. In the event, of course, she was well ahead of me, and by the time I returned she'd already imposed an exclusion zone in a wide enough radius around us to seriously irritate the local traffic controllers.[1]

As we rose higher, away from the city itself, I was able to get a better view of the landscape surrounding it, a wilderness of snow and ice through which hills and escarpments in muted tones of black and grey rose to pierce the leaden clouds above them, so that it was hard to tell where rock ended and vapour began. Somewhere out there was the highest point on the planet, but which of the vague blobs in the distance it was I couldn't tell even if I'd cared.

Then, suddenly, with shocking abruptness, the landscape vanished. I just had time for the briefest of glimpses of a sheer cliff face of quite staggering proportions receding into the depths beneath us, which were swallowed by the all-enveloping murk, before we were cocooned in a bubble of mist that wrapped itself around our fragile little craft and blotted out the world.

HAPPILY, OUR FIRST sight of Principia Mons was far more propitious. As we descended the clouds grew thinner, merely whitening at first, until finally they broke altogether, allowing shafts of bright sunlight to break through, and revealing a sky of quite

---

1. *So much so that the prohibition was flouted several times by local civilians, until a 'warning shot' downed an aircar full of city aldermen returning from a banquet at the halls of the Fabricator's Guild, fortunately without doing serious injury to anyone of consequence. After that, it seems to have been followed to the letter.*

remarkably vivid blue. (Or so it seemed to me, but then I'd been stuck onboard a succession of starships for most of the last few months.) Jurgen seemed no more uncomfortable than usual, so I left him to his own devices, and glanced out of the window again, eager to see what the absence of clouds would reveal.

It's no exaggeration to say that I've seen some remarkable sights in my time, from the spires of Holy Terra itself to the aurorae of Fabulon, but the landscape of Periremunda was in a class of its own. Beneath us the last vestiges of rain evanesced into vapour, rising again to form more clouds without ever reaching the sere and barren surface of the world below, where bare, baking rock alternated with oceans of drifting sand.

Once we flew over a sandstorm, which would have stripped the flesh from the bones of an unprotected man within seconds, kilometres high, but still so far below us as to seem like a thin film of dust seeping across the planet's surface. The eye-stabbing flicker of electrical discharges sparked and flashed deep within it, an uncanny echo of the rolling sonic boom that trailed in the wake of our hurtling aircraft. And in all directions, as far as the eye could see, rose columns of rock, each separated from its nearest neighbour by tens or hundreds of kilometres, to stand proud and alone, like the trunks of some immense petrified forest.

From above they seemed refulgent, glowing with life, in stark contrast to the magnificent desolation surrounding them. As we passed close to a few I was able to discern forests and lakes, hills and valleys,

and the unmistakable signs of human habitation, all preserved in miniature, like the vivaria sometimes maintained by curious children or noble dilettantes.

We must have crossed or skirted some dozen or so of these remarkable spires on our journey, although most flashed past so quickly I barely had time to take in any details. Some were relatively open, appearing to support agricultural communities of some kind, while others seemed completely over-grown, choked by a profusion of tangled vegetation that only a Catachan could love. A few seemed to support communities the size of small towns, while others, barely a kilometre across, seemed completely uninhabited.

I dredged up from somewhere the statistic that roughly eighteen thousand of the plateaux scattered across the planet held a population of some sort or another,[1] and shuddered at the logistical problems that implied for the Imperial Guard forces waiting to be deployed in their defence. Even split down into individual squads, which would be absurd, a mere dozen regiments could never hope to cover a frac-tion of them. All we could do was wait, and hope our enemies showed their faces openly somewhere we could concentrate our forces against them. A pretty forlorn hope, of course, if they knew what they were doing, and what little indication we'd had so far seemed to confirm that they did. If ever a planet seemed ideally suited for guerrilla warfare, Periremunda was it.

---

1. *Which implies that, despite his assertion to the contrary, he probably at least skimmed through the briefing materials on the voyage out from Coronus.*

Perhaps fortunately I had little time for any more such pessimistic musings, as Jurgen finally roused himself with an expression of hopeful inquiry.

'Do you think that's it, sir?' he asked.

I nodded. 'Must be,' I said. There could only be a few truly urban areas on a world like this, and I doubted that any of the others would be quite as dense as this one. A faint tremor passed through the airframe of our tiny craft as, once again, we became slower than the sound of our passage, and the pitch of the engines fell, allowing us the leisure to contemplate the city as we drifted in towards the landing field.

Principia Mons was, in many ways, gratifyingly familiar, the surface of the plateau covered in the sprawling jumble of hab units, manufactoria, temples and other such structures that can generally be seen on the approaches to any reasonably populous city throughout the Imperium. A few open areas remained unbuilt on, chiefly bordering the precipitous drop edging this peculiar eyrie. There were a handful of parks scattered across the outer fringes of the city, and a further one almost in the centre, which seemed to have a fortified enclave of some kind in the middle of it[1], but for the most part the place seemed completely urbanised.

As we approached I could see that the top kilometre or so of the spire had been honeycombed with tunnels, leaving structures and industrial units

---

1. *The gardens of the governor's palace: unusually, these were divided into an inner garden, to which access was strictly limited to members of his household, and an outer park, open to the citizens of the city on festivals and holidays.*

clinging to the side of the rock. The effect was not entirely unreminiscent of a hive, and I felt a faint warm glow of nostalgia at the thought.[1] It didn't last long, though, being swiftly replaced by the realisation that despite its elevated position the planetary capital possessed an undercity to rival that of a more conventional community. In my experience troublemakers tended to gravitate into them like sump rats down a waste pipe, where they were Horus's own job to winkle out again.

Not my problem, though, I told myself firmly, having had more than enough of that sort of thing on Gravalax and Simia Orichalcae. In any case my place was with the 597th on Hoarfell, which, cold and uninviting as it was, at least had the advantage of being comfortably free of tunnels where heretics might go to ground. I had no more time for such musings, however, as a sudden surge of pressure against my spine told me that the landing thrusters had just cut in, and within moments, it seemed, we were back on terra firma, to Jurgen's eloquently unspoken relief.

We disembarked into a fresh breeze, lightly scented with the odours of burnt promethium and cooling metal, but welcome for all that, and I squinted reflexively. The sun was still some way above the horizon, and although the first blush of sunset was beginning to tint the clouds above us, it still seemed dazzling after the cheerless gloom of the snow clouds blanketing Darien. It felt pleasantly

---

1. *Cain alludes in many places throughout the archive to having been native to a hiveworld, but precisely which one remains obscure.*

warm, too, and I unfastened my coat, stepping
upwind of Jurgen as I did so. I'd served with him
long enough to realise that the sudden increase in
temperature would soon have a similar effect on his
body odour. I glanced around, orientating myself.

'We seem to have been expected,' I remarked. A
groundcar was making its way across the expanse of
rockrete between us and the terminal building,
flanked by a pair of outriders perched over the
wheels of their gently-humming monocycles,
pennants on its front wings bearing the device of the
Adeptus Arbites snapping in the wind. My aide
nodded, sidestepping a servitor, which seemed so
intent on recovering the packages from the courier
plane's hold that it didn't even register our presence.

'They're doing the thing in style,' he agreed, a hint
of approval entering his voice. If there was one thing
Jurgen relished, apart from porno slates, it was a
punctilious adherence to protocol, preferably with
as much pomp and ceremony as possible. A Salamander or utility truck would have done just as well
for me, to be honest, even more so if I'd known
what that simple little piece of courtesy was going to
lead to, but I have to admit to feeling rather gratified
at the time. I didn't travel by limousine all that
often, and the effusiveness of the welcome being
extended to me augured well for the meeting when
we arrived.

The groundcar hissed to a halt at the foot of the
boarding ramp, and a young man in a neatly
tailored uniform hopped out to meet us, with a
crisp salute to me, and a sidelong look of barely-
suppressed astonishment at Jurgen.

'Commissar Cain?' he asked, as though there could
be any possible doubt of the fact, and I nodded,
returning the salute in my best parade-ground
manner.

'That's right.' I indicated my malodorous companion. 'This is my personal aide, Gunner[1] Feric Jurgen.'

'Justicar[2] Billem Nyte.' The young man nodded at
Jurgen with as much courtesy as he could muster, no
doubt noting the contrast between his own immaculate uniform and the rather haphazard manner in
which my aide's seemed to be not so much clothing
his body as just hanging about in its general vicinity.
'Arbitrator Keesh sent me to pick you up.'

'That was very thoughtful,' I said, nodding a greeting to the outriders as I settled into a seat so
over-upholstered that for a moment I thought I'd
need my chainsword to cut my way out of it again.
Neither of our escorts seemed to notice me, although
the blank reflective visors of their helmets made it
difficult to be sure. I fought down a fleeting memory
of the necron warriors we'd faced so recently, and
opened the window as Jurgen squeezed in beside me,
unslinging his lasgun in order to fit it through the

---

1. *Jurgen had been serving with the 12th Field Artillery when Cain first
acquired his services, so his military rank was that of gunner rather than
the private or trooper more common among the line regiments of the
Imperial Guard.*

2. *The local name for law enforcers. As has been noted elsewhere the
accepted nomenclature for such officials varies widely from world to
world, and like many seasoned travellers Cain often refers to them simply as Arbites, despite the fact that they're merely subordinate to the
Adeptus rather than true members of it. In this case, however, as he usually does when he has contact with actual Adeptus Arbites functionaries,
he is precise about the distinction.*

door. (Like most troopers in the Guard, he would rather have cut his own arm off than go anywhere without it, an attitude I'd been more than grateful for on innumerable occasions.) 'I must say this is a great deal more comfortable than I was expecting.'

A small naalwood cabinet, which alone was probably worth more than the aircraft we'd arrived on, proved to contain six crystal goblets and a couple of decanters. Finding that one of them contained amasec of a quite exceptional age and piquancy I poured myself a generous measure and settled back to enjoy the ride.

'It's the arbitrator's personal vehicle,' Nyte told us with a hint of pride, no doubt revelling in his status as one of the few justicars allowed to play with it. 'I'm his amanuensis.'

'Then I'll be sure to thank him when I see him,' I said, noticing Jurgen's expression out of the corner of my eye, and moving quickly to forestall the inevitable jockeying for precedence that was bound to ensue between the two aides now that he'd realised Nyte was more than just a chauffeur. Nyte took the hint and returned to the driving seat, no doubt grateful for the sheet of armourcrys between him and the passenger compartment.

At first sight, Principia Mons seemed little different from any other Imperial city I'd visited in the last few years, apart from the visible lack of artillery damage. We hummed along a broad avenue between pleasingly proportioned buildings, the lack of space at the top of the plateau we were perched on not apparently having had an appreciable effect on the local architecture. I'd been expecting a rather more

jammed-together feel, but in general it all felt surprisingly open and uncluttered. After a while it occurred to me that this apparent contradiction explained the extensive undercity I'd noticed as we flew in: the Periremundans had simply built downwards instead of up. (Not something I'd have felt too happy about in their position, weakening the top of the pole I was perched on, but I supposed they knew what they were doing.)

All in all, then, it was a remarkably pleasant ride; at least until we got to the point where someone tried to kill us.

CHAPTER THREE

As AMBUSHES GO, I have to admit it was neatly and professionally executed. I suppose I should have expected something of the sort, having been warned before we left Coronus that the insurgents we faced appeared to be well organised and effective out of all proportion to their numbers, but the taste of unaccustomed luxury and the sheer normality of the street scene gliding past the window had lulled me into a false sense of security completely at odds with my normally reliable streak of paranoia.

Our outrider escort was clearing the way for us with flashing lights and wailing sirens, the constant flow of civilian traffic that would otherwise have impeded our progress scurrying out of the way with gratifying alacrity, so I wasn't too surprised to notice a larger, heavier monocycle trailing along in our

wake, taking advantage of the clear channel we were opening up to make much better speed than its rider could normally hope to manage along the crowded urban roads. I couldn't see much of his face, his head being protected by a helmet not dissimilar to those of our escorts apart from the vivid flame motif that flickered across it, echoing the red and yellow paintwork of his cycle and the crimson leathers both he and his passenger were wearing. The girl riding pillion with him was bareheaded though, apart from a pair of goggles, her auburn hair whipping back like a banner in the breeze of their passing, and I fought down the impulse to wave as they drew closer.

'What the hell...' Nyte said, his voice echoing in my comm-bead even as he jammed on the brakes with a suddenness that wrenched me from the embrace of the clinging upholstery and almost spilled my drink. There was a large transporter ahead of us, slewed across the carriageway, its cab section wedged against the supporting piers of an overhanging bridge. Evidently its driver had misjudged the distance in trying to pull over to let us pass, got stuck, and left the cargo trailer hanging out over the roadway, obstructing it. 'Get that thing out of the way!'

'I'm on it,' one of the outriders assured him, evidently on the same frequency, and accelerated away. A moment later he slewed to a halt next to the cab, and began a heated altercation with the driver.

'Something's not right,' I said, feeling the familiar warning tingle in the palms of my hands. The driver should have been getting out by now, assessing the damage at least, and deferring to the authority of the justicar haranguing him. Trusting my instincts

implicitly after all we'd been through together, Jurgen picked up the lasgun, which he'd left lying across his lap, and flicked the safety off.

'What do you mean, sir?' Nyte asked, an instant before the monocycle following us roared up alongside, and I found myself looking down the barrel of an automatic shotgun. The girl holding it smiled at me, the wide mouth in her angular face somehow seeming to hold too many teeth, and squeezed the trigger. A loud crack echoed around the luxurious cabin, and for a moment I wondered why I wasn't dead, before the distinctive smell of ionised air told me that Jurgen had managed to get his shot in first. The girl pitched backwards off the monocycle's pillion, and a heavy armour-piercing slug, evidently intended to shatter the armourcrys window they'd no doubt expected to be there (and which would have been, I suppose, had I been accompanied by anyone other than Jurgen), tore through the reinforced body shell centimetres from my shoulder instead.

'What the hell was that?' Nyte demanded, seeming rather slow on the uptake for an agent of Imperial justice, but then I suppose he was keeping his eye on the road.

'Ambush!' I said tersely, drawing my laspistol, but I never got the chance to use it on the rider beside us. Nyte reacted immediately, swinging the heavy vehicle, and ramming him off the road. Our would-be assassin hit the guardrail, performed an elegant parabola, and bounced off the support pier of the bridge ahead, which was still blocked by the frakking truck, of course.

'I can't get around it,' Nyte said, drifting into a skid that bounced us off another couple of groundcars and

left us coasting to a halt facing the wrong way and an apparently endless stream of gridlocked traffic, which began filling every square metre of rockrete in sight like water pouring into a bucket. A light cargo hauler belonging, according to the garish sign on its side, to a firm of sanitation engineers, slammed into the side of us, becoming inextricably wedged against the doors.

'This side's jammed too,' Jurgen offered helpfully, then fired another lasbolt at a civilian in a jacket patterned with a bile green and orange check, whose purple-dyed hair stood out around his head as though he'd just stuck a finger in a power socket. The jacket alone was offensive enough to justify his summary execution, although what had attracted Jurgen's attention was the rather more pragmatic matter of the shotgun he carried, the same type as the one the trick cyclists had tried to use on us a moment before, and no doubt would have done, if my perfectly understandable desire for fresh air hadn't allowed us to fire first.

'We're trapped!' Nyte said, sounding more angry than frightened, which I suppose would have been reassuring if I hadn't been panicking enough for the three of us. Vile Jacket dived for cover behind a car full of squawking civilians, who piled out and ran, and I glanced around hoping to catch sight of the confederates I knew must be around here somewhere. Fat chance of that, though, with my vision blocked in almost every direction.

'No we're not,' I said, thumbing my chainsword to maximum speed, and thrusting it over my head as I did so. The passenger compartment filled with sparks

and the smell of burning, but I was managing to cut through the reinforced metal, and after a moment I'd succeeded in removing a wide enough section of coachwork to worm my way out and up onto the roof.

I wasn't out there for long, though, you can be sure, as presenting an obvious target has never been very high on my list of desirable things to do. As I slithered down into whatever cover I could find, I tried hard to recall what I'd seen.

The shotgunner with the bad taste in jackets was in a good position to make life unpleasant for us the moment we raised our heads, or he was able to get a clear line of sight. I knew shotguns could be loaded with all kinds of surprises, and doubted that our antagonists, whoever they were, would confine themselves to anything as obvious as scattershot and slugs. The sheer number of milling civilians in the immediate vicinity made it almost impossible to guess just how many more of them were closing in on our position, but there was little doubt about where they were coming from. As I'd ducked back behind the reassuring bulk of the armoured limousine I'd seen the driver of the truck, which had blocked the road, leaping from the cab at last, a pistol of some kind in his hand.

'Seven hostiles closing on Rolling Justice,'[1] the outrider who'd been dispatched to deal with the obstruction in the first place reported. Then a crackle

---

1. *The regular call sign for the arbitrator's personal vehicle on Periremunda. Somewhat theatrical, but under most circumstances it was a pretty dull little world, so I suppose the justicars couldn't be blamed for trying to make a routine chauffeuring job sound a little more interesting.*

of gunfire erupted from that general direction. 'Correction, six moving, one down.'

'Rolin, Dawze, get back here!' Nyte ordered, his voice taking on the peculiar flat timbre of someone consciously working at staying in control, despite a jolt of adrenaline big enough to have woken a hibernating keth. 'All units in the vicinity, converge on these co-ordinates.'

'I'm still pinned,' the outrider responded, a crackle of small arms fire lending credence to his words. A second voice chimed in on the same channel, presumably the other one, wherever the hell he'd got to.

'I can see him, Dawze. He's behind that red speeder, your two o'clock. I can circle and take him.'

'Negative,' Nyte snapped. 'Get back here and guard the commissar.' Encouraging words, I'm sure you'll agree, but I'd got a good enough idea of the layout of things to realise just how much more easily said than done that was going to be. Rolin would have had a better chance of stopping an avalanche with a teaspoon than making any headway through the mess surrounding us, and that went for the reinforcements Nyte was calling in as well. If I was going to get out of this in one piece, I'd have to take care of matters myself, as usual.

Well, almost. A familiar odour behind me brought the welcome news that I'd been joined by the only assistance I knew I could rely on.

'The justicar's got one,' Jurgen confirmed, slithering into the gap between the rear bumper of our car and a motorised tricycle with a large metal box between its two front wheels. Judging by the aroma of soylens viridiens emanating from it, and the attire of its

startled rider, who goggled at us as though she'd suddenly been confronted by a pair of orks, the contraption was full of comestibles of some kind intended to be sold in the street. He raised his lasgun again, and spat a burst in the general direction of the shotgunner. 'Frak. Missed the gretch-frotter.' He glanced at the quietly bleating street vendor, and flushed. 'Sorry miss. Didn't realise there were ladies present.'

The sheer incongruity of his attempt at good manners seemed to reassure the girl that she wasn't hallucinating, at any rate, and she swallowed convulsively. 'Don't mind me,' she said, her voice quivering rather less than I would have expected. Apparently reassured as much as seemed feasible under the circumstances, she coughed nervously. 'Who are you people, anyway? And what in the warp's going on?'

'Ciaphas Cain, regimental Commissar, 597th Valhallan. My aide Jurgen. Terrorist attack,' I said, covering the basics as quickly as I could, and returning my attention to the important stuff. Dawze had at least disabled one, and was still engaged in a firefight with another. That left five hostiles potentially closing on our position. One of them we knew about, and he wasn't going anywhere, which left four unaccounted for. The palms of my hands began to tingle.

'Where are the other hostiles?' I voxed, hoping Rolin or Dawze might have a clue. No such luck.

'Lost them in the crowd,' Rolin said helpfully.

'Oh for frak's sake!' I said. 'Use your eyes! Everyone else will be running away!' A stubber round suddenly punched its way through the box on the trike, and its

owner squealed, diving behind my legs like a startled puppy. I looked up in time to see a young man in the robes of a low-level Administratum functionary standing on the roof of the sanitation truck, adjusting his aim. Before he could complete the motion I swung my chainsword up, taking his left leg off at the knee, and he toppled to the rockrete in front of us, where I was able to detach his head with a simple swipe. The snack-seller squealed again, the green streaks in her hair now augmented by a spatter of less flattering scarlet.

'One more down,' I reported. 'Nyte, where the hell are you?'

'On my way,' the justicar responded, appearing on the roof of the limousine at last, the heavy stubber in his hands accounting for the length of his absence; no doubt he'd been scrabbling in some carefully concealed weapons locker. He swung it, shredding the nose of the car behind which the shotgunner was sheltering with a hailstorm of high-calibre ordnance. Vile Jacket rolled out of the way, bringing up his own weapon, but before he could fire Jurgen took him in the torso with a short, controlled burst, and he twitched for a moment before lying still. Nyte turned to look at me, and flourished the stubber.

'Scratch three,' he said, a trace of smugness in his voice. Then before I could even say something helpful, like 'get the frak down, you idiot,' another shotgun blast took him full in the chest, and he fell heavily to the ground on the far side of the car. His torso armour seemed to have taken the brunt of it, but there was a lot of blood too. After a moment he hauled himself sufficiently close to vertical to slump

against the bodywork, still sitting on the carriageway, but he wasn't going to be putting up much of a fight from now on if I was any judge.

'Man down,' Jurgen said, as though it might have escaped my notice, but I suppose he could have meant it for our listening escorts.

'Engaging,' Rolin said, a moment before a crackle of small arms fire made that obvious. 'Two hostiles, female, look like they're carrying autoguns.' There was a moment's pause. 'One breaking for your position...' then his vox channel abruptly went dead.

'Rolin's down,' Dawze confirmed a moment later, 'and the hostile I've been engaging is pulling back.' A note of puzzlement entered his voice. 'Why would he do that? He had me pinned.'

'I don't know,' I said, the palms of my hands tingling in earnest now, 'but they seem remarkably well co-ordinated.' I looked at the rapidly cooling bodies of the terrorists we'd dispatched. None of them had any kind of comms gear with them that I could see. 'Can you spot anyone who seems to be in control?'

'Negative,' Dawze replied. A note of puzzlement entered his voice. 'Come to that, I haven't seen any of them so much as speak.' A horrible suspicion began to stir in the depths of my mind. I had no time to worry about that just at the moment, though, as a fusillade of incoming fire began rattling off the metal all around us.

'Emperor preserve us, we're going to die!' the snack vendor moaned, huddling so close to the rockrete she might have been trying to disguise herself as one of the road markings. Likely as that sounded, it was hardly helpful, so while Jurgen returned the favour

with a couple of unaimed bursts in the general direction most of the projectiles seemed to have come from, I looked her in the eye with my most commissarial expression of reassurance.

'We're not dead yet,' I said, with all the self-confidence I could muster, 'and we're not going to be. I swore an oath to protect the Imperium from the Emperor's enemies when I put this uniform on, and today, you're that part of the Imperium. All right…' I trailed off, suddenly remembering I had no idea what the girl's name was. She nodded, clearly divining my difficulty.

'Zemelda Cleat.' She took a deep breath, and straightened, picking up the stubber the young man had dropped when I trisected him. 'And I can take care of myself, thank you very much.'

'Good girl,' I said, reflecting that at least she might draw their fire, even if the chances of her hitting anything with the clumsy weapon were minimal. 'Tuck that into your shoulder, pull the trigger gently, and Emperor guide your aim.' She followed my instructions somewhat gingerly, wincing at the noise and the recoil, and then a feral grin stretched across her face.

'Brisk!' she said approvingly, and spat a steady stream of shot at our enemies, who, now I came to think of it, seemed remarkably reluctant to take advantage of their still superior firepower.

'Why aren't they advancing?' Jurgen asked, not really expecting an answer. 'They've got us completely boxed in.'

'Maybe they're waiting for us to panic,' I said, trying to sound as though that was a remote possibility

rather than the current state of affairs, at least so far as I was concerned. 'Break cover and try to run for it.' That would have been suicidal, of course, but it happens more often than you'd credit. The fight or flight reflex is deeply ingrained in the human psyche, and tends to surface at the most inconvenient moments, which is why our Guard troopers are so well trained to override it, and they have people like me looking over their shoulders in case that turns out not to be enough.

'We'd have to be pretty stupid,' Jurgen pointed out unnecessarily. 'We can hold them off all day from here.' It was perfectly true, we were in an easily defensible position, even if that was more by luck than judgement; even more so now that the last of the innocent bystanders (apart from Zemelda) were rapidly-diminishing dots on the horizon, and anyone not wearing a justicar's uniform was an obvious target. My aide shrugged, developing his theme in rather more detail than I would have appreciated. 'Unless they've got grenades or a flamer, of course.'

'Of course,' I echoed, a thrill of horror running through me at the thought. Suddenly their tactics made a lot more sense: keep our heads down while someone edged close enough to lob a couple of fraggers over the barricade of metal protecting us. Unless some of the shotguns they seemed to favour were loaded with inferno rounds, in which case they wouldn't even need to get that close, just line us up in their sights and start the barbeque. I voxed Dawze. 'Any of them carrying grenades that you can see?'

'No.' His voice changed, taking on a tinge of curiosity. 'I can see movement in the truck again. Two,

maybe three more of them. I'm circling round for a better look.'

'Be careful,' I said, the little warning voice in the back of my head positively screaming. I cracked off a couple of shots from my laspistol at a flicker of movement behind a blocky blue utility truck some four or five vehicles away, and was rewarded with a sudden scurry of motion as whoever it was ducked back into cover. A desultory stubber round or two, and a hail of scatter-shot, rattled against our refuge, then everything went quiet again.

'Definitely three of them, keeping under cover,' Dawze reported after a moment. 'Moving fast. Emperor's teeth, they're quick. Moving to intercept.'

'Stay back!' I warned, the suspicion I still didn't want to acknowledge rising again, leaving a tingle of fear in the pit of my stomach. I shook it off irritably. Things were bad enough already, without jumping at phantoms.

'It's OK,' Dawze reassured me. 'They don't know I'm here. I can drop the first one before they even...' His voice rose to a scream. 'Emperor on Earth, what the hell is th–'

His vox went dead.

'Here they come,' Jurgen said, as calmly as he reported everything from my bath being ready to the sudden appearance of a slavering daemon horde, and opened up with his lasgun. A moment later he ducked back beside me, bringing a powerful blast of his personal fragrance with him, and grimaced. 'They seem pretty determined.'

'No kidding.' Zemelda crouched down on my other side, her face white. A hail of incoming fire blistered

the air over our heads, and I could only hope that
Nyte had had enough sense to keep his head down as
well.

'They're not trying to kill us,' I said, taking no comfort from the idea. 'This is just to keep us from
shooting back.'

'Well, it's working.' Her jaw clenched grimly. 'Why?'

'So they can close. They must know help's on the
way, so they need to finish it fast.'

Jurgen nodded. 'Suppressive fire, we call it. When it
stops, they'll make their move.' We looked at one
another with grim understanding.

'So the moment they do, we fire,' I explained, keeping it as simple as I could for the civilian. 'Shoot
everything and anything that looks like a threat. Got
it?'

'Got it.' Zemelda looked as green as her hair, but
nodded anyway.

'Good.' Abruptly the noise stopped, and we rose
together, looking for targets. Jurgen found one immediately, two women both carrying autoguns, charging
towards us with the berserker fury of orks. One was
dressed as a medicae orderly, the other enveloped in a
sea-green smock that blurred the outline of her body,
but not enough to hide the subtle wrongness of its
shape, a subtlety which all but vanished as I noticed
the third hand emerging from its depths to replace the
depleted magazine.

'Genestealer hybrids,' Jurgen said, recognising them
instantly after our run-in with their brethren on
Gravalax, opening up on full auto and catching them
both in a blizzard of lasbolts. The faux medicae went
down, plates of chitin armouring her thorax becoming

visible as her robe tore, while the three-armed horror dived for cover again behind an abandoned car. Zemelda began blowing holes through the metal protecting it with her stubber, an expression of stunned horror on her face.

Forewarned by a flicker of movement in the corner of my eye, I turned, just in time to take another assailant, as garishly dressed as the late fellow with the shotgun had been, squarely in the face with a bolt from my laspistol. He screeched and fell back, dropping from the roof of the sanitation truck with a wet, meaty thud, and another figure in a pair of nondescript overalls leapt at me, clawed hands poised to rend and tear. Unfortunately for him, my chainsword had a far longer reach than he did, and he expired in several pieces before he got close enough to use them.

'What are those things?' Zemelda asked, still playing bullet tag with the hybrid behind the car, while Jurgen tried to get a clear line of sight on the one disguised as a medicae.

'Xenos,' I said, 'crossed with humans, who didn't even know they'd been tainted with alien genes. We've been finding them hidden on worlds right across the sector.' I glanced up, and froze. Three purestrain 'stealers were hurtling towards us, bounding across the tangle of stalled metal with all the malignity of hunting dogs catching the scent of something small and furry. I rounded on Jurgen. 'Forget the hybrids!' Dangerous as they were, they were barely worth considering compared to the real threat. I'd seen purestrains shredding Terminator armour aboard the *Spawn of Damnation*,[1] and I knew

that if they got within arms-length of us we were all dead.

We concentrated our fire against the oncoming creatures, but they were hellish fast and agile, and most of our shots went wild. We managed to down the first one momentarily, but it rose again almost at once, while the others swept on past it without even breaking stride. Just to make things even worse, we came under fire again from the autogun-armed hybrids, which made us keep our heads down and prevented us from aiming properly. Looking into those slavering jaws, I had no doubt that we would all be dead in moments, and as so often happens in these situations, I found myself preternaturally sensitive to every detail of my surroundings.

Perhaps it was that which first alerted me to the faint trembling in the rockrete beneath my bootsoles, as though something large and fast was passing below my feet. In any event I distinctly recall feeling that faint tremor of movement, but before I could remark on it to my companions I became aware that something was happening on the road ahead of us. A bright yellow flatbed in the path of the oncoming 'stealers seemed to be shifting and rising up, and for a moment I found myself suspecting warpcraft of some kind. Then as it rose even higher I caught a glimpse of something standing beneath it.

'Emperor be praised!' Zemelda said, with every sign of sincerity, and I have to admit I could scarcely

---

1. *A space hulk Cain boarded with the Reclaimers Astartes Chapter, while serving as the Imperial Guard liaison officer to them during the Viridia campaign.*

have been more surprised if he'd put in an appearance in person. The lorry was being pushed aside by
something roughly human-sized, but completely
encased in finely wrought metal, from which the sun
struck the unmistakable refulgence of gold. Smaller
than the suits worn by one of the Astartes, but power
armour nevertheless, and even at this distance it had
clearly been crafted by a master artificer whose skill
would certainly have impressed Tobamorie.[1]

As we watched, scarcely daring to believe what we
were seeing, the gilded warrior tipped the heavy truck
over on top of the charging 'stealers, crushing two of
them against the other vehicles with a scream of
rending metal. After a moment, rancid ichor began
to drip through the tangle of wreckage, making it
obvious that neither was getting back up again in a
hurry.

'Where did he come from?' Jurgen asked, his habitual expression of mild bafflement almost comforting
under the circumstances.

'Down there would be my guess,' I said, indicating
a manhole cover lying on the carriageway next to a
dark hole in the rockrete. 'He must have come
through the undercity.' I had no time for further
speculation, as the sole surviving purestrain charged
at the golden warrior, and the breath caught in my
throat; but the armour-clad figure evaded the
creature easily, with a casual grace that looked more
suited to the ballroom than the battlefield, catching
one of its wickedly-taloned arms and ripping it clean
out of its socket. The 'stealer screeched, and tried to

1. *The armourer of the Reclaimers, who seem to have considered Cain
as close to a friend as was possible for anyone outside his Chapter.*

rally, but the foe it was facing seemed as agile as it was. As the chitinous horror tried to charge home once again, the mysterious warrior levelled its right arm, which proved to have a heavy bolter built into it. One short burst was all it took to reduce the hideous creature to a messy stain.

'Well, that was lucky,' I said, trying to sound casual for Zemelda's benefit, but I needn't have bothered. She was still so stunned by this unexpected turn of events that I doubt she'd have noticed if the Emperor Himself had tapped her on the shoulder at that point.

'But who is he?' Jurgen asked. I shrugged.

'I think we're about to find out,' I said. Sure enough our mysterious saviour was walking towards us at an unhurried pace, pausing just long enough to dispatch the remaining hybrids with a couple of casual bolter bursts. They tried to make a fight of it, but it was a futile endeavour really, their bullets just pattering off the gleaming golden armour like summer rain.

I have to admit to a prickle of apprehension as the refulgent figure approached us, allowing me to take in the full splendour of its armour for the first time. It was, as I'd immediately surmised, the work of a master, of that there could be no doubt. The elegance of its construction was all too obvious, at least to anyone who'd spent as much time as I had listening to Tobamorie rhapsodising over some tech-sorcerous toy or other. It had barely been scratched by the hybrids' bullets, the full intricacy of its decoration undimmed and undamaged.

It was not, as it had first appeared, made entirely of gold, (which given the softness of that particular metal wouldn't have given much protection to its

wearer anyway). Rather, the gold was etched onto a polished surface of much darker metal, forming intricate filigree, which in turn twisted around icons of the saints and well-known scenes from the life of Him on Earth. For all its beauty, though, there was no disguising its deadliness, the muzzle of the bolter on its right forearm and the faint crackle of ozone around the power fist on its left mute testament to the destructive power its wearer was able to wield.

The figure halted a couple of metres away, and, to my astonishment, addressed me by name.

'Hello Ciaphas,' it said, through a vox unit on its chest. The voice sounded familiar, although I couldn't be entirely sure until a golden gauntlet rose to push back its visor. It opened, with a hiss of breaking atmosphere seals, and a well-remembered face, framed with golden hair, grinned at me, devilment dancing as always in the depthless blue eyes. 'We really must stop meeting like this.'

Clearly enjoying my stupefied expression, which by this point I'm bound to admit would have done credit to Jurgen, Amberley's smile widened still further.

CHAPTER FOUR

WITH ALL DUE modesty, I have to say that I recovered remarkably fast under the circumstances.[1] I resheathed my weapons, while Jurgen slung his lasgun across his shoulder and went to look for a primary aid kit before Nyte bled to death. Fortunately the limousine seemed well equipped with more than just hidden weaponry, and he was able to begin cutting the straps holding what was left of the justicar's body armour in place free with his combat knife after only a moment or two spent rummaging in the wreckage. Nyte was looking distinctly the worse for wear, and Jurgen cracked a vial of smelling salts under his nose, blissfully unaware of just how pointless that was in his case.

---

1. *So he says. I recall a distinct resemblance to a stuffed fish for quite some time.*

'Last time was more pleasant,' I admitted, having spent the bulk of it chatting about the necron threat in the palatial surroundings of her hotel suite, before the obvious question occurred to me. 'What in the warp are you doing here, anyway?'

Amberley smiled again. 'The same as you, I imagine. Trying to save Periremunda from a 'stealer infestation. Although I was hoping Keesh would have had a chance to explain what's going on before you found out about it for yourself.'

'I'd have preferred that too,' I said feelingly, before the full implication of what she'd said got through to me. 'You mean the Arbites know about this already?'

'Of course they do. Why else do you think they insisted on the Imperial Guard being sent in to contain it? You know the PDF's bound to be compromised.'

I nodded slowly. I'd seen the same thing on Gravalax, and Keffia before that. 'The infestation's well established then?'

Amberley nodded as best she could inside the collection of ironmongery surrounding her. 'Worse than Gravalax, if I'm any judge. We've taken out the patriarch, so that ought to slow them down a bit, but another purestrain will evolve to replace it before too long, you can bet on that.' She turned a little, with a faint humming of servos, and glanced at Zemelda, who was still standing behind me with her mouth hanging open, the stubber dangling slackly from her hand. 'Who's your little friend, by the way?'

'Zemelda Cleat,' I said, looking from one woman to the other as though we'd all just met casually in a ballroom somewhere. 'An unfortunate bystander.

Zemelda, this is Inquisitor Vail, an old friend of mine.'

'Inquisitor?' Zemelda's face paled even further, if that were possible, and she looked for a moment as if she was about to make a run for it on general principle, but commonsense reasserted itself and she remained rooted to the spot. Amberley nodded, and smiled at her, the warm friendly grin most people seemed to find reassuring.

'Of the Ordo Xenos. So unless you're an alien, you needn't worry about anything I might do.'

'I see.' The snack vendor clearly didn't, but smiled hesitantly in turn nonetheless. 'No one will ever believe me, you know, about meeting a real live inquisitor, and a commissar.' She glanced at me again, and something seemed to click behind her eyes. 'Oh wow, I've just realised, you're *that* commissar. Cain: the one who liberated Perlia, and all that other stuff.' Flattering as it was to be recognised by, now that I had the leisure to appreciate the fact, quite an attractive young woman, I began to feel a little concerned. The way she was babbling looked to me like nothing so much as delayed shock, which I suppose wasn't all that surprising under the circumstances. 'That settles it, they'll definitely think I'm making it all up.'

'I'm afraid you won't be able to tell anyone,' Amberley said kindly, no doubt coming to the same conclusion as I had. 'My presence here's a secret, and so is the real nature of the enemy.' She raised the right arm of the power suit, and for a moment I found myself wondering if she was simply going to solve the problem with a quick burst of bolter fire,

but she was merely reaching out to open the food locker on Zemelda's somewhat battered-looking tricycle. She extricated a lump of something encased in greyish pastry with surprising dexterity given the bulk of the mechanical claws encasing her hands, then stopped, with a rueful expression. 'I'm sorry, I haven't got any change. No pockets in this thing. Ciaphas, can you lend me a couple of credits?'

'I think so.' I rummaged in the depths of my coat for a handful of currency. Zemelda shook her head.

'Forget it. You just saved my life. That ought to be worth a portion of glop at least.' She shrugged. 'Besides, the insulation's been punctured, so they won't stay hot long enough to sell anyway. Just help yourselves.'

In truth the snacks didn't seem all that appetising to me, but Amberley had evidently had a strenuous afternoon of it (quite how much I was to discover later), and piled in with almost as much alacrity as Jurgen did once he'd realised there was free food on offer.[1]

'He'll live,' my aide reported around a mouthful of reconstituted protein, with a final glance back at Nyte, who was looking a little happier now the bleeding was staunched and his rescuer comfortably downwind again. 'Do you want me to check on the others?'

'No point.' Amberley licked a trickle of gravy from the corner of her mouth, and consulted an auspex screen embedded in her helmet. 'I'm not picking up any more life signs in the vicinity, so we might as well get moving again.'

---

1. *Actually, I only ate two, and they weren't that large to begin with. And I'd expended a lot of energy; cleansing a genestealer nest can really take it out of you.*

'Moving where?' I asked.

Amberley glanced at the manhole cover she'd emerged from a few moments before. 'Where do you think?' she asked, hoisting Nyte over her shoulder with one hand as she spoke.

'What about the bodies?' I asked. 'If the 'stealer presence is supposed to be a secret...'

'Not a problem,' she assured me cheerfully, detaching something from a clip on the power suit and lobbing it casually away. 'There's so much spilled promethium around, it'll incinerate all the evidence.' She took a couple of steps towards the dark hole in the carriageway, and glanced back in our direction. 'I'd step it up a bit if I were you. That inferno charge only had a two minute timer.'

Well that was enough to get me moving, you can be sure of that. Pausing only to grab Zemelda by the arm and urge her into motion, as I'd already had one jaunt through a 'stealer infested undercity with Amberley and wanted as many warm bodies between me and potential trouble as possible, I sprinted for the relative safety of the tunnels. We barely made it, shrugging the heavy metal plate into place behind us, before the ground shook over our heads and a faint pattering of dust drifted down from the ceiling to discolour my cap.

Zemelda coughed diffidently. 'Excuse me,' she said, looking rather lost in the glow from the luminators built into Amberley's suit, 'but what do we do now?'

WELL THAT WAS a pretty good question, of course, but to my complete lack of surprise Amberley was well on top of it, setting off at what looked like a leisurely pace, but

which left the rest of us trotting to keep up. The tunnels were broad and high, lined with cables and ducting, which meant nothing to me, but which I assumed had something to do with the infrastructure of the city above our heads.

The local techpriests were obviously frequent visitors, judging by the fresh wax seals set on junction boxes every dozen metres or so, and the faint lingering scent of burned incense that hovered in the air, almost obscured by the fresher ones of dust and damp. A couple of times we passed shrines to the Omnissiah, and I took fresh heart from their presence. I've never really understood the doctrinal aspects of the clockwork model of the Emperor the cogboys[1] worship, but if they were down here as often as those icons implied, there wouldn't be much risk of running into a 'stealer cult. (Not that I'd really expect to this close to the surface, they tend to go to ground in the lower depths, but by now, as you'll appreciate, I was hardly in the mood to take anything much for granted.)

It was at about that point I noticed another light in the distance, moving towards us, and began to draw my weapons again. Amberley didn't seem terribly concerned, though, just glancing in my direction with a faint moue of amusement, before calling out a cheery greeting.

'I found them,' she said.

'Splendid.' I recognised the speaker at once, although he hung back in the middle of the group, his scribe's robes looking even more incongruous than usual in this utilitarian environment. Even if I

---

1. *A mildly disparaging nickname for techpriests and enginseers common among the Imperial Guard.*

hadn't spotted his face and his distinctive attire, his dry, pedantic voice would have identified him immediately, not to mention his logorrhoea. 'I would have estimated your chances of an opportune arrival, given the maximum sustainable speed of that armour and a relatively unencumbered route to the surface, at approximately eighty-seven and two-thirds per cent, although my observations of the tunnel system as we followed the path you took would probably reduce that to somewhere in the order of eighty-six and a quarter...'

'Hello Mott,' I said, and Amberley's savant finally stopped babbling for long enough to nod a cordial greeting.

'Commissar Cain. A pleasure to see you again.' I braced myself for another torrent of verbiage, but apparently the phrase didn't trigger any more random associations in his peculiar augmented mind, for which I was profoundly grateful. As we drew nearer to the little knot of people, I wasn't surprised to find another familiar face, hanging back as far as possible. Divining the reason for her reticence I nudged Jurgen back to the rear of our party too, trying to maximise the distance between them.

'And Rakel. How are you keeping?' Mad as ever would be my guess, but Amberley's pet psyker seemed as lucid as she ever got, simply staring at Jurgen with a degree of loathing even more profound than most

---

1. *Cain's not exaggerating here. Jurgen was a blank, one of those incredibly rare individuals with the innate ability to nullify any psychic or sorcerous influence in the vicinity. It was Rakel's reaction to their initial meeting on Gravalax that first brought his gift to my attention.*

people's. But then most people wouldn't actually pass out or go into convulsions if he got close to them.[1]

'I feel the shadow,' she mumbled, her flat nasal tones setting my teeth on edge as usual, 'and it's hungry.' She was dressed in fatigues, which, like most of the clothes she seemed to possess, looked a little too small for her, displaying rather too much of her generous décolletage as a result. But by her standards, I suppose, they were practical. To my surprise she was carrying a laspistol. I'd have thought with a weapon in her hands she'd be more of a danger to anyone with her than to the enemy, but if Amberley believed she could be trusted with it I wasn't going to argue.

'That's a shame,' I said dryly. 'We could have brought some more of those pasties with us if we'd known.'

'Ciaphas.' Amberley looked at me reprovingly. 'Don't tease the psyker. She's had a hard day.'

'We all have,' a cheerful young man with an unruly blond fringe said. There were three members of the party I didn't recognise, two of them the kind of hired muscle Amberley had employed briefly on Gravalax until the 'stealers got them, while the third was enveloped in the robes of a techpriest. I nodded a cordial greeting, feeling a great deal happier for being surrounded by people with guns. (Apart from Rakel, of course, but unless she pointed it at me or Jurgen there didn't seem much point in objecting.)

'I'll look forward to hearing about it,' I said, 'as soon as we get to wherever we're going.'

'Didn't I tell you?' Amberley asked ingenuously, Nyte still lolling across her shoulder like a feebly twitching scarf. 'We're going to the Arbites building.'

She grinned at me again. 'I'd hate you to miss your appointment.'

'How very considerate,' I said, determined not to seem too surprised by anything she told me. 'Is that where you entered the undercity?'

'That's right,' the young fellow confirmed. He had an autogun slung across his shoulder, and a bandolier of magazines around his chest. Like Rakel he was dressed in plain fatigues, although his fitted properly, and hadn't been left unfastened to an indecorous degree. He seemed to have appointed himself Zemelda's guide, which she certainly wasn't objecting to, his affable demeanour matched by a face which, if not exactly handsome in the conventional sense, was pleasant enough, accentuated by the shock of blond hair that fell into his eyes constantly. Every time it did so he twitched it away, with a gesture so automatic he seemed genuinely unaware of it, and which I assumed accounted for his nickname until the first time I saw him fade into a patch of shadow. 'The name's Pelton, by the way, but my friends call me Flicker.'

'What do your enemies call you?' Zemelda asked archly, and Pelton shrugged.

'Haven't got any,' he said, 'I killed them all.' Zemelda laughed, but I felt a shiver go down my spine. Back on Gravalax Amberley had recruited a group of murderers and psychopaths for a raid on a genestealer nest, and one of them had turned on us at the worst possible moment.

No doubt sensing my unease, Amberley smiled at me. 'Flicker's harmless,' she assured me. 'Unless I tell him not to be.'

I nodded at the other man, who had taken point next to Rakel, either by prior arrangement or on his own initiative. 'What about him?' I asked.

If anything her smile grew broader. 'Simeon? Oh, he's dangerous all right. Mostly to himself, though.' I had no trouble believing that. The man was slightly built, but seemed to burn with a nervous energy that was almost a visible glow in the gloom-enshrouded tunnels. He wore a sleeveless vest festooned with equipment pouches, and his lank, greasy hair just failed to hide the thin, flexible tube running into the base of his skull from somewhere beneath it. 'I found him in a penal legion, one where they use chemical injectors to keep the cannon fodder in line. 'Slaught, psychon, blissout, you name it, he's addicted. Remove his implant, and he'll die. Sooner or later he will anyway. In the meantime, the automatic systems keep him more or less stable by varying the proportions of the cocktail.'

'I can see how someone like that would be useful,' I said slowly. 'For as long as the tranqs work, anyway.'

'He earned his keep in that 'stealer nest,' Amberley said. 'Gave him a quick blast of 'slaught and let him go. It was all I could do to keep up with him, and in this thing, that's really saying something.' I nodded.

'Why didn't you use the power suit on Gravalax?' I asked. Amberley shrugged, the servos whining as they tried to match the movement, and Nyte's recumbent form swayed slightly across her shoulder.

'That was supposed to be a recon sweep,' she reminded me. 'This thing's all very well when I'm expecting a stand-up fight, but it's not exactly tailored for sneaking around in.' The servos whined

again. 'Besides, it's not entirely reliable. Keeps breaking down at inconvenient moments.'

'There's nothing wrong with the suit,' the techpriest admonished, in the distinctive burr of the Caledonia system. 'If you will keep standing in the way of heavy weapons fire, I can only do so much to keep it running.' He waved a dismissive mechadendrite in my direction. 'While she was running about on Gravalax with you, I was rebuilding the primary fluid link and re-sanctifying the fusion bottle.'

'I didn't hear you complaining while you were standing behind me,' Amberley replied, her bantering tone enough to confirm that the techpriest had evidently been a part of her retinue for at least as long as Mott and Rakel.

The techpriest shrugged, a surprisingly human gesture for one of his calling, although it seemed a little stiff, hinting at extensive augmetic enhancements beneath his grubby white robe. A pair of mechadendrites waved lazily above his shoulders, and the eyes beneath his hood were blank and reflective in the light from the luminators. 'A true servant of the Omnissiah gives thanks for his protection whatever form it comes in,' he shot back. 'And bolters are bad for my health.' His silver eyes regarded me thoughtfully. 'As it seems my lady can't be bothered with introductions, I'm Cogitator Yanbel.'

'Ciaphas Cain,' I said automatically. I gestured in the general direction of my aide, who seemed to have found another of Zemelda's snacks in one of the utility pouches he was habitually festooned with, and was getting most of it more or less into his mouth. 'And that's Jurgen. Don't be fooled by your initial

impression, he is tolerable most of the time. If you don't stand too close.'

'The blank.' Yanbel nodded. 'I know. She's gone to a lot of trouble to get you both here.' He broke off as Amberley gave him a sharp look, and then turned her dazzling smile on me. The news the techpriest had let slip hardly came as a surprise, but it wasn't exactly welcome. Although the prospect of spending some time with Amberley before she dragged me off on whatever suicidal escapade she had in mind went a long way towards making up for it.

'That's flattering,' I said, addressing her directly. 'But I can't help wondering why.'

'All in good time.' The coquettish expression I knew all too well was on her face now, and I knew there was no point pressing the matter. 'Keesh will explain. There's a lot more going on here than I can sum up in a couple of sentences.' The sparkle of mischief was in her eyes again. 'Besides, I wouldn't want to spoil the surprise.'

'Surprise?' I asked, trying to keep the undertone of trepidation out of my voice. Amberley nodded.

'You'll see,' she said cheerfully.

CHAPTER FIVE

A SHORT WHILE later we came to a halt outside a heavy iron door, like many of the others we'd passed on our walk from the site of the ambush, and Simeon flattened himself against the wall as though anticipating another attack. His febrile gaze kept flickering back and forth along the tunnel, alert for any signs of movement that might betray an enemy, and I noticed for the first time that his pallid face and arms were seamed with old scar tissue. He carried a shotgun, presumably because he wasn't able to make use of anything that required much in the way of accuracy, and he kept it held close to his body, ready to bring it to bear with the unthinking ease of a combat veteran.

Every time his eyes swept across me as he shifted his gaze from one direction to the other he seemed

to flinch, and, as you'll appreciate, I found this a trifle disconcerting given his evident mental state and the fact that he was armed. I mentioned this to Amberley, and she shook her head.

'It's not you,' she said, pushing against the door. The metal bent a little, but failed to move, and she took a step back, sighing with irritation. 'It's your uniform.' Well, that made sense, I supposed, it would have been his regimental commissar who'd consigned him to the living hell of the penal legions in the first place.

'What did he do?' I asked, curious in spite of myself, and Amberley shrugged, with the whining of servos I was beginning to become so familiar with.

'Cracked under pressure. He ordered an entire platoon executed for failure to salute a superior officer in the middle of an artillery barrage, and shot seven troopers himself with his sidearm before he was brought down. Tragic.'

'It happens.' I shrugged too. 'Some junior officers just can't take the pressure of combat. That's why we have commissars.'

'He *was* a commissar,' Amberley said, and I looked at the poor wretch with a curious amalgam of horror and pity. You hear stories about members of the Commissariat who go off the deep end, but no one ever pays them much mind, and it was the first time I'd ever seen one of my compatriots brought so low. I had little time to brood about it, though.

"Scuse me.' Yanbel glided smoothly past us on little wheels attached to the soles of his augmetic feet and started doing something complicated to one of the ubiquitous junction boxes with his mechadendrites, his regular hands busy with a small incense burner

and, to my surprise, a viridiens pasty apparently scrounged from Jurgen. He met my gaze and shrugged. 'Been a while since lunch,' he explained indistinctly.

Reflecting that most techpriests of my acquaintance had been indifferent to the flavour of food, viewing it simply as fuel for the body (which I suppose under the circumstances was just as well), I took his impromptu snack as confirmation of the impression I'd long since formed that at least a mild degree of eccentricity was an essential requirement for joining Amberley's entourage.[1] 'Ah, that's got it.' With a hum of servos, the slab of metal began to move aside to let us in, and the techpriest grinned at Amberley. 'Thirty-seven seconds. Perhaps we should tell the arbitrator it's time he updated his security protocols.'

'I'll bear that in mind,' Amberley said dryly, leading the way into the brightly lit space beyond.

I followed, finding myself in a utility area not much different to those in the cellars of buildings throughout the Imperium: dust, pipe work, a scurrying rodent or two, and a staircase leading upwards. The main difference from most of the others I'd seen was the group of justicars aiming guns at us, but Amberley didn't seem too bothered by that, and with most of her entourage between me and the weaponry I wasn't either, at least as soon as I'd noticed that most of them were beginning to relax now that the heavy door to the undercity was beginning to close behind us.

---

1. Not as such, but as most of my fellow inquisitors will undoubtedly agree, the nature of our work tends to bring us into contact with a higher than average proportion of people whose view of the galaxy is somewhat unconventional.

'The inquisitor has returned,' the squad leader reported crisply, presumably to some higher authority through a voxcaster built into his helmet, as the fact was blindingly obvious to everyone in the room. Then his voice faltered a little. 'With additional... personnel.'

'I'm Commissar Cain,' I said, stepping forward to seize the initiative before he could get the impression that I was just another of Amberley's underlings. 'The arbitrator's expecting me. I'm afraid I got a little sidetracked on the way to our meeting.'

'That sounds like an interesting story,' a new voice chimed in from the top of the stairs. I glanced up, seeing a grey-haired man in the unmistakable black uniform of an arbitrator senioris gazing down at us with an air of mild curiosity. 'I look forward to hearing the details in more salubrious surroundings.'

'We need a medicae,' Amberley said, slipping Nyte off her shoulder and handing him casually to a couple of nearby justicars. Arbitrator Keesh stood back to let them pass, and resumed his position at the top of the stairs.

'What about the other two?' he asked.

'They didn't make it. Sorry.' Amberley glanced in my direction. 'Ciaphas will fill you in, I'm sure.'

'Aren't you sitting in on the briefing?' Keesh asked.

Amberley shook her head. 'I'll join you as soon as I've changed into something more comfortable,' she said, and led her band of misfits, now apparently augmented by Zemelda for the foreseeable future, up the staircase and out of sight. Accustomed as I

was to reading people's body language, I could hardly help noticing the way Pelton and Keesh avoided eye contact with one another, each of them positively bristling as they passed, Pelton's conversation with the green-haired snack-seller apparently becoming the most engrossing piece of small talk in the galaxy, while the arbitrator's attention was taken up completely with routine status reports.[1] There was no time to wonder about that either, as Jurgen and I were approaching the top of the staircase ourselves by this time.

'Commissar Cain.' Keesh stuck out a hand to shake mine, which I took automatically, and smiled with every sign of sincerity. 'Welcome to Periremunda. I'm sorry your reception wasn't quite as cordial as we would have liked.'

'That's all right,' I said smoothly. 'I'm sorry we dented your car.'

'IT MUST HAVE been a simple case of mistaken identity,' Keesh said, once we were comfortably settled in his office and I'd run through a quick and concise summary of our adventures on the way in from the aerodrome. It was a large, well-appointed room several storeys up, with a spectacular view across the city and the open wilderness beyond, the sky flaring red and gold as the sun finally set behind the spires of rock on the horizon. 'The insurgents obviously thought it was me in the car, and hoped my removal would cripple our efforts to root them out.'

'That sounds plausible,' I agreed, sipping a goblet of amasec of even finer quality than the vintage I'd

---

1. *Which Cain presumably overheard on his comm-bead.*

found in the decanter that had been vaporised by Amberley's firebomb. 'I've hardly been here long enough to have made any enemies of my own.'

'Other than the one we're all facing,' Amberley said dryly. She was sprawling on a sofa against one of the walls, having donned a gown of a smoky grey colour, which set off the blue of her eyes very nicely, a delicate porcelain cup of recaf in her hand.

I nodded in agreement. 'Just how deeply entrenched is the 'stealer infiltration?' I asked.

'Deeply enough,' Keesh said, staring out at the luminators beginning to spark into life across Principia Mons. 'Judging by the number of cells we've uncovered in the last year, they've been here for generations. No one even suspected their presence until they began their campaign of insurrection.'

'Which raises the question of why now?' I glanced at Amberley. 'We're in big trouble, aren't we?'

'We are.' She shrugged, setting up ripples in the misty material, which fell away from her shoulder. 'At least we've taken out the brood lord, which ought to leave them disorganised, here at any rate. There are bound to be others, in nests on other plateaux.'

'Like Hoarfell?' I asked anxiously, and to my relief she shook her head.

'We can't rule it out, of course, but that seems unlikely. We've had no reports of unrest there yet.' She looked at me appraisingly, no doubt divining my main concern. 'Of course they're bound to have a cell of hybrids in place. Darien's a large enough city for them to hide in, even without a tunnel complex below it.'

'That's true,' I agreed, the memory of the sprawling conurbation I'd seen from the air filling my mind. There was no point worrying about it at the moment, though. 'Can I tell Colonel Kasteen what we're really facing?'

'You might as well,' Amberley conceded, after a quick exchange of glances with Keesh, who was clearly unhappy about that but understandably disinclined to argue with an inquisitor. His disquiet had obviously registered with her, however, as she returned her gaze to the arbitrator almost at once. 'The 597th helped to clear up the 'stealer infestation on Gravalax,' she explained, 'and they've fought tyranids before too. They'll be far more effective if they know what they're dealing with.'

'I see.' Keesh nodded, somewhat mollified. 'Then by all means tell them, commissar. I assume you can rely on your colonel's discretion?'

'Of course,' I said, trying not to sound nettled at the question. I'm sure I'd have asked the same thing in his position.

'Very well.' Keesh turned, and activated a hololith built into his desk. A slowly-rotating image of Periremunda appeared, flickering slightly in the manner of most such devices, blue icons marking the major population centres, and red ones the locations of cult cells tracked down and eliminated in the last year or so since they'd begun to show their hand. Amber dots marked the ones where some members were believed to have escaped the cleansing zeal of the justicars and the PDF, and a rash of sickly purple ones the locations where the existence of cells was suspected, but unproven. He nodded at Amberley. 'I

can see why you insisted on that particular regiment
being assigned here if that's the case.'

'It seemed prudent,' Amberley said, with the faintest
of glances at Jurgen, who sat uncomfortably in the
corner of the room, chewing absently on yet another
of the snacks he'd squirreled away in the depths of his
uniform. Divining her hidden meaning, I couldn't
help agreeing with her. My aide's peculiar gift had disrupted the telepathic bond of the brood we'd
discovered in the tunnels beneath Mayoh,[1] and it
might prove equally effective here. Of course that
implied that she expected us to get close enough to
the damn things for his abilities to kick in, which was
somewhat disturbing in itself. To distract myself from
the thought, I indicated the hololith.

'Can we see the disposition of our own forces on
that?'

'Of course.' Keesh manipulated the controls, and a
reassuring number of green icons appeared. I recognised the identifying code of the 597th easily enough,
and the other Guard regiments seemed as well
deployed as could be expected under the circumstances, two of them being stationed right here in the
capital. The vast majority of Imperial units register-
ing, however, were PDF ones, and I noted how many
of them were deployed in close proximity to amber or
purple contacts with a fair degree of trepidation.

I indicated them with a wave of my hand. 'I take it
these units are considered potentially unreliable?' I
asked, and Keesh nodded.

'Of course,' he said. I felt a shiver of apprehension
as I took in the full scale of the problem. Not all of

1. *The planetary capital of Gravalax.*

those PDF units would be compromised, of course, but enough of them would be to make assigning them anywhere something of a risk. I'd seen infected troopers turning against their own comrades without a second's warning on Keffia and Gravalax, and even the possibility that it might happen would have a corrosive effect on morale. Worse still, as the scale of the problem became steadily more apparent, the escalating levels of mistrust among the ranks would inevitably lead to clashes and friendly fire incidents between units completely free of infection.

I contemplated the turmoil about to descend on our heads with a growing sense of trepidation. If even a fraction of what I was seeing here was true, Periremunda was on the brink of collapse into an abyss of anarchy far worse than anything I'd seen on Keffia or Gravalax. On those worlds the genestealer infiltration had been discovered in time, and effectively neutralised before the boil could burst, so to speak, but here it was already beginning to suppurate. It was at that point I noticed an unfamiliar icon among what was beginning to look like a pitifully small proportion of healthy green smudges, and pointed to it in some perplexity.

'What's that?' I asked. 'It's not Guard or PDF.'

'It's a convent,' Keesh explained, evidently surprised that I hadn't recognised the sigil. 'The Order of the White Rose[1] keep a small chapter house here, blessing Periremunda with their presence.' He shrugged. 'That is indeed fortunate for us, under the circumstances.'

---

1. *One of the orders minoris, which split away from the Order of the Sacred Rose in the latter part of M39.*

'Quite,' I said diplomatically. That was all we needed, a bunch of psalm-singing fanatics in power armour getting in the way of a properly co-ordinated military response. I hadn't had much personal contact with the Ecclesiarchy's orders militant in the past, but on the few occasions I had done, I'd found their undeniable martial prowess so closely allied with the worst kind of Emperor-bothering tunnel vision that deploying them effectively in anything resembling a coherent battle plan was all but impossible. The best you could hope for was to point them in the vague direction of something important to the enemy, shout 'heretic!' and leave them to it. If you were lucky they'd put a useful dent in the opposing forces, and even if they didn't, at least you'd got them out of the way before they started preaching at you.

'I'm sure we can find something useful for them to do,' Amberley said, clearly no more convinced of that than I was.

Something about the way she spoke started the palms of my hands itching again, and I looked at her narrowly, a sudden ghastly suspicion beginning to stir at the back of my mind. 'There's something else you haven't told me, isn't there?' I asked, meeting her gaze. After a moment she nodded.

'There is, but it's still highly classified. You can tell your colonel, and Major Broklaw if you see fit, but if it goes any further than that before the official briefing I'm going to be quite seriously put out.'

'I see.' I nodded, not wanting to picture the consequences of Amberley losing her temper. 'And this information is?' I was by no means sure that I wanted to know, but I could hardly back down now without

losing face. I was certain Amberley had more than an inkling of my true character by this time, but Keesh certainly still believed the legend of Cain the Hero, and disabusing him looked like being a very bad idea.

Amberley took a decorous sip of her recaf. 'You heard Rakel back in the tunnel,' she said, and I nodded. It had seemed like the usual gibberish at the time, but now, knowing what I did about the scale of the infestation, her words made a horrifying kind of sense.

'She said something about a shadow,' I said, trying to look as though the mouthful of amasec that followed those words had simply been a thoughtful pause rather than an attempt to hide a panic-stricken gulp, 'and that it was hungry.'

I stared at the rash of icons marking the known and probable 'stealer cults, scarcely daring to believe the conclusion I couldn't help drawing from the evidence. 'They've started calling, haven't they?'

'They have.' Amberley nodded in confirmation, placing her recaf cup on a nearby occasional table, as apparently unperturbed as if we'd merely been chatting about the weather. 'Rakel noticed it a few days ago. That's why we raided the nest, hoping to disrupt it by taking out the patriarch.'

'Has it worked?' Keesh asked, and to my inexpressible relief Amberley nodded.

'To some extent. The telepathic network between the 'stealers and hybrids is still in place, of course, but without the brood lord to act as a link to the hive mind it's not acting as a beacon any more.' She shrugged. 'Of course this was only the strongest signal, but we can hope the other nests are so much

weaker they're not getting through yet. Maybe that will give us enough time to shut them down too.'

'If Rakel can stand the strain,' I said, feeling an unexpected pang of sympathy for the psyker. True she had a voice like fingernails on a blackboard, and was almost completely round the bend even on a good day, but being subjected to the unholy keening of a genestealer feeding call in her head couldn't have been an awful lot of fun. And to have to go actively seeking it again, Emperor knew how many times, seemed an awful lot to load on her fragile mind and chubby shoulders. 'I take it that was why she was with you?'

Amberley nodded. 'Led us right into the heart of the nest,' she said, and grinned. 'They couldn't have been expecting visitors, there were hardly any guards in the way.'

Recalling my own frantic duel with the patriarch of the Gravalax cult, chainsword against claws quite capable of ripping their way into a Baneblade, I shook my head ruefully.

'I don't suppose they thought they needed any,' I said, as insouciantly as I could. 'In my experience a brood lord can take care of himself.'

'He made a fight of it,' Amberley agreed, the flicker of darkness in her eyes momentarily at odds with the conversational tone of her voice. 'But the suit helped, and the others kept the purestrains off my back while I finished him off.'

Despite her casual air, I couldn't help picturing something of the horror of that pitched battle in the shadows beneath our feet, and nodded slowly. She and her companions had been lucky to get out alive,

and there was no guarantee that they'd be so fortunate the next time. Of course if she hadn't, or hadn't been monitoring the justicars' vox frequencies and heard what was going on as they neared the surface, Jurgen and I would both have been killed as well, and events on Periremunda would have taken a very different course.

'But she can still feel the shadow,' I said, returning to the psyker's words. 'Does that mean…'

'Yes.' Amberley nodded bleakly. 'We've cut it off all right, but the signal's already been heard. We might have bought ourselves a little more time to prepare, but there's a hive fleet on the way, and there's nothing we can do to stop it.'

Editorial Note:

Since not everyone reading this will be as familiar as the members of my own ordo (or for that matter Cain himself) with the state of the tyranid threat as we perceived it in the early 930s of M41, the following extract may prove helpful, particularly in elucidating the precise role of the genestealer infestations which generally precede the onslaught of their hive fleets.

From *The Abominable Chitin: a Concise History Of The Tyrannic Wars* by Arten Burrar, 095 M42

FOR MOST OF the concluding quarter of M41 it was possible to believe that the tyranid threat to the Imperium had been, if not completely eradicated, at least effectively contained. True, isolated splinter fleets from Hive Fleet Behemoth continued to appear

from time to time throughout the eastern fringe, tiny shards of the all but unstoppable juggernaut of destruction that had been halted at such terrible cost by the Ultramarines in the desperate battle to save Macragge, but, formidable as they were, they could generally be dealt with by the combined might of the Navy, Astartes, and Imperial Guard. Only rarely did they succeed in overrunning a world completely, but every time they were able to do so, replenishing their store of biomass in the process, they grew in strength. Thus the prevailing strategic doctrine, from the defeat of Behemoth in 745 right up until the horrifying discovery in the last decade of the millennium of two new fleets, each alone greater and more lethal than their predecessor by an order of magnitude, had simply been to seek out and eliminate every trace of these diabolical organisms wherever they could be found.

Given the vastness of the Imperium, and the unimaginable gulfs between the stars composing it, it was hardly surprising that these splinter fleets were to prove more than a little elusive. The tireless defenders of the Emperor's blessed domains did have one significant advantage, however, which enabled them to predict the appearance of these swarms with a fair degree of success.

It will be remembered that one of the first and most shocking discoveries made after the appearance of Behemoth was the presence of genestealers among the bewildering variety of organisms encountered by the gallant defenders of the Imperium. The insidious nature of these creatures had long been known:

worlds without number had been infested with their changeling progeny, and only the vigilance of the Holy Inquisition, rooting out such cancers in the body of the Imperium with the ceaseless diligence for which we should all give thanks,[1] preserved many more from being irretrievably contaminated. For the first time it became apparent that these creatures were in fact the vanguard of the hive fleets, seeking out worlds ripe for plunder, and in some way calling down the tyranid hordes to feast upon them.

For decades the exact mechanism by which this was achieved remained a mystery, but after Inquisitor Agmar's perceptive analysis of the Ichar IV incident, presaging the appearance of Hive Fleet Kraken, much that had previously been little more than conjecture at last became clear. It seems that when a genestealer brood successfully infiltrates the population of a human occupied world (or, for that matter, one tainted by the presence of one of the lesser sentient races such as the orks, tau or eldar), it remains hidden, quietly building up its numbers and influence until it reaches some critical proportion of the population at large. Then the brood's telepathic link becomes so powerful that it begins to radiate outwards through the warp, acting as a beacon to the malefic entities that spawned it.

Although the unprecedented size of the Ichar IV infestation made it the first occasion on which this signal became readily detectable by astropaths across the subsector, vindicating the theory beyond all possible doubt, some inquisitors of the Ordo Xenos had

---

1. *Although in my experience gratitude for our efforts isn't exactly common.*

already speculated that precisely this mechanism was at work, and a few even claimed to have used sanctioned psykers to successfully disrupt it on more than one occasion.[1] Even those who doubted the truth of the matter, or proposed alternative explanations, were forced to accept the incontrovertible fact that wherever a genestealer cult grew strong enough to begin moving openly against the Imperial authorities a hive fleet was liable to show up within a matter of months. It thus became a matter of policy for both Munitorum and Admiralty alike to monitor such outbreaks closely, and move as many resources as could be spared from other battlefronts to the vicinity of these worlds with all due dispatch.

It must be remembered, however, that our glorious Imperium is huge, and not all the worlds so threatened were fortunate enough to be relieved in time.

---

1. *At which point a lesser woman might be tempted to say 'I told you so.'*

CHAPTER SIX

WITH ALL THAT to digest, you'll appreciate my return
to Hoarfell was a grim one, my mood not exactly
lifted by the fact that when I eventually left the
Arbites building I immediately found myself surrounded by a gaggle of halfwits from the pictcasters
and printsheets waving imagifiers in my face and
shouting increasingly fatuous questions at me. How
they'd known I'd be there I had no idea, but I har-
boured a pretty strong suspicion nonetheless.
Amberley's presence on Periremunda was supposed
to be a deep, dark secret, so a genuine Hero of the
Imperium (at least so far as anybody else knew)
hanging around in the general vicinity would prove
to be an invaluable distraction. In any event I hid my
irritation with the ease of a lifetime's dissembling,
and trotted out a few platitudes about my original

reason for being there. (Which, under the circumstances, I'm sure you'll appreciate was far from being
the most important thing on my mind at the time,
but it still needed sorting out nevertheless. In the
event, I'd got Jurgen to hand all the paperwork over
to someone in Keesh's office, reflecting that at least
it'd give Nyte something to do while he was lounging
around the place recuperating.)

'Have you any comment to make about this afternoon's terrorist attack on the starport approach
road?' someone shouted, and I smiled blandly for
the pict recorders.

'Anyone who threatens the Emperor's loyal subjects
in any way is nothing less than a heretic in my book,'
I said, deciding to play the bluff soldier, which I
knew the civilian sheep would lap up. I struck a
heroic pose, one hand on the hilt of my chainsword.
'I don't care how well hidden the traitors think they
are, they'll be rooted out, and made to pay the full
price of their treachery. You can be certain of that.' All
good rabble-rousing stuff, I'm sure you'll agree, the
sort of stuff I've been spouting by rote since I got my
scarlet sash, and I never expected anyone to take it
seriously; not seriously enough to try to kill me, at
any rate.

But I'm getting ahead of myself. At the time I
thought no more of the incident, dismissing it as just
another minor annoyance in what was shaping up to
be a pretty bad day overall, despite the unexpected
pleasures of seeing Amberley again so soon and
working my way through Keesh's collection of well-
matured amasec. After deflecting a few more
questions with vague but reassuring platitudes, I

followed Jurgen to the somewhat less luxurious car Keesh had laid on to take us back to the aerodrome, my aide's distinctive miasma parting the scrum of squabbling news gatherers almost as effectively as a burst from his lasgun would have done, and made the most of the sombre journey back to rejoin the regiment. I had a strong suspicion that it would be the last hour or so of relative peace and quiet I'd be able to enjoy for a long time to come.

'GENESTEALERS,' BROKLAW SAID, nodding slowly, with the expression of a man who'd just bitten into a bit-terroot pastry thinking it was filled with sweetbriar. At least he didn't say 'Are you sure?' which a lot of men in his position wouldn't have been able to resist, but both he and Kasteen knew me well enough by now to know I wouldn't exaggerate about something like that. (Or at least they believed I wouldn't, which amounts to the same thing.) 'I suppose we should have guessed.'

'At least we'll know what to look out for,' Kasteen said, taking the bowl of tanna Jurgen was handing to her as she spoke. We'd convened in her new office, which was starting to look positively lived-in already, with a litter of data-slates across the surface of her desk, and a stack of empty tanna bowls teetering precariously on one edge. The command post below was looking a bit more businesslike as well, auspexes, vox units and cogitators up and running, and the usual complement of troopers scurrying about. Most of the enginseers had disappeared, which indicated that they'd got all their gadgets working as well as they ever did, and gone off to tend to our wargear, which

was always a comforting prospect. The last thing we needed if the enemy mounted a surprise attack was to find half our kit malfunctioning.

I nodded, taking my own drink, and stifling a yawn. Despite my assurances to Kasteen and Broklaw before setting off for Principia Mons, the strenuous activities of the day were beginning to catch up with me. At least the loading doors in the distance had been closed, so the howling draught I'd noticed before was absent, but it had evidently been snowing constantly in Darien the whole time I was away, and the room was distinctly chilly so far as I was concerned. I warmed my fingers around the bowl gratefully. (Apart from the augmetic ones, of course, which could barely tell the difference.)

'Pass the word down to the troopers discreetly,' I advised, 'and not a word to the local PDF.'

'Of course,' Kasteen said, leaning back in her chair. We all knew that if they'd been compromised, which was a pretty safe assumption given how widespread the 'stealer infiltration clearly was on Periremunda, tipping them off that the game was up would be certain to spark a mutiny among the contaminated units. Far better to gather what information we could quietly, pinpoint the infested ones first, and strike before they realised we were on to them.

'It sounds as though the inquisitor knows what she's doing, anyway,' Broklaw said.

Knowing Amberley as well as I did, and having already gleaned a little more than I was comfortable with about the way the Inquisition functioned (but a good deal less than I was going to discover before the battle for Periremunda was over), I found this far less

reassuring than the major evidently did. I felt it would be unfair to disabuse him, however, not to mention unwise, so I held my tongue.

'Did she say anything else?' Kasteen asked, eyeing me narrowly through the steam from her tanna bowl.

Until then, to be honest, I still hadn't made up my mind whether or not to share Amberley's final bombshell with my comrades, but now she was asking me directly I couldn't see any good reason to withhold it. I trusted the two of them as much as anyone apart from Jurgen, and at least I wouldn't be the only one fretting about the news.

I nodded slowly. 'She did, but it isn't to leave this room.' I looked at them each in turn, underlining the need for discretion with all the subtlety of a second-rate actor playing to the back row of the gallery. 'She told me specifically that you two were the only other people I could trust with the information.' Kasteen and Broklaw nodded solemnly, barely even bothering to hide how smug they felt at being let in on a secret most of their superiors would remain blissfully ignorant of for the next few weeks. Of course their satisfaction probably didn't last more than the next couple of minutes, but that was hardly my fault. I made a show of glancing at the door, to make sure it was closed, and the expressions of eager expectation grew on my colleagues' faces.

'You can rely on us,' Broklaw said.

'That's what I told the arbitrator. Inquisitor Vail, of course, knows that already,' I said.

Kasteen inclined her head at the implied compliment. 'You can assure her that her confidence wasn't

misplaced,' she said. I was never quite sure how much of my personal association with Amberley she'd deduced, but she generally seemed to take it for granted that we were at least keeping in touch, and may have suspected that I was one of her loose association of covert agents. (Which of course I was from time to time, since there was no way of getting out of it: I'm sure most of the men in the galaxy are familiar with the sinking feeling that accompanies the words 'Do you think you could do me a little favour, darling?', but when the woman asking the question is an inquisitor it's even less wise than usual to say 'No'.) At least if she did think that, of course, it diverted attention from Jurgen, who was probably the biggest asset Amberley possessed, as well as the most unlikely-seeming candidate for the job.

'Good,' I said, lowering my voice instinctively, 'because if any of this gets out, the unrest we've seen so far will seem like a couple of drunks brawling in the street. The entire population will panic, and with the PDF unreliable, we'll never be able to contain it.'

'The hive fleet's been sighted, hasn't it?' Kasteen asked, her face even paler than usual.

'Not yet,' I said, 'but Amberley's convinced it's on the way. Rakel seems to think she can feel its presence in the warp.'

'Then we haven't got long,' Broklaw said. He seemed, if anything, more rattled at the news than the colonel had been, but the two of them were rallying fast, and I could hardly blame them for being somewhat disconcerted. The 597th had been formed from the depleted remnants of two other regiments, the 296th and the 301st, after the defence of Corania

had reduced both to less than half of their original complement. It had been a tyranid swarm that had butchered their friends and comrades, and if the thought of facing any enemy of the Imperium was likely to give them pause, it would be the scuttling horrors of the hive fleets. Come to that, I'd seen more than enough of the hideous creatures to last me several lifetimes by that point myself. 'I'll start putting together a contingency plan for keeping the plateau free of any spores they start dropping. If we can do that we can hold out up here pretty much indefinitely.'

'Good thinking,' Kasteen said, glancing in my direction with every sign of her usual confidence. 'One thing you can say for this frakked-up geography, it gives us a fighting chance. Most of their spores will drop into the deserts or the lava pits, where they'll have nothing to consume. We'll lose some of the plateaux, no question about that, but the uninhabited ones we can just sterilise from the air, and win back the others the old-fashioned way.'

'Well that sounds like a plan,' I said, trying to hide my own sense of relief. She was right, of course, the very conditions that made Periremunda such a nightmare when it came to rooting out the 'stealer infestation would play right into our own hands when it came to fighting the 'nids themselves. I hoped. Something told me it wasn't going to be quite as easy as that, but the thought was a comforting one, and it would do to be going on with.

'We'll start working on some immediate action drills for tackling the most common creatures too,' Kasteen added. 'If we work them in to the standard

counter-insurgency training no one outside the regiment should notice, and it'll be good for the morale of our own people.'

'I'll get the company commanders preparing the ground,' Broklaw agreed. He glanced at me. 'As soon as they know we're hunting hybrids they'll want to start practising anti-tyranid techniques anyway. We don't have to tell them we already know they're going to need them.'

'Agreed,' I said, relieved to hear that our people would be as ready as possible for the coming storm without having to break the letter of my agreement with Amberley. Most of the troopers would remember all too well how the desperate battle for Corania had begun as a routine operation to clear out a genestealer cult, which had escalated rapidly into an all-out battle simply to survive once the splinter fleet the 'stealers had called arrived in orbit. Only the fortuitous presence in system of a Naval flotilla and the relative weakness of the tyranid swarm prevented the siege from turning into something far worse.[1] If anything, they'd be more suspicious if we weren't taking precautions against the same thing happening again. 'I'll leave it with you, then.'

Unfortunately, of course, it wasn't quite that easy. I found my way to the quarters Jurgen had found for me, a tolerably comfortable room in a quiet corner of the garrison, which most of the Valhallans were avoiding because of the heat emitted by the power

---

1. *Cain had presumably heard the story from the survivors, as these events took place before he joined the regiment. Anyone wanting a fuller account of them is referred to chapter eighty-seven of Arten Burrar's* The Abominable Chitin, *cited earlier.*

plant in the basement, and I fell into bed gratefully enough. But sleep was a long time in coming, and when it did was troubled by dreams of the tyranid swarms I'd encountered before, sweeping across deserts and through cities like a tide of scuttling death.

CHAPTER SEVEN

FOR THE NEXT few days, despite my understandable trepidation, Darien remained unrocked by civil insurrection: a circumstance which should have been comforting, but which just left me feeling restless and uneasy. My paranoid streak, normally so reliable, kept insisting that the longer things remained quiet the worse they were likely to be when everything finally went ploin-shaped, so I was unable to appreciate the lull as much as I'd have liked, despite the happy discovery that Darien possessed a reasonable number of good quality restaurants and discreet gaming establishments only too eager to acquire the cachet they apparently believed would be conferred by the patronage of a Hero of the Imperium. As a result my leisure time was spent pleasantly enough, despite the freezing

temperatures, which my comrades in arms still seemed to think were positively sultry.

'We've completed our deployment,' Broklaw reported, gesturing to the image in the hololith, his sleeves rolled up to the elbows despite the way his breath misted into visibility with every word.

I leaned across it, brushing away the thin film of snow that my cap had acquired on the short journey from my quarters as I did so, noting the disposition of our forces. They'd been scattered all around the plateau with a speed and efficiency that I doubted anyone other than native-born iceworlders could possibly have matched, and at a first glance I could find nothing to criticise.

Two full companies, first and second, had been given the job of defending Darien, continuing to operate out of our makeshift garrison, and if that strikes you as being somewhat excessive under the circumstances you should bear in mind that the city was the largest concentration of life on Hoarfell, and would attract any tyranid organisms that made it to the surface as surely as Jurgen to an 'all you can eat' buffet; not to mention being the site of the starport, which represented our only line of retreat if things started going really badly.

Stuck on the top of a thin spire of rock as we were, we had precious little room for manoeuvre, and if it looked as if we were about to be overrun our only option would be to run for the shuttles and Horus take the hindmost. Not for the first time I found myself blessing the foresight of whoever had decided to billet us as close as we were to the landing field. I nodded approvingly.

'You've got the city well covered.'

'I think so,' Broklaw agreed. 'I thought about detaching a couple of platoons from first company to bolster the outer picket lines, but if things get bad enough to need them there we'll need them here even more desperately to help defend the civilians.' He spoke as if that were possible, but we all knew they'd be easy prey for the 'nids, and if the swarm ever made it into the streets of the city we'd have our work cut out just trying to survive ourselves. Any civilians managing to make it through would just be a welcome bonus.

'Fourth and fifth[1] look more than capable of holding the line,' I reassured him, and Kasteen nodded her agreement.

'That's what we thought,' she said briskly.

There were a handful of outlying villages scattered around the hills and valleys, most of them playing host to a platoon or two, which between them looked able to respond to any incursion within as short a time as anyone could reasonably expect given the rugged and wintry terrain. 'We've managed to overlap most of the patrol areas, so the chances of anything that makes it down staying undetected are reduced as much as possible.'

'Good thinking,' I said. I didn't really give much for anyone's chances of finding a lictor or one of the other specialised scout organisms unless the creature fancied a quick snack, but the strategy should make

---

1. *Third Company was the regiment's logistical support arm, made up mostly of transport, medicae, sapper, and other specialised units. Though just as capable of fighting as any other troopers at a pinch, they would only be deployed in the front line in the direst of emergencies.*

it more difficult for ordinary gaunts and the like to
sneak through our lines unnoticed. I indicated a few
scattered hamlets and mining stations with no icons
marking the presence of friendly troops. 'What about
these?'

Kasteen shrugged dismissively. 'Settlements with
fewer than a hundred souls: barely a dozen, some of
them. Not worth the effort of trying to defend.'

Well, I supposed the inhabitants might feel rather
differently about their homes, but I couldn't fault the
military logic, and nodded my agreement. 'We've told
the locals to evacuate to the nearest population centres. Some have, some are insisting on staying put.' She
shrugged again. 'It's their call. If they want to play 'nid
bait, I'm not risking any of our people to hold their
hands.'

'Quite right,' I agreed, happy to have as many heavily armed troopers standing between me and the
chitinous hordes as possible. I turned away from the
flickering display. 'Are we making any progress on the
other matter we discussed?'

'Not much,' Kasteen said, turning to lead the way up
the staircase to her office. The matter in question was
a little too sensitive to talk about openly where any of
the common troopers might overhear us, although I
was pretty sure most of them could join the dots for
themselves now word had filtered down the ranks to
keep an eye out for any sign of genestealer activity. She
waited until I'd closed the door behind us, reducing
the never-ending chatter of the command centre to a
muted murmur, before continuing. 'We've been
liaising with all the usual agencies, but so far we can't
say for sure which of the local PDF units have been

compromised.' She shrugged, handing me a data-slate, which said the same thing at much greater length, and which I replaced on her desk after a cursory glance. 'Of course we can't entirely trust any of our sources either. It's entirely possible the hybrids have infiltrated the justicars, the Administratum, starport security, and for all I know the local ecclesiarchs and refuse collectors too.'

'Pretty much what we'd expected,' I conceded, trying not to sound too disheartened at the limitless vistas of distrust her words had opened up.

Broklaw looked at me in a speculative fashion. 'Could your friend in Principia Mons be any help in narrowing it down?'

I looked thoughtful. Amberley might have some more solid information, but if she did she wasn't sharing it, and if that was the case she'd undoubtedly have excellent reasons for not doing so. In either event, I wasn't about to ask her. Need to know is practically a twenty-third verse of the creed[1] to most inquisitors.

'I doubt it,' I said. The matter was pretty moot anyway as she'd been out of touch for over a week, cleaning out any other nests of purestrains she'd been able to track down, in an attempt to block whatever psychic signal Rakel thought she could feel the brood lords channelling into the void. 'Besides, she's out of town.'

'I see.' Kasteen looked mildly disappointed. 'Perhaps if you made a personal approach to the arbitrator?'

---

1 *The version most widely used by the chaplains of the Imperial Guard is the abbreviated twenty-two verse one, as services in the field tend, of necessity, to be as brief as possible.*

'I could try,' I said, without much hope. Keesh had been making precious little headway with the problem before we arrived, and would certainly have passed on anything new he'd uncovered that affected our position. On the other hand setting up a meeting with him would give me an excuse to return to the more equable climate of Principia Mons, at least for a short while, and after freezing my extremities off on Hoarfell for what felt like eternity I wasn't about to let the chance of even the briefest of respites go by without grabbing at it. 'I'll get Jurgen to make the call.'

'We might as well face it,' Broklaw said, 'the only people on the entire planet we know we can rely on are the ones in this regiment.' He glanced at me. 'That is still the case, isn't it?'

'Yes,' I confirmed. After my experiences on Keffia, where the infiltrating 'stealer hybrids had managed to infect scores of the Guardsmen sent to eradicate them by the simple expedient of running bars and bordellos where likely victims could be isolated and implanted, I'd placed all such establishments firmly off limits as soon as I'd returned to Hoarfell with the unwelcome news of what we were actually facing. The troopers had grumbled, of course, but for the most part had complied with the restriction. Only a few of them had actually seen me executing the infected soldiers among our own ranks on Gravalax, but the story had got round fast enough, and no one seemed keen to be the next in line. There had been the inevitable few who'd gone ahead regardless, out of bravado or sheer stupidity, but none of them had shown the telltale wounds of

implantation when the justicars had returned them
to us, and I'd made sure that however much fun
they'd had the night before the morning after definitely hadn't been worth it. After that, the problem
had more or less petered out.

'Well, that's something anyway,' Kasteen said.

THE RESPONSE TO my request for a meeting with
Keesh was as gratifying as it was unexpected, my
aide rousing me early the next morning with a mug
of tanna and the news that the arbitrator himself
was on the vox asking to talk to me. Hauling myself
out of bed and grabbing the comm-bead from its
accustomed place under my pillow, next to the
laspistol, I screwed the little transceiver into my ear
and took a mouth-scalding gulp of the fragrant
drink while Jurgen handed me my trousers.

'Cain,' I said as crisply as I could while gulping for
air. 'Thank you for getting back to me so quickly.'

'Our mutual friend made it very clear that we
ought to co-operate,' Keesh said, too astute to
mention Amberley's name or title even over an
encrypted link. 'So I thought I'd give you some
advance notice of something you'll be hearing
through the usual channels in the next hour or two.
We've just had an astropathic message from
Coronus.'

'That's excellent news,' I said, sipping my tanna a
little more carefully this time. The mere fact that a
message had got through at all meant that the hive
fleet was either still some distance from Periremunda, where the shadow it cast in the warp wasn't
able to disrupt communications with us yet, or

weak enough for the area of interference to be significantly smaller than usual. Keesh's voice took on a more cautious tone.

'Yes and no,' he said guardedly, and I felt the palms of my hands begin to tingle again. Despite his attempt to sound unruffled, he was obviously seriously perturbed by something. 'I'm sure you'll be pleased to hear that we have reinforcements on the way.' Well, that was cause for optimism anyway. He hesitated.

'I sense a "but" coming,' I said, managing to mask my own unease a great deal more successfully.

Keesh cleared his throat. 'My department has uncovered some fresh intelligence, which casts a disturbing new light on things. I've been invited by the lord general to brief all the regimental commanders in person,' he said, the implication obvious. This was something else he didn't want to talk about over the vox. 'The Imperial Guard commanders anyway.'

Better and better. Keeping the PDF out of the loop only confirmed the sensitivity of whatever he wanted to tell us. My palms began to itch worse than ever. 'And the commissars too, of course.'

'Of course,' I echoed, making a mental note of the time and security arrangements he began to rattle off. As the link went dead, I found myself wondering if it was too late to crawl back into bed and pull the blankets over my head until it all went away, but of course there was no chance of that. Pausing only to finish my tanna, and the hot grox bun Jurgen had managed to find for me somewhere, I went to give the colonel the good news.

CHAPTER EIGHT

'ANY IDEA AT all what this might be about?' Kasteen asked, more by reflex than because she expected an answer.

I shook my head. 'He wasn't very specific,' I replied, cursing the wind that was sweeping across the starport from the lip of the plateau, barely a kilometre away from where we were standing. We'd had a number of similar exchanges over the last few hours, none of them going anywhere, and had run out of increasingly wild speculation some time back. That was probably just as well, we were only making ourselves feel worse. Although it must be said that neither of us had managed to get anywhere close to just how bad the news we were going to hear as soon as we made it to the capital would turn out to be. I huddled a little deeper into my greatcoat, and tried not to shiver too visibly.

Sandy Mitchell

We were standing at the edge of a pad in the middle of the aerodrome, the engine of the Chimera that had conveyed us there rumbling quietly in the background, tainting the air with the scent of burned promethium, while a chill wind threw flurries of grubby snow in my face whichever way I turned to avoid it. None of the Valhallans with us seemed at all inconvenienced by the freezing temperature, of course, which was still positively balmy by their standards. Most of the squad accompanying us, which I'd thought to be a reasonable precaution after my last visit to Principia Mons, were wearing the greatcoats and fur hats most often associated with regiments from their homeworld, but all of them had left the heavy garments unfastened, revealing the standard issue flak vests beneath. (Apart from Kasteen, come to think of it, who had donned a dress uniform for the occasion, and didn't want it getting soggy before meeting the arbitrator.)

'Any sign of the shuttle?' I asked Jurgen, and he shook his head mournfully, already anticipating the discomfort of being airborne again.

'I'll chase them up, commissar,' he promised dutifully, and began talking with his usual blend of calm reasonableness and unshakable tenacity to someone on his comm-bead.

'Thank you.' I glanced at my chronograph. 'I wouldn't want to keep the arbitrator *and* the lord general waiting.' Of course technically I could keep both of them hanging about indefinitely, my position alone ensuring that, never mind my fraudulent reputation, but I was reluctant to do so. For one thing I wanted to hear whatever bad news

Keesh had for us as quickly as possible, so I could start worrying about something real instead of all the horrible possibilities my imagination kept presenting me with, and for another I seemed to have made a reasonably positive impression on the lord general when we'd met back on Gravalax, and I was keen to reinforce it. In my experience it never hurt to be well in with the people in charge, especially when their decisions could materially affect my chances of getting through the next twenty-four hours with my body still in possession of most of its component parts. Mostly, though, I just wanted to get aboard the shuttle, which was ten minutes overdue already, and out of that pox-rotted wind.

'There seems to be a bit of a problem in traffic control,' Jurgen reported after a moment. 'They've got everything in a holding pattern while they try to sort it out.'

'What sort of a problem?' I asked, cutting into the right frequency to hear for myself, my sense of trepidation immediately reinforced by the unmistakable flat tones of suppressed panic in the traffic controller's voice.

'HL 687, respond. This is Darien Down,[1] calling HL 687. You are continuing to deviate from your assigned trajectory. Correct course and respond immediately.'

'They've lost track of one of the heavy lift dirigibles,' Jurgen explained helpfully. 'It was delivering a cargo of promethium to the storage tanks on the edge of the plateau, but its mooring lines broke, and it's drifting across the field towards the city.'

---

1. As opposed to Darien High, the orbital part of the starport facilities.

'Drifting my arse,' Kasteen said, shading her eyes and looking upwards. A vast shadow blotted out the opalescent haze forcing its way through the snow clouds, plunging us into a partial eclipse. 'That thing's moving under power.'

'You're right,' I said, the shiver of apprehension rippling though me at the realisation even more acute than the effects of the wind. A low drone of engines reverberated from the snow-dusted rockrete around us. I glanced at the idling Chimera. 'Lustig, can we bring it down with the heavy bolters?'

'We can give it a try,' the veteran sergeant in charge of the squad assented, running for the vehicle. 'Jinxie, with me.'

'Sarge.' Trooper Penlan, whose nickname I have to admit wasn't entirely unmerited, doubled in her squad leader's wake, the flash burn scar on her cheek flushing with the sudden exertion. Despite her reputation for being somewhat accident-prone, I felt Lustig had made the right choice. She was a solid and competent trooper, unlikely to lose her head, and we were going to need a steady hand on the heavy weapons if we were going to bring the gas-filled behemoth down without touching off its volatile cargo. That reminded me...

'This is Commissar Cain,' I broadcast, cutting in on the traffic control frequency with my commissarial override code. 'In view of the clear and present danger to the civilian population, I'm bringing this matter under military jurisdiction at once.' In actual fact I couldn't give a flying frak about the civilian population, of course, but it sounded good, and if I was any judge the aerodrome staff would be only too

eager to pass the problem on to anyone else daft enough to put their hand up, which of course they were. 'How much promethium is that thing carrying?'

'Three kilotonnes,' the controller told me, making my blood run even colder than it had seemed to on Simia Orichalcae. 'If it detonates…' His voice trailed away, and I could hardly blame him; an explosion that size would level most of the city, taking the starport and our garrison along with it. With a vertiginous lurch of horrified understanding I realised at last why Amberley and Keesh hadn't been able to uncover any 'stealer cult activity in Darien. The damned hybrids had fled the place in preparation for this atrocity, which would surely spark panic and rioting all over the globe if it succeeded. More to the point, though, I'd be barbequed along with the rest of the city. Whatever it took, the dirigible had to be stopped.

'Aim for the gas cells,'[1] I voxed Lustig and Penlan, noticing with a surge of relief that the envelope containing them extended some distance beyond the cluster of fuel tanks slung beneath the taut fabric, each one of which was large enough to have parked a whole company's Chimeras in with room to spare. The hail of heavy explosive ordnance should rip the relatively fragile material apart with ease, releasing the gas, and robbing the airship of lift. I turned to the other troopers. 'Target the engines.' They were a little more solid, it was true, but unarmoured all the same,

---

1. *The gas bag keeping the dirigible aloft would have been subdivided into several compartments, so that it would remain in the air in the unlikely event of one or more being accidentally torn.*

and the lasbolts from our small arms ought to do a
reasonable amount of damage.

'Sounds good to me,' Kasteen agreed, drawing her
sidearm, and placing a couple of shots squarely into
the front starboard engine, which began to leak fluid
and a trickle of smoke. Only then did I remember she
habitually carried a bolt pistol, but she didn't seem
to have blown us up yet, so I left her to it and headed
back towards the Chimera, Jurgen trotting at my
heels as always. I'd be able to supervise things a lot
more effectively without the wind throwing snow in
my face every few seconds, possibly distracting me at
a crucial moment, and if things did go horribly
wrong I stood a slightly better chance of escaping the
worst effects of the fireball behind a nice thick slab of
armour plate. (Not an appreciably greater one, it's
true, but give me the choice between virtually certain
death and its absolute guarantee and I'll take the forlorn hope every time.) I half expected Kasteen to
follow, but she seemed to be having too much fun
playing pop the balloon with the troopers, who had
all opened up with their lasguns, knocking holes
through the labouring engines with every sign of
enjoyment.

I dived inside the sturdy little vehicle just as Penlan
opened up with the bolter in the turret, Lustig
joining in a moment later with the forward mounted
one, although he couldn't have got much elevation
on it. Not that it mattered, I suppose, the target was
certainly big enough. Even though it was practically
on top of us by now, I could still see Lustig ripping a
line of holes along its trailing edge as I stuck my head
out of the top hatch to see what was going on. (A

little foolhardy, perhaps, but I could always duck back inside if things looked like getting uncomfortably warm, and if I was going to preserve my unmerited reputation for leading from the front I'd need to be visible.)

'Frak,' Lustig said, the rear of the dirigible finally passing the point where he could bring our secondary armament to bear. Penlan was having no such difficulty, her eyes glued to the targeting auspex, swinging the turret around beneath me to cleave a long, jagged tear along one flank of the wallowing behemoth.

'Jurgen,' I called. 'Get this thing turned around!'

'Right you are, sir,' my aide agreed, and a moment later our idling engine roared fully into life, the Chimera's tracks flinging up a spray of freezing slush as it slewed on the spot, bringing our forward-mounted weapon to bear again. 'How's that?'

'Good enough,' Lustig said, confirming the fact a moment later by chewing another hole through the gasbag.

'It's working!' Kasteen reported, her voice echoing tensely in my comm-bead, and glancing up at the perforated dirigible I was forced to agree. It was definitely losing lift, the fabric loose and flapping in several places where once it had been taut with the pressure of the gas within, not quite crippled, but undeniably wounded. Two of its engines were trailing smoke, but none of them had cut out yet, the fans canted downwards to provide as much extra lift as possible while maintaining its inexorable progress towards the unsuspecting city. 'Keep firing!' Possibly the most unnecessary order she'd ever given, but

everyone complied with undiminished enthusiasm nevertheless, Penlan whipping the turret around to tear another handful of gas cells open so fast I almost lost my balance.

It was at that point I became aware of another danger, which had escaped me in the more immediate prospect of immolation. As the slowly descending leviathan lost ever more altitude, the mooring lines dangling beneath it were beginning to scrape along the ground like the tendrils of a vast jellyfish, raising small blizzards of ice and snow as they came. Mindful of the fact that anyone becoming entangled in one would be ripped apart, and therefore in no position to go on ensuring my safety, I issued a general warning over the vox.

'Mind out for the mooring lines,' I broadcast, with another glance upwards as I did so. That last burst of bolter shells seemed to have done the trick, anyway, the dirigible was definitely losing height and manoeuvrability, wallowing this way and that as it descended.

'Very good, sir,' Jurgen responded, taking my words as literally as he always did, and slammed the Chimera into reverse.

'Frak!' Taken unawares by the sudden jerk, Penlan's hand tightened on the traverser, swinging the turret wildly with a whine of abused servos. The hail of bolter shells veered off target, impacting somewhere in the tangle of metalwork shrouding the ominous bulk of the tanker module, bloated with its volatile cargo. She snatched her finger away from the trigger as though it had suddenly become white hot, and stared up at me, her startled eyes wide beneath her

enveloping hat. 'Sorry sir, that took me a bit by surprise.'

'Me too,' I admitted, forcing a carefree smile past the rictus of terror that seemed determined to plaster itself across my face. 'No harm done...'

'I can see flames,' Kasteen reported, her voice tenser than ever. A chill hand seemed to clamp itself around my heart, squeezing as it did so, and I forced myself to look upwards. It was true, a vivid orange bloom had appeared on the starboard tank, and, merciful Emperor, it was spreading even as I watched. Any moment now the whole cluster would blow, taking the entire starport to perdition, and us along with it. Even if we could somehow get aboard the thing and overcome the hybrids manning the flight deck we'd crippled it so badly that we'd never be able to fly it to somewhere it could detonate harmlessly, let alone manage to escape in one piece if we made the attempt.

It was at that moment inspiration struck. Glancing around desperately for some way of saving our necks, or mine at any rate, I saw one of the mooring lines scoring its way across the landing pad in front of us, a little cloud of snow, steam, and pulverised rockrete rising around it like a miniaturised foretaste of the apocalypse to come.

'Jurgen!' I shouted. 'Ram the mooring line!'

I've no doubt that most men in his position would have at least hesitated, probably wondering if I'd lost my wits, but not least among my aide's well-hidden virtues was a dogged deference to authority, and he responded without question or a moment's pause. The Chimera rocked on its suspension as he

slammed it back into a forward gear so high no other driver would even have considered attempting it, gunned the engine to a high-pitched scream that would have set the teeth of an eldar banshee on edge, and let in the clutch. Despite the abuse it had suffered the Chimera leapt forward like a hound off the leash, throwing me back against the lip of the hatch so hard I felt a bruising impact even through the thickness of my greatcoat, and found myself wishing briefly that I'd thought to don my own body armour beneath it, before all my attention became caught up in the urgent necessity of regaining my balance and hanging on. My companions at least were in seats, which protected them from the worst of the buffeting, but I didn't dare leave the vantage point of the cupola. We'd have only one chance at this, and a slender one at that. Timing was going to be absolutely crucial.

'Penlan,' I said, hoping to the Golden Throne that her wits hadn't been too addled by Jurgen's typically robust driving, 'get ready to rotate the turret on my mark. As fast as you can, and don't stop whatever happens. OK?'

'Right sir.' She nodded, her face grim, too seasoned a campaigner to ask any questions at so critical a juncture.

'Brace for impact!' Lustig called from his station next to the driver's seat, and forewarned I did so, just as Jurgen ploughed us into the dangling hawser, thicker than my forearm, which was still gouging a shallow channel across the solid rockrete of the landing pad. The whole vehicle shook with the violence of the collision. From my vantage point in the top

hatch I could see the thick frontal armour buckling, and for a panic-stricken moment I thought it would kill the engine or turn us over, but Jurgen fought for control and our tracks bit into the solid surface beneath the thin coating of slush. Then the writhing cable was falling across us, threatening to take my head off as it lashed about, anchored for a fleeting moment by the weight of our treads.

'Now!' I howled, dropping through the hatch for my very life, and Penlan began to swing the turret, rotating it faster than the enginseers who maintained our vehicle pool would either have believed possible or approved of. For a moment I thought my desperate gamble had failed, as it completed two full turns, then with a sound of rending metal it came to a sudden halt, filling the passenger compartment with the smell of burning insulation.

'Sorry sir,' Penlan said, looking at me dolefully. 'It's stuck.'

'Good.' I poked my head up again, just to make sure, and my heart leapt. The dangling cable had fouled the turret, just as I'd hoped it would, wrapping itself around it and all but tearing off the bolter, which now dangled uselessly from what remained of its mounting. 'Jurgen, drop the ramp!'

'Very good, sir.' My aide complied, his voice as unconcerned as though the order was nothing more unusual than a request for more tanna, and the boarding ramp clanged down behind us, scraping against the surface of the pad as the dangling hawser jerked us around like a fish on a hook.

'Lustig, Penlan, out!' I bawled, wishing I could follow them, but that wasn't going to be possible just

yet, and the two troopers obeyed at once, discipline and their unaccountable confidence in me combining to get them moving even faster than I'd expected. As they baled out past me I drew my chainsword, and began hacking at the heavy hinges supporting the thick slab of metal. 'Jurgen, go! Head straight for the edge!'

'Ciaphas?' Kasteen's voice sounded a little strange for some reason, less crisp and incisive than usual. 'What the hell do you think you're doing?'

'I'm not entirely sure,' I admitted, as my screaming blade began to cut through the hinges in a shower of sparks almost as spectacular as the one being left in our wake by the dragging ramp. With our engine howling in protest we began to move, painfully slowly at first, our hull booming as though from a series of heavy weapon strikes as the abused metal took the strain of the tangled cable and the immense inertia of the slowly falling dirigible. Abruptly the boarding ramp fell free, and we lurched forwards, picking up speed. 'But it's all I can think of.'

'Emperor be with you,' Kasteen said, and fighting down the suspicion that it could very well be the other way round in a few more minutes if my luck didn't hold, I waved at her as insouciantly as I could and hurried back to the seat so recently vacated by Lustig.

'Which way, sir?' Jurgen asked, his vision slit all but obscured by the dangling cable and the spider web of cracks radiating across the armourcrys. Truth to tell, the gunner's station wasn't much better, but I could see enough through the sights of the bolter to guide us, and to my immense relief the weapon still

appeared to be functional. That would make things a little easier, at least.

'A bit more to the left,' I said, catching sight of one of the vivid orange reflectors marking the boundary of the landing field, and taking us as far away from the promethium dock as I could. There was no point in making things even worse than they already were, if that was possible. The battered APC responded to his nudge on the controls with what sounded like a groan of resignation.

'Ciaphas!' Kasteen's voice was urgent in my commbead. 'It's losing height faster than ever. It's going to come down right on top of you!'

'Then we'd better make this quick,' I said, fighting the impulse to look up and see just how close three thousand tonnes of burning promethium was getting. 'How's the fire?'

'Spreading fast,' she said grimly. Better and better. Forcing the matter to the back of my mind by an act of will that vaguely surprised me, I returned my attention to the sights of the bolter, and the narrow strip of snow-powdered rockrete I could see through them. I was only going to get one shot at this.

'Can you jam the throttle open with something?' I asked Jurgen, and he nodded, directing a blast of halitosis in my direction as he glanced over to reply.

'No problem,' he assured me, beginning to rummage through his motley collection of pouches and webbing with his free hand. 'Oh, I wondered what had happened to that.' He pulled out what looked suspiciously like the fossilised remains of one of Zemelda's pastries, although as I was concentrating on the bolter at the time, and

understandably disinclined to bring the thing in his hand any further out of my peripheral vision than I had to, I might have been mistaken. At any event he jammed whatever it was into the slot of the throttle control, and nodded in evident satisfaction. 'Firm as our faith in the Emperor,' he said cheerfully.

'Good,' I said, hoping it was a good deal firmer than mine, but now was hardly the time to consider the matter. The perimeter wall of the starport was looming up ahead of us, and I triggered the bolter, hoping the barrier was as fragile as I'd deduced. Often they're more like fortifications than boundaries, intended to contain the blast of a shuttle accident, but here there would be no point in taking that kind of precaution. The only thing beyond the wall was a sheer drop of Emperor knew how many kilometres, and it was only there at all to keep the occasional starport employee visiting the outlying installations from falling off the edge. With any luck it had been put together as cheaply as possible, and no more solidly than most civilian constructions.

To my immense relief, I was right: the wall ahead of us disintegrated in a hail of heavy ordnance and brick dust, revealing a terrifyingly narrow strip of snow-dusted scrub, with a vertiginously disconcerting vista of cloud tops beyond.

'Ciaphas! It's right on top of you!' Kasteen shouted, her voice shrill in my comm-bead, and I leapt out of my seat.

'Run for it!' I yelled to Jurgen, and we pelted for the yawning gap at the back of the Chimera, our boots ringing on the floor plating almost loudly enough to drown out the complaints of its battered bodywork

and overloaded engine. We jumped almost simultaneously as the floor beneath us lurched and fell away, bounding over the rubble where the wall had been and disappearing over the lip of the bottomless chasm.

For an instant I wondered if we were going to make it. Then my boots impacted on frost-slick grass, and I lost my balance, falling heavily to my knees. For a panic-stricken moment as I scrabbled for purchase I thought I was sliding back over the rim of that terrible abyss. Then my hands caught hold of a bush clinging tenaciously to the edge of the world, and my heart began to slow. I took a deep breath, my aide's familiar miasma informing me that he'd made it too, and staggered to my feet.

'There she goes,' Jurgen remarked conversationally, seating himself on the remaining stub of wall as the blazing dirigible scraped the top of the undamaged sections on either side of the breech we'd made, dislodging a small avalanche of bricks as it went. My breath caught in my throat, and I found myself thankful I hadn't been able to see just how far the flames had spread during our wild ride across the apron. They were licking greedily all round the promethium tanks, the metal glowing red with the heat, and disaster must surely be imminent.

Slowly the wounded behemoth toppled into the abyss, faster and faster as the last remaining vestiges of gas escaped, weighed down by its own lethal cargo and the swinging plumb bob of our gallant Chimera.

'Ciaphas! Are you there?' Kasteen asked in my ear, and I took a deep breath, steadying my voice as best I could.

'I'm fine,' I assured her, 'Jurgen too.' Something rumbled like distant thunder, and a moment later a blast of heat scorched past our faces, flashing the snow around us into steam. Far below, the clouds glowed ackenberry red, as though the sun were somehow setting beneath our feet. I took another deep breath, trying not to cough as I inhaled the warm mist surrounding us. 'But I'm afraid we're going to need another Chimera.'

Editorial Note:

The following is appended without comment, other than that it was typical of innumerable other such effusions published at the time.

From *Periremunda Today: The News That Matters to Your Planet*, 224 933 M41

COMMISSAR HERO SAVES DARIEN!
FIERY APOCALYPSE AVERTED!

SOURCES CLOSE TO the Arbites office in Principia Urbi[1] have confirmed the rumours, rife since mid-morning, that the terrorists waging their despicable campaign against all that is good and holy on our

---

1. *A newsgleaner hanging around on the pavement outside.*

Emperor-blessed globe have been thwarted in their most audacious attack to date by none other than Commissar Ciaphas Cain, the celebrated Hero of the Imperium, whose recent vow to personally crush the traitors in our midst did so much to hearten our beleaguered citizenry.

The valorous commissar was present at the aerodrome in Darien when a promethium tanker, whose crew had been infiltrated by the heretic scum, was directed towards the heart of the city in a suicidal attempt to detonate the cargo it was carrying, obliterating both a strategically vital starport and over a million innocent lives. Acting on the instant, with never a thought for his personal safety, Commissar Cain attached a mooring rope from the dirigible to a nearby tank, driving it over the lip of the plateau, and dragging the deadly cargo to its destruction scant moments before the explosion, which would have dealt so mortal a wound to that defenceless community.

Fortunately for Periremunda, and the Imperium of which our beloved homeworld is such a vital part, Commissar Cain was spared by the Emperor's grace from sharing in the fate of those whose fell design he so heroically thwarted, escaping unscathed to continue his unrelenting quest to uncover and eliminate His Divine Majesty's enemies wherever they may be hiding.

Commissar Cain's outstanding courage and devotion to duty was witnessed by Colonel Regina Kasteen, the statuesque redheaded Valkyrie who

commands the regiment to which he is attached. Asked if there is any truth to the rumours of a romantic liaison between them, she coyly declined to comment.[1]

---

1. *Extremely unlikely, knowing Kasteen, although anything she did have to say in response to such a question would certainly have been unsuitable for publication.*

CHAPTER NINE

NEWS, IT SEEMED, travelled fast on Periremunda, and once again I found myself wondering if Amberley had given it a little nudge.[1] When we arrived at the aerodrome on Principia Mons we were almost immediately surrounded by a scrum of pictcasters and printscribes baying like orks about my supposed heroism back on Hoarfell. Luckily Kasteen and I had retained our escort, despite the loss of the Chimera, and we were able to walk through the horde unmolested, while Lustig and his troopers kept them at arms length by the judicious use of gun butts and profanity. Perhaps equally fortunate, from my point of view, was the fact that the Valhallans regarded the climate this low down as uncomfortably sultry to say the least, which meant they'd discarded their

---

1. In this instance it hadn't proved necessary.

greatcoats, and Kasteen's light summer dress uniform showed off her figure to considerable advantage, thus deflecting a fair amount of attention in her direction.

'Commissar. Colonel.' Nyte was waiting for us at the entrance to the concourse, looking a bit frayed around the edges but reasonably fit under the circumstances, surrounded by a knot of armed justicars. Clearly he was determined not to make the same mistake twice, and I began to regret the loss of our Chimera a little less. He nodded a formal greeting, pointedly ignoring Jurgen. 'I hadn't expected you to bring quite so large an escort.'

'I could say the same,' I riposted, conscious of the number of eavesdroppers surrounding us, and determined to play the part everyone seemed to expect of me. Mentioning the reason for our mutual caution was, of course, out of the question. I nodded towards the exit. 'Shall we go?'

'By all means,' Nyte said, leading his superfluous justicars outside. To my surprise, instead of the groundcar I'd been expecting, the squat armoured shape of a Rhino was waiting for us, its engine grumbling, and the aquila symbol of the Adeptus Arbites fluttering from pennants bedecking it in a manner that reminded me at once of Keesh's ill-fated limousine. He looked at it dubiously. 'I'm not sure there'll be room for everyone.'

'Team one[1] can ride outside,' Lustig volunteered, with a glance at the colonel. 'Keep our eyes open for any sign of trouble.'

---

1. Like many regiments with extensive experience of urban warfare, the 597th routinely divided its squads into two fireteams of five troopers each.

Kasteen nodded. 'That should be perfectly satisfactory, shouldn't it?'

'Of course,' Nyte said, his tone managing to convey precisely the opposite. While the designated troopers scrambled up top, finding convenient stanchions to hang on to, the rest of us clambered inside through one of the side doors, which clanged shut behind us with reassuring solidity.

I glanced round, orientating myself almost at once. It had been some years since I'd last set foot in a Rhino, but the layout was almost the same as the ones I'd hitched a lift in from time to time during my brief period of attachment to the Reclaimers, apart from the fact that the benches were fixed at a more comfortable height for mere humans instead of the armour-clad giants of the Astartes. In their vehicles I'd always found my legs dangling in the manner of a child attempting to sit in an adult-sized chair, which had always left me feeling oddly self-conscious. The ceiling was as high as I remembered, though, with more headroom than I was used to in a Chimera, in order to accommodate the greater bulk of Astartes power armour. The only real difference I noticed was the weapon rack on the bulkhead dividing the crew and passenger compartments. Instead of bulky bolters, too heavy and ill balanced to be wielded effectively by anyone with muscles unaugmented by techno-sorcery, it held riot guns, tanglers, and stubbers.

'Are we taking the same route as before?' I asked, as we jerked into motion, and Nyte shook his head.

'The highway's still closed for repair.' He directed a wan smile at me. 'It seems we put quite a dent in it.' I

nodded, realising he didn't want to mention Amberley's presence here in front of the common troopers, and probably his own people as well, come to that.

Kasteen nodded too. 'Commissar Cain's told us all about it,' she said, with just enough stress on the 'all' to settle any doubts he might have had as to whether I'd taken her into my confidence. Nyte inclined his head, taking her meaning at once, and Kasteen carried on with all the smooth assurance of a diplomat evading questions of policy. 'I'm glad to see you've recovered so quickly from your injuries.'

'I'm well enough to carry out my duties for the arbitrator,' Nyte assured her. Jurgen muttered something about data shuffling and watering the office plants, which I pretended not to have heard.

After a relatively short period of jolting around inside the APC, which was no more uncomfortable than most rides I'd had in one, and a considerable improvement on many (at least no one was shooting heavy ordnance at it) we came to a halt and the hatch clanged open. I followed Nyte and Kasteen outside, to be greeted by a somewhat windswept Lustig.

'No sign of any trouble,' he reported, saluting both me and the colonel in one fluid movement.

'Best get your people together, and go and find something to eat,' I said. I suspected, rightly as it turned out, that the briefing was going to go on for some time. I glanced at Kasteen. 'We should be safe enough in here.'

'I imagine so,' she replied, a trace of amusement flashing in her eyes.

We'd come to rest in an underground bunker, no doubt in the rock beneath the Arbites building, where a number of Rhinos like the one that had brought us

here were parked. They looked blocky and functional in the harsh light of the luminators suspended from the ceiling, their weapon mounts gleaming where highlights were struck from them, and a couple were being fussed over by enginseers. A thick adamantium blast door was sliding closed behind us, sealing the exit ramp. 'I had no idea the local law enforcers were so well armed.'

'This equipment belongs to the Arbites,' Nyte informed us, leaving one of his subordinates to take care of Lustig and his troopers, and leading the way down a rockrete-lined corridor behind a more conventionally sized door. 'We're only granted access to it in the event of a major civil emergency.'

'I imagine the present situation more than qualifies,' I said, and he nodded soberly.

'I'm afraid it does.' Anything more he might have been about to say would have to be kept to himself, however, as a cheerful voice hailed us from somewhere up ahead.

'Ciaphas. You made it after all.' Amberley was waiting beside a plain wooden door, which might have led anywhere. She was simply but strikingly dressed, in a mottled grey tabard over the sort of bodyglove I was more used to seeing on Arbites officers, although hers was a rich, deep red rather than midnight black. Her hair was drawn back into a ponytail with a ribbon of the same colour, which almost exactly matched the rubies set into the eye sockets of the tiny skull in the centre of the stylised letter 'I' of the Inquisition sigil that hung around her neck, wrought in gold and no larger than my thumbnail. 'You look surprised to see me.'

'I am,' I admitted, 'and very pleasantly too,' which happened to be the truth, and her smile spread a little.

'You're a shameless flatterer,' she said, 'but thanks anyway.' She pushed the door open, and stepped through. 'I'm afraid we don't have much time to socialise, though.'

I followed, finding myself in a corridor almost ankle deep in carpet, lined with portraits I assumed depicted the luckless arbitrators previously assigned to this backwater world (unless they'd been shipped in as a job lot when Keesh or one of his predecessors took over the building). Tapestries depicting notable judicial decisions or quoting some fine point of law in High Gothic filled the spaces between, so that glancing back I was unable to tell where the service door by which we'd entered the public side of the building had been located. Amberley slowed her pace a little, to fall into step beside me, and took my arm.

'Nice work this morning,' she said. 'If that fuel barge had gone off it would have made things rather awkward.'

'It certainly would have been for us,' I said. Amberley shook her head, and her eyes clouded for a moment.

'I'm talking about the bigger picture. If things are as bad as we think they are, we're going to need Darien.' She squeezed my arm in a friendly fashion, and grinned again. 'Not to mention our assets there.' She nodded at Kasteen as she spoke, implying that she meant the regiment, but her eyes were resting on Jurgen, who was a pace or two behind me as usual.

Noting that, I felt a faint, premonitory tingle in the palms of my hands as the thought occurred to me that there was a lot about this situation I still hadn't been told. But then that's what this briefing was supposed to be about.

Before I could formulate an adequate response we'd entered a wide lobby, and Amberley had paused before a pair of ornately carved double doors, from behind which I could hear a muted babble of conversation.

'Here we are,' she said, standing aside. She might have been about to say something more, but the vox unit built into the pendant around her neck chimed softly, and a faint voice murmured something I couldn't quite catch. 'She's absolutely sure?' she asked, and listened again. 'I know, she's never exactly clear, but… I'll be right there.' She returned her gaze to me. 'I have to go. Planet to save, you know how it is.'

'Aren't you staying for the briefing?' I asked, bemused.

Amberley shook her head, with a trace of amusement. 'My presence here's a secret, remember? I'm not about to stand up on a stage in front of half the planet.' She shot a dazzling smile at me, her eyes sparkling with mischief. 'Don't tell anyone I was around; I'd hate to have to kill you.'

'I'd prefer it if you didn't have to as well,' I assured her, trying to sound as if I was joking, and not entirely sure that neither of us was.

'I'll try and catch you afterwards,' Amberley said, hesitating on the verge of turning to go, 'and if I can't, I'll be in touch as soon as I can. You'll

understand a lot more when you've heard what Keesh has to say.'

'I'll look forward to it,' I said, and reached out a hand to open the door.

'This is as far as we go,' Nyte said, stepping forward hastily to bar Jurgen's progress. 'The briefing's restricted to personnel of command rank only.' Jurgen's habitual expression of placid imbecility began to harden into the mask of obstinacy that had kept admirals and generals on hold until I could be bothered to deal with them, and he gave Nyte a withering look.

'I go with the commissar unless he tells me otherwise.' Conscious of the barely-concealed smirk on Amberley's face, I nodded judiciously.

'Technically you're right, of course,' I told Nyte. 'Jurgen's military rank is too low to permit him to accompany me.' In actual fact it was about as low as it was possible to get and still consider him a Guardsman rather than a piece of ancillary equipment, but that was beside the point. 'However, since he's here as my aide, he's a representative of the Commissariat rather than the Imperial Guard, which means he has *carte blanche* to go anywhere his duties demand. Is that not the case, inquisitor?'

'Indubitably,' Amberley agreed, keeping a straight face with some difficulty.

'I see.' Nyte coloured a little, no doubt regretting having started this conversation in the first place. 'I'll leave you to it, then.' He disappeared down the corridor, and Jurgen looked at me placidly, all trace of truculence gone.

'Anything I can do for you, commissar?'

I shook my head. 'Nothing springs to mind,' I admitted.

'Very good, sir.' He commandeered one of the sofas scattered around the place with a sigh of satisfaction, and fished a thermal flask of tanna and a porno slate out of his collection of pouches. 'I'll wait for you here then, shall I?'

'That's probably best,' I conceded. After all, he'd had a busy day of it so far, so he might as well put his feet up while he could. Suppressing a twinge of envy, I turned to Kasteen, and gestured towards the door. 'Shall we?'

'By all means.'

I swung it open, with a last regretful look at Amberley's departing derriere, and we stepped through together.

The noise was the first thing to register, a babble of overlapping voices that echoed from the domed ceiling overhead, and then my eyes caught up with my ears. We were in a large amphitheatre, tiers of well-padded seats falling away to a podium on which Keesh was already seated, chatting to the unmistakable figure of Lord General Zyvan, the military leader of our little expeditionary force. He clearly remembered me from Gravalax. Glancing up, he made eye contact briefly, and inclined his head in greeting. Of course this just drew everyone else's attention to us, and several scores of heads turned in our direction, the ambient noise dropping off considerably as the assembled notables registered the presence of the hero of the hour. I glanced around, looking for somewhere to sit, while every eye in the room swivelled in my direction.

'Commissar,' Zyvan said, a friendly smile elbowing its way past his neatly clipped beard. 'A pleasure to see you again.' He nodded to Kasteen. 'And you too, of course, colonel.'

Suddenly aware that we were the only two people in the room still standing, Kasteen nodded formally. 'My lord general,' she said, her search for a seat becoming as unobtrusively urgent as my own.

'Allow me.' A nearby techpriest budged up a little, making room for the two of us, and Kasteen and I slipped onto the bench beside him gratefully. His robe concealed a few odd, solid protrusions, which nudged me uncomfortably from time to time, but at least I wasn't standing there like a practice target on the firing range any more. His lower jaw had been replaced with metal, a grille of fine mesh where his mouth should have been, but in spite of being unable to smile he nodded a greeting, which seemed sincere enough, and his voxcoder unit managed to inject an affable tone into his speech. 'Magos Lazurus, at your service.'

'Commissar Cain,' I replied, as if he hadn't already known, and indicated my companion. 'And Colonel Kasteen, of the 597th Valhallan.'

'Your reputation precedes you, commissar,' Lazurus said, with a trace of amusement. Reminded of the necessity of reinforcing it while I was still the centre of attention, I caught Zyvan's eye again.

'My apologies for delaying you all,' I said, projecting my voice clearly through the now muted hum of conversation the way I'd been taught to as a callow young cadet. 'I'm afraid our pilot was unable to depart on schedule.'

'That was quite fortunate for us, it seems.' Zyvan accepted the apology with the good grace I'd expected, then to my surprise smiled at me. 'Perhaps you'd be kind enough to fill in the details for me over dinner before you leave.'

'It would be my pleasure,' I assured him, having no doubt that his personal chef would be far more creative than the cooks of the 597th.

'If there are no more late arrivals expected, perhaps we can begin,' Keesh said, scanning the room, and Zyvan nodded his agreement.

'Seal the chamber,' he said, and a squad of his personal guards took up positions around the theatre, covering the exits, their hellguns ready for use.

As they moved up the aisles, I took the opportunity to scan the people present, surprised a little by their diversity. There were plenty of Guard uniforms, of course, the colonels of every regiment currently on Periremunda, some of them accompanied by a selection of their senior officers, and almost all with their commissars in tow. I recognised a few familiar faces from other wars, but most were strangers to me. Apart from Lazurus there were few tech adepts to be seen, but those that were here seemed clustered around him, as though they were part of the same party.

After the doubts Keesh had expressed about the loyalty of the PDF I wasn't surprised to find them conspicuous by their absence, but one local institution seemed to have been taken into the Arbitrator's trust. Down by the podium, watching him and Zyvan intently from the front row, was a small knot of figures in bright silver power armour, the black

surplices wrapped around them broken only by the image of a single white rose.

'Battle Sisters,' Kasteen said, her voice taking on a tinge of awe.

I nodded. 'I suppose if any planetary force can be considered uncompromised by the 'stealers it would be them,' I conceded. After all, they were hardly likely to pass on the taint even if they were infected, and in the atmosphere of Emperor-bothering piety in which they lived I doubted that anyone touched by the xenos would escape detection for long.

'By the Emperor's grace,' Kasteen said, and I nodded again, rather less happy to see them than the colonel evidently was. I'd seen the Sororitas let loose on the battlefield before, and as I've said, they've always struck me as something of a blunt instrument tactically speaking, whereas what I thought we needed now was subtlety. Of course that opinion was about to change markedly, but I had no inkling of that at the time.

'As most of you have already been informed,' Zyvan said, while a hololith flickered erratically into life, projecting a map of the subsector above his head, 'we've received a message from Coronus. A further two divisions of the Imperial Guard have been successfully mustered and are expected in system in a little over a week, along with a reinforced battlegroup from the sector fleet, if the warp currents remain favourable.'

'Praise the Emperor for His deliverance,' the woman in the most garishly decorated set of power armour said, and the others made the sign of the aquila at the sound of the holy name.

Zyvan nodded curtly. 'Indeed. However, we haven't been delivered yet. The hive fleet is also inbound, and as near as we can estimate its location from the warp shadow our astropaths have detected, is somewhere around here.' A vague blob appeared, swallowing a large chunk of space. 'As you can clearly see, depending on where in the shadow the bulk of the tyranid fleet actually is, it could arrive anything up to a week before our reinforcements, or a fortnight afterwards. There's simply no way of telling which until they get here.'

A ripple of unease began to slosh around the room, and I thought it was time to remind people what a hero I was supposed to be again.

'I've faced tyranids before,' I said, 'and so has the colonel here. They're formidable enough, I grant you, but we're both living proof that they can be beaten.'

'Well said.' Zyvan looked at me with something like approval. 'But there's an additional complication to take into account.'

'The 'stealer cults,' I said, nodding. 'We need to purge the PDF before the 'nids get here, so we can throw them into the fight with confidence.'

'We're doing all we can to speed up the process,' Keesh assured us, 'but that in itself has revealed a new problem.' Something about the way he spoke started the palms of my hands itching again, and I simply nodded, waiting for him to continue, unsure of whether I could trust my voice not to betray my sudden rush of apprehension.

'Quite so,' Zyvan said. His steely gaze swept the room, the force of his personality washing over everyone in turn. 'What you are about to hear is

highly sensitive. It's no exaggeration to say that the survival of this world may depend on your discretion.'

Better and better, I thought. I already had some inkling of Zyvan's flair for the dramatic, a trait I was to grow a great deal better acquainted with in the years to come, but something about his body language told me that in this instance he meant every word of it. He nodded to Keesh.

'Last night we uncovered a brood of hybrids, which had successfully infiltrated the System Defence Force,' the arbitrator began without preamble. 'The purge is still continuing, but among the facilities compromised was this one.' The hololith flickered, and began projecting a wobbly image of the Periremunda system, one of the outer orbitals highlighted in red.

'Argus five orbital,' Zyvan put in helpfully. 'One of the eight aether platforms making up the system-wide auspex net.'

'Exactly,' Keesh said, returning to his theme. 'Of course the moment we realised so sensitive an installation had been under the control of the enemy we began an immediate review of the datalogs. The results of which were disturbing, to say the least.'

'Disturbing how?' the woman in the gaudy armour put in again, the unspoken 'get on with it' resonating around the room. Despite its source, it was a sentiment I felt myself warming to. Whatever the arbitrator was leading up to it was nothing good, of that I was certain, and I felt an intense desire to hear the worst and at least get it over with.

'Canoness Eglantine.' Keesh nodded, acknowledging her presence with a weariness that hinted heavily

that they'd met before and seldom saw eye to eye,
which I suppose was hardly surprising: the law dealt
in hard evidence, the Ecclesiarchy in matters of faith,
and the common ground between the two was generally pretty narrow. 'You have something to add?'

'Merely that a true servant of the Emperor should
feel no disquiet, however dire the news,' the woman
said. 'He protects.' She bowed her head, and the rest
of her entourage did the same. Before they could turn
the whole thing into a prayer meeting, Keesh got to
the point, which was probably what Eglantine had
intended all along.

'The datalogs had been tampered with,' he said, 'to
conceal the fact that the machine spirits of the auspexes had been blinded across a narrow arc of the
entire system.'

Something which might have been a sharp intake
of breath rattled the chest of the techpriest next to
me, the thought of the blasphemous desecration
wrought on the cogitators of the Argus station clearly
distressing to him. The hololith changed again, a
thin violet funnel appearing like a scratch across the
face of the Periremunda system, linking the planet to
its outer reaches. With grim inevitability the image in
the hololith began to shrink, Periremunda, her sun,
and the other planets and habitats dwindling to a
single point as though floating in bathwater being
sucked down a drainage pipe.

'The area of darkness only extended as far as the
halo,'[1] Zyvan said, 'but our tech adepts and Naviga-
tors were able to extrapolate the line it drew beyond
the limits of the auspex web.' With a grim sense of
inevitability I watched the image continuing to

shrink until the previous view of the subsector had been restored. As I'd known it would, the thin violet line extended several parsecs from Periremunda, finally vanishing into the ominous shadow surrounding the tyranid hive fleet.

'How long ago was this treason committed?' I asked, impatient to hear the worst. Keesh looked directly at me, his manner as serious as I'd ever seen it.

'The records were tampered with on 847 932,' he said heavily. I began to calculate the amount of time that had elapsed, a chill of apprehension shivering down my back, but before I could reach an answer Keesh saved me the bother. 'So it seems highly probable that something from the hive fleet landed undetected around six months ago. The tyranids aren't just coming, ladies and gentlemen. They're already here.'

---

1. *The fringe of cometary debris marking the nominal boundary of a solar system.*

CHAPTER TEN

WELL, THAT GOT everyone's attention, you can be sure, the ensuing clamour at least giving me time to mask my own terror. This was far worse news than even the most pessimistic scenario Kasteen and I had been able to imagine during our chilly wait at the aerodrome back in Darien.

The colonel looked at me, her lips tight. 'This is going to affect our strategy,' she said, with commendable understatement. 'We've been working on the assumption that we'll be dealing with an invasion from space. If the 'nids are already on the ground, we're going to have to fortify in depth.'

'Once we know where they're coming from,' I agreed. If they were already on Hoarfell, the scout creatures could be lurking anywhere. Deception and camouflage were what they were bred for.

There was a slim chance that we might be able to deduce their presence, though, if only by inference. 'As soon as we get back, we'll need access to all the PDF and justicar files on Hoarfell for the last six months. Missing persons, auspex glitches, friend of a friend tales, anything odd or suspicious.'

Kasteen nodded. 'If we can trust the files,' she said, raising the old question of how much we could rely on institutions that might well have been infiltrated by the 'stealer cults.

'For now we're going to have to,' I said. 'They're all we've got.'

Kasteen nodded again, looking far from happy. 'I'll get Ruput on it as soon as I can get a message out,' she said. Contacting Broklaw now would be impossible, the security measures Keesh had put in place for this meeting effectively blocking any outgoing vox transmissions.

'Good,' I said, and raised my voice over the babble of sound. 'If I might ask a question?'

As so often in these cases, one man sounding as if he knew what he was doing was sufficient to make everyone else take a deep breath, at least metaphorically speaking, and start to calm down. The fact that in this case it was backed up by my fraudulent reputation for remaining calm and decisive in a crisis probably didn't hurt either.

'By all means, commissar,' Keesh said, his tone relieved, although whether this was due to the fact that everyone was starting to attend to the matter at hand again, or that I seemed to have forestalled the Sororitas delegation from launching into the

second verse of *He Clasps Us to His Bosom Bright*,[1] I couldn't be sure.

Conscious that, once again, I was the centre of attention, I affected an air of unassuming modesty. 'Has any trace of a tyranid vanguard actually been detected on any of the plateaux?' Amberley's words about needing Darien were coming back to me, and from a tactical viewpoint they only made sense if other plateaux with starport facilities were felt to be under greater threat. After all, with two divisions of Imperial Guard in the warp, we'd need somewhere to offload them when they arrived.

'No,' Keesh admitted, his evident relief at the answer spreading little ripples of reassurance around the auditorium. 'That at least indicates that whatever infiltration there has been, it's on a small scale.'

'How can you be so sure?' Eglantine asked, a trace of asperity in her voice, as though one of her novices had failed to memorise some cherished piece of dogma correctly. Keesh looked at her almost pityingly.

'Because of the unique geography of this planet, your devoutness. The habitable surface of Periremunda is a minute fraction of the whole, and for the most part densely populated. If an infiltrating force has made it down, it must be small enough to evade detection under such conditions, or isolated on one of the lesser plateaux, and effectively trapped there. The lord general and I incline to the former view,

---

1. *A hymn invoking the Emperor's protection in times of peril; somewhat mawkish to modern tastes, but still popular among the pious of a traditional disposition.*

and anticipate little difficulty in dealing with them
once they reveal themselves.'

Eglantine looked less than convinced. 'If they
landed on any of the plateaux at all,' she pointed out.
'Most of the planet is wilderness. If they came down
in the desert, they could be anywhere.'

'If they came down in the desert they'll be dead,'
Keesh assured her. Having seen how tough the chitinous horrors could be I wasn't quite so sure about
that myself, and from his dubious expression it
seemed that Zyvan shared my opinion.

'Nevertheless,' I interjected, 'a thorough orbital
scan to make sure couldn't hurt. Perhaps our ships in
orbit could do the job?'

'They already are,' Zyvan assured me, with an
approving nod. 'So far they've found nothing,
although much of the lower depths are hard to get an
accurate auspex image from.' Remembering the vast
sandstorm I'd flown over on my first visit to Principia
Mons, I nodded. Anything could be hiding under
that, or the smoke from the equatorial volcanoes.
Nevertheless, the fact that they'd failed to find the
scuttling horde we all dreaded offered at least a
crumb of reassurance.

Now their minds had been relieved of the prospect
of being engulfed under a tidal wave of chitin the
moment we set foot outside the auditorium, everyone's attention returned to the more mundane
matters of tactical disposition. This basically boiled
down to all the regimental commanders being given
a free hand to secure their assigned plateau in whatever manner they saw fit, contingency plans for
evacuating the bulk of the civilian population to

peaks defended by the Guard if the hive fleet arrived or the putative infiltrating force showed their hand (or talons, or rending claws) before our reinforcements showed up, and a progress report from Keesh on the painfully slow process of identifying which PDF units were definitely free of the 'stealer taint and could be relied on to fight without having someone looking over their shoulder ready to call down an artillery barrage at the first sign of treachery. The number above suspicion was still depressingly low, and it seemed all too probable that we'd be forced to rely to an unsettling extent on the units in the next most trusted category, which Keesh had rated as no more than reasonably reliable. It was when the hololith displayed this second, much larger, list that Eglantine interrupted once again.

'This is tantamount to questioning the loyalty of my own sisterhood!' she declaimed, with a fine ear for the dramatic. It seemed she'd spotted the name of the Gavarrone Militia, the PDF unit based on the plateau where the Order of the White Rose had its convent, and since Gavarrone was an Ecclesiarchy fiefdom technically independent of the planetary government, subject only to canon law, had chosen to interpret the fact as a thinly-veiled attempt to call into question the loyalty of the church itself.

To be honest I've no doubt that Keesh had relished the chance to get a little dig in at his rival in the never-ending squabble between church and state, but under the circumstances he was too sensible to make an issue of it, merely bowing to the furious canoness.

'I'm sure no one here would wish to do such a thing,' he assured her, his voice studiedly neutral. 'If

your faith in the men of the Gavarronian PDF is as strong as it is in your Battle Sisters, then you may deploy them as readily as you see fit.'

Unable to pass back the buck Keesh had so neatly dropped in her lap without tacitly endorsing the doubts she'd objected to, Eglantine nodded tightly. 'We prevail by the grace of the Emperor,' she said.

'Then our victory is assured,' Keesh said blandly, twisting the knife, and the meeting dragged on into the late afternoon.

ALL DULL THINGS come to an end, thankfully, and at long last Keesh and Zyvan bade us farewell, a few final words about the need for absolute secrecy still ringing in our ears. Truth to tell there was little need for this, as I don't think anyone present was unaware of the consequences if word of the tyranid menace were to leak out to the civilian population before all our preparations were in place. They were spooked enough already at the notion of traitors and heretics running around detonating random bits of the land-scape, and if they got even an inkling of the real threat hanging over their homeworld the panic and civil disorder would be all but impossible to contain.

I regained the relatively fresh air of the lobby grate-fully, my head throbbing with boredom and fatigue, and glanced around for Jurgen, but he seemed to have vanished completely, leaving only the faintest reminder of his presence floating in the air around the sofa he'd occupied. There was a little more solid evidence that he'd been there as well: a tray contain-ing a delicate porcelain tannapot and bowl, both empty, and a matching plate decorated with the

squashed remains of what had possibly once been an ackenberry éclair. A cordon of crumbs and less identifiable detritus enclosed the space where his feet would have been.

'Commissar?' Lazurus was standing next to my shoulder, something under his robe humming faintly. 'Is something troubling you?'

'Not really,' I said, masking my irritation as best I could. The sight of the remains of Jurgen's impromptu picnic had reminded me of how hungry I was getting. Where he'd found it I had no idea, and knew better than to ask. 'I was just wondering where my aide had got to.'

'I'm sure he'll turn up,' Lazurus said blandly, his voice dropping to a level where no one else around us could hear it. 'Inquisitor Vail seems to have considerable faith in your ability to find that which is lost.' He studied my face for a reaction, which I like to think I was too practiced to give him, despite the sudden shock of hearing Amberley's name on the lips of a stranger (which he didn't actually have, as I've already mentioned, but you know what I mean).

'We were lucky on Gravalax,' I said, as blandly as I could, too experienced a dissembler to take refuge in an easily challenged lie. He was evidently aware that Amberley and I knew one another, if nothing else, and could easily have been fishing if he only suspected her presence here. Obviously knowing how the game was played, Lazurus nodded affably.

'So I heard. Good luck with finding your minion.' He began to turn away, then, as I'd half expected, being no stranger to the use of that particular technique myself, glanced back as if with an afterthought.

'Oh, that reminds me. Any promising leads on Metheius yet?' Of course I hadn't a clue who he was talking about, but I was just tired and hungry enough not to be able to resist the urge to tease him a little.

'Nothing concrete,' I said, with just enough hesitation to make him think I was holding out, and he nodded again, as though I'd confirmed something.

'Of course. You'll need to talk to the inquisitor first.' He nodded affably again, and made the sign of the cogwheel. 'May the Omnissiah regulate your systems.'

'And yours,' I said blandly, wondering what else Amberley hadn't been telling me.

'Looks like you've made a friend,' Kasteen said, moving a little closer now that the techpriest had gone. For some reason cogboys always gave her the creeps, even our own enginseers, although she could conceal it well enough if she had to. That didn't mean she had to like being around them, though, and she tended to find something else to concentrate on in their presence if she could. While I'd been having my bizarre *tête-à-tête* with Lazurus she'd been chatting to her opposite number from one of the Harrakoni regiments, and perhaps fortunately had missed the entire exchange.

'Possibly,' I said, a little guardedly, and glanced around for Jurgen again. The crowd in the lobby area was beginning to thin out, and wide gaps were beginning to appear between the bodies, but still no sign of my errant aide. I turned my head, catching sight of a flicker of movement in the corner of my eye, but when I looked in that direction I could see nothing there. The last of the Imperial Guard contingent moved away, standing aside to make

room for Eglantine and her escort, leaving Kasteen and me to our own devices. 'You'd better go on ahead. I'll catch up when I've found him.'

'Right.' Kasteen nodded briskly, conscious as I was of the need to get things moving back on Hoarfell as quickly as possible, and disappeared down the corridor, tapping her comm-bead. 'Lustig, we're moving out. I want a vox relay to Major Broklaw as soon as we're clear of the damping field.' Left on my own I sighed with impatience, and glanced around, hoping to find some clue as to Jurgen's whereabouts. He couldn't have gone far, the tannapot was still warm.

That simple little piece of deduction saved my life. As I inclined my head and bent forward at the waist to reach out and touch the piece of porcelain I became aware once more of that flicker of motion in my peripheral vision, and a chill breeze flashed past my cheek. That was a sensation I was all too familiar with, an edged weapon of some kind striking a great deal too close for comfort, and I drew my chainsword by reflex, flourishing it around me in a defensive pattern I'd practised so often it went beyond conscious thought. Whirling round, looking for a target, I found myself facing an empty room.

My mouth went dry, and on the back of my tongue I could suddenly taste the ozone crackle of sorcery. I'd faced psykers before, of course, but almost always in the company of Jurgen, and I fought down a rising tide of panic. Pushing it away into a corner of my hindbrain, where it could usefully speed my reflexes without getting in the way of my prospects for survival, I scanned the room, looking for that telltale blur of motion again.

I caught it flickering in my peripheral vision in the nick of time, and blocked instinctively, feeling rather than seeing the blow, and was rewarded with the unmistakable whine of diamond-hard teeth slicing into steel.

'Frot!' said a voice close to my ear, an edge of aggrieved surprise in it, and I cut at the source of the sound, but of course my invisible assailant had the advantage of being able to see the humming weapon in my hand, and evaded it easily.

'Jurgen! Kasteen!' I bawled, 'get back here!' but static hissed in my comm-bead, blotting out everything else. It seemed that the psyker, whoever he was, had the eldritch ability to block communications as well as my senses.[1]

'You're on your own, hero,' the voice taunted me, and I flicked through a guard position purely by instinct, being rewarded again with another jolting impact as I deflected a strike no more effective than the previous one had been. 'Oh very good, or very lucky.' The voice had the whining timbre of someone insignificant and ineffectual who finally gets the chance to pick on someone they think is even weaker, and the sudden surge of anger that accompanied that realisation was strong enough to drive out most of the fear I felt. After all the monstrous foes I'd faced and bested, I wasn't about to be beaten by some pathetic nonentity.

'I've fought daemons and real witches,' I said, keeping my voice light and easy. 'A three-for-a-credit psyker's not much of a challenge.' You might think

---

1. *Quite probably; the human brain operates on minute electrical impulses, so it's perfectly possible that his masking field would also affect anything electronic in the vicinity.*

goading the fellow was hardly sensible, but under the circumstances I thought I didn't have a lot to lose. Sooner or later he'd manage to get past my guard, and the best chance I had was to keep him off-balance and hope he'd make a mistake, with any luck one that revealed his precise whereabouts long enough for me to cut the legs out from under him.

'I'm powerful enough to gut you!' Well, the getting him angry part of the plan appeared to be working. His voice rose in a petulant whinny, and a nearby armchair rocked a little as something banged into it. I struck out instantly, releasing a cloud of stuffing as my shrieking chainblade sliced through the grox hide upholstery, and was rewarded with a muffled curse. I could only just have missed him.

Stepping into the gap, following up my advantage by instinct, I suddenly found the flickering outline of a human figure solidifying like mist in front of me, wavering in and out of visibility like a badly-tuned hololith. There was an abrupt crash somewhere behind me as something ceramic shattered with an unmistakably expensive sound, and a familiar and surprisingly welcome odour filled the room.

'Hold on, commissar! I'm coming!' Jurgen bellowed, but the mere fact of his arrival was enough. Abruptly the ozone tang of sorcery was gone, replaced by the reassuring blend of old socks and flatulence, and a weasely little fellow, waving a wickedly-serrated combat blade as though he barely knew which end to point forwards, was standing in front of me, his eyes wide with shock.

'What did you...' he began, in tones of outrage, before my gently humming blade detached his head

from his shoulders. He continued to stare at me for another instant, trying to comprehend his own death, until the pressure of his heartbeat pushed a fountain of blood through his neck and sent his head bouncing into a corner.

'Where were you, Jurgen?' I asked, trying to sound calm as I cleaned and resheathed the blade that had just saved my life yet again.

My aide shrugged, and indicated a tray on the floor, which contained the shattered remains of a tanna service not unlike the one he'd been using, and a spilled mound of sandwiches. 'I saw the guards on the door standing aside to let everyone leave, so I went to get you and the colonel some refreshment. I thought you could do with it after all that talking.' He contemplated the wreckage of his errand for a moment, and re-slung the lasgun he'd readied across his shoulder. 'I'd better go and get you some more.'

'Thank you,' I said, more by reflex than because I wanted the tanna, and turned to join him. 'I'll come with you and save you the trouble.' There didn't seem much likelihood of another unnatural assassin lurking in the vicinity, or they would have attacked me together, but I wasn't in the mood to take any more chances than I had to.

'Commissar?' Lord General Zyvan was emerging from the auditorium, Keesh at his shoulder, and a squad of his personal guard levelling their hellguns as they took in the unexpected vista of carnage. He glanced at the dead psyker, and raised an eyebrow. 'I can see our dinner conversation is going to be even more interesting than I'd anticipated.'

CHAPTER ELEVEN

'It seems whoever was trying to kill you, he wasn't a hybrid,' Zyvan said, handing the data-slate he'd been glancing at across the table to me. The aide who'd delivered it bowed formally and disappeared again, leaving us to our recaf. The dinner preceding it had more than lived up to my expectations, and although I was to become a great deal better acquainted with the genius of Zyvan's personal chef in the years to come, up until that point I'd seldom tasted anything to compare with it.

The lord general had proven to be an affable and engaging host, which reinforced the positive impression I'd already formed of him after our initial meeting on Gravalax. All in all I'd found myself enjoying a remarkably pleasant evening, one that had improved even more after Amberley joined us.

Her appearance halfway through the first course, with polite but guarded apologies about having been unavoidably detained, had come as a most pleasant surprise, and the enthusiasm with which she began making up for lost time as soon as she got hold of a fork hinted that whatever she'd been called away to do earlier in the day had proven to be somewhat strenuous. She didn't volunteer the information, and I knew better than to ask, as did Zyvan, of course, unless he knew already.[1]

Both had listened to my account of the day's activities with every sign of interest, interrupting only to ask pertinent questions or for someone to pass the condiments. I'd started with the incident at Darien aerodrome, resisting the temptation to embroider things, because I knew from long experience that the more matter-of-fact I sounded about my supposed heroism the greater the credit tended to snowball.

'Keesh's people are following up on the crew of the dirigible,' Amberley said, through a mouthful of sautéed grox heart. 'Several key workers in the transport company have already disappeared, which seems significant, but no one they've netted so far seems tainted with the 'stealer genes.'

'So at least they won't be trying that again,' I said, more in hope than expectation, and to my relief Amberley nodded.

'Keesh is stepping up security checks on all commercial air crews, so no one flies from now on without a gene scan.' She ladled a spoonful of grated radish onto the fragrant offal filling her

---

1. *He didn't.*

plate. 'I must say he seems pretty efficient for an arbitrator assigned to a backwater dirtball like Periremunda.'

'Maybe he annoyed the wrong people,' I said. It happens in every branch of the Imperial service, able and ambitious individuals getting sidelined by the nervous incompetents above them, or just backing the wrong side in the endless round of internal politics and getting their careers derailed as a result. Whereas I, who would have liked nothing more than to sit out my years of service in a pointless sinecure as far from harm's way as possible, kept getting entirely the opposite. That just goes to prove what I've always suspected: the Emperor has a nasty sense of humour.

'Either way, it's been good luck for us,' Zyvan said. He'd invited Keesh to join us as well, but the arbitrator had declined, preferring to follow up on our mysterious psyker as quickly as possible before the trail went cold. I hadn't been all that surprised when his preliminary report arrived, and our would-be assassin turned out to be fully human (in so far as the phrase can ever be applied to someone touched by the warp, of course). None of the 'stealer spawn I'd encountered previously had shown any talent for warpcraft, and I mentioned as much.

'It's never been documented,' Amberley agreed, which is as close as an inquisitor will ever get to dismissing something as impossible.

'That raises the question of where the fellow came from,' Zyvan pointed out, with a fastidious sip of his recaf, 'and why he was so determined to kill the commissar.' I nodded in agreement.

'I was wondering about that myself,' I said. 'I would have thought you or Keesh would have been the obvious targets.'

'Then I take it you haven't seen a pictcast lately,' Amberley said dryly. I hadn't, of course, taking no more interest in the mundane gossip of the indigenous civilians here than I had on any of the other planets I'd visited, and the attractive inquisitor lost no time in filling me in, amusement sparkling as always in the depths of her eyes. 'The newsbands are full of you, and so are the printsheets. So far as the Periremundan in the street goes, you're the public face of the Imperial Guard here.'

'I see,' I said slowly, taking a sip of the bitter liquid in my cup, and feeling as though I'd suddenly sprouted a target icon between my shoulder blades. In my experience civilians had only the sketchiest idea of how the military actually functioned, and it seemed horribly feasible that some halfwit insurrectionist would think removing me from the equation would somehow undermine our ability to fight them.[1] That brought me right back to the most fundamental question. 'So who was he, and who could have sent him?'

'Well, he was evidently a psyker,' Amberley said, 'and a relatively weak one at that.' I nodded, trying to look as though I was keeping up, and fortunately Zyvan asked the obvious question before I could.

'How do you know he was weak?' He glanced at the data-slate again. 'According to the autopsy he was at

---

1. *In actual fact, given his popularity among the Imperial Guard contingent, Cain's assassination would have had a noticably adverse effect on morale, something which, typically, seems not to have occurred to him.*

least forty years old, possibly close to fifty. He must have successfully concealed his curse for decades, or he would have been picked up by a black ship long ago.' I nodded too. According to the received wisdom, the taint of the warp usually appeared with the onset of puberty, and I mentioned as much.

'That's generally true,' Amberley admitted, 'but there are exceptions.' She shrugged, her pale yellow gown slipping across her skin in a fashion that distracted me very pleasantly for a moment or two. 'You'd have to ask someone in the Malleus or Hereticus about that, though, rogue psykers are their department. But I do know enough about them to recognise a witch who can't really control his powers.' She nodded at me. 'You kept seeing flickers of movement in his general vicinity, you said.'

'That's right.' It had all been in my original account of the incident, and managed to explain away how I'd been able to bisect the bastard without revealing Jurgen's extraordinary gift. So far as Keesh and Zyvan knew, I'd just got lucky with a speculative swipe. 'And I kept him talking, which helped me get an idea of where he was.'

'Exactly.' Amberley nodded again. 'If he was used to his powers he would have kept quiet, maximising his advantage, and he would have learned how to move without revealing his position. The reason you kept getting glimpses of him out of the corner of your eye was because he was too excited to concentrate on keeping whatever aura he was projecting around himself whole.'

'That makes sense,' I said. 'Sort of. Which leaves us with a nameless nobody who suddenly discovers he's

a psyker and sets out to kill a man he's only ever seen on the picts. What are the chances of that?'

'Not high, I would say.' Zyvan placed his empty recaf cup down on the table, and began to pass round a decanter of amasec at least equal to anything in Keesh's collection. 'I'll ask the arbitrator if there are any Chaos cults active on Periremunda. Wherever there are witches...'

'A good point,' I said, having come to much the same conclusion myself. We both looked at Amberley, who shrugged again, with the same pleasing effect as the last time.

'There's bound to be at least one,' she said, in a casual tone that I for one found vaguely disturbing. 'Probably several.' All right, her branch of the Inquisition was meant to deal with alien threats, like the one facing us at the moment, but I would have expected her to be a little more concerned at the possibility of a bunch of heretics running around the place performing their blasphemous rituals and summoning who knew what horrors from the warp. Something of what I was thinking obviously showed on my face, because Amberley smiled at me. 'Most so-called cultists have no idea of the true nature of Chaos. They band together more because they feel alienated from society than because they really want to bring down the Ruinous Powers on the galaxy.' Her eyes grew hard for a moment. 'There are exceptions, of course.'[1]

'And you think one of the exceptions is active on Periremunda?' I asked.

---

1. *Which is why we have the Ordos Hereticus and Malleus. Although it must be said that some of the more Radical members of both are barely distinguishable from their prey, even in their degree of apparent sanity.*

Amberley shook her head. 'I doubt it. We'd have found traces of them before now. But it's perfectly possible that one of the less dangerous groups is entrenched here. Even if all they do is enact a few meaningless rituals they've picked up from horror picts, they'd be a natural refuge for any rogue psykers on the planet. People like our anonymous friend here.' She glanced in the direction of the slate. My would-be killer had been carrying no identification, and had been dressed in the sort of gaudy clown costume that anywhere else would have made him stand out like an ork in a ballet dress, but which the Periremundans seemed to think was bordering on the conservative. No doubt Keesh would find out who he was in the end, but by that time his associates would probably be long gone.

'So in your considered opinion,' Zyvan said slowly, trying to digest the new and unwelcome information Amberley had just presented us with, 'whatever group this man belonged to is no real threat to our operation here?'

Amberley rolled her eyes despairingly, and sighed. 'Of course they're a threat, they're Chaos-worshipping loonies. Just a great deal less of one at the moment than the hive fleet, which is poised to devour every living thing on the planet.' She sipped at her amasec. 'Once we've dealt with the immediate problem, we can worry about the little things.' I was by no means reassured to hear a Chaos cult, even one an inquisitor seemed to consider relatively ineffectual, being referred to as a little thing, but I took her point.

'Let's look on the bright side,' I said. 'Maybe the 'nids will eat them all for us.' Amberley laughed mellifluously.

'Maybe they will,' she said.

'The thing I don't understand,' Zyvan said, glancing at the slate again, 'is why they'd reveal themselves now. He must have known there was a chance he'd get caught.'

'He probably wasn't the most rational person on the planet,' I said, thinking of Rakel, and most of the other psykers I'd ever met, 'and he thought he was undetectable, remember. He probably thought he'd be able to stroll into the Arbites building, carry out his assignment...' for some reason I found myself reluctant to use the phrase 'kill me', as it reminded me a little too forcefully of how close he'd come to succeeding, 'and walk straight out again. If he'd managed to pull it off the insurgents would have got the blame, and no one would even have suspected the existence of his cult.'

'That's what I mean,' Zyvan said. 'If they hadn't shown their hand this afternoon, we still wouldn't know they were there. Why bother?'

'We've been lifting a lot of stones looking for the 'stealer broods,' I pointed out. 'Maybe they were just afraid that we'd start pulling their people in as well, and get on to them that way. So they panicked, and thought they'd disrupt the counter-insurgency effort before we stumbled across them by accident.'

'That sounds plausible,' Zyvan said. Well it was no more irrational than anything else I'd seen the minions of Chaos do over the years, and I couldn't think of any other explanation, so I just nodded and let it go.

The rest of the evening passed in a pleasant haze of small talk, a regicide game with Zyvan (which I won

quite comfortably, despite Amberley leaning over my shoulder suggesting alternative moves every five minutes), and enough of the lord general's excellent amasec to reinforce the mood of light-hearted merriment despite the terrible danger hanging over us. All in all it had been a long time since I'd felt quite so relaxed, despite the rigours of the day, and Zyvan clearly felt the same. From then on I was to receive periodic invitations to dine with him whenever our respective duties permitted.

At length, however, the evening wore itself out, and I offered to escort Amberley back to her hotel suite. Not that she required escorting, of course, being perfectly capable of decking an ork if she had to, but it was the polite thing to do, and it would enable me to spend a little more time in her company. After a moment's consideration she nodded, smiling.

'That would be nice,' she agreed.

ZYVAN HAD SET up his headquarters in the Arbites building, more for the security it offered than from any other consideration I suspected, and Amberley led me through a twisting maze of utility corridors until we found ourselves back in the underground chamber our Rhino had come to rest in a few hours before. A gleaming speeder the size of a limousine was parked there now, its windows blacked out, hovering a couple of centimetres above the stained rockrete floor with its grav units humming faintly.

'Very nice,' I said, taking in the thing's sleek lines and air of barely restrained power. I wasn't terribly *au fait* with civilian vehicles, but I doubted anything

that efficient and expensive-looking had originated on Periremunda.[1]

As we approached it the door hissed open, and Pelton grinned out at us, a chauffeur's cap perched incongruously on his mop of wheat-coloured hair. 'Home, milady?' he asked, playing the part about as convincingly as a marionette, and Amberley nodded, sliding across a rear seat almost as wide and well padded as the one I'd occupied in Keesh's mangled limousine.

'Home, Pelton.' She glanced up at me. 'Coming?'

'Of course.' I masked my surprise with the ease of long practice, and clambered in beside her. I raised an eyebrow as the rear door hissed closed. 'Milady?'

Amberley nodded, as Pelton fed power to the motivators, and the long, sleek vehicle began to move, turning on the spot as it rose to about a metre above the floor and humming towards the blast door. 'I'm travelling as the Lady haut Vail, minor aristocracy from the Krytenward system. It explains the servants and other riff-raff hanging around my suite.' The last sentence was delivered in the bored drawl of the nobility, and Pelton grinned again, apparently enjoying the joke.

'That's us,' he explained, in case I hadn't got it, and returned his attention to the controls. 'Whoops, didn't see that coming.' He kicked a little more power to the repulsors, bouncing us over a Rhino that was just emerging from the access tunnel, with barely a

---

1. A *D'Lorien Raptor*, fabricated on Rubica, if anyone cares. Extensively modified by Yanbel, of course; the standard model comes without communications gear, weapons, or armour plate.

centimetre to spare between us, the blocky armoured vehicle, and the roof of the tunnel.[1]

'Flicker, stop showing off for the commissar,' Amberley said, her tone indulgently reproving.

'Sorry boss.' We shot out of the tunnel like a shell from the barrel of an Earthshaker, and headed skyward at a pace that would undoubtedly have tried Jurgen's stomach had he still been with us: mine too, to be honest, if the aircar hadn't been fitted with inertial dampers. As it was the ride seemed smooth enough, and I settled back to enjoy it.

'I met Lazurus at the briefing,' I said conversationally. Amberley regarded me with cool detachment, giving nothing away beyond a barely concerned acknowledgement of the name. 'He asked how you were.'

'Did you tell him?' Amberley asked casually. I shook my head.

'I said you'd seemed well enough when I saw you on Gravalax.' To my surprise she actually laughed out loud at that, as mellifluously as ever.

'You really do have a talent for this sort of thing, don't you?'

'I'm not sure,' I said cautiously. Amberley knew me as well as anyone in the galaxy, and saw further beneath the mask I usually presented to it than anyone else, but I was still not sure quite how far that was. 'It depends what sort of thing we're talking about.'

'Diplomacy, misdirection, sneaking about.' She grinned happily at me again. 'You know, inquisitor stuff.'

---

1. *Cain's exaggerating here. There were at least three centimetres to spare all around.*

'You'd know more about that than I would,' I said, and she laughed again.

'See what I mean?'

'He seemed to think I was looking for someone called Metheius,' I said, refusing to be deflected. 'Why would he think that?'

'Because he knows I am, and he knows you're an associate of mine. Lazurus and I are working together, sort of.'

'Sort of?' I asked, looking out at the lights of Principia Mons below and around us. The night was humming with life, and the thought of the ravening swarm about to descend on all those happy, oblivious people was a depressing one. Amberley nodded.

'The Mechanicus and the Ordo Xenos have a joint project running. It's been going on for decades, but about a dozen years ago it ran into a bit of a hiccough, on Perlia.' She looked at me narrowly, and after a moment a sudden horrified understanding burst over me.

'The Valley of Daemons,' I said, the memory of the hidden Mechanicus shrine I'd stumbled across while leading my ragtag army to safety surfacing for the first time in years. The facility had been gutted when we found it, everyone and everything dead apart from a single surviving combat servitor, which had given me an anxious few moments, and at the time I'd been too busy trying to fend off an army of blood-maddened orks to think too much about the mystery. I did so again now, though, in the light of this new and disturbing information.

'That's right,' Amberley said evenly, no doubt waiting to see how much I'd be able to work out for

myself. I tried to dredge as much detail out of my memory as possible, seeing again the vast dam collapsing, the tidal wave we'd unleashed scouring its way down the valley, and the ork army besieging us being swept into welcome oblivion. But it was what I'd seen before that that had been, in its own way, even more disturbing.

'Everyone had been killed,' I said slowly. 'We thought the orks had done it at first, but there wasn't enough damage for that. The place had been hit cleanly and surgically.' I remembered something else. 'All the databanks in the cogitators had been wiped, and something had been taken from a vault there. It looked like a melta had been used on it.'

'That was Metheius's doing,' Amberley said. She leaned forward to tap Pelton on the shoulder. 'Take the scenic route, Flicker.' Understanding what she meant, Pelton peeled away from our original heading to begin a leisurely circuit of the palace gardens, where it seemed the governor was holding a ball. Lanterns flickered in the ornamental shrubs beneath us, and elegantly dressed couples strolled arm in arm along illuminated paths or rotated around one another on the dance floor floating in the centre of the lake. No one glanced up as we passed, apparently taking us for just another late arrival, if they even noticed us at all.

'All by himself?' I asked, finding that hard to credit.

Amberley shook her head. 'Of course not. He had help, and outside contacts, but for a long time he was one of the most senior magi working on the project.'

'Which was what, exactly?' I asked. Amberley hesitated, as if wondering how far to take me into her confidence.

'While the dam was being built,' she said at last, 'the Mechanicus unearthed an artefact. It was unlike anything they'd ever seen before, so they brought it to the Ordo Xenos, to see if we might be able to help them identify it.'

I felt a prickling sensation in my scalp. There could be only one explanation for such a discovery. 'Let me guess,' I said. 'It predated humanity's presence on Perlia.'

Amberley shook her head slowly. 'It predated humanity's presence in the galaxy,' she said quietly. 'Us, and every other race we know of, except possibly the Necrontyr.' She paused for a moment. 'And it was still functional.' The tingling sensation worked its way down my spine in a far from pleasant fashion.

'What does it do?' I asked, unable to keep a note of awe from my voice.

'We still don't know, even after generations of study, but what little data we were able to recover once the orks were eliminated and we could return to the site would seem to indicate that Metheius had made some kind of breakthrough.'

'Which he seems reluctant to share,' I concluded.

Amberley nodded grimly. 'Quite. He must have had confederates within the facility for their attack to have succeeded so completely. Eight of his fellow techpriests vanished along with him, so it's not hard to guess who they might have been.'

'The damage we saw was consistent with an assault from the outside,' I said. 'So he must have had help there too. A mercenary band, something like that.' The memory of the dead techpriests and their guards came back to haunt me once again. 'A competent one

too. There was hardly any collateral damage. Even a squad of Astartes could hardly have been more precise.'

'That's what we concluded,' Amberley said, 'and in the confusion surrounding the orkish invasion, they were able to get clean off-planet before anyone knew they were gone.'

'I see,' I said, my head spinning. 'And you think he's taken refuge on Periremunda.'

'It's a possibility,' Amberley said. 'I came here to check it out, and found Lazurus following up the same lead. We've been sharing our findings ever since.' She chewed her lower lip, looking mildly vexed. 'Unfortunately this tyranid thing complicates matters a bit. I can't really sit back and leave the 'stealers to bring the sky down on our heads, so Lazurus is getting a clear run at Metheius while I'm out bug-swatting.'

'I thought you were on the same side,' I said, confused. Amberley looked at me thoughtfully.

'You know how it is. The Inquisition and the Mechanicus are meant to be equal partners, but whichever of us recovers the artefact gets to be a bit more equal than the other.'

I sighed, and shook my head. 'It's a lot simpler in the Guard,' I said. 'See the enemy, kill the enemy. We don't have to worry about all this political stuff.' That wasn't entirely true, of course, but life was certainly a great deal less complicated where I usually sat.

'No doubt,' Amberley said, not fooled for a moment. She shrugged. 'So there it is: unimaginably ancient xenos artefact somewhere on the planet in the hands of a renegade, the hive fleet poised above

our heads ready to rip this world apart, hidden 'stealer broods everywhere making an early start on their behalf, and now a bloody Chaos cult crawling out of the woodwork just in case we were getting bored.' She forced a carefree smile to her face, with an effort few people other than me would have been able to detect. 'Welcome to my world, Ciaphas.'

Editorial Note:

While Cain was running around the planetary capital, getting himself tangled up in my investigation, the rest of the Imperial Guard was reacting to the dire news Zyvan had just imparted to its senior commanders with its usual efficiency. Since, almost inevitably, Cain doesn't bother to mention any of this in his own account I've appended the following extract from the memoirs of Jenit Sulla, who at the time was a mere lieutenant in the 597th, in the faint hope that it might prove illuminating. As always where this particular author is concerned, readers with a refined appreciation of the complex and subtle nuances of which the Gothic language is capable may wish to skip this passage entirely.

From *Like a Phoenix on the Wing: The Early Campaigns and Glorious Victories of the Valhallan 597th* by General Jenit Sulla (retired), 101 M42

MY READERS CAN readily appreciate the consternation with which Colonel Kasteen's news was greeted upon her return from the capital, and the keenness with which we felt the absence of Commissar Cain, whose steady demeanour and steely resolve in the face of even the most dire of crises was so unfailingly inspirational to those of us who were privileged to serve alongside him. I for one, however, took heart from the fact that he would soon be among us once again, and resolved that upon his return he would not find me, or any of the women and men under my command, any the less prepared to confront this most terrifying of foes than he would be himself. After all, we had faced and bested the tyranid fiends on Corania, albeit at the most terrible cost, and I had no doubt that we would prevail once again, under the steadfast leadership of our colonel and the inspiring presence of our commissar.

By the time he returned, his habitual jaunty demeanour somewhat muted by the heavy responsibility he must now have felt,[1] our preparations to meet this fearsome foe were well advanced. Colonel Kasteen's foresight in anticipating that the presence of genestealers on this fascinatingly fractured world might presage the arrival of a splinter fleet had been well founded, and I like to think that the 597th was by

---

1. Or, more likely, a hangover of monumental proportions.

far the most prepared of all the regiments on Perire-munda for the onslaught to come. For my part, I had been drilling my platoon in the painfully learned lessons we had acquired on Corania ever since the colonel had issued her far-sighted order to practise them, and felt nothing but confidence in the women and men under my command.

When the flesh-moulded abominations of the hive fleets dared to show themselves openly, they would not find us wanting in fighting spirit, of that I had not the faintest scintilla of doubt. But when the foe even-tually appeared in front of our eagerly waiting weapons, it was to be far from the comforting chill of Hoarfell, and in a manner none of us could possibly have anticipated.

CHAPTER TWELVE

MAKING THE MOST of her pose as an aristocratic parasite, Amberley had taken over the penthouse suite of the most exclusive hotel in Principia Mons, which, among many other amenities, boasted its own landing pad, tucked away behind a small but pleasantly-scented roof garden. Pelton conveyed us there without further ado, coasting to a halt and popping the rear doors of the luxurious speeder with all the aplomb of the chauffeur he was pretending to be. The scent of hegantha and callium drifted inside the aircar, both blooms, I recalled, of which Amberley was particularly fond. I found myself wondering for a moment if she'd chosen the penthouse because they were already growing there, or if she'd had them planted after she'd arrived.[1]

'Very nice,' I commented, stepping out into the cool night air. The city was spread out almost as far as the eye could see, until it ended abruptly at the lip of the

---

1. *Well, if you have to play the spoiled little rich girl, you might as well embrace the role. Nothing convinces people you've more money than sense quite as effectively as indulging a ludicrously expensive whim.*

plateau in a sudden cessation of light and motion as sharp as a knife-edge. Most of it was far enough below us for the never-ending noise to be muted, and the ground cars scuttling around like glowbugs seemed to skitter silently along the luminated thoroughfares in the distance.

Amberley nodded. 'It'll do. It fits my cover, and the flight pad means we can come and go as we please without exciting any more comment than necessary.'

I nodded too, picturing her walking though the lobby in power armour, and suppressed a grin. The staff of such an establishment was discreet, I had no doubt, but there were still some things that would raise a few eyebrows. 'I'm sure it does,' I said.

Amberley shrugged. 'They're used to all kinds of eccentric behaviour here. They'll tolerate pretty much anything if you pay them enough, and they won't ask too many questions. Even so, it never hurts to be circumspect.'

'I'm sure it doesn't,' I said. I got a bit more used to her methods over the years, as she dragged me into her covert activities time and time again, but I never quite managed to shake off the feeling that she tended to adopt disguises and elaborate cover stories more for the fun of it than because they were strictly necessary.[1] Amberley laughed, took my arm, and led me inside

---

1. *That, of course, is entirely a matter of opinion. Some inquisitors believe the Emperor's work is best done by charging around the place like a grox in a ceramic emporium, leaving a trail of carnage and destruction in their wake, while others prefer not to let the enemies of all that's good and holy get away clean by making it blindingly obvious that they're coming for them.*

while Pelton powered the luxurious speeder down. 'Modest little place you've got here.'

The main living room was huge, tinted windows looking out and down at the urban panorama, the neat, comfortable furnishings supplemented by plants in tasteful ceramic urns and a surprising amount of weaponry left lying around the place. Amberley shrugged as my eyes fell on the scattering of ordnance.

'It pays to be prepared,' she said cheerfully.

'That it does,' Yanbel agreed, doing something with his mechadendrites to the barrel of the heavy bolter I'd last seen attached to the forearm of Amberley's power suit. He held it up to the light, squinting along its length with a faint whirring sound as his augmetic eyes focused on something too minute to see, and emitted a grunt of satisfaction before reaching for a small jar of sanctified oil with one of his natural hands and beginning to bless the thing.

Over in the far corner, Rakel looked up from what looked like a hushed conversation with Simeon (they seemed to spend a lot of time together, I noticed, probably because in their differing ways they were both as marginally sane as one another), and shot me a venomous look.

'It's you,' she informed me unnecessarily, her eyes skittering around the space behind me as she spoke. 'But I don't feel the void.'

'Jurgen's still back at the Arbites building,' I said, taking my best guess at what she was blathering about. If Keesh came up with anything else about our mysterious assassin, or Zyvan learned anything new about the tyranid threat, I wanted to know right away,

and I wanted my aide on the spot as a visible and odoriferous reminder to both of them to keep me in the loop. The psyker relaxed a little.

'The shadow's hungry,' she told me seriously, then turned back to Simeon. 'His mind's all shiny, like a mirror.' I hadn't a clue what to make of that, so I just smiled politely.

'Commissar. Mainly brisk of ya!' Zemelda entered the room, looking like a bad actress in a drawing room farce, her crisply-starched maid's uniform at incongruous odds with the green fringe hanging over her face, and the bulge of a badly concealed laspistol just below her left breast. She seemed genuinely pleased to see me, despite making no more sense than Rakel, and I smiled in return.

'It's good to see you too,' I said, taking my best guess at the meaning of the Periremundan street slang, and the erstwhile snack vendor beamed at me as though I'd just told her she'd won a thousand credits. 'I see you're settling in all right.'

'You bet.' She nodded vigorously. 'Best job I ever had. Beats the hell out of flogging gristle pies or fly-posting for slash gigs,[1] I can tell you.'

'I'm glad to hear it,' I said, trying to mask my bemusement.

Zemelda nodded again, with undiminished enthusiasm. 'It's like when we were juves, playing games, but this time it's for real, you know?'

I nodded, not really trusting myself to speak. It was the same eager enthusiasm I was used to seeing in the

---

1. *No, I don't know either.*
2. *An Imperial Guard slang term for raw recruits. It's apparently a phonetic rendering of FNGs, which I'm told stands for Frakking New Guys.*

fungs² just arrived from the recruiting stations on
Valhalla, all fired up with martial zeal and the
supposed glory of combat. The bright ones wised up
fast, kept their heads down, and got on with the grim
business of survival. The rest became heroes or dead,
quite often both, and almost instantly forgotten by
their squadmates. With an unexpected pang, I found
myself wondering which category Zemelda would
fall into.

'She's being a big help,' Amberley said, with an
indulgent grin at her eager new assistant. 'The sort of
inbred imbecile I'm supposed to be wouldn't be seen
dead without a ladies maid to run errands for her,
and Zemmie fits the bill perfectly.' She nodded at the
psyker in the corner. 'Rakel doesn't really look the
part, even on a good day.'

'And I look like a kleeb in a dress,' Pelton added,
following us into the room. That conjured up an
image I'd rather not have had inflicted on my
synapses, and I nodded slowly.

'I can believe that,' I said. Zemelda had gravitated
towards him the moment he appeared, and I
couldn't help noticing the half-smiles they'd
exchanged as they registered one another's presence.

Pelton shrugged. 'Joking aside, she's got a real apti-
tude for dark ops.' Zemelda coloured slightly at the
words of praise. 'She can live a legend as well as a
pro, and she's getting to be a pretty good pistol shot.
Took down a hybrid the last brood we raided with a
single lasbolt, just as it was drawing a bead on
Simeon.' The familiar easygoing grin appeared on his
face. 'Not that I suppose he'd have noticed even if he
had been shot.'

'That's beside the point,' Amberley said, her tone mildly reproving. 'I prefer my associates unperforated. They're more useful that way.' Not for the first time I found myself impressed by the easy camaraderie she seemed able to inspire in the motley rabble she tended to surround herself with. I saw a lot of faces come and go over the years, but all of them seemed to share it, however diverse their lives and backgrounds had been before they found themselves swept into her orbit.

'You won't get any argument from me,' Pelton agreed, and the two of them wandered off, leaving Amberley and me to gaze out at the night-shrouded city together.

'They seem to have hit it off,' I said, and Amberley nodded.

'No bad thing,' she said. 'If she's going to hang around with us she'll need a good grounding in combat techniques, and Flicker's the only one in the group proficient enough to teach her.' A self-mocking grin appeared on her face. 'Apart from me, of course, and I don't have the time to baby-sit.'

'He seems to know a lot about undercover work,' I said. Amberley nodded again.

'He was in deep for a long time, infiltrating a shadow cartel in the Torredon Gap. Too long, probably. He had to do some questionable things to maintain his cover, and there were suspicions he'd turned.' I nodded slowly. Much of the Torredon subsector was riven by warp storms, leaving only a few safe routes for the merchant vessels plying the trade routes there, and piracy was a never-ending problem.

'So he was with the Naval Provosts before you recruited him?' I asked.

Amberley shook her head. 'He was an arbitrator, until the chastener running him decided he'd become more of a liability than an asset, and tried to reel him in. Flicker disagreed with that assessment, and it ended badly.'

'How badly?' I asked.

Amberley sighed. 'There were a lot of bodies. Flicker thought if he was going to be yanked out of the field he was going to clean house first, and started taking out all the key players he'd identified in the cartel.' A note of grudging admiration entered her voice. 'He was smart, I have to give him that: set one of the senior directors up as a pretender to the high seat, took out a couple of the second echelon, and pointed the finger. It was a bloodbath. By the time his handlers caught up with him the cartel was in shreds and anyone capable of repairing the damage was dead.'

'So what was wrong with that?' I asked, in honest perplexity. It sounded to me as if he'd done the galaxy a favour.

Amberley looked at me pityingly. 'Think about it. An arbitrator stepping outside the law, however laudable his motives, isn't something the Arbites can take lightly. Luckily I happened to be around when they were getting ready to flush him, and thought a talent like that shouldn't go to waste.'

'I see.' I nodded, reflecting yet again how relatively uncomplicated things were in the Imperial Guard. On the battlefield you do whatever it takes to win, and that's the end of it. 'Well, at least it seems Zemelda's in good hands.'

Amberley looked at me speculatively. 'I'm hoping she won't be the only one tonight,' she said.

WE WERE ENJOYING a leisurely breakfast the next morning when Lazurus arrived unexpectedly, a clattering ornithopter bearing the cogwheel sigil of the Adeptus Mechanicus settling onto the flight pad beyond the hegantha bushes with all the fluttering grace of an iron chicken. Amberley looked up from her ackenberry waffles as he entered through the patio doors, and nodded a cordial greeting.

'Pull up a chair,' she invited, a trifle indistinctly, while Zemelda, still apparently revelling in her impenetrable disguise, poured a cup of recaf and placed it on the table in front of him. Emperor alone knows how she expected him to drink it, what with not having a mouth and all, but it was the sort of thing a servant was supposed to do, so she probably thought it added to the solidity of her cover or something. The simple task accomplished she went to poke the dish of salma kedgeree on the sideboard with a serving ladle, and try to look as though she wasn't listening avidly to the conversation around the table.

Lazurus inclined his head courteously as he took the proffered seat. 'Thank you, but I've already ingested nutrient this week,' he returned, with an obvious effort at good manners. He glanced in my direction, but if he was surprised to see me there, made no sign of the fact. 'Commissar, you look well. I trust your interaction with the inquisitor has proven satisfactory?'

'It has,' Amberley said, with a barely perceptible grin in my direction, 'but I fear you've had a wasted

journey. Ciaphas has no more idea of Metheius's whereabouts than either of us do.'

'That's most disappointing,' the magos said, managing to sound as if it was anything but. 'I had hoped a man of his apparent resourcefulness could open a few of the doors that have so far remained closed to us.'

'As had I,' I assured him blandly, as if I'd been privy to the search for the renegade cogboy since the beginning, and as I spoke I found a number of possibilities suggesting themselves. 'My position in the Commissariat gives me access to all the intelligence being analysed by the Guard and the Arbites, for instance.' I glanced at Amberley. 'Unless, of course, you've already taken Zyvan and Keesh into your confidence?'

'Not about this,' she confirmed. 'They have enough to worry about with the 'stealers and the hive fleet.' She shrugged, pushing her plate away, and taking a sip of her recaf. 'Besides, the *shadowlight*–'

'The what?' I interrupted, a forkful of kedgeree halfway to my mouth.

Lazurus chimed in helpfully. 'The xenos artefact Metheius absconded with. Since his departure we've uncovered more items in the Valley of Daemons, including a selection of metal tablets of unknown composition containing fragments of script, one of which appears to refer to it by that name.'

A familiar dry cough announced the arrival of Mott, who had been listening to the latter stages of the conversation, and seemed unable to resist verbalising the torrent of related information encoded within his augmetically enhanced cerebellum any longer.

'The language has never been reliably deciphered,' he put in, reaching for the insulated jug of recaf Zemelda had recently put down on the sideboard and pouring himself a cupful without seeming to look at it. I flinched, anticipating scalded fingers and the crash of the cup on the carpet, but he judged it to a nicety and carried on talking without apparently pausing to draw breath. 'However, a few earlier examples have been discovered scattered across the galaxy, and a rough attempt made to assign meaning to some of the symbols. The main difficulty with this is that the examples so far recovered, though uniformly ancient beyond imagining, appear to originate from different points within a span of aeons, so it's by no means certain that any established symbology would have remained unchanged during the lifetime of the civilisation that produced them.'

Remembering the fractured Gothic Zemelda lapsed into when she forgot no one else present was from around here, I could well believe that, but suppressed the urge to nod in agreement. Once Mott got going, the last thing you wanted to do was encourage him. 'On the other hand, the regularity of the script, and the uniformity of workmanship of the few artefacts and other fragments recovered across such a diverse range of sites would seem to indicate that it was a remarkably stable society, as well as long lasting, so it's by no means beyond the realm of possibility that at least a fair degree of consistency was maintained.'

'Thank you, Caractacus,' Amberley said, glaring at me with a 'now look what you've done' expression on her face. 'As I was saying, the existence of the arte-fact, whatever it might have been called, is a secret

known only to a few, and both we and the Mechanicus would prefer to keep it that way.' Lazurus nodded his agreement, but my mind was only just catching up with the last thing he'd said before Mott's logorrhoea got triggered, and I stared at him in some perplexity.

'Hold on a minute,' I said. 'You've found more of this stuff? When did that happen?'

'When do you think?' Amberley asked, reaching for a slice of buttered toast. 'While they were rebuilding the dam you blew up, of course.'

Lazurus nodded again. 'The resulting flood rearranged the topography of the valley quite substantially.' A warning glance from Amberley forestalled Mott from filling us all in on quite how much that was, how much topsoil had been removed in the process, and how many orks had got their feet wet. 'In particular a new site was revealed, containing quite a lot of interest to us, including further devices that, as yet, have failed to yield up their secrets.'

'Which is all very interesting,' Amberley put in, bisecting her toast with a small, precise bite, and spraying me with crumbs as she completed the sentence, 'but we're drifting away from the point.' She looked at me speculatively. 'How do you think your access to the military intelligence grid can help us to pinpoint Metheius? Preferably before he becomes indigestion for a 'nid.'

'Because the analysts are looking for evidence of 'stealer infestation,' I pointed out, 'and nothing else. The fact that they missed the Chaos cult that tried to kill me last night proves that.' I glanced at Lazurus as I spoke, but he betrayed no surprise at my words.

Not that I expected to see any, cogboys of his rank are more clockwork than human anyway, but I imagine that whatever conversation ensued between him and Amberley after I left the room would have been interesting to overhear. 'If I ask Zyvan for access to the raw data, I might find something they missed, because it fell outside the parameters they were looking for.'

'It's worth a try,' Amberley said, nodding thoughtfully. 'I've only been getting the filtered stuff, and asking to look at the source material myself would only give rise to awkward questions. So far as the Guard is concerned, I'm just here to advise on the tyranid problem.'

'Regrettably, I find myself in a similar position,' Lazurus agreed. 'I may be advising the lord general on the most judicious use of the Omnissiah's bounty in the furtherance of our cause, but, as a mere civilian, any intelligence I may be privy to is strictly on a need to know basis.'

'I'll talk to Zyvan,' I said. 'Keesh too. If I tell them I'm looking for leads on our mystery assassin, they ought to co-operate.' I glanced at the elaborate chronograph on the wall, which was ten minutes fast and encrusted with far too many gilt angels. 'I'll have to swing by the Arbites building anyway, to pick Jurgen up.'

In all honesty the only thing I expected my offer of help to lead to was an excellent excuse to visit Amberley every few days to report in person on my regrettable lack of progress, and enjoy a pleasant few hours of her company. But, as so often seems to happen, that apparently trivial gesture was to fling me

into a maelstrom of danger and treachery far beyond
anything I could possibly have imagined.

CHAPTER THIRTEEN

THE NEXT FEW days were as unnerving as you might imagine, the nebulous outline of the shadow in the warp continuing to creep towards the feeble glow of the Periremunda system centred in the imaging field of our hololiths, until the morning it engulfed us altogether. I happened to be in the command centre at the time, with Kasteen and Broklaw, and all three of us exhaled audibly as the boundary of the zone of darkness lapped around the flickering pinpoint of light at last, and began to draw it ever deeper inside itself, like an amoeba digesting some microscopic piece of flotsam.

'That's it,' Broklaw said laconically, and I found myself glancing up at the skylights in the roof of the old warehouse, an irrational corner of my mind half expecting us to be plunged into literal darkness.

Nothing of the kind actually happened, of course. Ironically, the almost perpetual cloud cover had lifted across most of Hoarfell that day, and bright sunlight lanced down into the seething mass of soldiers going about their business from a blue sky dappled with blotches of cloud. Of course it was still far too cold outside for my liking, the wind cutting straight to the bone even through the weave of my greatcoat, and just as inevitably the Valhallans had cranked the big doors open a little to make the most of it. I'd found the relief from the usual dank murkiness positively cheering, at least until I'd dropped by to see what was going on among the senior command staff.

'Any luck yet?' Kasteen had greeted me as I'd arrived, and I'd shaken my head ruefully. As I might have expected, Zyvan and Keesh had accumulated an impressive amount of raw intelligence between them, with more coming in all the time, and I'd normally have found the task of wading through it onerous in the extreme, not to mention impossible without help. Luckily I'd been able to pass the bulk of the files over to Mott, who positively relished that sort of thing, and he'd reduced most of the data to neatly cross-referenced summaries before lobbing it back to me for my expert evaluation; which, so far, I'm bound to admit, had come up with precisely nothing.

Nevertheless, I'd been grateful for the distraction, as otherwise I'd have had little else to do apart from worrying about the hive fleet approaching us, and whatever its still undetected advance guard might have been up to. So I suppose it was just sheer bad luck that I happened to stop by to ask Kasteen for a progress report at almost exactly the same moment

that the shockwave in warp space preceding the 'nid swarm engulfed the system.

'We're on our own,' Kasteen agreed with her subordinate, watching the stain spread further across the wavering and insubstantial starfield projected above the hololith table. This was quite literally true. Now that we were inside the shadow there could be no hope of any astropathic communication from Coronus, or from the flotilla of starships hurrying to our aid. We could still estimate the fleet's position, though, and I stared at the little cluster of contact icons, willing it to arrive before whatever tide of chittering death was lurking inside the pool of darkness that was now swallowing us whole. Of course that was even more problematic now than it had been, as the warp currents themselves would be affected by the mass of the hive fleet, although whether that was going to speed or hinder our would-be rescuers only the Emperor could say.

'Better step up our alert status,' I suggested, and Kasteen nodded tightly.

'Already on it. Whenever they show themselves, we'll be ready.' She nodded at the hololith. 'Irrational I know, but I half expected them to start pouring out of the woodwork as soon as the shadow arrived.' Her tone was light, but in the slightly forced way that revealed an element of barely-contained fear. Knowing the regiment's history, I could hardly blame her for that: both the former units that now made it up had been chewed to pieces on Corania. Kasteen had been a mere company commander at the time, and had ended up being saddled with the responsibility for an entire regiment by the simple

fact of being practically the only senior officer to survive. It was the merest good fortune that she'd turned out to be so levelheaded and gifted a leader.

'Me too,' I admitted, and we shared a moment of wry amusement, although I don't suppose she thought I was anywhere near as sincere as I actually was. I'd fought tyranids before too, and the idea of facing wave after wave of genetically engineered killing machines was a sobering one to say the least.

'We stopped them before, we can stop them again,' Broklaw said briskly, and we all nodded gravely as though we believed it.

'Colonel.' A vox operator looked up from her control lectern, and waved to attract our attention. 'A message from the lord general.'

'My office. Put it through.' Kasteen acknowledged the woman briskly, as though the moment of hesitation had never been, and led the way towards the metal staircase giving access to the mezzanine. As we hurried up the clattering stairs she glanced back at Broklaw and myself. 'Looks like it's going to be sooner rather than later.'

In that, to everyone's unspoken relief except mine, she was completely wrong. Zyvan's voice was clipped and incisive as he acknowledged her greeting.

'Colonel. Is Commissar Cain with you?'

'He's right here.' She glanced across at me, and I tapped the comm-bead in my ear, joining the conversation.

'How can I help you, general?' I asked, trying to ignore the faint flutter of apprehension that flickered in my gut. In my experience, whenever someone

powerful and well connected asks for you by name, it seldom presages anything good.

'I've a message from Inquisitor Vail,' Zyvan said, almost succeeding in masking his irritation at acting as an intermediary. It made sense, though. If she still wanted to keep her presence on Periremunda a secret, there could be fewer more secure lines of communication than going through the lord general's office. 'She's on her way to Hoarfell, and wants you to meet her at the aerodrome.'

'You can tell her I'm on my way,' I said, with as much enthusiasm as I could muster. Even the prospect of seeing Amberley again wasn't quite enough to outweigh the near certainty that she was about to drag me deeper into whatever it was she was really here to do. Refusal being completely out of the question, though, I took refuge in the public persona of Cain the modest hero. I turned to Kasteen and Broklaw, who both looked vaguely stunned by this unexpected turn of events, not to mention a little awestruck by the sudden reminder of my exalted connections. 'I'm afraid you'll have to manage without me for a while,' I told them.

'We'll manage,' Kasteen assured me gravely, as if my presence there would make the slightest difference to her battle plans. 'Any idea what this is all about?'

'Not a clue,' I admitted, trying to sound as though the prospect wasn't almost as terrifying as facing the 'nids. I shrugged, in as carefree a manner as I could contrive. 'I'll tell you when I get back, if it's not too highly classified,' I said breezily, hoping I'd live long enough to get the chance.

* * *

THE JOURNEY TO the aerodrome was as brief and eventful as such trips generally were with Jurgen driving, our scout-pattern Salamander carving its way through the civilian traffic as though they were enemy foot soldiers although with fewer casualties. Jurgen was as familiar with the sturdy little vehicle as he was with his lasgun, and although his approach to driving was as robust as ever, we never actually hit anything sharing the road with us. We came pretty close at times, but since we were surrounded by armour plate, and the civilian traffic wasn't, neither of us found the occasional near miss unduly alarming.

As we rattled and roared our way along the main access road to the landing field, leaving a turbulent wake of profanity and blaring clarions behind us, I noticed that the melta he habitually carried when things got even more dangerous than usual was tucked into the driver's compartment beside him. He was clearly expecting trouble too, which was no bad thing.

There was no one else in the galaxy I'd rather have covering my back if we turned out to be right, and the heavy weapon had made a crucial difference to our chances of survival on more than one occasion.

I'd taken what precautions I could as well, fitting fresh power cells into my chainsword and laspistol, and strapping on the carapace armour I'd acquired on Gravalax beneath my greatcoat, which concealed it nicely.

'Do you think that's them now?' Jurgen asked, swinging us around a wallowing heavy transporter with what looked like the guts of a shuttle engine

protruding perilously from the flatbed on every side, and I ducked reflexively as a tangle of pipe work thicker than my forearm all but brushed the cap from my head. He took his hand from the throttle for a moment, to point a grime-encrusted finger at a sleek Aquila class shuttle descending on the pad we'd been told to head for.

Ignoring the eloquent hand gestures of the startled driver behind us, I nodded. 'Must be,' I said. In keeping with her desire to remain incognito as much as possible Amberley tended to avoid plastering her personal transport with Inquisition sigils, but the crimson and grey colour scheme was a fair indication of its ownership to anyone familiar with the organisation she worked for. I found myself wondering for a moment if the presence of a space-capable shuttle meant that her old associate Orelius was orbiting patiently somewhere above our heads, but doubted that. Periremunda was a small and provincial kind of place, and the presence of a rogue trader in the system would hardly have gone unnoticed for long.[1] I glanced at my chronograph. 'She's punctual, at any rate.'

I should have known better than to verbalise the thought. As I've mentioned innumerable times before in the course of these memoirs, Jurgen's adherence to protocol had a tendency to border on the obsessive. Now, no doubt considering it in some way essential to be waiting on the pad when the shuttle grounded, he accelerated, flinging me

1. *In fact it was from my personal yacht, the* Externus Exterminatus, *which was waiting in orbit as usual, broadcasting the ident code of an ore barge from Desolatia.*

back against the heavy bolter on its pintel mount, and scattering the gaggle of PDF troopers manning the checkpoint at the aerodrome perimeter. Glancing back, I saw one of them yelling excitedly into a vox unit, but at least none of them had the wit to fire at us,[1] which was an unexpected blessing. Thanking the Emperor for small mercies I clung to whatever handholds I could find, while Jurgen slalomed us around an obstacle course of fuel bowsers, slack-jawed enginseers, and cargo-handling servitors as though trying to avoid an incoming artillery barrage shell by shell. My comm-bead crackled.

'Commissar Cain, this is Darien Down.' The traffic controller's voice was tense, which was hardly surprising under the circumstances. The poor frakker probably thought we were about to be blown halfway to the Golden Throne again, and I was in another frantic dash to avert disaster. 'Is there an emergency we should be appraised of?'

'Everything's fine,' I assured him, with all the soothing sincerity I could muster while my fillings were being shaken loose by Jurgen's driving. 'Vital military dispatches to collect, that's all.'

'I see.' He clearly didn't, but then in my experience civilians never really expect to understand military matters. All that mattered to him was that whatever I was up to had nothing to do with the safety of the starport, and that was that.

---

1. *In fact they probably recognised Cain, who was a familiar figure across the entire planet, especially in Hoarfell, where his actions in the fuel tanker incident had made him an even greater hero to the local populace.*

Despite Jurgen's heroic efforts the shuttle touched down a few seconds before we reached the pad, its cargo ramp descending as it came, so that the lip of it kissed the rockrete a mere heartbeat behind the landing skids. I looked at it expectantly, waiting for Amberley to appear at the top of the dull iron gradient, but the cargo compartment remained empty, and the engines continued to scream, throttled back just enough to keep the whole thing from lifting again. Recognising the telltale signs of a pilot prepared for a rapid dust-off in a hot LZ,[1] I ducked instinctively below the level of the armour plate surrounding me, my eyes scanning our surroundings for any sign of a threat.

'Get aboard as fast as you can,' Amberley's voice said in my ear, and taking her words as literally as he did any other instruction Jurgen gunned the engine again, hurtling towards the narrow ramp at a speed anyone else would have regarded as insane.

Even inured as I was to his cavalier handling of the little vehicle by a decade and a half of familiarity, I found myself flinching as we bounced up the metal incline, our spinning treads millimetres from the edge, and into the tight confines of the miniscule cargo bay. Even now I find it hard to believe that we didn't just bounce off the bulkhead facing us, but as always my aide had judged it to a nicety, slamming the abused gears into reverse, and bringing us to a halt with barely a centimetre to spare. As he cut the engine our pilot fed full power to his own, and I felt

---

1. *Taking off quickly from a dangerous landing zone. Sometimes I think Imperial Guard should be classified as a distinct dialect of Gothic all by itself.*

a familiar surge of acceleration at the base of my much-abused spine. As I clambered out I caught a final dizzying glimpse of Darien Down receding into the distance before the rising ramp thudded into place, and sealed us in. I took an unsteady breath, redolent of Jurgen.

'Nice driving,' Amberley said, entering the narrow hold through a door in the forward bulkhead.

Jurgen scratched his head, beaming at the unexpected compliment. 'Thank you miss,' he said, blushing beneath the grime.

Amberley smiled at me, and I returned the expression as best I could. She was dressed in a skin-tight bodyglove, which would normally have been more than enough to raise my spirits, but unlike the one I'd seen her in at the Arbites building in Principia Mons this one was midnight black and festooned with sockets and truncated power cables. It just had to be the dermal interface layer for her power armour, and that realisation was enough to start my palms tingling in earnest. Wherever we were going, she thought she was going to need it.

'I always thought it was impolite to keep a lady waiting,' I said, trying to sound as relaxed as I could, and Amberley grinned at me, probably not fooled for a second.

'Come on through,' she said, indicating the door behind her. 'You might as well be comfortable while we get where we're going.'

'Which is where, exactly?' I asked, following her into a compartment that might almost have been the lounge of a small hotel suite, if it hadn't been for the sets of crash webbing on the generously padded

seats. I dropped into the nearest, one of a group around a crystal-topped beverage table, and Zemelda leaned across it to deposit a welcome goblet of amasec in front of me, still apparently playing the servant with undiminished enthusiasm.

'Thought you might need this,' she said.

'You thought right,' I agreed, swallowing half of it too quickly to fully appreciate so finely aged an example of the distiller's art, and taking in her appearance with vague surprise. Like Amberley, the former snack vendor was dressed for trouble, in dark fatigues stippled with hive-pattern camo,[1] a bandana of the same material keeping her hair, which seemed brighter and greener than ever by contrast, out of her eyes. Her laspistol was holstered openly at her waist, and a couple of frag grenades hung from the utility vest around her torso, next to a wicked looking combat blade. Amberley dropped into the seat opposite me, and smiled indulgently at her protégé.

'Our little girl is growing up,' she said cheerfully.

'So I see,' I said. I glanced around the compartment, the barren wastes of the Periremundan landscape hurtling past beneath us too quickly to distinguish any details, the occasional plateau there and gone in a mere flicker of shadow. Most of her entourage were here, Pelton dressed almost identically to his green-haired girlfriend and cradling his autorifle protectively, while Simeon glowered at us from the corner, twitching a little now and again as his automatic implants regulated the flow of chemicals coursing through his system. His shotgun was across

---

1. *Dark greys, blues, and black, intended to let the wearer blend into the shadows of the underhive.*

his lap, and he kept touching the spare magazines of reloads hanging from the bandolier across his chest, muttering something too low to be audible, but which had the cadences of the prayer of accuracy. Rakel stood next to him, her face even more strained than usual, directing a pained and venomous glance behind my head. My nose apprising me of the reason, I turned to Jurgen. 'Perhaps you'd better check out the Salamander,' I suggested. 'We might need it when we land.'

'Very good, sir.' Jurgen's arm twitched in the vague semblance of a salute, and he vanished through the door in the bulkhead. As he disappeared behind the thick metal plating Rakel's expression relaxed into something approximating her usual air of distraction, and she nodded as though listening to a conversation only she could hear.

'The wind's blowing again,' she said, 'and its teeth are sharp.'

'I'm glad you're feeling better,' I said diplomatically, resolving to keep Jurgen out of the way as much as possible. Not that I really gave a frak about the barmy little spook, of course, but she was armed again, and I didn't want her becoming so agitated by his presence that she might think of alleviating the discomfort of it by using her laspistol. For one thing my aide's peculiar gift had saved my life several times already, and I had every expectation of it continuing to do so for as long as he remained around, and for another I didn't fancy the idea of her popping off a gun in such a confined space. It wouldn't breach the hull, of course, that was proof against the heat and stresses of re-entry, never mind a puny little lasbolt,

but it could easily ricochet off the metal, putting my life in danger.

Mott was sitting at the table too, a mug of recaf in his hand, and a vaguely expectant air hovering about him that seemed to indicate that he was itching to start explaining what we were all doing here as soon as Amberley let him. Yanbel was in a corner next to the small door leading to the flight deck, doing arcane things to Amberley's power suit, which loomed over everything like an Astartes captain at a garden party. As everyone's presence registered with me, the obvious question occurred (apart from 'what the frak are we doing here,' of course, which I knew better than to ask a second time. I knew Amberley well enough by now to know that she'd explain what was going on when she was good and ready, and no power in the galaxy could hurry her up).

'Who's flying this crate?' I asked.

Amberley shrugged. 'Pontius, I think,' she said, as though the name would mean anything to me.

Pelton flicked a stray lock of hair, which had escaped his bandana, out of his eyes. 'Ex-Navy, like most of the boss's crew. He's good. If he has to he can fling this thing around like a fighter in a fur-ball.'

'Then let's hope he doesn't need to show off his skills,' I said, assimilating this latest piece of news as calmly as I could. So, Amberley had her own star-ship. Well, it wasn't that surprising, I suppose, inquisitors need to get where they're needed as fast as possible. It simply hadn't occurred to me before now, probably because the first time I'd met her she'd been with a rogue trader, and since then I'd somehow

assumed she just used the authority of her office to commandeer a vessel whenever she needed one.[1]

'That rather depends on what we find when we get there,' Amberley said, getting to the point at last.

'Which would be where, exactly?' I asked, sipping the remains of my amasec, and trying to look as relaxed as possible.

Amberley gestured to Mott. 'A mining station, on one of the lowest of the plateaux. Caractacus will explain.' She smiled indulgently at her savant. 'After all, he uncovered the lead we're following.'

'Thanks in no small measure to you, commissar,' Mott began, in his dry pedantic voice. 'Your request for access to the Arbites files was answered in the fullest possible fashion, and one of the items appended was the working notes of the medicae who performed the post mortem examination of the psyker who attempted to assassinate you.'

'I thought you'd already seen the autopsy report?' I asked Amberley, and she nodded.

'Of course. Keesh passed it on as soon as it was completed, and there was nothing in it to help us, or so it seemed at the time. What Caractacus has been looking at, though, is the data the report was compiled from, and it seems the medicae missed something significant out of the final summary.'

'Deliberately?' I asked, and Amberley shook her head, her blonde hair sweeping across her shoulders.

'Probably not. Keesh is investigating, of course, but it looks like a genuine oversight.'

---

1. *Which works too, of course, especially when you need something with enough firepower to put a dent in a planet, but it's nice to have somewhere cosier to call home.*

'Quite understandably, too,' Mott put in. 'There were merely trace amounts, barely detectable, and our medicae colleagues could hardly have been blamed if they'd missed them entirely. That they did not was the greatest good fortune, even though they failed to realise the importance of the discovery.'

'Traces of what?' I asked, suspecting I was going to regret prompting the savant for an answer. Luckily, however, the question seemed to be specific enough not to have triggered a quincunx of random associations.

'There were minute particles of dust in the cadaver's lungs,' Mott said. 'All quite normal, of course, but a few showed unusual characteristics. Cross-referencing them with the geophysical data of Periremunda, it became quite obvious to me that he had to have visited one particular plateau in the relatively recent past.'

'Where there's a mining station,' I said. I nodded thoughtfully. 'Isolated, self-contained, a long way from civilisation. What would he have been doing there?'

'That's what we're going to find out,' Amberley said. 'Keesh tried the subtle approach, voxing to ask for their personnel records, but no one's answering.'

'I see.' I nodded again, the palms of my hands beginning to tingle in earnest. On a world like Periremunda, regular contact with other population centres was vital, and any isolated outpost would be certain to have backup systems to deal with a simple vox failure. 'Does this interesting mining camp have a name?'

'Hell's Edge,' Amberley said, grinning happily.

'Sounds delightful,' I said, looking around the compartment for the decanter of amasec.

CHAPTER FOURTEEN

I HAVE TO concede that, if nothing else, Hell's Edge lived up to its name. I've seen less inviting places in a century or more of rattling around the galaxy, but damn few of them, and even fewer when no one was shooting at me. For one thing, as Amberley had said, the plateau was one of the lowest on the planet, which meant that it was pretty much on the margins of habitability. As we disembarked, the hot, thick air seared my lungs, and I hastily tied my sash around my face as a makeshift breathing mask, feeling a faint pang of envy at the thought of the cool recycled air inside Amberley's power suit.[1] As well as being

---

1. Which, as anyone who's ever worn one of the things can readily attest, is actually tainted with the lingering bouquet of Emperor knows how many centuries of old sweat and flatulence. That said, it's still a major improvement over a great many external environments, including Hell's Edge.

viscous and clogged with grit, the air was rank with the stench of brimstone, which was hardly surprising considering where we were.

As Pontius brought the shuttle swooping low over the thin stalk of vertical rock I'd tensed involuntarily, reminded of far too many combat drops, and of our precipitate arrival on Simia Orichalcae thanks to a lucky shot by an ork with a portable rocket launcher. This time, however, no flashes of light strobed from the ground to greet us, and as we banked around for another pass I got my first proper look at our destination.

'I can see how it got its name,' I said dryly. The massive outcrop on which the colony stood was perched on the bank of one of the equatorial lava flows, a thick soup of dully glowing liquid rock lapping around its base on the better part of three sides. Pipes and other manmade excrescences ran down the flanks of the plateau, apparently disappearing beneath the surface of the lava. I pointed them out, and Mott nodded thoughtfully, his augmented synapses flooding with related information at the sight.

'The flow here is rich in a number of metals, which can be readily extracted in their molten state,' he began. 'Normally the difficulty would lie in filtering the useful material from the magma in which it's suspended, but the peculiar conditions here make that task considerably easier. Of particular interest is the manner in which…'

Ignoring the rest of the monologue, I looked out over the surface of the plateau. It was small by the standards of most of those I'd seen. Although I'd

only set foot on Hoarfell and Principia Mons so far, I'd caught sight of several of the others from the air, and nothing as small as this had seemed to support a community of any significant size. Hell's Edge was no more than a kilometre across in any direction, and the largest open area I could see was the inevitable landing field. Roughly the size of a scrumball pitch, it would just about take a heavy lift shuttle if it had to, although a dirigible mooring mast at the far end indicated that most of the processed material would be leaving at a rather more sedate pace for a final destination somewhere else on the planet.

Like its grown-up cousin in Darien the landing field sprawled up to the edge of the plateau, but in this instance with no sign of a wall or fence to guard against an incautious misstep. Picturing a plunge of two or three klom into a pool of molten rock, I shuddered, and determined to remain well away from the brink. The rest of the surface was covered with buildings, mainly manufactoria of one sort or another that I took to be the processing plants where the useful material was extracted and cast into ingots, storage facilities for the blocks of cooled metal, and a scattering of hab units.

'Anything on the vox?' I asked, as we clattered down the ramp together, Rakel keeping as far away from Jurgen as she could, and most of us with guns in our hands. Jurgen carried his beloved melta, of course, his standard issue lasgun slung across his shoulder, the all-pervading stench of brimstone robbing me of my usual method of keeping track of his whereabouts. I scanned the desolate ground around us, alert for any signs of ambush. Amberley

shook her head, grimaced as the tainted air hit her nostrils, and sealed her helmet.

'Nothing,' she said. 'Pontius is continuing to scan, but there's no signal traffic this side of Aceralbaterra.'[1] To my unspoken relief our pilot was doing a good deal more than that, keeping the shuttle's engines idling just in case we needed to beat a hasty retreat. There was no point in unshipping the Salamander; comforting as I would have found its armour plate and heavy weapons right now, there was simply nowhere to go in it.

'That pretty much rules out a vox problem,' I said, little firecrackers of paranoia chasing themselves around my synapses every time I thought I caught a glimpse of a moving shadow.

Pelton nodded in agreement. 'We should have seen a welcoming committee by now,' he concurred, following my example, and hastily converting his bandana into a makeshift facemask. A moment later Zemelda followed suit, her green hair tumbling in untidy profusion, almost as disordered as Pelton's blond thatch, as she removed the strip of cloth restraining it. Jurgen simply ignored the foul air stoically, as he did most sources of discomfort, although being an iceworlder he undoubtedly found the place even more unpleasant than the rest of us did.

'We should,' I agreed, hefting my laspistol in sweat-slick fingers (apart from the augmetic ones, of course, which at least allowed me to keep a tight enough grip on it to aim properly), and wishing I'd had the

---

1. *The nearest plateau with a sizeable population, some three hundred kilometres to the south, apparently named for the explorer who first catalogued this patchwork globe.*

foresight to jettison my greatcoat while I'd had the chance. Despite the stifling heat, thin chills of ice water seemed to be chasing one another down my spine. There was no sign of life here at all, which meant something was terribly wrong. 'How many people are supposed to be here?'

'Two hundred and thirty-seven,' Mott said, his voice apparently unaffected by the heat and dust. Like Yanbel, he seemed to have been insulated from the worst effects of the environment by his array of augmetic enhancements, while Rakel and Simeon just seemed too out of it in their respective fashions to care, but that was nothing new. 'A hundred and ninety-six employees, forty-one ancillary staff, and eighteen dependants, of which seven are still minors.'

'Then where the hell are they?' Simeon gripped his shotgun with whitening knuckles, his paranoia rising along with his chemically enhanced alertness.

Rakel shook her head vehemently. 'All gone, no one home.' It came out in a childish singsong, and I bit back the obvious rejoinder. After all, it wasn't her fault she was barmy, and this was hardly a good time to be irritating Amberley. Instead, I made my voice as calm as possible, hoping I might prise a little more sense out of her that way.

'What do you mean, gone?' I asked, and she glared at me as though I'd just mistaken her for a joygirl and offered her a credit.

'Not here, idiot. Don't you speak Gothic?'

Well, there was obviously no point getting into a slanging match with a loon, so I just shrugged and let it go, trying not to notice the grin on Simeon's face or picture the one on Amberley's.

'We'll split up,' the inquisitor said, her voice still remarkably calm in my comm-bead, although I suppose it's easier to ignore the possibility of a sudden ambush if you're clumping around inside a couple of centimetres of ceramite. (Not that it does to get too complacent even then. I've seen genestealers ripping terminator armour apart like Jurgen with a plateful of shellfish, both of which are sights I'd rather not see again.) A black and gold arm rose with a faint whine of servos. 'Flicker, take Rakel, Simeon and Zemmie and check out the hab blocks. Anything at all out of place, vox me a description of it, and wait for the rest of us to arrive before you start poking around.'

'Got it.' The former arbitrator nodded once. 'Don't worry, boss, I'm not about to trip any booby traps, or start prodding Chaos sigils with a stick.'

'Good.' Amberley's voice held a faint hint of amusement. 'Rakel should be able to pick up any psychic residue, so you're unlikely to blunder into anything like that without warning, at least.' She turned to the rest of us. 'Everyone else with me. We'll start in the processing plant.'

'We could cover more ground if we split into pairs,' Zemelda suggested diffidently, a glance at Pelton indicating which partner she had in mind for herself. Amberley shook her head, the gold-chased helmet rotating smoothly on its bearings.

'No,' she said. 'I want everyone in teams large enough to deal with anything unexpected we might stumble across. Yell for help at the first sign of trouble, and run like frak if you have to. Dead heroes are no help to me.'

'Yes, boss.' Zemelda nodded, and fell into place at Pelton's shoulder. After a moment Simeon and Rakel followed, and the four of them began making their way towards the hab units, exploiting whatever cover they could find on the way. Pelton seemed confident enough in his own leadership, and he and Simeon kept their advance covered with an efficiency my years attached to the Imperial Guard had left me well able to appreciate. Zemelda was doing her best to imitate them, and to my surprise showed every sign of being able to give a good account of herself once the shooting started. Rakel, of course, just slouched along, her eyes as unfocused as usual, either confident enough in her prediction of lifelessness not to fear any enemy presence or too bonkers to care if she was wrong.

'Come on.' Amberley turned towards the nearest industrial block. 'Let's go and see if we can find out where all the people went.'

'If they really have gone,' I said, angling myself to keep the bulk of her power armour between me and a row of pipe-festooned gantries any halfway competent sniper would have leapt at the chance to hole up in. 'How much can you trust Rakel on something like this?'

'She's pretty reliable,' Amberley reassured me, before undercutting the effect by adding 'usually'. Getting a sudden blast of my aide's distinctive aroma, even through the all-pervading stench and the sash around my face, I nodded, the reason for her caution now clear. 'She does seem pretty definite.'

'For once,' Yanbel said dryly. The nearest processing plant was a few score metres to our left, and we made

straight for it, angling towards a pallet of dull metal ingots stacked on a motorised trolley on the fringe of the landing field. My only thought at first was to use it as cover. It was only as we got closer that a nagging sense of wrongness about it began to worry at my subconscious.

'What's this doing here?' I wondered aloud. 'Shouldn't it be in one of the warehouses?'

'It certainly shouldn't be parked out in the open,' the techpriest confirmed. 'All this dust and ash in the air will degrade the motivator units. It'll need stripping down and re-consecrating, that's for sure.' He shook his head. 'The enginseers shouldn't have been that negligent.'

'Maybe they were expecting to get it straight back inside,' Jurgen volunteered, his habitual expression of vague bafflement mirroring my own behind its makeshift mask.

'Makes sense,' I agreed. 'If they were bringing the ingots out to load in a shuttle...'

'We'd have seen a shuttle,' Amberley pointed out reasonably. Her burnished helmet, its decoration dulling already beneath a thin veneer of pale grey ash, turned, taking in the sight of our Aquila squatting in the centre of the pad, most definitely alone. I shrugged.

'Maybe the people went with it?' I suggested, not believing my own words for a moment.

'Most interesting.' Mott ran a finger through the patina of volcanic fallout on the edge of the pallet, and held it up to his face. I almost expected him to taste it, but he just squinted at it for a moment before wiping the digit clean on the hem of his robe. 'Judging by the depth of accumulated detritus, and assuming a

uniform rate of deposition, this conveyance was abandoned approximately five days ago.'

'Not just abandoned,' I said. I'd reached the driver's seat, little more than a thinly padded shelf next to the control lever that seemed to govern direction and speed. Ash was accumulating in jagged rents torn into the fabric, and although it was hard to be sure under the thin grey coating, some dull brown residue seemed to make splash patterns against the backdrop of stacked metal bars. 'That looks like blood.'

'It is,' Amberley concurred after a moment, no doubt spent consulting the enhanced senses built into her power suit. Jurgen prodded the gashes in the seat with the barrel of the melta.

'Bit big for a gaunt,' he said. 'Lictor, you reckon?'

'It's possible,' I said, having recognised the distinctive pattern of talons in the slash marks. Despite the furnace heat of this desolate place, my blood ran cold. None of us had any doubt that we'd found the reason Hell's Edge had fallen silent, but an even more disturbing possibility kept insinuating itself into my mind. I turned to Amberley. 'Can Rakel detect 'nids as well as 'stealers?'

'I assume so,' Amberley said, which wasn't exactly the resounding reassurance I'd been hoping for. 'She says she can feel the shadow of the hive fleet, but we've never faced a swarm on the ground together before.' Her voice altered slightly, taking on the timbre of command. 'Flicker, stay alert. We've found signs of tyranid activity.'

'Confirm that,' Pelton voxed back. 'We're inside the hab units. No sign of anyone, but plenty of personal effects. It's as if they all just got up and left.'

'Look out for any signs of battle damage,' I put in helpfully. 'If the 'nids have hit the place, they're bound to have left traces of some sort.' I tried to picture ten score civilians mounting any kind of effective resistance to an onrushing swarm of scuttling death, and dismissed the possibility at once. They'd all have been slaughtered within moments, their corpses devoured on the spot, or dragged off to be broken down into raw biomass for the hive fleet.

'Eew!' Zemelda's voice broke in suddenly, her disgust audible in the wordless syllable. 'The floor here's covered in bugs. All dead.'

'Fleshborers,' I said, my guess confirmed. Realising she wouldn't have a clue what I was talking about, I went on to explain. 'Ammunition from their guns. They shoot these little insect things that eat their way through you. Luckily they die almost at once.'

'Mucoid,' Zemelda said, which I took to be an expression of revulsion, and a perfectly understandable reaction under the circumstances.

'Quite,' Amberley agreed dryly. 'Keep looking, and stay alert.'

'Got it,' Pelton confirmed.

Since the pallet-shifter wasn't going to tell us anything more we moved on towards the manufactorium we'd originally been heading for, Amberley leading from the front, which was fine by me. I trotted behind her, feeling the need to show willing, and reflecting that at least that kept her heavy bolter between me and any trouble that might be lurking up ahead, while Jurgen stuck close to me as always, his melta tracking steadily as he swept his eyes back and forth in search of any threat to our

wellbeing. The savant and the cogboy trailed in our wake, Mott prattling endlessly about tyranid anatomy and physiology, and bemoaning the fact that the ubiquitous scattering of ash had obliterated any tracks that might have let him estimate their numbers and subspecies, while Yanbel glanced at our bleak surroundings as though wondering what an Omnissiah-fearing servant of the Machine God was doing in a place quite so untidy as this.

I don't mind admitting I'd felt uncomfortably exposed during our trek across the landing field, and a sense of relief began growing in me as soon as we reached the main portal of the manufactorium. Intellectually, of course, I knew that the 'nids could be lurking in ambush just as easily within as out here in the open, but my primitive hindbrain equated inside with safety, and I hurried through the gaping metal doors after Amberley as quickly as I could.

The air inside was surprisingly clean, and I wound the sash from around my face with an exquisite sense of relief, despite getting a full-strength blast of Jurgen's halitosis in the process. The vast hall was astonishingly quiet, the complex machinery filling it shut down completely, although who had done so, and why they would have taken the time to deactivate them in the middle of a tyranid attack, was beyond me.[1]

'What's this?' Jurgen asked, prodding what looked like a random accumulation of scrap metal scattered around the floor with the barrel of his melta. Yanbel scooted over to join him, the wheels on his feet

---

1. *More likely they'd been switched off by automatic systems, in the absence of any fresh raw material to process.*

apparently working a great deal better in here than in the thick layer of dust outside, and apparently indifferent to the thickening miasma that was beginning to surround my aide now that we were being spared the worst of the brimstone. He picked up the nearest piece of twisted orichalcum, and examined it carefully, nodding to himself.

'Biometric relay.' He scooped up another piece of metallic detritus. 'Lymphatic interface link.' He nodded decisively, sure of his conclusion. 'It's a servitor, or it was, before something ripped out all the sanctified parts.'

'Or spat them out,' I said, feeling distinctly uncomfortable at the thought. Something had consumed the biological components of the melded flesh and metal construct completely, picking the non-organic parts clean in the process.

'Probably.' Amberley's voice was still steady, although I thought I could detect an undercurrent of uncertainty in it that was far from reassuring. 'But the 'nids are only of secondary importance right now. We're here to look for evidence of a Chaos cult, remember?'

I nodded soberly. The chitinous horrors were at least a known quantity, however perturbing their presence, but whoever had sent the rogue psyker after me wasn't, and we couldn't afford any more surprises that might undermine our ability to defend this world. If there was any indication at all to be found here of who the mysterious assassin had been, and who had sent him, uncovering it had to be our main priority.

I activated my comm-bead. 'Pelton, find anything yet?'

'A whole lot of nothing,' the former arbitrator told me cheerfully. 'If there really was a Chaos cult hiding out here, it was the most Emperor-fearing one I've ever come across.'

'What do you mean?' Amberley asked, and Pelton's voice instantly became more businesslike.

'We must have checked out thirty accommodation units by now, icons of the Emperor in all of them. Devotional pamphlets and lives of the saints in going on half. If there were any Chaos worshippers here, they must really have liked living dangerously.'

'Are miners usually that pious?' I asked. I hadn't met that many, of course, but somehow I doubted it. On the other hand, I could readily appreciate how living in a place like Hell's Edge might incline someone to invoke the Emperor's protection with a little more enthusiasm than usual.

Amberley shook her head. 'I don't know. I'll look into it.'

We pressed on, passing through a labyrinth of mechanisms larger than a Chimera, the purpose of which I couldn't even begin to guess at, our voices and Amberley's resonant tread echoing around us as we moved.

'What the frak?' I asked, taken by surprise as we rounded the corner of one such mysterious device, and a stinking waft of sulphurous air washed over me. At first I thought that someone must just have left a door open, then as my eyes focused again after filling with water as the rank smell punched its way into my sinuses, I realised the truth. A hole had been blasted through the thick rockrete wall, large enough to drive our Salamander through, littering the floor

with chunks of detritus in the process. I glanced at Amberley. 'I think we've found a bit of that battle damage I mentioned,' I said.

'Me too,' Jurgen confirmed, as constitutionally immune to sarcasm as always. He eyed the breach appraisingly. 'Someone's taken a couple of heavy bolters to it. Melta too, by the look of things.'

'Not something you'd normally expect to find in a civilian facility,' Amberley agreed, clanking forward to examine the breach more closely.

Yanbel nodded, taking in the scene with whatever augmented senses lay hidden beneath his cowl. 'Someone was certainly desperate to get in,' he remarked.

As he spoke the memory of the violated Mechanicus shrine I'd found in the Valley of Daemons on Perlia rose to the surface of my mind, and I nodded too, my mouth going dry. Then the thought dissipated almost as soon as it had come, as something about the pattern of debris forced its way out of my subconscious and into my forebrain.

'Desperate to get out, more likely,' I said. 'The damage was inflicted from this side of the wall.'

'You're right.' Amberley nodded in turn, putting the picture together in her own mind, and glanced around the high, echoing chamber. We'd made our way to this point by a series of zigzags, keeping as much of the machinery as possible between ourselves and any wide open space where a 'nid swarm might mass. I'd seen the value of channelling them into narrow firelanes, where they could only come at you a few at a time instead of taking full advantage of their numbers to overwhelm you, often enough to

have followed Amberley's lead in this without argument, although I must admit to having kept my eyes open for ambushing 'stealers or the like as we'd followed our winding path through the thickets of ironmongery. Now she took a few paces back from the gaping hole in the wall, and pointed. 'Thought so. Look.'

I joined her, the others clustering round too, and glanced in the direction she was indicating. A wide, clear corridor between the banks of hoppers, control lecterns, riveted iron, and Emperor knew what else stretched from where we were standing to the doors by which we'd entered, through which I caught a comforting glimpse of our shuttle still sitting patiently on the pad. Rather less comforting was the condition of some of the machinery bordering the open area. Scorch marks and dents abounded, and in a few places holes had been punched clean through the thick metal plate.

'Bolters,' I said, recognising the pattern left by the explosive armour-piercing projectiles, and Amberley nodded sombrely.

'Flamers too, by the look of it,' she said, indicating a wide, scorched area on the floor, about twenty metres beyond where we stood.

As I took a step towards the nearest damaged machine, intending to examine it more closely for some clue as to what had happened here, something on the floor crunched beneath my bootsoles. I glanced down, with a shiver of apprehension, already certain of what I was about to find. The carcasses of tiny beetles, too many to count (although no doubt Mott could have given me a reasonable

estimate of their numbers if I cared enough to ask), were scattered everywhere I looked. 'Fleshborers,' I said unnecessarily.

Amberley nodded tightly. 'It's pretty clear what happened here,' she said, and I nodded too, concurring with her assessment. Someone had been attempting to leave the building, and found their way blocked by a swarm of onrushing gaunts, too many to fight through even with the impressive amount of firepower they'd clearly had at their disposal. So they'd laid a temporary barrier of blazing promethium, buying enough time to blast their way through the wall behind us in order to escape.

'Whoever fought their way out of here was impressively well equipped,' Mott said. 'I would estimate that, judging by the impact patterns left on the machinery surrounding us, at least half a dozen bolters were employed in addition to the heavy weapons, the traces of which are all too obvious.'

I felt another shiver work its way down my spine. 'That sounds like a fully-equipped Astartes squad!' I said in horrified astonishment. A dreadful possibility began nagging insistently at my forebrain. 'Could the witch have been in league with one of the Traitor Legions?'

'I doubt it,' Amberley reassured me. 'Their presence tends to be rather more obvious.'

'Skitarii, perhaps?' Yanbel offered. That sounded plausible. I nodded, recalling again the crimson-garbed bodies of the Mechanicus foot soldiers littering the hidden laboratory on Perlia.

I looked at Amberley again. 'Does Lazurus have a bodyguard with him?' I asked. I couldn't imagine any

other reason why a squad of skitarii would be on a planet as far from the major warp lanes as Periremunda.

'Not that I'm aware of,' she said.

Jurgen coughed loudly, and hawked a gobbet of phlegm into a corner. 'Besides,' he said, as though the point was obvious (which I suppose it was as soon as he'd verbalised it), 'the clockwork soldiers carry hellguns, don't they?'

'Usually,' I agreed. I'd seldom seen one with a bolter, that much was true. 'And what would they be doing in a midden like this in the first place?'

'That's what we're here to find out,' Amberley said. After a moment she turned, and began plodding deeper into the complex. 'They must have come from this direction.'

Well I could have told her that, of course, there was only one obvious avenue of approach to the point where the battle with the tyranids had occurred. Further speculation would be pointless, however. The only way to find out who the mysterious warriors were, and what they were doing in Hell's Edge, would be to find out where they had come from. With a rising sense of foreboding I took a tighter grip on my laspistol and set out after her, hoping that the answers we sought wouldn't have to be paid for in blood.

CHAPTER FIFTEEN

WE FOUND IT after another half an hour or so of poking into corners and, in my case at least, jumping at shadows, wondering if a lictor was about to leap out on us from some place of concealment, its jaws slavering, but we were all still uneaten when Amberley paused in front of a section of wall that looked to me like any other, and regarded it quizzically.

'Nice work,' she said, then without warning she drew back her power fist and punched a hole clean through the solid rockrete partition, revealing a thin metal lining beyond. After a moment or two she'd enlarged the breach to a ragged hole, and shouldered her way inside, dislodging a small cascade of rubble as she stepped over the uneven lip of the gap she'd made. After a moment, sure the place had been abandoned, she popped the seal of her helmet,

apparently intent on examining the place with her own eyes.

Yanbel and Mott followed, bounding over the obstruction easily with their augmetic legs, and after a moment's hesitation I scrambled awkwardly after them. There was, after all, safety in numbers, even if that just meant keeping the sage and the cogboy between me and a hungry 'nid. Jurgen followed, of course, manhandling his clumsy heavy weapon through the hole with his usual expertise and a deal of *sotto voce* profanity, but I had little attention to spare for my aide's travails. I was too busy standing in dumbstruck astonishment, like some hick from the sump getting his first look at an uphive trading post.

The chamber we'd found ourselves in was much smaller than the halls full of machinery that we'd been labouring though until now, but no less choked with the Omnissiah's bounty for all that, data-lecterns and cogitator banks lining the bare steel walls, and arcane mechanisms I couldn't even begin to guess the purpose of littering the floor in a fashion that seemed both functional and virtually random. Yet again I was reminded of the hidden laboratory I'd stumbled across on Perlia, and the grisly secret it had concealed, but this place was mercifully devoid of eviscerated corpses to mar its air of pristine functionality.

Picking my way carefully over the rat's nest of cables linking everything together I went to join Amberley and Yanbel, who were discussing our discovery in hushed tones. They both seemed as surprised as I was at what we'd found, which I wasn't quite sure how to take. On the one hand it dispelled the conviction that

had been growing in me from the start of this little jaunt that everyone else in the party (apart from Jurgen, of course) knew a great deal more than I did about what was going on, but on the other I'd been deriving a certain amount of solace from the assumption that at least Amberley was on top of things, and the idea that she was as far out of her depth as I felt hardly seemed reassuring. So, as usual in this sort of situation, I just adopted an air of calm self-confidence, and tried to make sense of what they were saying to one another.

'It certainly looks as if he's been here,' Yanbel agreed, a trace of doubt still audible in his voice. He gestured to the analytical engines surrounding us. 'This is the kind of equipment he'd need to continue his researches, no doubt about that. But why would a mining colony be hiding him?'

'Emperor alone knows,' Amberley said, a trace of asperity entering her voice, 'but he must have gone to ground somewhere away from the main population centres, and why else would all this stuff be here?' A faint whine of servos underlined a sweeping gesture, which nearly took the techpriest's head off. 'It's got his presence written all over it!'

'Metheius, you mean?' I asked, being able to add two and two as quickly as the next man, and Amberley turned to look at me with a faint air of surprise, as if she'd forgotten I was there.

'It's beginning to look that way,' she said.

'I'll see what I can recover from the cogitators,' Yanbel said, 'but don't hold your breath.' He moved away, and started the ritual of data retrieval at a nearby lectern.

Mott coughed diffidently. 'This chamber appears to have been abandoned at the same time as the rest of the facility,' he pointed out, 'and in something of a hurry, too.' He gestured towards the door to the hidden chamber, clearly visible on this side, a metre or so from the makeshift one Amberley had so thoughtfully provided us with. 'I can see a genecode scanner and an intrusion alarm linked to the access point, both of which whoever left here last neglected to set.'

'I imagine they had other things on their minds,' I pointed out dryly, 'what with the whole place swarming with 'nids and all.' I should have known better, of course. Mott nodded thoughtfully.

'That's highly probable,' he conceded. 'Given the human brain's response to abnormal levels of stress, particularly in a life-threatening situation, I would have thought it extremely likely that the individuals in question had no immediate goal beyond simple survival. On the other hand, the residue of the skirmish we found would seem to indicate that they were extremely resourceful, and highly motivated–'

'Quite,' Amberley said, cutting him off before he could bore us all into a coma, 'but that still doesn't tell us who they were.'

'The records have all been wiped,' Yanbel reported from his station at the data-lectern, his tone clearly adding a non-verbal 'I told you so', and I nodded slowly.

'Just like Perlia,' I said. Whoever had been here clearly didn't intend coming back, but then given the circumstances in which they'd left, that was hardly a surprise. Amberley nodded grimly.

'Search this place thoroughly,' she said, then grimaced at me. 'I can't believe I just said that. It's not as if we'll find the *shadowlight* just lying around the place, but we'd better make sure before we go. I don't want to give Lazurus the chance to claim we frakked up.' She activated the vox unit built into her suit. 'Flicker, we've found a bolthole. Looks like Metheius has been hiding out here.'

'Are you sure?' Even over the vox link, the incredulity in Pelton's voice was palpable. 'Why would a techpriest be consorting with psykers?'

'I've no idea.' The edge of irritation in Amberley's voice was growing again. 'When we catch up with the gretch-frotting boltbag and put him to the question you can ask him, all right?'

'Fine, boss.' Pelton's voice was conciliatory, which was hardly surprising under the circumstances. Hacking off an inquisitor isn't among the brightest of things to do, even if you work for her. 'We've got you on auspex, be with you in five.' The link went dead, and Amberley sighed, glancing at the techpriest with a faintly apologetic air.

'Sorry about the boltbag remark,' she said. 'It's getting to be a rather stressful day.' Of course it was about to get a great deal more so, but at that point, mercifully, we were all still blissfully ignorant of the fact. Yanbel glanced up from the lectern, still muttering prayers and tapping keys in the hope that he might be able to coax a shred of forgotten data back into existence, but Metheius had known the system well, and had evidently covered his tracks just as skilfully as he'd done in the Valley of Daemons so many years before.

'No offence taken,' he assured her, no doubt reflecting that a servant of the Omnissiah was supposed to be beyond such petty reactions as annoyance, even if the tone of his voice hinted otherwise.

'Pelton does have a point, though,' I ventured cautiously. 'Even if Metheius is a renegade, would he really be associating with a Chaos cult? Those loonies are about as far from the ideal of the machine as it's possible to get.' Amberley sighed deeply, and appeared to count to ten under her breath.

'In my experience, enemies of the Emperor take whatever help they can get. Maybe he traded them the weapons for a place to hide.' I nodded in a conciliatory fashion.

'That sounds reasonable,' I conceded. It still didn't sound right to me. I would have thought a mere handful of bolters would hardly be sufficient inducement to provide a facility as lavishly equipped as this, but she was the expert, and if her fuse was getting shorter I didn't want to be the one to press the detonator.

'I'm getting movement on the auspex,' a voice cut in on the vox, and after a moment I recognised it as Pontius's. It seemed our pilot had been doing more than just putting his feet up while we'd been strolling around Hell's Edge admiring the scenery. His intonation took on a trace of puzzlement. 'Northwest sector. That's on the lava side.'

'Back to the shuttle! Move!' Amberley's voice took on the ring of command, no doubt drawing exactly the same conclusion as I had, and, to my inexpressible relief, reacting in exactly the same manner as I

would have done (though no doubt from far nobler motives than mere self-preservation.)[1] 'Flicker, get your team aboard now! Pontius, get ready to lift!'

'Powered up and ready for dust-off,' the pilot assured her, while Pelton acknowledged the change in our plans in a few terse words. Pausing only to rip the now obvious door off its hinges, Amberley led the way back through the labyrinth of corridors and idle machinery towards the open air at a pace that left me gasping in the warm and foetid air. I wasn't about to lag behind, though, having more than an inkling of what we would find waiting for us on the surface of this barren spur of rock, and knowing all too well that to be trapped inside the building would mean certain death.

At length, however, we entered the echoing hall by which we'd first entered the complex, and the breach in the wall left by our mysterious predecessors gaped ahead of us, the stench of brimstone getting stronger all the time as we approached it. Without pause or hesitation Amberley swung off to our left, making straight for the wide open doors, the welcome silhouette of our Aquila waiting patiently for us beyond them.

As we left the shelter of the building the tainted air punched me in the chest, gouging its way into my lungs. Amberley sealed her helmet at once, but there was no time to waste tying a rag around my face again.

I glanced around, taking in the scene surrounding us, instincts honed on battlefields throughout the segmentum kicking in and assessing the immediate

---

1. *In all honesty, looking back, none spring to mind.*

threat. Pelton's group had almost made it back to the shuttle, double-timing it as though Horus himself was after them, little puffs of grey dust being kicked up by their hurrying feet, and their weapons at the ready. Simeon was clearly in full combat mode, his movements preternaturally quick, his head snapping around in all directions so violently I half expected it to come clean off his neck and begin rotating like the auspex sensoria of a command Chimera.

It was hard to be sure over the shriek of our Aquila's engines and the constant low rumble of the geothermal activity, but I thought I could hear an ominous scuttling sound away to our right, and turned my head to face the main cluster of industrial buildings. As I did so a flicker of movement caught the corner of my eye, almost hidden by the clouds of noxious fumes drifting from the fumaroles littering the ground beneath our narrow spire of rock.

'Simeon, five o'clock high!' I shouted, barely in time, but his reactions were boosted to preternatural levels by whatever foul alchemy was polluting his blood and he turned faster than I would have believed possible, bringing up his shotgun as he did so. The flat boom of it echoed across the open landing field, and a ball of something cartilaginous, trailing tentacles like some languid aquatic invertebrate, burst messily in midair, spraying some sort of loathsome ichor all around itself. Where it hit the thin carpet of ash the ground sizzled, exuding foul fumes. An instant later another pair of detonations echoed from the buildings ranged around us, as two more of the vile constructs exploded into oblivion without finding targets of their own.

'What the hell was that?' Zemelda asked, her voice understandably a little shriller than usual.

'Spore mines,' Amberley replied tersely, clearly not wanting to waste any more time in idle conversation.

'Some kind of bio acid, by the look of it,' Mott added helpfully. 'Fortunately every one in a cluster tends to detonate at the same time, which means they're relatively easy to guard against if one remains sufficiently alert–'

'Duck!' I snapped at him, cracking off a shot with my laspistol, which took out another deadly balloon swooping at his head. Once again the rest of the swarm went off with it, sending a few shards of something hard and dangerous-looking pinging off Amberley's armour and making the rest of us flinch.

'And that would appear to be a form of frag analogue.' Mott sounded no more than mildly intrigued by our close brush with death. 'I'd need an intact specimen to examine to be sure, of course, but my guess would be that the outer shell consists of small segments of chitin, bonded together with cartilage, or perhaps muscle fibres–'

'Shut up and run,' I suggested, suiting the action to the word, and not a moment too soon. The sight I most dreaded, a heaving mass of chitinous armour and razor-sharp talons, was bearing down on us from the direction of the manufactoria, so dense and so shrouded in the dust being raised by innumerable claw-edged feet that it was virtually impossible to tell where one malevolent life form ended and its neighbour began.

'Keep an eye out for the larger ones,' I counselled, breaking into a sprint towards the distant shuttle. 'If

you can take them down the swarm will lose cohesion.'

'Fine idea in theory,' Pelton said, his team taking whatever cover they could in the shadow of the boarding ramp, and beginning to shoot enthusiastically in the general direction of the approaching tide of talon and mandible. 'Picking them out might be a bit more difficult, though.' He was right, of course, but that was hardly helpful. The mass of chittering predators was bearing down on us like a tsunami, the fusillade of covering fire from the direction of the shuttle, welcome as it was, seemed about as effective as lobbing pebbles. The horde of nightmarish creatures carried on scuttling towards us at a rate that would have seemed impossible had I not seen it with my own eyes all too often before (and run like a startled sump rat too when I could, but that's beside the point).

On the other hand the swarm was so densely packed that there could be no question of missing, even at a range so extreme that normally there would be no chance at all of acquiring a target. Following our comrades' lead we began shooting too, pouring lasbolts and explosive projectiles from Amberley's heavy bolter into the middle of the scuttling swarm; to no real effect if I'm honest, but it took no extra effort and made us feel better (if that were possible under such dire circumstances). Jurgen's melta might have made a difference, I suppose, but if he'd stopped running long enough to fire the cumbersome heavy weapon he'd have been gaunt chow for sure within a second. Why he didn't just ditch the thing and un-sling his lasgun I have no idea, but that was Jurgen for you, once he'd

got an idea stuck in his head that was that (and lucky for us too, as things turned out).

'They're not going to make it!' Zemelda said, an edge of panic beginning to enter her voice, which was hardly helpful, I thought, although it was hard to disagree with her. The horde of slavering killing machines was hideously close now, a front line of hormagaunts bounding clear of the pack, their scything claws extended eagerly to rend our flesh as they leapt towards us. The termagants behind them were moving a little more sedately, and my bowels spasmed at the sight of their fleshborers swinging towards us, taking clear aim in our direction. Behind them a larger silhouette loomed, rending claws and a deathspitter ready to do their deadly work, but the real danger the warrior form represented was its ability to focus the will of the hive mind, co-ordinating all these disparate creatures into what amounted to a single entity, fixated on our destruction.

'Pontius,' Amberley said, with what I thought was a surprisingly pettish cast to her voice considering the peril we were in. 'If you're *quite* ready?'

'Just waiting for you to get a little closer,' the pilot responded calmly, and I felt a sudden flare of hope. The Aquila's primarily a workhorse, of course, but it's also a mainstay of the Navy auxilia. Amberley's might look like a standard civilian model, but that was no guarantee that it was unarmed, as I'd assumed from its external appearance. Almost as soon as the thought had formed, concealed gunports slid smoothly aside to reveal the welcome silhouettes of twin lascannons, flanking the stubby snout of the sturdy little shuttle. 'Targets coming into optimum range… now.'

The lascannons spat their heavy bolts, smashing into the onrushing tide of chitinous death, felling half a dozen of the vile creatures in an instant, but the rest came on with undiminished fury.

'Flicker! Board now!' Amberley snapped, and with a final volley that actually succeeded in downing another couple of gaunts, which were promptly mashed flat by the onrushing horde behind them, Pelton's team scurried up the ramp to safety. My lungs burning, and my feet slithering in the thin drift of ash, I pounded towards the blessed sanctuary offered by the Aquila's hold, intent on nothing more than reaching it alive. The lascannons fired again, reaping another bountiful harvest of tyranid flesh, but as always the relentless monstrosities came on regardless, indifferent to their own losses.

'Hurry!' Zemelda was hovering at the top of the ramp, sending laspistol bolts whining around our ears, her commendable desire to help somewhat diminished by the reflection that she could well end up doing the 'nids' work for them. Yanbel and Mott clattered up the incline to join her, and I flinched as a volley of fleshborer bugs missed me by centimetres, spattering off the portside landing skid, where in the absence of anything to devour they twitched feebly and expired.

'Still with you, commissar,' Jurgen reassured me, pausing on the lip of the ramp to turn and aim his melta. My own bootsoles rang on metal at last, and I turned to see what had happened to Amberley.

It wasn't good. The warrior directing the swarm had evidently determined that she was the greatest threat, and concentrated most of their ranged fire against her

power suit. The intricate engraving had been scored by a myriad of tiny abrasions where innumerable flesh-borer and deathspitter shots had struck, mercifully without finding a weak spot that would allow their living ammunition to work their way inside, but they'd clearly been chewing away at the armour's joints. She was moving stiffly now, more slowly than she had been, and the bolter on her arm had expended all its ammunition. A crowd of horma-gaunts was pressing her hard, their scything claws scoring visible rents in the ceramite beneath the ornate decoration on the surface of the suit, and once again the image of the Reclaimer terminators being ripped to shreds aboard the *Spawn of Damnation* rose to the surface of my mind. These were no 'stealers, of course, but their sheer weight of numbers was begin-ning to tell, and it could only be a matter of time before they found a weak point and managed to get at the woman inside.

A second later, to my vague astonishment, I found myself moving into the attack, my laspistol picking off the nearest of the biological constructs as my trusty chainsword left the scabbard, howling like one of the tyranids themselves as its teeth bit deep into chitin, and my boots crunched once again in the carpet of volcanic ash. What was uppermost in my mind then, I honestly couldn't say. I'd like to believe that, just for once, my innate pragmatism had been outweighed by the affection I felt for her, but I'm bound to admit that it had also occurred to me that Pontius wouldn't get the Aquila off the ground until Amberley was safely on board it, and every second we delayed was another chance for the tyranids to cut me down too.

'Jurgen, the big one!' I shouted, blessing the fact that the warrior seemed to be holding back, content to let the cannon fodder wear Amberley down before it closed for the kill itself. My aide nodded, and, forewarned, I closed my eyes for a moment as the actinic flare of the melta burst like a second sun a few metres to my left. When I opened them again the warrior had vanished, along with a handful of its attendant minions, to be replaced by a few gobbets of steaming meat and a stench of charred flesh that even managed to punch its way through the all-pervading stink of Hell's Edge.

'Nicely done,' Amberley said, ripping a gaunt's head off with her power fist. I disembowelled another with my chainsword, and the swarm surrounding her fell back, all sense of purpose draining away. I dispatched another with a quick lasbolt to the thorax, and they began to break, scuttling away in the manner of their kind when the controlling influence of the overmind is removed. Amberley followed me back up the ramp, and into the welcoming bowels of the shuttle. 'Pontius, you can lift when ready.'

'Very well, ma'am.' The note of our engines deepened, and the ground began to fall away beneath us. The survivors of the swarm were heading for the corner of the plateau by which they'd entered it, and glancing down through the gap left by the closing ramp I just had time to catch a brief glimpse of a narrow isthmus of rock stretching across the lava flow before the thick slab of metal slid smoothly into place. No doubt that was how the swarm had been able to cross the lake of liquid rock

and surprise us. Amberley discarded her helmet with a hiss of breaking atmosphere seals.

'Thank you, Ciaphas,' she said, shaking her hair free. 'I thought I was in trouble there for a moment.' I shrugged, still unsure of my motives and uncomfortable with her gratitude, which I felt I didn't really deserve.

'Glad to help,' I said, taking refuge in the pose of modesty that had served me so well for so many years, and she smiled at me with what looked like genuine affection. Fortunately I was spared any further awkward exchanges by Yanbel, who scooted forward to examine the armour with an audible intake of breath.

'You won't be wearing this for a while,' he said, shaking his head. 'I'll need to strip it down completely, bless the components, and Omnissiah alone knows where I can find a new fluid link this side of the Gulf.'

'I'm sure you'll do your best,' Amberley said, shrugging her way clear of the breached exoskeleton and stretching gratefully, in a manner that showed off her skin-tight bodyglove to considerable advantage. She smiled at me again, and led the way through the bulkhead to the lounge.

'I don't know about you,' she said, reaching for the decanter, 'but after all that excitement I could do with a drink.'

'I thought you'd never ask,' I replied gratefully.

'What I don't understand is how they knew we were there,' Zemelda said, dropping into a nearby seat, and staring out of the viewing port. The survivors of the swarm had scuttled down the face of the

plateau with their usual alacrity, and were already almost halfway along the narrow causeway they'd crossed to reach us. Pontius swung the shuttle round a few degrees, and hovered in place.

'They must have seen the shuttle land,' I said. 'They're bright enough to know that our arrival meant more people to consume, so they sent out a small scouting swarm to finish us off. After taking the miners so easily they wouldn't have expected us to be as well armed as we were.'

Amberley nodded, sipping her amasec with every sign of satisfaction. Below us the narrow spine of rock disintegrated under the impact of a fusillade of lascannon shots, and the remaining 'nids vanished under the lava flow, flaring briefly into patches of greasy smoke as they did so.

'They're building up their biomass reserves,' she said. 'Now the hive fleet's in range they'll be creating an army to consolidate their beachhead, and pave the way for the main invasion force.'

I felt a faint chill of dread as I pondered the implication of her words. 'That means they'll strike again,' I said. 'Raid more settlements.'

Amberley nodded grimly. 'I'm afraid you're right.' She drained her goblet, and poured another drink, a large one. 'Hell's Edge was only the beginning.'

Editorial Note:

Cain, of course, doesn't bother to expand on the consequences of this development for the planet as a whole, or for the campaign to defend it. I have therefore appended the following extracts from other sources, in the hope that they will go some way towards filling in the gaps in his narrative.

From *Periremunda Today: The News That Matters to Your Planet,* 264 933 M41

TERRORISTS ARE XENOS INFILTRATORS! KEEP WATCHING THE SKIES!

In a startling announcement, endorsed by no lesser eminence than Lord General Zyvan, commander of

the Imperial Guard heroes charged with eradicating the taint of un-mutual deviance from our fair world, Arbitrator Keesh today revealed the shocking truth that the campaign of terrorism that has rocked Periremunda for so long has an even more sinister purpose than simply challenging the benevolent rule of the Emperor's divinely appointed regents. Far from being mere traitors and heretics, a crime that in itself deserves no less than utter annihilation and eternal damnation, the perpetrators are something even more foul: the changeling offspring of the vile xenos species known as genestealers, which taint the pure bodily essences of the Emperor-fearing, thus perverting them to the cause of the world-devouring tyranids.

Though one of the dreaded hive fleets is reported to be on its way to Periremunda, all true human citizens may take heart from the knowledge that so is a taskforce drawn from the very cream of the Imperial Navy, and the redoubtable warriors of the Imperial Guard, which between them is more than powerful enough to obliterate the cancer of the xenos presence from our blessed corner of the galaxy. Moreover, we still have the unceasing vigilance of Commissar Cain and his valiant comrades-in-arms to protect all true followers of the Emperor.

As for the xenos-tainted vermin still lurking among us, let them tremble in fear, knowing that their inevitable extermination is naught but a matter of time.

IS YOUR NEIGHBOUR A GENESTEALER?
2O WAYS TO TELL!
(See page 7)

Transcript of an address by Planetary Governor Merkin W. Pismire the younger, 266 933 M41

MY FELLOW PERIREMUNDANS, it's with a heavy heart that I address you all tonight. Um, unless you're in a different time zone, of course, when I guess you'll be having breakfast. Or sleeping, or whatever. Erm...

By now you'll all have heard what's really been going on for the last few months, and no doubt you were as surprised as I was when I first saw the news picts this morning. Um, that's to say my daughters saw them, and lost no time in bringing me up to speed. Um...

You may all rest assured that I voxed Arbitrator Keesh as soon as I became aware of the situation, and demanded a full report, which, I'm sure, will prove extremely reassuring as soon as it arrives, or the young man I spoke to has time to pass on the message.

Anyway, I can state quite confidently that things are completely under control. We've all heard these silly rumours about low altitude settlements suddenly losing contact with the rest of the planet, and I'm quite sure there's no truth to any of them. It's probably just these genestealer scallywags spreading scare stories to undermine our morale.

I mean, if the enemy was already here in force, I'm sure I'd know all about it. My staff is pretty good at keeping on top of the important stuff.

So goodnight, and Emperor bless you all. You can rest assured that everything that can be done will be done.

Erm... How was that? Gubernatorial enough? Or should we go again?

Err... What do you mean, it was live?

CHAPTER SIXTEEN

AMBERLEY WAS RIGHT, of course. Over the next two days we lost contact with another seven outposts, all of them situated among the lowest altitude and most marginally habitable of the plateaux, which at least meant that relatively few people had vanished into the maw of the tyranids,[1] to be used as the raw material for spawning another generation of their hideous kind. That raised a whole new set of questions, of course.

'You must have some idea of where their digester pools are,' I said. I was sitting in Kasteen's office, along with the colonel, Major Broklaw, and a portable hololith, in which the disembodied heads of our counterparts from the other regiments on-planet

---

1. Estimates vary between about 1,500 and just over 3,000. Records of that time are, understandably, somewhat fragmentary.

flickered uneasily, orbiting Zyvan's face and upper torso like cherubs round a high-ranking ecclesiarch. There was still no sign of the hive fleet, or our promised reinforcements, and, under the circumstances, ordering the senior command staff to Principia Mons for a face-to-face briefing would have been the height of folly. Zyvan shook his head.

'We've been looking, believe me, but the sandstorms are still blocking too many of our orbital imagers, and our recon flights haven't turned anything up either. By the time we've established the loss of another settlement and sent a response team in, the wind has obliterated any tracks that were left in the desert.'

'The commissar does have a point though,' Kasteen put in, backing me up loyally, even if that did mean coming perilously close to sounding as though she had doubts about Zyvan's strategy. 'On Corania they clustered round the pools, depositing the dead they'd collected and spawning new creatures. Bombing from the air while they were vulnerable made a big difference, and denied them reinforcements. For a while at least.'

'I quite agree,' Zyvan said, 'and the minute they're located, our ships will commence an all-out bombardment from orbit. It's the only way to be sure of eradicating them.' He permitted himself a wintry smile. 'One thing you can say for this place, we won't have to worry too much about collateral damage.'

Several of the faces around him nodded in agreement, and I recognised a few from the Gravalax campaign a couple of years earlier, whose names I'd never caught. Kasteen and Broklaw were looking

vaguely cheered by the remark as well, and I'm
bound to say I appreciated the point as much as they
did. Despite our best efforts we'd put quite a dent in
the planetary capital there, and it had gone against
the grain to be killing and maiming so many of the
civilians we were supposed to have been protecting.
(Although, to be fair, a good half of the ones who
didn't turn out to be 'stealers were rabid xenoists
who would have sold us out to the tau in a heartbeat,
so I suppose we weren't hurting nearly as many loyal
subjects of the Emperor as we might have done.)

'That's some comfort, at least,' I said, taking shameless advantage of my position to consolidate the
good opinion he evidently still had of me. After leaving Hell's Edge behind us, Amberley had ordered our
pilot to head straight for Principia Mons, where we'd
lost no time in briefing the lord general about what
we'd found in the ill-fated settlement. (The 'nid presence, at any rate. She never said a word about the
hidden laboratory, and I knew better than to raise the
subject myself.)

Zyvan had been as courteous a host as before,
politely ignoring the fact that we were both as malodorous as Jurgen (other than offering us the use of
his bath, which was more like a swimming pool with
soap, and sending my uniform out to be cleaned
while we ate), and asking a number of pertinent
questions about the numbers and types of organisms
that had attacked us, which I did my best to answer.
My input had evidently proven satisfactory, as he'd
gone so far as to shake my hand when Jurgen and I
had departed to meet the courier shuttle he'd
ordered to meet us at the aerodrome.

'Can't we at least narrow it down?' Kasteen asked, worrying at the point she'd raised like a kroot with a bone. 'We know where they've struck, and at roughly what times. Surely we can estimate where the swarms are originating from.'

'Our analysts have been trying to do just that, of course,' Zyvan said, nodding in approval, and clearly grateful for having at least one regimental commander to hand with some idea of what we were facing.[1] 'Unfortunately it seems that the settlements the 'nids have hit are scattered right across the planet, and given our best knowledge of how fast they can move, the timing isn't consistent with the activities of a single swarm.'

'More than one.' Broklaw added something under his breath that the lord general pretended not to have heard. 'Can you at least give us some idea of how many we're dealing with?'

Zyvan shook his head. 'Our best guess is at least three distinct swarms,' he said heavily, provoking a flurry of consternation among his halo of floating heads, 'but that's just going by the number of raids we've discovered so far. We're also assuming that the swarms are sufficiently numerous to have sent out more than one group of organisms at a time, and that each pack has already created a digester pool to process the biomass they're harvesting.' I noted the euphemism with faint surprise. Zyvan had always struck me as fairly blunt in his mode of expression, a

---

1. *The 597th was the only regiment currently on Periremunda with previous experience of fighting tyranids, although the Karthelan 463rd had taken part in the cleansing of the Taragon underhive following the discovery of a recently established genestealer cult there in 929 M41.*

personality quirk he was renowned for, and I hadn't expected him to shy away from the fact that it was the corpses of slaughtered civilians he was talking about.[1] 'If they haven't begun digesting the material they've collected after all, and are simply consuming it for energy, then we're looking for a greater number of randomly roving swarms with no focus for their activities beyond finding the next pocket of life on this benighted globe and snuffing it out.' He shrugged, clearly thinking he might as well give us all the bad news in one go. 'If the worst case estimate turns out to be the right one after all, we're going to find five of the damned things running around loose out there.' That provoked further consternation among the hololithic heads. 'Assuming there haven't been even more raids we don't know about yet, of course. That could revise the numbers even further upwards.'

'Emperor on Earth,' Kasteen said, her face pale even for a Valhallan.

I nodded judiciously. 'It makes good tactical sense,' I said. 'The hive fleets often infiltrate an advance force, to tie up the defenders before the main assault begins, and this planet's tailor made for them to do just that. They could be pretty much anywhere, while we're deployed in a few major population centres, waiting for them to come to us. We daren't spread ourselves any thinner, either, which leaves the majority of the plateaux completely undefended.'

---

1. *In fact Zyvan probably chose his words carefully to reflect the fact that it wasn't just humans the tyranids were taking: the settlements they'd attacked were denuded of all forms of life, including plants and domestic animals.*

'Apart from the local PDF garrisons,' an eager young commissar I didn't recognise pointed out. He was assigned to one of the Harakoni regiments, and his uniform cap was embellished with one of the blue feathers commonly affected by veterans of a grav chute combat drop, so he clearly wasn't the sort to either shirk his duty or feel he was too grand to ignore the traditions of the troopers he served with. Despite his air of puppy-like enthusiasm, which reminded me disconcertingly of Lieutenant Sulla, the keenest and most irritating of our platoon commanders,[1] I was inclined to listen to the lad. 'Are any of them sufficiently reliable to deploy?'

'The arbitrator informs me that roughly two-thirds of the PDF regiments are now believed to be free of genestealer infiltration,' Zyvan said dryly. 'How well founded that belief is, however, remains to be seen; and of course the loyalty of the Gavaronian militia has been personally vouched for by the Canoness Eglantine.' The faint pause before he continued said all he needed to about that particular assurance. 'So I suppose we can expect most of them to mount some kind of effective resistance when push comes to shove.'

'Sounds like Keesh has been busy,' I said, surprised and relieved to hear that so much of the PDF had been effectively purged in so short a time.

Zyvan nodded. 'Apparently his office has received a great deal of first-hand intelligence gleaned during a

---

1. *Despite the eminence to which she would later rise, Cain's attitude towards Sulla remains, at best, one of mild antipathy throughout his memoirs. She, ironically, appears to have remained in lifelong ignorance of his actual opinion of her, clearly regarding him as something of a mentor.*

series of raids on hidden 'stealer nests,' he said. Realising who had carried them out, and the wisdom of
circumspection in this regard, I returned the gesture.

'Then let's hope his sources are accurate,' I said,
knowing full well that they were.

'Indeed,' Zyvan replied, diverting matters on to
safer ground with as much finesse as a diplomat. 'If
they are, we'll have a fighting chance of holding on
until our fleet arrives.'

'Assuming the hive fleet doesn't get here ahead of
them,' the Harakoni colonel put in, and I was pleasantly surprised to notice the young commissar
nodding in agreement. A realist as well as a populist,
maybe he was going to turn out to be one of those
rare examples of our calling who don't end up dying
heroically on the battlefield leading from the front,
or taking a lasbolt in the back from a disgruntled
trooper goaded once too often with the threat of execution or the lash.

'That might depend on how many of the unpurged
regiments turn out to be loyal after all,' he pointed
out reasonably.

'Then we'll have to hope that it's most of them,'
Zyvan said. 'I'm deploying them in the outer defensive perimeters in any case.' Where our artillery could
drop shells on them at the first sign of treachery, and
the 'nids would be into them first regardless. Selling
that to the high command of the local forces
wouldn't be an easy or pleasant job, and I didn't envy
whoever had got it. But there were enough bright,
eager scions of the Imperial aristocracy whose fami-
lies had bought them commissions cluttering up
Zyvan's general staff for him to be irritated by one of

them on an almost daily basis, and I had no doubt that a suitable candidate had made himself obvious at just the right moment. (The obvious solution, assigning the whole pack of them to the front line somewhere, where if the enemy didn't take care of them their own men probably would, didn't seem to have occurred to him, nor would it, in all the years we were destined to serve together.)[1]

'If it's the splinter fleet I encountered in the Desolatia system,' I said, more to remind everyone who the real hero was supposed to be around here than because I thought it was strictly relevant, 'it will be relatively weak. Our warships killed around seventy percent of its vessels before they could escape into the warp, and we dealt with the 'stealers on Keffia and Gravalax[2] effectively enough to prevent it being summoned there. It's been over a dozen years, I admit, but I doubt it's found enough to consume in the meantime to regain much of its strength.'

'Quite so.' Zyvan nodded in agreement. 'Where the tyranids are concerned nothing can be certain, of course, but it does seem likely that this is the same fleet.'

1. No doubt it did, frequently, but Zyvan was too conscientious a servant of the Emperor to risk Imperial interests, or the lives of the ordinary soldiers under his command, simply to rid himself of a trifling nuisance. Besides, there would always be plenty more to replace them, so any respite would have been fleeting at best.

2. In actual fact, later events would point to a quite different interpretation of the Gravalax incident. The 'stealer cult there, as Cain points out in his own account of the affair, was intent on provoking a war of attrition with the tau, which would have seriously weakened the Imperium's defences throughout the Damocles Gulf and its neighbouring sectors. Given the line of advance of Hive Fleet Kraken, it now seems more than probable that they were intending to prepare the way for this massive invasion force rather than a mere splinter fleet.

He smiled mirthlessly again. 'I'd certainly prefer to believe that it's the only one in this part of the galaxy.'

'Then we should be able to hold out,' I said, nodding judiciously, and trying to sound more certain than I felt. 'For a few days, at least. It's already weak and wounded, and our reinforcements should be able to finish it off for good.' That's always a pretty tall order when you're dealing with 'nids, of course, they pop up again just when you think it's all over with a persistence even a necron would envy, but it was what everyone needed to hear, and the expressions and voices of everyone in the link became a lot more confident and decisive after that.

'All we need now is a strategy for holding out,' Broklaw remarked, as though this would be nothing too difficult, and Kasteen nodded her agreement.

'We'll need to be ready for rapid deployment, so we can get stuck into them wherever they appear.' The familiar self-confident smile was back on her face now that her old fear of the 'nids had been replaced by a genuine conviction that we could win. 'At least requisitioning enough shuttles won't be a problem on a world like this.'

'The commerce commission will raise merry hell about it,' Zyvan pointed out, with enough of a grin lurking behind his beard to make me suspect that another young subaltern with razor-sharp creases in his uniform and an unfortunate tendency to irritate the lord general was about to have his diplomatic skills tested to the limit. 'But they can frak off to the warp so far as I'm concerned. We've a war to win, and if they don't want to help us do that, they can sit outside the perimeter and bitch about it to the 'nids.'

'We can't defend everywhere,' Broklaw pointed out. 'Even if every regiment becomes air mobile, it'll take time to respond to an attack.'

'Precisely,' Zyvan said, 'which is why we're implementing a strategy of phased reinforcement.' He smiled, looking more relaxed than he had done since I'd left him in earnest discussion with Amberley the evening before to return to Hoarfell. 'Not unlike the way the Guard responds to an attack on the Imperium itself, as it happens, but on a much smaller scale, of course.'

'I'm not sure I follow,' the young commissar said.

'It's fairly straightforward,' Zyvan assured him. 'When the 'nids attack a populated plateau, the local PDF garrison will respond, and report the situation. Reinforcements from the nearest plateaux with PDF garrisons will start arriving at once, giving the nearest Guard regiment time to put its own rapid response force into the air.'

'That should work,' I agreed. If nothing else, it would buy Keesh's people a little more time to evacuate the civilians, and the PDF gaunt fodder should at least slow down the 'nids long enough for the real soldiers to get there. All in all I couldn't think of a better plan, although if I'd realised Zyvan was inadvertently setting me up for another attempt on my life, no doubt I'd have been a good deal less sanguine about it.

CHAPTER SEVENTEEN

FOR THE NEXT couple of days Zyvan's strategy seemed to be working. So far as we could tell the 'nids were still confining their depredations to the lowest lying and most sparsely populated plateaux, as our analysts had anticipated, and I have to confess to finding that curiously reassuring, Hoarfell being neither of those things. That wasn't to say that we were at all complacent about the possibility of an unexpected attack on our own position, of course: the one thing we all knew from experience was that the scuttling horrors were nothing if not unpredictable, and Kasteen kept the regiment on high alert in case a lictor or a purestrain 'stealer brood had somehow managed to sneak onto the plateau despite our vigilance.

Apart from that unnerving possibility, of course, there was the constant looming threat of the hive

fleet to worry about. Though its advent was expected hourly it still seemed in no hurry to arrive, which was fine by me, as once it emerged from the warp we could expect the entire planet to be blanketed in spores and battle to be joined in earnest wherever we happened to be.

The one piece of good news was that we didn't have any more guerrilla attacks by 'stealer hybrids to worry about, the security precautions we'd imposed in the wake of the fuel tanker incident apparently proving enough to prevent them from re-establishing a presence in Darien, although hitherto unsuspected broods were emerging elsewhere around the planet to commit acts of sabotage aimed at undermining resistance to the swarms. I heard little from Amberley during this tense interlude of sporadic fighting, her attention apparently entirely taken up with rooting out the cancers in our midst, or following up whatever leads she'd discovered in Hell's Edge that might lead her to the missing techpriest before the tyranids found him first (or Lazurus and his team managed to locate him, which she seemed to regard as almost as bad).

Keesh hadn't been idle either. He and his justicars were attempting to evacuate the settlements deemed most at risk from the tyranid swarms roaming the desert, relocating the populations of the lowest plateaux to higher and safer ground (at least until the hive fleet turned up, and 'safe' ceased to have any meaning other than a large metal box with a lock on it), a strategy which, in addition to saving countless lives, would also deny the invaders the resources they needed to increase their numbers. It was a massive

undertaking, though, and all too frequently the dirigible fleet arrived too late at some luckless community to find nothing of it remaining beyond the kind of desolation we'd discovered in Hell's Edge.

While all this was going on, the regiment was getting its first taste of action against the chittering nightmares that continued to besiege us. Several of our platoons had been airlifted to bolster the sagging resistance of the PDF when the 'nids moved against towns or industrial zones large enough to be worth defending, and, I'm pleased to say, had given a good account of themselves in the process, despite the trauma of facing their most dreaded foe once again.[1]

Of course the more successful we were at evacuating the smaller colonies the more we were forcing the 'nids to mass their forces against larger, more vital targets, so in retrospect I suppose each victory we gained was somewhat pyrrhic, merely forcing us into another more desperate battle within a matter of hours, but the grim statistics of attrition seemed to be marginally in our favour. There was no doubt in my mind that we were making the tyranids pay for every centimetre of ground they gained in ichor. Any other foe would at least have been given pause by the pounding they took, but true to type they took no more notice of their own casualties than we would of an expended

---

1. *Elements of the 597th were deployed in support of the PDF on three separate occasions during this period, managing to repulse the tyranid attack entirely on one of them, and holding it off for long enough to successfully complete the evacuation of the surviving civilians before retreating in good order themselves in both of the other engagements. Their previous experience of fighting this particular xenos breed no doubt stood them in good stead, and the positive effect on morale these victories had went well beyond the regiment itself.*

power cell. Nevertheless, just as we would have been handicapped by a shortage of ammunition, every hole we blasted through their ranks represented a marginal degradation of their ability to fight, and our policy of burning every 'nid corpse we could recover (to say nothing of our own) denied them the opportunity of replenishing their ranks. If the hive fleet that spawned them hadn't arrived when it did, I suspect, we might even have been able to force our advantage past the tipping point, and succeeded in cleansing them entirely from the surface of Periremunda unaided.

That didn't happen, of course. The fleet did arrive, along with our own reinforcements, and the focus of the campaign shifted to a more conventional system-wide engagement, where the battle in space became as important as events on the ground. (At least so far as the official record goes. The events I was to become involved in could well have changed the face of the entire galaxy, although just how far-reaching they were I'd have no idea until decades later, at the turn of the millennium, when Abbadon's insane assault on the heart of the Imperium began.)[1]

But I'm getting ahead of myself. What I meant to be talking about was the day all hell broke loose, my shadowy enemies made another attempt to kill me, and I discovered far more than I ever wanted to know about the true nature of the Holy Inquisition.

IT ALL STARTED innocently enough, although in my experience it usually does when I'm about to be

---

1. *Cain's account of his exploits during the 13th Black Crusade, though fascinating, need not detain us at this juncture.*

pitched yet again into mortal peril and bowel clench-
ing terror. I'd been hanging around our command
centre, trying, like everyone else, not to look as
though I was staring at the hololith for the first sign
of the hive fleet emerging from the warp, and discussing our state of readiness with Kasteen. So far
we'd deployed four platoons in support of the PDF,
and they'd all returned in high spirits, despite the
inevitable casualties they'd taken.[1] I complimented
the colonel once again on her decision to practise the
anti-tyranid tactics the veterans among us had
learned at so great a cost on Corania, and she nodded gravely.

'It seems to be paying off,' she conceded. I glanced
at the status board. Second company was on standby
for rapid deployment at the moment, a couple of
platoons already sitting out at the aerodrome waiting
for a vox message to pile into the transport shuttles
we'd requisitioned, along with a couple of civilian
pilots who seemed less than thrilled to be hopping
in and out of war zones pretty much on a daily basis,
but understandably disinclined to argue with an
awful lot of people carrying guns. The dropships
from our troop carriers would have been preferable,
of course, but in the nature of things there were far
fewer of those to go round than there were regiments
demanding their use and our position on Hoarfell

---

1. *Or perhaps because of them: they all seem to have lost around fifteen
per cent of their initial complement (the vast majority of the fatalities
being the inevitable 'fungs'), a remarkably low total considering the
nature of their foe. Not to mention the heartening effect that seeing the
tyranids break and run must have had on the survivors of the massacre
on Corania.*

made us a low priority. Zyvan had decided that the company-sized transports would be better employed shifting troopers who were nearer to the enemy (which meant more of them could be plucked to safety if things went seriously ploin-shaped, but of course no one would have been tactless enough to mention that to the civilian authorities). I nodded approvingly.

'We've got by far the best survival rate of any of the Guard regiments,' I said, which happened to be true. The Harakoni had taken a real mauling that morning, and I'd found myself wondering briefly how their young commissar had fared. I didn't even want to start thinking about the PDF. There was no doubt that Zyvan's strategy was effective, but it left under trained and ill-equipped militia units holding the line against the tyranid horrors until the real soldiers could get there, and there was no doubt at all that the price they were paying was a heavy one. If the peculiar topography of their homeworld hadn't made it impossible I've no doubt that many more of them would have broken and run than actually did.

Since they had nowhere to go in any case, and were fighting for their homes and loved ones, which I've observed time and again will make even the meekest civilian stand his ground like a Terminator, they remained at the front, and died in droves. Even allowing for our own people's remarkable ability to engage the chitinous nightmares and emerge unscathed, these battlezones sounded extraordinarily unhealthy places to be, and I resolved to stay as far away from them as I could, at least until the spores started falling, and I couldn't avoid the 'nids wherever I was.

Luckily no one had challenged my assertion that my place would be at the regimental headquarters when that ghastly prospect occurred (where, of course, I'd have a full company of troopers to hide behind), and that traipsing off on one of these periodic hit-and-run raids made it all too possible that I'd be wrapped up in what amounted to a glorified skirmish when the sky started falling. From years of practice I'd managed to sound a little wistful as I'd pointed this out, contriving to give the impression without actually saying so that I'd have liked nothing better than to charge off to face an endless tide of malevolent chitin, but my sense of duty was strong enough to override such a selfish impulse, leaving me no alternative but to skulk around our heavily fortified compound drinking tanna and generally getting underfoot while the troopers got on with defending the civilians like they were supposed to.

'So far,' Kasteen said, looking around us, her expression dour. Whatever doubts she might be feeling, this was no place to discuss them. The command centre was swarming with men and women going about their regular duties, and we both knew morale wasn't going to be helped if they got even an inkling that the senior command staff was less confident of our ultimate victory than we appeared. By mutual, unspoken agreement we began to walk towards the staircase leading up to the gallery where her office was. 'But we still have to face the hive fleet. That's going to be a very different game.'

'True,' I said, standing aside to let her mount the stairway first, 'but our reinforcements can't be far behind them.' My attention was quite pleasantly

distracted for a moment by the callipygian spectacle ascending past my eye level, and as I placed my foot on the lowest tread I couldn't help tilting my neck back a little to continue appreciating it for a moment longer.

Minute as it was, that movement was to save my life, as without it I'm sure I'd never have noticed the faint flicker of motion high in the girders supporting the roof. My first thought was that a bird of some kind had entered the vast enclosed space through the massive doors at the far end, which, as usual, had been left open to admit a howling draught and the occasional flurry of snow so essential to the Valhallan notion of wellbeing. That didn't seem terribly likely, though, as the constant noise would have prevented any self-respecting avian from roosting comfortably, and if there was such an intruder it would almost certainly have left some trace of its presence on the room below. The palms of my hands began to itch, and, mindful of my recent experience with the psyker assassin, I craned my head for a better view, wondering where the hell Jurgen had got to now that I really needed him.

'There's something in the rafters,' I said, drawing my laspistol, and trying to focus on the faint impression of movement in the shadows over our heads. Kasteen glanced up too, and reached for her sidearm. Around us I could see little ripples of alarm and consternation, most of the troopers on vox and auspex duty glancing at the lasguns resting against their control lecterns. Whatever the thing was, it was small, and I found myself reminded all too vividly of the spore mines that had attacked us in Hell's Edge.

'I see it too,' Kasteen said grimly, aiming her bolt pistol. Then her gaze skittered off to one side. 'And another one.'

'Arm yourselves!' I called, although the advice seemed somewhat superfluous by now, all the troopers I could see with a weapon having them to hand already. Then, as if suddenly becoming aware of our scrutiny, the mysterious intruders swooped to the attack.

'What the hell?' Kasteen said, surprised, as they came into view for the first time. An echelon of servo skulls, five in all, was dropping towards us, and her aim wavered indecisively. She turned to a loitering enginseer, his face predictably blank beneath the cowl of his Adeptus Mechanicus robe, and glared at him. 'Who let those things in here?'

'They're nothing to do with us,' the techpriest assured her, in the level voxcoder drone of so many of his kind. Something whirred behind his eyes, as he appeared to focus on something the rest of us couldn't see. 'The idents don't match any of the local Mechanicus shrines–'

Whatever else he might have been about to tell us was lost in the sudden bark of what sounded like a bolt pistol, and his torso disintegrated in a shower of blood and shrapnel, which no doubt had been part of his augmetic systems before the explosive projectile had rearranged them. I returned fire at once, and I wasn't the only one. Every trooper in the hall who could grab a weapon opened up on the macabre intruders like a bunch of drunken aristos on a shooting party who'd just caught sight of a flock of widgeon. The skulls were hellish fast and agile,

though, jinking through the barrage of lasbolts like those flying platter things the tau use when they've got more sense than to stick their own heads over the parapet. Only one went down, smacking into the rockcrete floor with enough force to shatter bone and weapon alike.

'Keep firing!' I shouted unnecessarily, and the troopers complied with a will. I scurried into cover behind the staircase just in time, another couple of bolter rounds exploding against the metal mesh where I'd been standing an instant before, while Kasteen, her retreat cut off, sprinted upwards to the gallery, shooting as she went. She didn't manage to hit anything, but the stray rounds from her bolt pistol punched a constellation of miniature stars in the roof of the command post, and the leading skull veered away from the fusillade of explosive projectiles.

I expected at least one of the swarm to turn on the colonel now that she was exposed on the narrow walkway outside her office, even though she'd ducked behind the balustrade to take as much advantage of the available cover as she could, but they all ignored her, dropping past the level of the mezzanine, and with a thrill of horror I realised that every single one of them was heading straight for me. Indeed, if it hadn't been for the sheer volume of fire making them evade as they came, they would have been nose to nose with me by now. (Well, strictly speaking none of them had noses any more, but you know what I mean.)

There'd be plenty of time to worry about what it all meant later. Right now my priority was survival, and

I studied the airborne assassins carefully, searching for any kind of weakness. Two of them appeared to have bolt pistols built into them, the barrels protruding grotesquely from between their teeth like inside-out suicides, and if they hadn't been forced to dance around to make themselves harder to hit, with the inevitable deleterious effect on their own accuracy, I have no doubt that I'd have shared the fate of the luckless enginseer. A third had a chainblade humming away beneath it, apparently in the fond hope that its gun-slinging brethren would have been able to keep me busy long enough for it to part more than my hair, while the fourth seemed to be completely unarmed for some reason.

That was the one. If it wasn't carrying a weapon, it had to be there to direct the others. Taking careful aim I steadied my arm against the metal of the staircase, thankful yet again for the augmetic fingers that let me hold my laspistol more firmly on target than even the most skilled duellist could have managed, and squeezed the trigger.

To my immense relief the shot struck home, and the bone casing shattered, spilling lumps of auspex gear and the sensorium array attached to it across the floor. By some strange freak of chance the tiny antigravity unit that had kept the skull aloft shot upwards, still functioning and no longer weighed down by its payload, to shatter one of the skylights over our heads and vanish into the thin grey murk that kept Hoarfell almost perpetually wrapped in its chilly embrace. Looking up after flinching instinctively away from the shower of broken glass rattling against my refuge, and the flurry of snow that

followed it, I tried to acquire another target, only to find the specimen with the chainblade swooping at my head.

I reacted at once, drawing my chainsword by reflex, not even consciously aware that I was doing so until I'd batted the thing aside. It bounced off one of the girders supporting the gallery, an ugly gash along its jaw where my blade had bitten deep into the bone. By sheer luck I seemed to have severed the power cable leading to its lift unit, and it lay inert on the rockrete, buzzing angrily and attempting to saw its way through the floor, until a couple of troopers put it out of its misery with a flurry of well aimed las-bolts.

The two gun-skulls hovered uneasily, apparently unsure of their target now the hunter unit that had led them to me was out of commission, and so many other people in the vicinity were popping off rounds at them. After a moment of frantic bouncing around, which enabled them to avoid vaporisation by something approaching a miracle, they suddenly turned and shot upwards, disappearing through the hole in the skylight.

'Someone really seems to have it in for you,' Kasteen remarked, descending the staircase again, somewhat gingerly as she tested the treads where the bolts had struck. 'First an invisible psyker, and now this.' She stared at me quizzically, the curiosity she was too polite to express openly all too visible on the faces of the troopers surrounding us. Suddenly becoming aware of their scrutiny, she gestured abruptly to the nearest non-com. 'Sergeant, get this mess cleaned up.'

'Yes, ma'am.' He saluted smartly, and began rounding up everyone who hadn't taken the hint and found urgent business back at their assigned station quickly enough. 'You and you, get a body bag. The cogboys'll probably want to organise some kind of send off for Sparky, so we'd better keep him fresh.' It seemed our erstwhile enginseer had been popular enough among the troopers to have acquired a nickname, which vaguely surprised me. Struck by an afterthought, the sergeant called the solemn faced troopers back as they turned to comply. 'Better get a mop as well, he's leaking a bit.'

'They're determined, all right,' I said, replying to Kasteen. I glanced at the hole in the ceiling through which the automated assassins had fled, an uncomfortable thought forcing its way to the forefront of my mind. 'They must be to have found a way through our security here.'

'We'll find out how they managed it,' the colonel assured me grimly.

I nodded, trying to look calm and analytical. 'No doubt we will,' I said, 'but those things can infiltrate almost anywhere.' Come to that, the ones that had retreated could come back for another go pretty much whenever they felt like it. My only option seemed to be to get the hell out of there before they rallied and tried to complete their programmed assignment, and as I glanced around the command centre the perfect bolthole seemed to present itself. 'Whoever's behind these attempts on my life must know I'm here, and they could try again.'

'Let them,' Kasteen said, as though looking forward to taking out another would-be assassin in

person. 'I've no objection to helping traitors commit suicide.'

I smiled, in a self-deprecating manner. 'I appreciate the sentiment, Regina, but you've got far more important things to worry about than ensuring my safety. Our overriding priority is the defence of this planet, and another attack on our headquarters could undermine that, perhaps fatally.' I paused, timing it just long enough to underline the seriousness of our responsibility. 'I'm not willing to risk compromising the operational effectiveness of the regiment just to keep myself out of harm's way.'

'What have you got in mind?' Kasteen asked, no doubt impressed by my dedication to duty, and veiling her concern behind a thin façade of brusque efficiency.

I gestured towards the status board I'd noticed before. 'We've got two platoons sitting out at the aero-drome. I'll go and join them for the time being.' Whoever sent the servo skulls could turn our head-quarters upside down searching for me, so far as I was concerned. Chances were they'd never think of looking among such a small detachment, and even if they did, I'd still have around a hundred troopers to hide behind.

Kasteen nodded slowly. 'Makes sense,' she conceded. She paused. 'Anything else we can do before you leave?'

'Get a complete pict record of those servo skulls,' I said, indicating the debris of the battle, 'and have it downloaded to a data-slate. I'll take it with me when I go.'

'I see.' Kasteen looked thoughtful. 'Do you really think you might be able to get some idea of where they came from by examining the picts?'

I shook my head. 'No,' I said slowly, 'but I know a woman who can.' After all, it was her fault in the first place for sticking me in front of the pictcasters, and giving every halfwit insurrectionist on the planet the impression that I was gunning for him in person, so it only seemed fair that she keep them off my back now. I was right too, this would all turn out to be a result of her activities on Periremunda; but in a manner which, at the time, I couldn't possibly have guessed.

Editorial note:

The following, mercifully short, extract fills in a brief elision in Cain's own account of events. After some deliberation I've decided to include it purely for the sake of completeness. Readers preferring to skip it are at perfect liberty to do so, if not actively encouraged.

From *Like a Phoenix on the Wing: The Early Campaigns and Glorious Victories of the Valhallan 597th* by General Jenit Sulla (retired), 101 M42

IT WILL COME as no surprise to those readers who have followed my account of the heroic exploits of our regiment thus far to hear that the women and men under my command were as eager as ever to confront the monstrous enemy we faced, not least because our

gallant comrades in First Company had already been fortunate enough to drive back the inhuman horde on no fewer than three occasions. At last, however, Second Company was placed on standby, ready and waiting to respond to the call to arms, and to our barely concealed delight Third Platoon was one of those selected to wait at the starport in Darien in anticipation of an immediate departure to wherever we were needed to deliver the Emperor's vengeance to the scuttling hordes that dared to pollute his most blessed demesne.

I would be somewhat lax in my duties as a chronicler of events, however, if I failed to admit to a degree of trepidation underlying our eagerness to engage the tyranid swarms. For all too many of us, the last time we'd faced these vat-spawned monstrosities had been a nightmare of slaughter in which we'd lost friends and comrades in uncountable numbers, and despite the unshakeable resolve our faith in the Emperor conferred upon us the memories of Corania remained fresh in our minds. Therefore the news that we were to be joined by none other than Commissar Cain was as welcome as it was unexpected, every woman and man of us determined to prove worthy of the leadership of so stalwart an example of the military virtues.

CHAPTER EIGHTEEN

'Fascinating,' Lazurus said, his metallic face flickering in the portable hololith aboard third platoon's command Chimera. I'd arrived at the aerodrome around half an hour before, no further threats to my life having manifested in the interim beyond Jurgen's habitually uninhibited driving style. After negotiating the obstacle course of the landing field at his usual breakneck pace he'd hurled our Salamander up the loading ramp of the nearest shuttle with almost as much alacrity as we'd boarded Amberley's Aquila, much to the consternation of the rapidly scattering troopers left on guard around the base of it.

Only as he brought us to a halt next to the Chimeras already parked in the hold, their noses angled towards the exit ramp for a rapid deployment, did I realise that their markings were those of third

platoon, and my heart sank. Lieutenant Sulla was trotting across the cargo bay towards us, positively bristling with the disconcerting enthusiasm she habitually displayed at the prospect of getting into action, and I began to wish I'd told Jurgen to head for the other aircraft instead of simply getting us under cover as quickly as possible. Lieutenant Faril, the officer in charge of fifth platoon, was a good deal less impulsive, and I'd have stood a much better chance of staying in one piece surrounded by the troopers of his command. Sulla was just as likely to take it into her head to order a suicidal charge at the nearest hive tyrant as stay comfortably behind cover potting away at it from a safe distance, and for some reason the troopers under her would just follow her into the fray, screaming their lungs out like maddened orks, and probably reducing the thing to bloody chunks before it even got over its astonishment at their temerity.[1]

'Commissar.' She saluted smartly, her narrow face, ponytail and toothy grin making her look more like a cartoon horse than ever, positively fizzing with excitement. 'I take it your arrival here means we're about to get stuck in at last?'

'If the Emperor wills it,' I said, thinking there was never a spore mine around when you really needed one. 'There isn't much for me to do back at HQ at the

---

1. *Despite Cain's cynicism, Sulla did indeed enjoy the confidence and respect of the troops she led, almost to the extent that he claims. She undeniably had a tendency to take risks a more cautious commander would think twice about, but as is so often the case her willingness to seize the initiative often proved decisive at a critical juncture, and the concomitant slightly higher casualty rates in her platoon seemed to have been more than offset by its members' astonishingly high morale.*

moment, apart from routine paperwork, so I thought I'd tag along on the next deployment if you or Faril don't mind hauling a bit of dead weight with you.' As always I spoke with the common troopers in mind, a bevy of which had popped out of their AFV hatches, like snow weasels sniffing for predators, to see what all the fuss was about. No harm in playing up to my image of modest heroism, especially if I was hoping to keep them between me and the 'nids.

'Happy to have you,' Sulla assured me, edging away from Jurgen as unobtrusively as she could, the aroma of his presence beginning to thicken noticeably in the confined space between the parked vehicles. 'Is there anything we can do for you while we're waiting?'

'I'd appreciate the use of your command vehicle,' I said, after a moment's thought. 'I've some sensitive material to transmit to Principia Mons for analysis, and I may have to discuss it with the lord general. Obviously I trust the discretion of everyone here, but security regulations...'

'Of course.' Sulla looked even more like a pony being offered a sugar lump than ever, completely bowled over by the prospect of being involved, however peripherally, in the affairs of the high command. I've often wondered if, in the years to come, she was disappointed to discover just how tedious most of them actually were.

Anyhow, the upshot of all this was that I ended up in the platoon command vehicle, comfortably secure from prying eyes and ears, while Jurgen fiddled about with the vox unit and brought me mugs of tanna at regular intervals. I had plenty of leisure to drink

them too, as Zyvan took at least twenty minutes to track Amberley down through whatever arcane channels of communication existed between his office and the roving inquisitor, but after what seemed like an interminable wait her face appeared in the hololith, followed almost at once by Lazurus, who had apparently dropped into her hotel suite for another non-exchange of information.

'That's very helpful indeed,' the senior techpriest said, amplifying on his original reaction, and glancing slightly to one side of the imager, where, presumably, the pict records of the servo skulls I'd transmitted from the data-slate had just appeared. He and Yanbel had begun to pore over them as soon as they'd come through, exchanging remarks in the peculiar twittering language of their caste.[1]

'Can you tell where they came from?' I asked bluntly.

Lazurus nodded slowly. 'It's merely the best estimate I can give you, of course, but judging from the configuration of the flux capacitors, I'd say that at least the hunter unit shows signs of having been manufactured on one of the forge worlds in the Hephastus cluster, around six or seven hundred years ago. I could have been a lot more precise if you'd managed to recover one of them intact.'

'I'll try to bear that in mind if they come after me again,' I said, but Lazurus merely nodded, as apparently immune to sarcasm as my aide.

---

1. *Binary, as it's apparently known, remains a complete mystery to anyone outside the Adeptus Mechanicus. Despite decades of intensive study, the sisters of the Ordo Dialogous have yet to establish even the most rudimentary rules of grammar and syntax.*

'That would be helpful,' he said, 'although I wouldn't have thought that's too likely now. Having failed with the servo skulls, he'll probably try something else next time.'

'Who will?' I asked, my astonishment at finally getting something akin to a straight answer not too great for me to pounce on it like a kroot spotting a nice juicy corpse. Lazurus looked as surprised as it was possible to with only half a face.

'Metheius, of course,' he said, as though that was the most obvious thing in the galaxy. 'Who else did you think?'

'Oh, I don't know,' I said, my irritation finally getting the better of my tongue. 'The Chaos cult with the invisible psyker? A cell of genestealer hybrids? I seem to have been walking around with a target on my back ever since I arrived on this Emperor-forsaken rock, so why shouldn't your renegade cogboy join the queue?'

'He's obviously afraid we're getting close to him,' Amberley said speculatively, 'and like everyone else on the planet, he must have got the impression that you're personally co-ordinating the hunt for hidden traitors.' She shrugged, the hint of a mischievous grin quirking at the corners of her mouth. 'Just goes to show that you shouldn't believe everything you read in the printsheets.'

Refraining from pointing out whose fault it was that every subversive idiot on Periremunda was labouring under that delusion, by what I considered to be something of a heroic effort, I merely nodded curtly.

'He must have been panicking to send those things after me in the middle of our compound,' I said. 'The

chances of them getting through several hundred troopers undetected were always going to be slim.'

'He probably had no idea that's where you'd be,' Amberley pointed out cheerfully. 'Most of the pict-casts have shown you in the capital, standing around in the open, and civilians expect commissars to be with the troopers in the front line, where you'd have been an easy target for a sneak attack. Just his bad luck you happened to be in such a secure location when his little messengers caught up with you.'

'Quite,' Lazurus agreed. 'They could have been homing in on you for days.' He pointed out a lump of something metallic, fused by my lasbolt, in the corner of one of the picts. 'That's a genecode scanner or I'm an ork, and I'd bet a Martian upgrade it was tuned to your DNA.' I shuddered, not entirely due to the Valhallan levels of air-conditioning inside Sulla's mobile command post. The notion of those silent assassins drifting through the skies of Periremunda, mindlessly intent on striking me down, was an unnerving one.

'So I assume there's no way of telling where they were dispatched from?' I asked, already sure of the answer.

Yanbel shook his head. 'None at all,' he said cheerfully. 'Those power packs are good for decades. They could have been sent from anywhere on the planet.'

'Wonderful,' I said, wondering how many more hitherto unsuspected factions were going to crawl out of the woodwork and take a crack at me before all this was over. At least with the 'nids things were

straightforward enough: kill or be killed. I began to feel a modicum of sympathy for Sulla's uncomplicated view of things. 'I suppose you still haven't a clue where he might be hiding?'

'We're narrowing it down,' Amberley assured me, which I felt was less helpful than it might have been. After a few more perfunctory words in both directions I broke the link and wandered outside, intending to clear my head by walking around on the landing pad for a few minutes. That should be safe enough, we were too far from any reasonable cover to fear a sniper shot, and the wide open skies around our idling transports would surely prevent any more airborne assassins from sneaking up on me unobserved.

No sooner had I reached the top of the boarding ramp, though, than I found my progress impeded by Sulla, her eyes shining like a juve who'd just been asked out on a hot date by the captain of the schola scrumball team. A sense of foreboding settled itself in my stomach, like the residue of a stale ration bar. In my experience there was only one thing that got her that excited: the prospect of imminent combat.

'Commissar, we've got a go from the colonel.' She hesitated. 'I would have told you before, but given the sensitivity of your discussions…'

'Thank you, lieutenant.' I nodded gravely, while the last of the pickets from the bottom of the ramp double-timed past us, their bootsoles ringing on the metal mesh, most of them glaring at Jurgen as they passed. 'Your discretion does you credit.' I retuned the comm-bead in my ear, hearing Faril's characteristically breezy tones confirming that all his

people were aboard and lifting. A moment later the deck beneath my feet lurched, and a familiar falling sensation in the pit of my stomach confirmed that we too had left the ground. Jurgen's jaw clenched in mute discomfort as he caught sight of the landing field dropping away beneath us, and then, perhaps mercifully, the rising ramp hid the vertiginous view. 'Where are we heading for?'

'Aceralbaterra,' Sulla informed me, in the briskly efficient fashion of all junior officers who've absorbed the briefing slate and relish the chance to prove it. I'd heard the name before somewhere, and after a moment I managed to dredge the context out of the mire of my memory. Amberley's shuttle pilot had mentioned it, during our eventful little jaunt to Hell's Edge. I nodded, as though I'd recognised it at once.

'That's down near the equator, I believe.'

'That's right, sir.' Sulla nodded eagerly. 'Fascinating place, by all accounts. One of the largest agricultural zones on the planet, although it's too low and hot for most conventional crops. Jungle everywhere, apparently, and it just keeps growing like a Catachan grotto, so there's no point in even trying to plant fields.'

'What do they use it for, then?' I asked, already dreading the answer.

Sulla shrugged. 'Grazing. The locals imported thousands of sauropods from Harihowzen, and they just roam around chewing lumps out of the vegetation. Big as Titans, some of them.' Well, that was something of an exaggeration. I'd seen similar creatures before and most of them were barely half that

size, but even allowing for an element of hyperbole the idea was enough to make my blood run cold.

The tyranids needed biomass to swell their armies, and they'd just discovered the motherlode. If Aceralbaterra fell, then Periremunda would fall right along with it. Far from finding a refuge, it seemed, I was about to be pitched into the most decisive battle of the entire war.

CHAPTER NINETEEN

ACERALBATERRA TURNED OUT to be just as uninviting as
Sulla had made it sound in our earlier conversation,
and I'd be lying if I didn't admit to quailing inwardly
as we approached it, flying low and fast to avoid the
dense clouds of gargoyles flocking around the outskirts of Konnandoil, the plateau's principal
settlement. Unlike the villages the 'nid swarm had hit
before, Konnandoil was a fair-sized town, and as we
swooped in over it I could see signs of fighting everywhere, surging tides of claw and mandible being
thrown back by the dogged resistance of the defenders, or, in all too many places, being swamped by it
altogether.

'There.' I pointed to a wide-open plaza, fronting the
aquila encrusted façade of what had evidently once
been the main Administratum building of this

benighted town. It was bordered on the other three sides by a colonnaded walk, which in happier times had evidently sheltered a scattering of brightly painted market stalls from the near constant drizzle.[1] Our pilot nodded, far from happy at the prospect, but astute enough to realise that the spot I'd picked was far enough away from the main bulk of the swarm to afford him a pretty good chance of getting away again before the hive mind recognised the presence of a fresh threat and turned to meet it.

I'd prevailed on the authority of my office to install myself on the flight deck for the duration of our journey, which had the twin advantages of avoiding both Sulla and the effect that being airborne was bound to have on Jurgen's physiology. Thus it was that I had something of a panoramic view of the plateau we'd come to relieve, and was able to form a remarkably cohesive picture of it.

As I think I mentioned before, our pilot, though merely a civilian inducted into Imperial service along with his shuttle, evidently had enough common-sense to have learned some basic survival skills. I can't claim that a Navy veteran wouldn't have been a whole lot sharper, but he did his best, bringing us in below the level of the plateau and popping up over the lip of it at the last possible second. I must admit to flinching a little as that vast spire of rock loomed closer and closer in the viewport, only to be pressed back in my seat by a sudden surge of acceleration as he tilted the nose up and shot us over the rim in an

---

1. *Though barely high enough to receive much in the way of rainfall, the dense mat of foliage covering Aceralbaterra respired moisture constantly, which condensed almost at once in the thick, humid air.*

elegant parabola. Reflecting on the effect this manoeuvre would undoubtedly have had on my aide's tender stomach, and thanking the Emperor quietly under my breath that I wasn't there to hear him express his opinion of it, I glanced down, to find that we were skimming over the treetops of a jungle so lush it could almost have been Catachan itself.[1]

My first impression of luxuriant foliage as far as the eye could see wasn't to last for much longer, though. A few manmade structures broke the smooth flow of vegetation, a scattering of outlying hamlets, no doubt the habitations of the hardy souls who herded and processed the sauropods that grazed on its inexhaustible abundance, and the occasional road slashing through the trees and undergrowth, but for the most part the fecund flora seemed to hold unchallenged sway.

Indeed, to my surprise, it seemed Sulla had hardly been exaggerating about its vigour. In a couple of places the highways through the jungle were already choked with overgrowth, and I began to apprehend that in more normal circumstances keeping them clear would be a constant chore. One such blockage seemed to be surrounded by servitors, hacking and burning away at the encroaching vegetation with single-minded diligence, blissfully unaware that the world had changed irrevocably around them, rendering their efforts to restore order to it entirely futile.

Then, in a second, the landscape altered completely. Great ragged gashes had been torn through the carpet of undergrowth, bare earth showing where the 'nid

---

1. *No doubt Sulla's earlier mention of the verdant deathworld had stuck in Cain's mind.*

swarms had scoured their way through the once verdant jungle, forming an arrow-straight highway from wherever they'd clambered up the precipice straight to the heart of the town. The scattered remains of gigantic bones showed where a herd of sauropods had been too slow to escape the tyranids' relentless advance, and as we neared our destination I saw another of the luckless behemoths overwhelmed by the scuttling horde. Despite its huge size, almost as big as our shuttle, it was brought down in seconds, engulfed by a remorseless mass of talon and mandible. Scores of the things died beneath its massive feet, or were shredded by jaws that could have bisected a Leman Russ, but the sheer number of gaunts that swarmed over it told in the end, and the gigantic creature vanished entirely within an instant, becoming nothing more than a spasmodically twitching mound of chitin, which began to diminish rapidly in bulk.

'Emperor's bones.' The pilot's face was ashen. 'Did you ever see the like?'

'All too often,' I said, keeping an eye out for a suitable landing site. Remembering my duty to boost morale, and mainly to take my own mind off the ghastly sight we'd just witnessed, I gave him an encouraging smile. 'But we've got more guns than the lizards.'

'I guess.' The pilot didn't seem any more convinced than I was, but returned his attention to the flight controls, which was one source of worry out of the way at any rate. I began to study the approaching town a little more carefully, making a mental note of all the hotspots, and trying to form an overall view of the battle to defend it.

The tyranids had evidently struck Konnandoil in a single mass, overwhelming the outlying districts on the side they'd attacked from in an unstoppable tsunami of cold malevolence. The PDF garrison had responded by setting up a defensive line on the fringes of the outer hab zone, giving the no doubt terrified civilians who lived there time to flee deeper into the town centre, where they could ultimately be eaten in a more salubrious environment.

There seemed to be little prospect of evacuating any survivors in the foreseeable future so far as I could tell, all our available air transport assets being fully engaged in ferrying more troops in. Nevertheless the line had held for a while, before the few surviving local PDF troopers had fallen back to join the second layer of defences, which had been hastily established by the first reinforcements to arrive, another PDF troop from a nearby plateau.

By the time we arrived the same grim dance had played itself out yet again, the surviving local units from around half a dozen scattered plateaux having consolidated at the third or fourth perimeter, which now encircled no more than two thirds of the besieged community.[1] Gathering from the sporadic local vox traffic that the vast majority of civilian survivors had been herded into the local temple, presumably in the hope that the Emperor would look after them as everyone else was too busy, I concentrated the bulk of my attention on the area

---

1. *Cain is presumably writing with the benefit of hindsight here, since, although the concentric rings of hastily prepared fortifications would be visible from the air, he would have had little detailed knowledge of the course of the battle up to this point.*

roughly equidistant between it and the defensive line in my search for a suitable landing site. (If the 'nids did break through they'd head for the temple with the single-minded determination of Jurgen spotting an 'all you can eat' buffet, giving us a chance to flank them, I hoped.)

Spotting the plaza of the bureaucrats I directed the pilot to it, as I've already related, and left the flight deck to retrieve Jurgen and clamber aboard our Salamander. It had somewhat belatedly occurred to me that having been the last to board the shuttle our sturdy little scout vehicle would be poised at the top of the ramp, effectively blocking anyone else from getting off before we did, which as you'll appreciate was a far from ideal state of affairs from my point of view. Nevertheless, there was nothing else for it, and at least I'd done all I could to make sure we'd be put down as far from the 'nids as possible, so I resolved to make the best of the situation.

And make the best of it we did, Jurgen flinging us down the metal incline like a sump rat abandoning a waste pipe, while I clung on to the pintel mounted heavy bolter I always like to have installed on my personal transport as a bit of extra insurance, trying to give the impression of leading from the front and being ready for anything.[1] Sulla's command Chimera followed us, and the troop transports fell into formation behind her, barrelling across the open space, which had been paved in an intricate pattern of multicoloured tiles before our shuttle's landing thrusters

---

1. *An impression certainly received by Jenit Sulla, whose prolonged description of Cain's 'noble bearing' in her account of the deployment is gushing in the extreme.*

and the treads of our vehicles had made rather a mess of it.

'Fourth squad, with me.' Sulla's voice was crisp in my comm-bead, every bit as efficient as she usually was when deploying her troopers, and for a moment I wondered if I should have hitched a ride in her command vehicle after all. That way I could have taken advantage of the vox and auspex systems onboard it to keep track of the ebb and flow of the battle, and maximised my chances of staying out of harm's way. I'd also have been surrounded by armour plate; the Salamander was open topped, and uncomfortably exposed by comparison. On the other hand the sturdy little vehicle was faster and more agile than anything else in our inventory, and I'd outrun a tyranid swarm in one before (albeit when there'd actually been somewhere to go), while hanging over the auspex in person would have meant being stuck in a large metal box with Sulla for the duration of the battle. On the whole, taking my chances with the 'nids seemed to be the marginally less irritating of the alternatives. The equine lieutenant went on. 'First and second, sweep out to the left. Third and fifth, you've got the right.'

A chorus of acknowledgements echoed in my comm-bead, and I leaned over the lip of the driver's compartment, raising my voice over the racket of our engine and the screaming of the shuttle's fusion jets as it rose over our heads and banked sharply away in the direction we'd come from.

'Stick with the lieutenant,' I told Jurgen, and he nodded once, accelerating smoothly to slot us in alongside the command Chimera. If I was going to

have to rely on Sulla to keep me out of the jaws of the tyranids, I wanted to be where I could keep an eye on her, and prevent her from doing anything too rash. A brief flurry of vox traffic in my ear told me that Faril was down too, and meeting a little resistance in his efforts to link up with the PDF elements we'd been sent to reinforce.

'Nothing we can't handle, though,' he informed us breezily, 'just a few gaunts. Our heavy bolters are chewing them up nicely.'

'Glad to hear it,' I told him. The data-slate I'd brought with me from Hoarfell bumped gently against my hip as Jurgen bounced us over the central island of a gyratory road junction, and an idea belatedly occurred to me: I didn't have to manage without access to the tactical displays just because I wasn't inside the command vehicle after all. I fished the portable cogitator out of my pocket, removed it from the anonymous Guard issue protective case, and muttered the litany of activation as I pressed what I hoped were the right keys. It had been some time since I'd needed to patch a slate into a local datanet myself, and I'd got used to having a regimental engineseer around to delegate that sort of thing to. Fortunately my memory proved to be accurate, and in a moment the icon I'd been hoping to see appeared on the little pict screen. 'Sulla, can your vox op[1] download the tactical display to my slate?'

'No problem, commissar,' her familiar eager tone reassured me, and a moment later a detailed plan of the town appeared on the screen, overlaid with tiny moving icons showing the disposition of our forces

---

1. *Vox operator, a common abbreviation among Guard personnel.*

and the dull, amorphous mass of the tyranid swarm. I noted with approval that Faril appeared to have joined up with what was left of the left flank of our defensive line, and that the 'nids' advance there appeared to have halted as a result, while the centre was holding on nicely. Indeed, our forces seemed to be gaining a little ground in that spot if anything, which was not only a welcome surprise, but also quite astonishing for mere local militia. Recognising the icon for the main command unit, whoever that was, I directed Sulla to join it.

'Good idea,' she said, apparently under some sort of illusion that I gave a frak what she thought. 'If we come in on their right we can broaden the salient. Otherwise they're going to get cut off, if they keep advancing at that rate without consolidating.'

'You're right,' I said, zooming in on the image on the tiny screen to get a clearer view of that section of the front line. With the larger, more detailed image of the portable hololith aboard the command vehicle to consult, Sulla had spotted what the reduced scale of the handheld display had made less obvious to me.

The unit gaining ground ahead of us, whoever they were, was advancing with a reckless disregard for their own safety, pushing deeper and deeper into the densely packed mass of tyranids facing them. Unless the flanking units followed, and started gaining a little ground too, the 'nids would be able to exploit the gap they'd opened up and surround them. More to the point, there was a more than even chance that part of the swarm would be able to sweep the other way too, gushing through the hole in our own lines

that the gung-ho idiots had ripped open, wreaking
Emperor alone knew what havoc in the streets behind
us before the next batch of Guard troopers arrived to
mop up the mess: assuming anyone could once our
defences had been breached. 'Follow up and reinforce, while I try to rein in those frakheads before they
invite the 'nids round for tanna and florn cakes.'

'You can rely on us, commissar,' Sulla assured me,
happy as ever to have something to shoot at, and
began issuing orders to her troops. 'You all know the
drill. Advance behind the Chimeras, use whatever
other cover you can, and watch each other's backs.
Concentrate your small-arms fire on the largest
creatures you can see when you get the opportunity,
but don't let the little ones get too close while you're
doing it, especially the 'stealers. Heavy weapons
concentrate on the big ones, and try to disrupt their
formations.'

'And don't advance too far,' I added. 'If that reckless
idiot out there gets too far ahead, leave him flapping
in the breeze and pull back to hold the line. Our highest priority has to be protecting the civilians.' Not to
mention my own tender skin, but it would hardly be
tactful to say so over the comm net, and I knew from
experience that practically the only thing likely to
keep Sulla on the leash once she started dealing out
damage to the enemy was an appeal to her overdevel-
oped sense of duty.

'Understood,' she said crisply, and went on issuing
more detailed instructions to her squad commanders.

By now we were approaching the battlefront, the
streets around us beginning to show clear signs of
damage, while the unmistakable sounds of mortal

combat wafted towards us through the moisture thick air, mingled with smudges of smoke and the rank smell of charred flesh. The Valhallans would find these humid conditions extremely uncomfortable, of that I had no doubt, but I knew them well enough to be sure that they'd fight just as effectively here as they would anywhere else, with the possible exception of a glacier field, where nothing or no one could challenge their superiority.

Jurgen slowed us a little, steering round a puddle of something viscid and greenish, which stank to the golden throne and seemed to have dissolved part of the roadway. As we skirted it I noticed a few pieces of metal in the middle of the mess, which looked suspiciously like the remnants of lasguns, hissing quietly as they sublimed into goo. More splashes of bio-acid had eaten through the façades of a couple of nearby buildings, and I breathed a silent word of thanks to the Emperor that whatever had vomited them up appeared to be long gone.

Leaving Sulla to continue her advance, and spotting a handful of PDF troopers in a rather more practically drab version of the local uniform than most of them seemed to favour,[1] I decided to speak to whoever was in charge and get an up-to-date assessment of the current situation. Tactical displays

---

1. *Every plateau's militia had its own colour scheme, generally as garish as the civilian fashions Cain noted earlier. The Aceralbaterrans, for instance, favoured orange fatigues under green and purple striped body armour, while the defence forces of Principia Mons appeared to prefer a combination of bright red and iridescent blue. As the tyranids generally rely on scent and vibration as much as sight to detect their prey, this bizarre predilection probably added less to their casualty rates than would have been the case with most other foes.*

are all very well, but if you really want to know what's going on at the sharp end, it often pays to ask the troopers dodging the lasbolts how things seem from their perspective. Most of the troopers looked up in a desultory fashion as Jurgen slewed us to a halt with his usual vigour, raising a small hailstorm of pulverised roadbed from beneath our tracks as he did so, regarding me through eyes hollow with exhaustion as I hopped down from the Salamander to greet them.

'Commissar Cain,' I said, injecting just enough of a parade ground snap into my voice to get the nearest man's attention without antagonising him needlessly. He had a corporal's chevrons pinned to the collar of his midnight blue fatigues, which were the only signs of rank I could see anywhere. The dark grey flak armour on his torso bore the unmistakable gashes of genestealer talons. 'Attached to the 597th Valhallan.'

After a moment, vague recognition stirred behind his fatigue-dulled eyes. 'I've seen you in the picts,' he said slowly. His posture straightened a little, and he glanced around at the motley collection of troopers surrounding him, all of whom bore minor wounds of one sort or another, mainly bites, claw or talon slashes, and in a couple of cases flash burns from what looked like the near detonation of bio-plasma bolts. 'Straighten up and look like soldiers, you dung shovelling rabble.'

Instead of saluting, as I'd expected, he made the sign of the aquila, and most of the others followed suit, shuffling into a rough approximation of attention as they did so. 'It's an honour, sir.'

'At ease,' I said, turning on the charm that normally served me so well. 'If anyone's earned the right to relax a little, it's surely the heroes who've endured so much to protect this place.'

'We can relax when the hell spawn have gone,' the corporal replied, looking at me a trifle oddly I thought. Then again, given what they'd evidently been through in the last few hours, it was hardly surprising if his elastic had gone a little slack. 'We're just regrouping, getting ready to follow up the main advance.'

'Your zeal does you credit,' I said, nodding approvingly, and doing some rapid analysis in my head. If his unit had suffered the usual attrition rate there could only be a few score effectives left by now, if that, and exhausted as they evidently were they'd have trouble fending off a flock of irritable butterflies, never mind a swarm of tyranids intent on ripping every living thing on the plateau into shreds. 'But the Guard are here now. Let us take up the slack, while you recuperate a little.' That way at least some of them might be in a fit state to fight again if my worst fears came to pass, and whoever was leading this suicidal charge into the heart of the enemy formation did overreach themselves and let the 'nids through our lines.

To my surprise, however, the corporal shook his head, a quietly determined cast settling across his features. 'We can't do that, sir, it wouldn't be right. It's our holy duty to follow where the Sisters lead.'

'Ah.' The coin dropped at last, and I finally registered the rosaries, *fleur de lys*, and icons of the Emperor that most of the troopers seemed to be

sporting somewhere about their person. Not all that unusual, of course, but now I came to think about it, in greater profusion and rather more prominently displayed than was perhaps the norm. 'You're from Gavarrone.'

'That's right.' The corporal nodded, a gesture echoed by most of the group around us. Reflecting that there would be no point in arguing with a bunch of religious fanatics, and that if they were that determined to throw their lives away they'd at least distract the tyranids while the Valhallans inflicted some real damage on the horde, I stood aside.

'Then by all means, do as your conscience dictates,' I said, making the sign of the aquila myself as I did so. (And, I may add, keeping a remarkably straight face in the process.) 'The Emperor protects.'

'And may he watch over you,' the whole bunch of them responded, for all the galaxy as if they were chanting the responses in some dull suburban chapel. Then they turned and shuffled away in the wake of our Chimeras.

I clambered aboard the Salamander, suffused with a new sense of urgency. The reason for the insane charge straight down the throats of the enemy was now completely clear to me. Eglantine's Emperor-bothering harridans wouldn't stop moving until they were cut to pieces, no doubt believing that every foot of ground they gained was a sign of personal favour from Him on Earth, and utterly heedless of the wider tactical implications of their actions. I wondered briefly why Zyvan would even have contemplated ordering them in and then dismissed the thought. No doubt he hadn't, the canoness having taken it

upon herself to order a squad or two of her Battle Sisters along to accompany the Gavarronian PDF detachments the lord general had requested. In any case, the reason they were there was entirely moot. The only thing that mattered now was calling them off, quickly, before their misguided fanaticism doomed us all.

CHAPTER TWENTY

AT LEAST THE troublesome Sisters were easy enough to find. I just had to look for the densest concentration of tyranids on the plateau, and, sure enough, as Jurgen swung us around the corner of what had apparently once been a fashionable shopping parade, there they were, merrily slaughtering their way through a dense thicket of onrushing hormagaunts, the bounding horrors' scything claws making little impression on the women's gleaming power armour. They'd taken some casualties of course, two or three of their number lying sprawled in the gutters, plainly beyond even the Emperor's help, let alone any mortal medicae, but the psychotic sisterhood seemed as indifferent to their own losses as the 'nids were to theirs, and an impressive number of chitinous corpses lay scattered around the place too. Gaunts by the score, which came as no

surprise, but several of the larger warrior forms as well, which probably accounted for their amazing success, at least so far. By luck or by judgement (almost certainly the former, although no doubt they'd claim it was the guidance of the Emperor), they seemed to have taken out all the creatures in the immediate vicinity relaying the influence of the hive mind, leaving them to face essentially mindless drones, which would continue to fall back slowly in the face of their fanatical advance until something capable of directing them intelligently came into range and brought them back under control again. Which it surely would do before long, as smoothly and automatically as blood clotting around a wound, the vast inhuman intelligence no doubt already aware of the gap that had appeared in its zone of control.

When that happened, of course, things would turn really nasty in a matter of seconds, as the entire horde became suffused with renewed purpose, and began acting as one again. Nevertheless, it seemed things weren't quite as desperate as I'd feared. I still had a little time to act before the overconfident Emperor-botherers found themselves suddenly facing a focused attack. A quick glance at the slate reassured me that Sulla was bolstering our flanks, so that if the worst came to the worst we should at least be able to hold the scuttling horde at bay until further reinforcements arrived, although that would be scant comfort to me if I'd been reduced to indigestion by that time, and I memorised the quickest routes back to our lines just to be on the safe side.

'We're holding position on the edges of the salient,' the lieutenant reported a moment later, the sound of

her voice in my comm-bead unusually welcome. 'Do you want us to move up and support you?'

Of course I'd have liked nothing better, especially as I was distracted for a moment before replying by the bothersome necessity of turning the heavy bolter on a flock of gargoyles that had spotted us and evidently thought we'd be easy pickings, but that could go horribly wrong too easily, despite the comfort having a squad or two of heavily armed troopers around me would have brought. If I had to run for it in a hurry I wanted somewhere to run to, where the platoon was well dug in and could provide adequate covering fire, rather than being cut to pieces around me while the 'nids broke through our overstretched defensive line and left me with nowhere to go.

'Better to dig in and reinforce the line,' I said, although it was hard to tell which of the two of us was the most despondent at the sound of my words. 'You'll get your chance to hunt bugs soon enough.' I paused, struck by an afterthought. 'There are some PDF survivors wandering around our rear, planning to follow the holy terrors into the breach. Stop them advancing any further if you can, and try to get them to dig in like proper soldiers. They won't be much help from what I've seen, but there's no point in letting them throw their lives away needlessly, and at least they can still shoot from cover.' That was to turn out to be a huge mistake on my part, of course, but I had no way of knowing that at the time.

'Yes, sir,' Sulla assured me, and I returned my attention to the immediate problem. Jurgen and I had emerged into another piazza, in which a fountain still played, somewhat incongruously, the wide basin

choked with genestealer corpses and the remains of a Battle Sister, who, judging by the wide distribution of her mortal residue, had detonated her entire stock of frag grenades in the moment of being finally over-run. The main battle had swept on since the poor girl's untidy demise, however, and seemed to be con-centrated at the far end of the plaza, where three narrow streets entered the wide open space, one at each corner, with the third equidistant between them. I glanced around, with a shiver of apprehen-sion. As I'd instantly surmised, the arrangement was repeated all around the square, which gave a grand total of eight potential entry points, although pre-dictably the Sisters were throwing themselves at the only three through which an enemy was visible, completely ignoring the possibility of being flanked.

'Which one's the command squad?' Jurgen asked, and I scanned the seething knots of power-armoured viragos in search of someone evidently in charge of this debacle. I'd had as little as I could contrive to do with the militant arm of the Ecclesiarchy over the years, and most of the contact I'd been unable to avoid had been with one or other of the Orders Majoris, so the specific iconography of the Order of the White Rose would be completely unfamiliar to me.

All the Sisters were dressed in the same dazzling silver armour that Eglantine had worn, with black or dark blue surplices bearing the symbol of their order flapping about them as they blazed away with their bolters or incinerated gaunts with hissing flamers, so that was no help. The squad in the centre seemed a little smaller in number than the others, though, and

the movements of its members a little better co-ordinated and more disciplined, which marked them out as veterans, and reasoning that the most experienced warrior on the battlefield would be in overall command I directed my aide to head in that direction with all due dispatch.

'Two squads of PDF have arrived,' Sulla told me, as Jurgen began threading the Salamander through the debris of the battle. Our treads crushed tyranid corpses pretty much everywhere we turned, and I found myself grudgingly impressed by the evident fighting prowess of the Battle Sisters, notwithstanding the fact that their single-minded zealotry still looked like coming within a hair of dooming us all. 'They're reluctant to accept our orders, though.'

'Then use your best judgement,' I said, not having any time to waste on this now. The battle was getting closer, and we were beginning to attract the attention of more of the 'nids. Sulla acknowledged me briefly, and cut the link, and to my immense relief I began to pick up a fresh source of signals almost immediately.[1]

'This is Commissar Ciaphas Cain,' I transmitted at once, swinging the bolter to take down a pack of hormagaunts that had leapt over the heads of the Sisters on the left flank and were now bounding towards us with baleful intent. I noted the sudden renewal of

---

1. *Although Cain would be able to contact pretty much anyone on the planet by relaying his signal through the vox equipment in Sulla's command Chimera, the sisters of the White Rose were apparently using their own communication system independent of the Imperial Guard network. Only as the two sets of short-range personal vox systems came into close proximity was he able to talk to them directly.*

their fighting spirit with trepidation. Clearly at least one synapse creature was coming within range and the tide of battle was about to turn, perhaps within a matter of seconds. 'Disengage and fall back!' The squad leader, who, now we'd come close enough to distinguish one psychotic psalm-singer from another, stood out from the others by virtue of the chainsword and bolt pistol in her hands, turned and looked in my direction. Like most of her Sisters she disdained the use of a helmet, despite the manifest foolishness of such a course,[1] and her narrow face was clearly visible, framed by the rather unflattering hairstyle common to most women of her calling. Dark eyes glared at me from beneath a crudely cropped black fringe, which didn't quite manage to hide the *fleur de lys* tattoo emblazoned on her freckle-spattered forehead.

Thin lips compressed in disapproval. 'We're servants of His Blessed Majesty,' she snapped, 'and not subject to the authority of your office. Go and shoot a few malingering Guardsmen like you're supposed to, and leave us to our holy task.'

'You're about to be overrun,' I said. 'Getting yourselves slaughtered isn't going to help the Emperor very much, is it?'

'Our destinies lie in His hands alone,' she responded, turning to disembowel a gaunt, which had just discharged its fleshborer at one of her comrades from point-blank range. The unfortunate woman shrieked as the living ammunition chewed most of her face away in an instant and began

---

1. *Given that the commissarial uniform has a cap rather than any more functionally protective headgear, Cain may be speaking from the heart here.*

burrowing down beneath her armour in search of a vital organ or two, which they seemed to find mercifully quickly, judging by the way what was left of her suddenly spasmed and collapsed. I'd have expected the others to react in some fashion, but the hideous demise of their comrade only seemed to make them even more determined to fight on to the death.

Well, frak them then, I thought, bringing the bolter to bear on a group of purestrain 'stealers emerging from one of the other alley mouths I'd noticed before. Time to be going. I gave it one more try.

'If you don't pull back now, you'll not only die for nothing, you'll let the swarm in through the hole you've left in our lines,' I said, fighting the feeling that I'd be better off talking to the 'nids. Then inspiration suddenly struck. 'And as soon as that happens,' I went on, 'they'll head straight for the temple and slaughter every civilian taking shelter in there, praying to the Emperor for deliverance. If you really want to report to the Golden Throne after allowing that kind of desecration to happen when you know you could have prevented it, I suppose that's a matter between you and Him on Earth.' I turned to my aide. 'Get us out of here, Jurgen. We've done what we can.'

'Right you are, commissar,' he agreed, as phlegmatically as ever, and swung the agile little vehicle around on its tracks.

As I caught my first clear sight of what now lay behind us, my bowels spasmed. My worst fears were being realised. A veritable flood of chitinous horrors was pouring into the square from the side streets, and we were almost cut off from safety already.

Leaving the Sister Superior to work out her own
salvation, I crouched as low as I could, blazing away
with the pintel-mounted weapon at anything that
seemed to get too close, searching frantically for the
larger creatures that would be imbuing the mass of
scuttling obscenity with direction and purpose. I cut
down one of the warrior forms as it aimed a
deathspitter at us, but it fired as it fell, spattering the
hull of our Salamander with foul smelling bio-acid
as its payload of maggot-like creatures burst against
the armour plate. A few stray droplets began eating
away at my greatcoat, but fortunately I was able to
shrug it off before it fully penetrated the weave,
wishing I'd had the foresight to don my precious set
of carapace armour beneath it.

'Jurgen, the flamer!' I ordered, and my aide complied, clearing our way with a gout of blazing
promethium, which fortuitously caught another of
the warrior forms in the backwash along with the
gaunts it was directing. It went down, shrieking as it
burned, and a moment later the Salamander lurched
as the hideous creature finally expired beneath our
treads. I ducked as another flight of gargoyles
swooped low over our heads, flinching in anticipation of a deadly rain of fleshborer beetles, but it
seemed they had another target in mind, the tyranid
intelligence no doubt considering that it had enough
flesh and chitin between us and safety to pick us off
with little difficulty, and right then I found it hard to
disagree. The gargoyles soared over one of the Battle
Sister squads, strafing them as they went, then beat
their wings lazily as they rose to go around for
another pass. Two of the women fell, and the others

returned fire with their bolters, bringing down a handful of the swooping monstrosities. The Celestians I'd spoken to were at least attempting to break out now, but I had a horrible suspicion that they'd left it too late. That was certainly true of their comrades on the right flank, half of whom had got themselves entangled in the flesh-ripping growth of a barbed strangler. One of them managed to trigger her flamer, burning her way free, but it was too late for her companions, strange thorned growths bursting out through their unprotected flesh. Why they never seem to bother to put the helmets on those power suits of theirs is completely beyond me.[1]

'Sulla,' I voxed, trying to keep an edge of panic out of my voice, 'we're coming in hot. The 'nids have broken through.'

'Acknowledged.' Her voice sounded infuriatingly calm, although for all I know she was working as hard at giving that impression as I was. 'We'll cover you as soon as you're in range.'

'I'm delighted to hear it,' I said, raising my voice a little over the racket of the hull-mounted heavy bolter, which Jurgen was using in conjunction with the flamer to clear a path for us. I swung the pintel-mounted weapon, taking full advantage of its all around arc of fire to keep the fleas off our backs as best I could, the main weapons on the sturdy little vehicle being fixed forward. (Not for the first time blessing my foresight in having the thing installed, I may add.) 'Any idea when that will be?'

---

1. *Apparently because most of them believe that their faith in the Emperor is armour enough. A couple of extra centimetres of ceremite probably couldn't hurt, though.*

'Any time now,' Sulla assured me, which, vague as it was, sounded pretty good. 'Fourth squad's moving up to support your retreat.' She paused. 'And the local mob insisted on going with them, for whatever that's worth.'

Not a lot, I thought, if they were all in the same state as the ones we'd met before, but every little helped, and even if they just ended up as 'nid bait, that would at least distract the creatures for a moment or two while we made a break for it.

'Commissar,' Jurgen said, 'really big one, two o'clock.' I turned in the direction he'd indicated, my heart hammering. True enough, just out of the line of fire of our main weapons, the unmistakable bulk of a hive tyrant loomed, pointing a venom cannon in our direction. I ducked reflexively beneath the armour plate surrounding me an instant before the deadly rain of poison shards pattered against it, bobbing up almost at once to grab the bolter before the creature could fire again. I managed to stitch a burst across its chest, and it staggered, but stayed on its feet, shrieking like a damned heretic.

'Hold on, commissar!' a new voice chimed in. 'We're on the way!' With a sudden flare of relief I recognised it as Sergeant Grifen, whose courage and competence I had good reason to trust, having passed through a necron tomb with her on Simia Orichalcae. True she'd lost most of her squad in the process, but that was hardly her fault, and she'd got me out in one piece, which was what mattered to me.

'Glad you could join us,' I said, conscious of having an image to maintain, and tried to get a line on the tyrant again. If I could only take it down, I thought,

that might just disrupt the swarm long enough for us to make it to safety. The hope was a forlorn one, of course, there would be plenty of other synapse creatures within range by now, but when it's the only one you've got, I've always found, even a forlorn hope can look pretty good.

The hulking monstrosity's shrieking intensified, and, forewarned, I ducked below the armour plate again just as it vomited a ball of bio-plasma at me and charged forwards, striking out with its rending claws. The thick slab of metal protecting me ripped like tissue paper, our hurtling Salamander slowed, and I rolled frantically, trying to evade the reaching talons. There was no time to reach the heavy weapon, even if I could have got round the massive bulk of the monster rearing over me. Instead I drew my chainsword, striking out with it purely by reflex, and was rewarded with a gout of foul smelling ichor as the blade bit deep. The creature roared with rage and made to strike at me again, and I parried instinctively, slashing across its thorax, deepening the wounds made by the bolter.

'I've got it,' Jurgen said, imperturbable as ever, turning in his seat as he spoke, and I just had time to glimpse the melta in his hands before the actinic flash of its activation and the smell of charred meat enveloped my senses. The thing fell back, and our battered but unbowed Salamander leapt forward, leaving the wounded colossus staggering in our wake.

'Well done,' I complimented my aide, breathing a little heavily I must admit, and regaining my feet a trifle unsteadily even considering the fact that his

driving was understandably more erratic than usual. He smiled, displaying teeth that would have made an ork recoil, and returned his attention to the controls. To my chagrin, though not I must admit to my complete surprise, the bolter was beyond use, fused and melted by the plasma burst, so I drew my laspistol and started plinking away at whatever targets presented themselves, more in hope than expectation.

'Heads up, commissar,' Grifen voxed, and to my immense relief fourth squad's Chimera appeared in the gap between a restaurant and a clothing shop, the window dummies of which continued to watch the battle with the air of elegant disdain in which they'd been posed, despite a couple of stray rounds from our remaining bolter taking the head off one, which appeared to be dressed in little more than a few square centimetres of gauze and lace. Jurgen triggered the flamer again, burning a path through what seemed like a solid mass of gaunts, and we both crouched as low as we could while fleshborers rattled off our armour plate like deadly hail.

Crushing a couple of the ghastly things that had fallen inside the crew compartment next to me under my boot heel, I ventured a cautious look over the rim, just in time to see the Chimera's heavy weapons open up, shredding the wounded tyrant, which had continued to charge doggedly in our wake despite the lead we were opening up.

'Good shooting,' I encouraged the unseen gunners, just as the spark and crackle of lasgun fire began to erupt from inside several of the buildings on that side of the square. I caught a glimpse of a couple of

our troopers behind a first floor window, evidently the residence of whoever owned the restaurant, aiming and firing methodically as they sought out the synapse creatures they could see from their elevated position. A warrior 'nid a few score metres away from us recoiled as their lasbolts hit home almost simultaneously. 'Thanks, Vorhees.'

'You're welcome, commissar,' the male of the pair assured me, the barrel of his weapon already tracking another target. 'Janny, eleven o'clock.'

'I see it,' Trooper Drere assured us both, managing to get her shot off an instant ahead of him this time, the faint hiss of her augmetic lungs audible in my comm-bead. 'Frak, it's fast!'

I turned, seeing another warrior sprinting towards us, an entourage of gaunts at its heels. No more tyrants around, thank the Emperor, and I began to believe we might actually make it. The surviving Battle Sisters had managed to cluster together, my old friend with the unbecoming haircut still keeping them in good order, although they seemed to have been whittled down to almost half their original number, and were forging their way back towards safety with relentless determination. Fair enough, the surviving synapse creatures still seemed to think they were the major threat, and were keeping the bulk of the swarm on the offensive against them, which was fine by me. If anything, I felt, it served the Emperor-bothering imbeciles right for dragging me into this mess in the first place.

More lasguns opened up, less disciplined and purposeful than the incoming fire from the Valhallans, but welcome nonetheless, and I caught a glimpse of

the blue and grey uniformed Gavarronians taking
what cover they could, or flattening themselves
against the walls of the side streets. Random as it
seemed, the fire they were putting out was at least
felling a few of the gaunts, and even the occasional
'stealer. More muzzle flashes betrayed the presence of
at least half of fourth squad behind the protection
afforded by their Chimera, their bare arms slick with
sweat[1] as they aimed and fired at the surviving warriors.

'Keep going!' I encouraged Jurgen, and he triggered
the flamer again, incinerating another brood of purestrains that was forging towards us with murder in
what passed for their minds. Even if we could disrupt
the hive mind again, the 'stealers would still remain
a potent threat if they were allowed to survive, still
functioning with a unity of purpose largely independent of the main overmind. I downed another with a
lucky pistol shot to the head, and the survivors scuttled away, apparently convinced we weren't worth
the effort. Or, more likely, just willing to let more of
their mindless brethren wear us down before moving
in for the kill. 'We're almost there!'

A couple of the PDF had heavy weapons with
them, I saw now, a two-man team manhandling their
rocket launcher into position for firing. I ducked
reflexively as their missile left the tube, hurtling past
us uncomfortably close, to detonate its payload of
frag in the middle of a dense pocket of gaunts closing in on the Sisters.

---

1. *Given the heat and humidity on Aceralbaterra, most of the iceworlders would have stripped down to little more than their body
armour, and trousers, of course.*

'That was a bit reckless,' Jurgen commented evenly, relying entirely on the flamer to get us through the press of chitinous abominations, as any bolter rounds we popped off would be as dangerous to our allies as to the enemy.

I nodded. 'Tell that idiot to watch where he's pointing his drainpipe,' I voxed, but before Grifen could respond the rocketeers fired again. This time the warhead dropped, detonating among the gaunts still peppering us ineffectually with fleshborers, shredding the majority of them most satisfactorily with its hail of shrapnel. Rather less satisfactory was the metallic clanging as several pieces of the warhead ricocheted from our severely battered armour plate, to be followed almost at once by an alarming rending noise.

The Salamander lurched abruptly to the left, banging my head painfully against the bulkhead separating the crew and passenger compartments, and then, to my horror, Jurgen cut the engine. 'One of the tracks is jammed,' he reported stoically, as though this was a misfortune on a par with the laundry shrinking a pair of my underpants. He hefted the melta. 'We'll have to make a run for it.'

'Great,' I said, shooting the face off a hormagaunt that had bounded up to us and attempted to remove my head. Our chances of getting out of here on foot were non-existent. Even the sainted sisterhood was having a hard time of it, and they were in power armour, for the Emperor's sake. I stood up to parry another scything claw with my gently humming chainsword, blessing my duellist's reflexes as I did so. That bang on the head must have been worse than I

thought. I felt weak and giddy, and if it hadn't been for the urgency of the situation making such a luxury too time-consuming, I'd probably have jettisoned my lunch. Blinking back the brown haze swirling in the corners of my vision I hacked and blocked like an automaton, no doubt displaying a complete lack of finesse that would have outraged old Miyamoto de Bergerac,[1] but which at least kept my head on my shoulders.

As the crowd of gaunts gave way, encouraged rather more by Jurgen's adroit use of his melta than my feeble efforts I'm forced to concede, I suddenly found myself facing something a whole lot worse. Another hive tyrant, apparently bred purely for close combat, reared up behind them, slashing down with its twin sets of scything claws. I tried to block the rain of blows, but stumbled, my legs giving way without warning as the dark cloud over my eyes rushed in, and I found myself pitching over the side of the Salamander to land on the cobbles at its feet.

The unexpected movement may, of course, have saved my life, the vile creature's flurry of strokes doing no more than inflict another massive dent on our sturdy little conveyance, but as I sprawled there I truly thought my last moment had come. Jurgen couldn't fire his melta while I was that close to it, he'd vaporise me as well, and there wasn't a heretic's hope in hell that he'd be able to reach his lasgun in time. Even if he did, he'd just annoy it. I struck out at its leg with my chainsword, hoping to cripple the thing just long enough to roll away, although if I did

---

1. *Cain's fencing tutor at the schola progenium.*

I'd only get ripped apart by something else, probably. The phantom cloud blanketed my vision, and a dull roaring sound filled my ears. I knew I was going to lose consciousness at any moment, and as soon as I did, that would be the end of me. At least I wouldn't be awake to feel it.

Frak that, I thought, the fierce survival instinct that has served me so well through so many desperate situations kicking in with a vengeance. If I am going to die, I'm going to take this walking obscenity with me. I rolled to my feet and staggered after it as it hopped back from my feeble strike, keeping inside the reach of its claws, and searching desperately for any sign of vulnerability. Emperor help me, if it had one I couldn't see it.

'Commissar, get down!' Grifen's voice barked in my ear, and I complied without thinking, my knees giving way again and pitching me onto the ground. The roaring noise was louder now, but only when it was joined by the unmistakable chatter of a heavy bolter did I realise that I'd been hearing more than the blood in my ears. Fourth squad's Chimera was charging to our rescue, both its heavy weapons chattering angrily as it came, and the looming monstrosity that had so nearly taken my life came apart in the middle like an overused practice dummy on the bayonet range. Lumps of offal pattered around me like obscene hailstones as the hideous creature slumped ponderously to the ground.

'Come on, sir.' A short, redheaded woman appeared through the haze obstructing my vision, hefting her lasgun one-handed as she fired it insouciantly at a nearby hormagaunt. She reached her

other hand down to me, and I took it gratefully, allowing her to haul me to my feet, where I stood, staring around in vague incomprehension. 'There you go, commissar, up we get.'

'Thank you, Magot,' I said, the fog growing thicker than ever. I swayed again, buoyed up by a sudden, and surprisingly welcome, burst of Jurgen's distinctive aroma. My aide appeared through the brown miasma, clutching my pistol and chainsword as well as his own weapons, an unaccustomed expression of concern on his grimy features.

'I've got your kit, sir. I'm afraid the coat's had it, though.'

'Get moving! Chat later.' Grifen took hold of one of my arms, Magot the other, and hustled me up the Chimera's boarding ramp, while its turret rotated, scything down most of the 'nids in the immediate vicinity.

'Much obliged,' I said, as the hatch clanged shut behind us, and our driver gunned the engine, hurling us back towards the relative safety of our lines. There was something I ought to say, I thought, or do, something important, but it wouldn't come to me what it was. Then the fog swirled in at last, and I lost interest in everything.

Editorial Note:

Quite understandably under the circumstances, Cain picks up his account of events after a gap of almost three days. Such lacunae are far from uncommon in his memoirs, of course, and I habitually fill them in from other sources whenever appropriate material is to hand. Although it must be said that in very few instances are such interpolations quite as essential as they are here. Once again I feel I should apologise for including more of Jenit Sulla's attempts to batter the Gothic language into submission, but as always her position on the fringes of Cain's activities has left us with a potentially revealing insight into the wider picture, which he so seldom considers himself.

From *Like a Phoenix on the Wing: The Early Campaigns and Glorious Victories of the Valhallan 597th*
by General Jenit Sulla (retired), 101 M42

THE NEWS THAT our gallant commissar had fallen was
greeted with a mixture of incredulity and horror. We
had all lost valued friends and comrades before, of
course, for such is the lot of the common soldier, and all
of us were equally willing to lay down our own lives in
the service of the Emperor, but our hearts froze within
us at the first intimation of these dolorous tidings.

My vox operator's voice trembled noticeably as he
informed me of the transmission he'd just received, and
I must own to suppressing a faint cry of distress myself.
Commissar Cain had forged and moulded the 597th, his
inspirational leadership bringing us victory time and
time again, even against the most hopeless odds, but it
wasn't just because of this that he embodied everything
that was good about our regiment. During those tense
few moments I found myself recalling innumerable
instances of his unfailing courage, his constant concern
for even the humblest trooper, and the many conversa-
tions we'd had in which his innate good humour, and
evident regard for my qualities of leadership, had done
so much to bolster my confidence in the dark times
when the spectre of self-doubt had threatened to impair
my effectiveness as a commander.

It was with no little sense of relief, then, that we
received the joyful intelligence from fourth squad that
their medic had examined him and pronounced him in
no danger. Surely it would take more than a small force

of tyranids to put paid to so redoubtable a warrior? The noble commissar, it seemed, had sustained a minor head wound, the effects of which had been exacerbated by the noxious fumes from a deathspitter round that had burst close to where he had fought so heroically against the tide of xenos-spawned corruption.

The Chimera conveying his unconscious form to safety rendezvoused with us before long, and I lost no time in ensuring that he was conveyed back to Hoarfell with the first transport shuttle to return with reinforcements, less than an hour later. By that time we had all too many wounded of our own to accompany him, but those of us who remained uninjured, or lightly enough so to continue discharging our duty to His Divine Majesty, persisted in the defence of Aceralbaterra, eventually prevailing by the grace of the Emperor.

It need hardly be said that Commissar Cain must take the greater part of the credit for this notable victory, for it was he alone who was responsible for dispatching no fewer than two of the hive tyrants directing the throng of scuttling foulness that beset us on all sides. Deprived of the guidance of these creatures the swarm began to lose cohesion, the remaining lesser creatures being too few in number to co-ordinate them effectively, and what had up until that point seemed an unstoppable advance began to falter.

As for the PDF lackwits whose ill-timed intervention had cost the commissar so dear, their fate remains shrouded in mystery. Loyal above all else to the righteous warriors of the Adepta Sororitas, to whose aid they had so disastrously gone, they remained to cover the

holy Sisters' retreat as best they could. Whether any survived, I couldn't truthfully say, preoccupied as I was by ensuring the most effective deployment of my own troopers, and by my understandable concern for the welfare of Commissar Cain.

What that may have been I have no idea, but suspect it was to give thanks for their deliverance. For which, impious as the assertion may seem, I consider they had our noble commissar to thank at least as much as they did the Emperor Himself.

From *Periremunda Today: The News That Matters to Your Planet,* 287 933 M41

PERIREMUNDA IS SAVED!
TYRANIDS FLEE AS RELIEF FLEET ARRIVES!

THE STOIC RESISTANCE of our beleaguered citizens was rewarded late last night with the long awaited news that the task force dispatched from Coronus Prime has just emerged from the warp on the fringes of our system, and that a mighty flotilla of warships now protects our beloved homeworld from the looming terror of the approaching hive fleet. Not only that, the war on the ground has taken a positive turn too, with the arrival of two fresh battalions of Imperial Guard veterans, eager to mop up the remaining tyranid interlopers that continue to befoul the sacred soil of our Emperor blessed globe. With such a mighty force at their disposal, it can surely only be a matter of time before Periremunda is cleansed forever of the taint of xenos contamination.

In a full and frank interview, Governor Pismire commented, 'Golly, that is good news. Are you sure about this? Who told you?'

Communiqué 47783/320/34598543, dated 292 933 M41

FROM: Admiral Bowe, commanding officer of Naval task force Divine Intervention.

TO: Lord General Zyvan, commanding officer Imperial ground forces, Periremunda system.

I'M PLEASED TO report that deployment of our Naval assets has gone according to plan, and that eight separate flotillas of both Capital- and Escort-class vessels are standing ready to intercept the approaching hive fleet the moment it emerges from the warp. Our transport vessels are inbound, and should begin offloading your men within the hour. I'm sure you'll know what to do with them.

Our astropaths can't be entirely sure, with the shadow still blanking everything, but our best estimate is that the bulk of the tyranid forces will arrive in no more than a day or two, so you'd better get them deployed fast.

Hope we can get together for a drink and a regicide game once the dust settles.

Regards,
Benjamin

From *Like a Phoenix on the Wing: The Early Campaigns and Glorious Victories of the Valhallan 597th* by General Jenit Sulla (retired), 101 M42

THE OPENING SALVOS in the final battle for Periremunda were to be fired before long, and as that storm broke around us, I found myself considering how frustrating Commissar Cain must have found it to be confined to the medicae facility while the regiment went into action against so vile and inhuman a foe.

The battle began, of course, in deep space, the living ships of the hive fleet vomiting forth from the warp as though even that abominable realm was unable to stomach their foulness, to be met head on by the cream of the Imperial Navy. The struggle that ensued in the never-ending night among the stars must have been titanic indeed. From our position on the ground we were able to discern quite clearly innumerable flashes in the heavens, as living behemoths of unnaturally sculpted flesh met metal hulls sanctified by the Adeptus Mechanicus in the name of the Emperor, the cleansing fire of their mighty weapons, and the indomitable courage of their crews.[1]

Though the fighting spirit of both crews and vessels alike remained undiminished the sheer number of tyranid organisms facing them eventually began to tell,

---

1. Given Cain's repeated references to the near-constant cloud cover over Hoarfell, we can quite safely conclude that Sulla is exaggerating here for dramatic effect. Readers wanting a rather more accurate account of the battle in space are referred to chapter 87 of Leander Kasmides's Swatting the Swarm: The Evolution of Imperial Navy Tactics Against the Hive Fleets.

in a manner strikingly similar to those instances when their ground dwelling monstrosities face the unyielding resistance of the Imperial Guard. Admiral Bowe quite properly concentrated much of the fire from his battleships against the larger behemoths, hoping thereby to diminish the effectiveness of the fleet as a whole, leaving the smaller tyranid creatures to his cruisers and escorts. Successful as they undoubtedly were in this task, despite the number of vessels crippled or destroyed by the vengeful monstrosities they faced, a goodly number of these insidious organisms were able to slip through the cordon, and, as we'd feared, begin to rain mycetic spores onto the planet below.

By great good fortune the vast majority of these seeds of destruction fell in the wasteland between plateaux, leaving relatively few to drop on the inhabited areas, many of which had been garrisoned by Imperial Guard troopers scarcely less able than those I was privileged to serve with. Suffice it to say that, whatever hopes of an easy victory the malign, inhuman intellect of the hive mind may have entertained, it was in for a rude awakening. Plateau after plateau was able to repulse the invaders, while those centres of population unfortunate enough still to be reliant on the Planetary Defence Forces for succour were evacuated as rapidly as possible.

On Hoarfell, I'm pleased to say, Colonel Kasteen's far-sighted preparations proved more than adequate, and only one incursion actually succeeded in posing a serious threat to our position in Darien.

CHAPTER TWENTY-ONE

'IT COULD SIMPLY have been an accident,' Kasteen said, a faint edge of doubt in her voice. 'You said yourself they were totally exhausted, and the PDF aren't exactly the best soldiers in the galaxy to begin with.'

Broklaw nodded, and handed me a bowl of tanna, which I took, grateful for the augmetic fingers that let me hold it steady enough to drink without spilling. That morning I'd finally had enough of being prodded and mauled by our medicae, despite the obvious attractions of lounging around in bed while the regiment took on the latest tyranid incursions without me, and hauled myself upright, trying to ignore the waves of nausea that continued to overtake me every time I turned my head too suddenly. The notion that the 'nids might be moving in on our garrison while I lay there oblivious, suffering from nothing worse

than what felt like a severe hangover, nagged at my innate sense of paranoia, to the point where nothing would settle my apprehension short of a trip to our command centre to check out the tactical situation for myself.

'I'd advise against it,' the chirurgeon had told me, holding up an indeterminate number of blurry fingers in front of my eyes. 'Concussion's a tricky thing.' He nodded at the pair of augmetic digits on my right hand. 'Frak up your brain, and I won't be able to replace it as easily as those.'

'I'll bear that in mind,' I told him shortly, and smiled to ease the sting of my unthinking retort. 'At least for as long as I've got one.'

'Well, if you're determined,' the fellow said, shrugging. I'd been expecting more of an argument, to be honest; only later did it dawn on me that, thanks to my undeserved reputation, he must have taken it for granted that I'd be itching to get back to the front line as quickly as possible and would be in no mood to take no for an answer. Either that, or the prospect of finally being able to rid his hospital of the health hazard posed by Jurgen, who had taken it upon himself to camp in the corridor outside my room for the entire duration of my stay, was too good to pass up. By the time my aide had appeared, a second or two after my nose had first registered his presence, bearing a clean uniform and my battered old weapons, I'd swung my legs off the bed and was beginning to feel more than satisfied with my decision.

It was only after we'd left, of course, that I began to doubt the wisdom of it, the first blast of a breeze, quite mild by Hoarfell's standards, making me stagger as the

outer doors swung closed behind us. Jurgen held out a supporting arm, which, after a moment's understandable hesitation, I took, reasoning that I was at least upwind of him, and that it would do the morale of the regiment, not to mention my status as a Hero of the Imperium, no good at all if I keeled over flat on my arse in front of a building full of sniggering troopers.

'Not far now, sir,' Jurgen assured me, leading the way to a comfortably appointed staff car that he'd managed to appropriate from somewhere, apparently having decided, quite correctly, that I was in no condition (or mood, come to that) to be bouncing around in the back of another Salamander at the moment. I settled into the soft upholstery with an involuntary sigh of relief, reminded of our eventful journey in Keesh's limousine so shortly after our arrival, although of course this particular vehicle was nowhere near as luxurious as the arbitrator's personal transport had been.

As Jurgen pulled away from the kerb I found myself recalling that earlier eventful trip, the first occasion after our arrival on which someone had tried to kill me without warning, in some detail. That time, at least, my assailants' motives had been clear enough. Keesh was the intended target, and I'd simply been the victim of an unfortunate case of mistaken identity.

The other attempts on my life had been very different, though, intended to kill me specifically without a shadow of a doubt, but that had been pretty much the only thing they'd had in common. Try as I might, I still couldn't see any reason why a renegade techpriest would throw in his lot with a coven of Chaos cultists.

Nor, for that matter, why either would go to so much trouble to eliminate me, who hardly posed much of a threat to either of them. At least no one had tried again.

My palms began to tingle, in that old familiar fashion I'd learned to trust over the years. The PDF troopers with the rocket launcher could simply have been over-excited or incompetent, of course, but they'd come within a hair of killing me just the same, and in a fashion no one could possibly consider deliberate; not unless they had a mind as nasty and devious as mine, anyway.

I voiced my suspicions as soon as I was alone with Kasteen and Broklaw, the two people in the regiment who were as close to friends as it was possible to be, given our respective positions, and the two whose judgement I was most inclined to trust.

Both officers listened in silence as I spoke, nodding as I finished speaking and sat back in my chair with an expectant air.

'If you are right,' the major said, resuming his seat and picking up his own tanna bowl, 'you're going to have Horus's own time proving it. If they really wanted to kill you out there, why not just lob a krak round at you and make sure of the job?'

Kasteen nodded her agreement. 'That would have taken out a Salamander pretty easily,' she pointed out. 'Frag warheads are next to useless against an armoured vehicle. It was just a fluke your tracks getting jammed like that.'

'Normally I'd agree,' I said, sipping the fragrant liquid gratefully, 'but I was in an open passenger compartment, standing up at the pintel mount. If

they'd hit a little closer, I'd have been taken out by the shrapnel as readily as the 'nids.'

'And don't forget most of fourth squad had a clear view of what was going on,' Broklaw added helpfully, having apparently been struck by a fresh idea. 'If it really was another assassination attempt, popping off a krak round against a dispersed target would have seemed distinctly odd to most of them.'

'Whereas a frag rocket was exactly what anyone watching would have been expecting them to use. If they had shredded me, no one would have suspected a thing.' I shrugged ruefully. 'Let's face it, I'd hardly have been the first commissar to be killed by a friendly fire accident.'

'That's true,' the colonel conceded, with a meaningful glance at Broklaw. It wouldn't be entirely true to say that as many of my colleagues fall at the hands of the men they're serving with as to the guns of the enemy, but far more do than is generally admitted, which, given the nature of our job, is hardly surprising. That, incidentally, is why I try to get the young whelps I'm responsible for these days to realise that they'll do far better by relying on tact and commonsense than the letter of the regulations. (Or at least last a bit longer.) 'But why would they want to? It's not as if you'd executed any of their friends, is it?'

'I don't know,' I admitted. I sighed, already regretting the impulse to get out of bed. My head was throbbing gently again, as though I'd drunk about three glasses of amasec more than was sensible, but without the consolation of having had the convivial time that ought to have left me feeling that way. 'But

why would a Chaos cult and a renegade techpriest I'd never heard of be gunning for me either?'

'I've no idea,' Kasteen said cautiously. 'I imagine that's more the sort of question your other contacts could answer.'

'I suppose you're right,' I said, knowing better than to expect any information from Amberley that she didn't want to part with. I rubbed my throbbing temples. 'I don't know. Maybe I'm overreacting.'

'Hard not to, when some frakwit nearly blows your head off and feeds you to the 'nids,' Broklaw said tactfully. He shrugged. 'If it was one of ours, of course, you could pull them in and question them about it.'

'I could,' I said, an idea beginning to form. Maybe it was the headache, but it seemed a pretty good one to me at the time. 'And I still might. The commissariat gives me wide powers of investigation where the security of the Imperial forces is potentially compromised. Can we really be certain that the Gavarronian PDF hasn't been infiltrated by 'stealers?'

'That canoness seemed pretty positive,' Kasteen reminded me.

'Exactly.' I nodded, then instantly regretted it. 'That means Keesh hasn't run the usual checks on them. If those trolls were hybrids they couldn't attack the Sisters without blowing their cover, but the chance to take out an Imperial commissar would have been too good to pass up.'

'Especially as the picts have been building you up as the single-handed saviour of the planet,' Broklaw added. He nodded judiciously. 'It does make a twisted kind of sense.'

'I'll take that as a compliment,' I said. I wobbled to my feet, leaning on Kasteen's desk for support as I did so, pretending I hadn't seen the flicker of concern that had passed between my companions. I smiled at Kasteen. 'If you don't mind, I'd like a vox link to the lord general's office whenever it's convenient.' Several of our platoons were currently engaged in running battles with 'nid swarms that had dropped from the skies while I'd been enjoying my enforced rest, and our comms net was pretty stretched as a result. Eager as I was to follow this up, it would have to wait until they'd been beaten back, at least for now.

'No problem.' The colonel looked a little puzzled. 'May I ask why?'

I smiled grimly. 'If I'm right, the Gavarronians should be pulled back from all front line duties at once, pending a full investigation.'

'I see.' Broklaw looked at me sardonically. 'Which you'll conduct, of course.'

'Who better?' I asked rhetorically.

AFTER A FEW more minutes of chatting quietly and sipping tanna in Kasteen's office I felt a little more like my usual self, and wandered down to the main command centre to see how the war was getting on. At the time, of course, I had no intention of actually participating in any more of the fighting, which, when you've experienced as much of it as I have, has considerably more appeal as a spectator sport. From long habit I'd slipped the comm-bead into my ear as I'd got dressed, as automatically as I'd buckled my weapon belt, and had been keeping half an ear on

the signal traffic even while I'd been speaking to Kasteen and Broklaw, so I had a rough idea of the prevailing tactical situation already. But looking at it in the hololith display made everything much clearer, just as I'd expected.

While I'd been taking my enforced nap, it seemed, the 'nids had been dropping spores all over Hoarfell (and just about everywhere else too, of course, but that wasn't my problem), and, naturally, obeying the genetically encoded imperatives of their kind, had swarmed towards Darien as rapidly as they could, drawn by the lure of the concentrated biomass the city represented. Kasteen had foreseen this, of course, and deployed our troops where they could harass them as they advanced, breaking up the smaller swarms before they could coalesce, and generally giving the scuttling horrors as hard a time as our people could contrive. And pretty successfully, too, if the display in the hololith could be believed. Most of the lesser broods had been eliminated piecemeal before they had a chance to join up with their siblings, and relatively few had made it through to reinforce the ones that had fallen on the city itself.

'We've kept them out of the streets, for the most part,' Kasteen said, indicating our deployment around the outskirts of Darien. 'The few that have made it into the urban areas are heading straight for the starport, trying to join up with the group there.' The ghost of a grin flitted across her face. 'That means we can ambush and eliminate most of those pretty easily.'

'So your only real problem's here, at the aerodrome,' I said, noting with some relief that the fears

that had driven me from my sickbed were apparently unfounded. So far, at least, none of the broods we'd detected seemed intent on attacking us in our garrison.

Broklaw nodded. 'You don't know the half of it. We've got nearly a thousand refugees trapped in the terminal building,' he said. 'Evacuated from lower down.'

'Most of them have been stuck there for days,' Kasteen added, 'waiting for genetic screening to weed out any hybrids among them, but the justicars have been a bit too busy to deal with that.'

'I can imagine,' I said dryly. The wide open spaces of the landing field had been tailor-made for an invasion force, of course, and our air defence assets could only bring down so many of the falling spores. If it hadn't been for the Navy keeping the bulk of the hive fleet otherwise occupied, we'd have had our hands a lot fuller than they actually were by now. Once again, though, Kasteen had anticipated this very contingency, applying the lessons so painfully learned on the battlefields of Corania, and deployed our forces to keep them bottled up.

'To be honest,' Kasteen said, 'the refugees are getting to be almost as much trouble as the 'nids. They can hear the fighting from where they are, and they're pretty much on edge. The PDF is trying to keep the lid on them, but it'll only take one idiot to panic and we'll have a riot to deal with on top of the bugs.'

'Not good,' I said, seeing the problem at once. The last thing the beleaguered defenders needed was a horde of panic-stricken civilians running around blocking our fire lanes, and driving the tyranids into

a killing frenzy. As soon as the creatures realised they were within spitting distance of a good square meal they'd surge forward, putting even more strain on our defensive positions. 'Are you going to reinforce the line here, just in case?'

Broklaw nodded again. 'We're moving another platoon up as soon as their Chimeras are refuelled and their ammo replenished.' A thought seemed to strike him, and with a sudden quiver of apprehension I knew even before he spoke what he was about to suggest. 'You could go in with them if you like.'

'That ought to calm the civilians down,' Kasteen agreed. 'Half of them seem to think you're the greatest warrior since Macharius.'

I looked at them both, cursing the impulse that had dragged me out of a nice cosy sickbed for no good reason, and which looked like dropping me straight into harm's way again. I could always plead fatigue and weakness, of course, but how much harm would that do to the image I'd acquired of indomitable courage, however unmerited it actually was, and to the loyalty it seemed to inspire among the regiment?

That's the trouble with reputations, once you've got one you need to maintain it. Kasteen and Broklaw were undoubtedly under the same delusion as the chirurgeon had been, that I'd left the sickbay because I was chafing to get back into action despite my wounds, and if I dispelled it I was going to undermine their confidence in me. Once that happened, my unquestioned leadership would start to crumble too. So I forced an easy smile to my face, as though I thought the idea a good one.

'Well,' I said, feigning just the right amount of reluctance to make them think I was actually eager to get back out there, 'holding the hands of a bunch of nervous civilians wasn't quite what I had in mind when I got up this morning.' That was true enough. I wobbled on my feet a little, just enough to remind them that I was in a far worse state than I was pretending, and was rewarded with another covert exchange of concerned looks. 'But I could do with a breath of fresh air, and I suppose I'd only be getting in the way on the front lines.' For a moment I wondered if I'd overplayed my hand, and had just bought myself a ticket into the war zone, but Kasteen and Broklaw were both nodding in agreement.

'With all due respect, Ciaphas,' Kasteen said, making it clear that she was talking as a friend rather than a comrade in arms, 'you look like something an ork spat out. I really wouldn't recommend you visit the combat zone today.'

'Well,' I said, permitting a little of the reluctance I felt to show through, and allowing them to think it was because I'd just been argued out of going off to take another pop at the 'nids, 'I suppose you're right, and I might be able to do a little good with the civvies.'

All in all, I thought, it could have been a great deal worse. I'd be getting a lot closer to the action than I'd have liked, but if the tactical display could be trusted there didn't seem much prospect of running into any actual tyranids, and I didn't suppose the refugees would be that much of a problem. Perhaps fortunately, I was blissfully unaware at the time of just how catastrophically wrong I would turn out to be on both counts.

CHAPTER TWENTY-TWO

GETTING TO THE starport terminal turned out to be simple enough, as Faril's platoon was just leaving the staging area to relieve Sulla's, who'd apparently been potting away at the chitinous horrors for the last day or so with a gratifying amount of success.[1] Jurgen and I managed to hitch a lift in the command Chimera, and although conditions there weren't exactly calculated to make me feel better, the usual noise and jolting hardly improved by my aide's close proximity in a confined space, I was glad enough of it. No doubt he could have found us another Salamander without too much trouble if I'd requested one, but after our experiences on Aceralbaterra I felt rather more comfortable entirely surrounded by armour

---

1. *Anyone caring to wade through the details can find them in Sulla's memoirs, in which she recounts the action at stupefying length.*

plate, and I was able to make use of the vox and auspex gear surrounding me to get a far clearer picture of
the way the battle was going than I would otherwise
have had.

To my relief, it seemed as though the situation had
hardly changed since my last look at the hololith in
the command centre. Our forces still held the
perimeter of the aerodrome and were advancing
steadily, slowly strangling the 'nid swarm in an ever-
tightening noose, driving them gradually closer to
the sheer drop over which I had so nearly plunged
myself a few short weeks before. Not that I expected
many to actually fall to their deaths, of course, they'd
shown on all too many other occasions that they
could clamber up the sheer sides of the plateaux with
astonishing dexterity, and I had no reason to believe
that they wouldn't prove equally adept at descending
if they had to. If anything the gap between the front
line and the terminal building had increased, and I
began to feel that this make-work errand might turn
out to be the best course of action after all, keeping
me well out of the way of any actual fighting while
contriving to give the impression that I was still leading from the front.

Thus it was, to my own vague surprise, with something approaching a light heart that I hopped down
from the Chimera with Jurgen, who was still lugging
his beloved melta around despite its weight, and
made my way up the steps of the terminal building.
Faril gave us a cheerful wave of farewell from the top
hatch, where he'd planted himself the moment Jurgen had boarded the vehicle in my wake, and
chugged away to look for something to kill.

'Who goes there?' A couple of PDF troopers, dressed in clashing lilac and puce fatigues, which even a Slaaneshi cultist would consider in screaming bad taste, aimed shaky lasguns at me. I tilted my head a little, allowing them the best possible view of the profile most favoured by the printsheets I'd seen.

'Commissar Ciaphas Cain,' I told them grandly. 'I'd like a word with your commanding officer.' The troopers lowered their weapons, and began conferring with several of their fellows who had emerged from the wide bronze doors behind them, which were decorated with aquilae intertwined with what I took for native avians and a crude-looking flying machine or two, and through which a wide, marble-floored concourse was visible. At least that's what I discovered once I'd ventured inside. From out here there was precious little sign of any floor space at all, practically every square centimetre of it appearing to be occupied by makeshift bedrolls and listlessly slouching civilians.

'It's him. It really is,' I heard one of the troopers muttering to his companion, before turning to the nearest of the newcomers. 'Don't just stand there, get the lieutenant!'

'Much obliged,' I said, reaching the top of the flight at last, and trying not to pant audibly as the designated trooper scuttled away. The one who'd sent him, who turned out to be sporting a lance corporal's single chevron, waved vaguely in what he no doubt fondly imagined was a passable salute. I returned it crisply, and smiled in a friendly fashion. 'Can you fill me in on the situation here?'

'Well, we're just sitting tight, sir,' the man said, clearly at a loss as to how to respond, 'in case the tyranids attack.' He tried to look a little more martial. 'We're not afraid to get stuck in, you know sir, but them in charge said to leave it to the Guard while we look after the refugees.'

'Quite the best thing,' I assured him, nodding gravely, and pleasantly surprised to find that my head wasn't throbbing quite as much as I'd expected afterwards. 'These people are the future of Periremunda. They have to be protected at all costs.'

'I hadn't really thought of it like that,' the fellow said, straightening visibly as some unsuspected residue of soldierly pride reasserted itself. Unfortunately the effect was rather spoiled a moment later as he got his first clear sight of Jurgen, and his mouth fell open like a startled squig. By that time, though, we were past the sentries and into the terminal itself, so any second thoughts he might have been having would have been far too late.

The interior of the building was, by any standard, a dismal sight, despite the garish fashion in which most of its occupants were dressed. Not as bad as some I've witnessed, of course, but pathetic enough: hollow eyed men and women bent under the weight of unbearable loss, apathetic children too bored and hungry to do much more than sit and whine instead of enjoying their carefree years as they should have been, and, permeating everything, the endless echoing roar of hundreds of voices no one was listening to. The smell was almost as bad as the noise, even my years of Jurgen's near constant companionship having done

little to prepare me for such a concentrated dose of pungent humanity.

As I advanced into the tiny area of clear space around the door, through which the ever-present wind and a few flakes of snow were drifting, I was struck by a sudden blast of heat, the press of so many bodies more than capable of overcoming Hoarfell's frigid climate. Most of the troopers I'd seen outside were sitting in front of a makeshift barrier separating this tiny cleared zone from the main concourse, apparently constructed from furnishings removed to make room for more of the ubiquitous bedrolls that carpeted the chill stone floor; desks, still bearing the sigils of one or other of the aerial transport companies that used to run regular services to other plateaux, a bench, and a recaf machine long since drained of the beverage it had once contained. Two of the PDF men were flanking a kind of gate made from the back of a cargo pallet, their lasguns held idly in their hands. From the way they kept scanning the crowd, rather than looking outwards for any sign of the tyranids, I suspected that they were more fearful of trouble from that quarter than anything the xenos might do.

And with good reason, I thought. The stench of desperation was almost as powerful as that of unwashed bodies, and I began to realise that Kasteen was right to be concerned. It would take very little to turn this sullen mass of humanity into a rampaging mob little better than a horde of orks, and if that happened a couple of lasguns would be no protection at all.

I had little time for such dispiriting musings, however, as a slightly overweight young man in the same lurid uniform as the rest of the PDF rabble was making his way through the crowd as quickly as he could, which wasn't very. He kept mumbling apologies as he dodged round the ragtag civilians packing the place out, instead of using his elbows and the authority of his position like a real officer would have done, and I began to see why he'd been saddled with this thankless task. No doubt his superiors thought he was the least likely junior officer to be missed in the front line.

'Commissar, it's an honour.' He raised his voice to greet me while still some distance away, and a few of the nearer civilians turned to look in my direction. As they did so, recognition sparked on their faces, along with something that made my blood run almost as cold as the snow outside: a renewal of hope. Before my horrified eyes the whisper rippled outwards, more and more faces turning in my direction, all clearly believing that my unexpected arrival heralded some kind of deliverance from the echoing limbo to which they'd all been confined for so long. As soon as they realised that I couldn't provide it, things were liable to turn pretty ugly.

'Lieutenant,' I returned, projecting as much easy confidence as I could. When all else fails, I've found, stalling for time never hurts. At the worst it gives you a chance to look for the nearest exit, and draw your weapon first if you have to, and if you're really lucky something unexpected happens that you can take advantage of. 'I hope you don't mind me dropping in like this, but I heard these people were stuck a little

closer to the action than seems entirely safe, and thought there might be something we could do about it.'

'I hope there is,' the chubby young officer said, looking almost as hopeful as the crowd beyond the barrier, which was drifting closer as we spoke. The troopers at the gate fastened it behind him, and tried ineffectually to wave them away. He said something else as well, but my attention was momentarily distracted by Sulla's voice in my comm-bead.

'Squad five, respond.' There was an uncharacteristic edge to her voice, and after a moment of hissing static, an uncertain voice replied.

'Five two responding. We've lost contact with team one,[1] lieutenant. It may be a vox glitch, but...'

'Fourth squad to sector five.' Irritating as I invariably found her company, I have to admit that Sulla reacted with commendable speed. 'Possible lurker, so move with caution. Marskil, hold position and stay alert.'

'Confirm,' the corporal responded, sounding highly relieved, and a moment later Grifen's familiar clipped tone acknowledged the order too.

'On it, lieutenant.' The palms of my hands began to tingle again. If the 'nids had managed to slip behind our lines, or an undetected genestealer brood infiltrate the city, the densely packed crowd around me would attract them like orks to gunfire. Perhaps I'd

---

1. *As I've previously mentioned, the 597th routinely split its squads into two fireteams of five troopers each. Team one would be under the command of the sergeant leading the squad, while team two would be led by the assistant squad leader, normally a corporal, when operating independently.*

be better off taking up the plight of the refugees with the local justicars, wherever they were quartered.

'We'll do everything we can, of course,' I assured the lieutenant, as though I'd heard what he'd said and gave a frak about it. I tried to recall the tactical maps I'd looked at aboard Faril's Chimera. Where in the warp was sector five anyway? Would trying to slip away just land me in the middle of another 'nid swarm, or a pack of genestealers?

'We'd really appreciate that,' the young officer told me, nodding earnestly. 'You can see for yourself that conditions here are far from ideal.' That earned a ripple of ironic laughter and a couple of catcalls from the audience we'd attracted, but to my relief none of it seemed overtly hostile. I knew just how easily that could change, however. Time for a bit of the old Cain charm, I thought, and turned to address the civilians directly.

'Citizens of Periremunda,' I said, raising my voice without apparent effort so that it cut through the babble of the crowd as easily as the noise of a battle-field. 'I can assure you that you haven't been forgotten, and neither has the tremendous sacrifice you've made in abandoning your homes for a short while to allow us to concentrate our forces more effectively against the tyranids. My presence here today should convince you of that. But I must ask you to remain patient for a little while longer. Even now the battle's raging to cleanse your world of the xenos taint.'

I couldn't have timed it better if I'd tried. Outside the massive building someone screamed, a short, choked-off cry of pain and terror, echoed a moment

later by a second voice, with only a single lasgun shot
between them.

I whirled around, galvanised by adrenaline, fear
and old reflexes combining to override the momentary surge of nausea that accompanied the
movement. I was staring at a walking nightmare,
looming twice the height of a man, slashing and tearing with its claws and talons, the thin film of slush
outside reddened with the shredded remains of the
corporal who'd greeted me and the trooper who'd
accompanied him.

'Fire!' I shouted, drawing my weapons without
thinking, and discharging a shot from my laspistol,
while the PDF troopers stood around uselessly, paral-
ysed by shock. The towering horror seemed to
shimmer as it moved, and my lasbolt gouged a harmless chunk from a pillar supporting the portico.
'Protect the civilians!' Not that I gave a flying frak
about them, of course, but if anything was calculated
to get the PDF off their collective arses and shooting
at the bloody thing it was probably that. I was right,
too. The chubby lieutenant drew his sidearm at last,
and the troopers finally snapped out of their stupor
and started blazing away at it, to no real effect that I
could see.

'Hold still, frot it!' Jurgen muttered at my side, trying to get a clear shot with the melta, but the lictor
moved too fast, and the PDF kept getting in the way.
Behind us the civilians scattered, howling in panic,
and very sensible of them too in my opinion. A couple more of the luridly uniformed militia went
down, spraying blood and entrails, and the chubby
lieutenant's head bounced on the marble close to my

boot, leaving a long, discoloured streak across the opalescent stone.

'Whenever you're ready,' I told my aide, unable to keep a touch of asperity from my voice, but as ever he remained immune to sarcasm.

'Almost got it,' he assured me, firing the heavy weapon at last, and vaporising a waste receptacle, a drinking fountain, and a hideously ornamented tub apparently intended to contain plants of some kind. Fortunately he managed to clip the lictor as well, charring the scything talon and rending claws on its left side into useless chunks of barbequed meat, despite its rapid evasion. That wasn't enough to kill it, of course, but it was certainly irritated. Screaming with rage it charged straight at me, bursting into the building and forcing me back against the PDF's makeshift barricade before I could get off another shot with my sidearm.

Cursing, I evaded its first rush as best I could, angling towards the side with the now useless limbs, and slashing at the steaming chitin with my chainsword. Jurgen had baked it nicely, it seemed, ichor and noxious streams of liquefied tissue leaking around the cracked plates of its hide, and the scream-ing blade bit deep, opening up a long slash across its flank. I knew better than to expect that to finish it though, and ducked, just as it whirled around and slashed at my head with its surviving scything claw.

'Back away, commissar!' Jurgen urged, unable to fire again for fear of hitting me, and I cannoned into one of the piled-up desks, the blood pounding in my ears. If the blasted barricade hadn't been in the way I'd have stood half a chance, getting a decent hack at

the thing's back as it barrelled on past me to start gorging on the civilians, but that wasn't going to happen now. Hemmed in by the pile of detritus, it could only be a matter of moments before I ended up as messily dead as the PDF troopers.

Suddenly, to my relieved astonishment, the thing staggered back, the fringe of tendrils hanging from its face twitching in agitation. For a moment I assumed that Jurgen's peculiar gift had somehow come to my aid again, but there seemed no reason why he should be affecting it; he certainly seemed no closer to either of us than before.[1] Then, trying to concentrate on my immediate surroundings through the haze of nausea that seemed to be closing itself around my synapses, I became aware of something going on behind me.

The civilians, as I've said, had scattered as the feral monstrosity first burst into the terminal building, but now, if anything, their cries of panic seemed to be intensifying. Risking a quick glance over my shoulder, which left my head pounding from the sudden movement but which somehow cleared it at the same time, I saw the crowd breaking and flocking to the sides of the concourse instead of getting as far away from the lictor as possible, which had been their first, and entirely understandable, impulse. Something else had them spooked, at least as much as the monstrosity I faced, and my first thought was that more 'nids had

---

1. *Whether or not a blank can affect the functioning of the tyranid hive mind is still a matter of some conjecture. Jurgen was certainly able to disrupt the brood telepathy of genestealer groups on more than one occasion, but, as in so many cases where anti-psyker phenomena are concerned, in a somewhat erratic fashion, and I can recall no instance where he unquestionably disrupted the overmind itself.*

appeared to flank us. If true, that would hardly have been unexpected, lictors tending to attract other predators in their wake once they locate a sufficient number of victims to make a concentrated attack worthwhile. But instead of a tide of gaunts, or purestrain 'stealers, I was confronted with something even more terrifying.

A trio of the refugees was advancing through the parting crowd, ignoring everyone else completely: an old man, a young woman, and a teenage boy. The woman and the boy were horrifying enough to behold, their eyes blank, and the hair around their heads waving wildly as though caught in a gale that no one else could feel, but the old man was a thousand times worse, levitating across the floor on bolts of lightning, which sparked and crashed around him. Cackling maniacally he flung out a hand, and the eldritch discharge enveloped the lictor. The creature reeled back, shrieking, and after a moment the girl muttered something, conjuring a bolt of seething plasma out of thin air. With a feral grin on her face she sent it spinning across the concourse with a flick of her wrist, to burst against the pile of furniture I was cowering behind.

'Avaunt, witch, in the name of the Emperor!' A balding middle-aged man in the robes of a minor ecclesiarch stepped out of the crowd, brandishing an aquila, his voice echoing resonantly around the concourse as he began to chant the rites of exorcism. The boy turned his head, an expression of contempt on his face, and stared at him as though the man was something he'd just found on the sole of his shoe.

'What's the Emperor ever done for us?' he asked, and the ecclesiarch fell to the floor as though punched in

the face, writhing and screaming like a man possessed. 'Only the True Powers can save us now.'

Panic-stricken, I glanced from one menace to another; the lictor, still wreathed in eldritch energy, striking out at random in its agony, and the trio of psykers, approaching me inexorably. At least the 'nid was out of the fight for the time being, however temporarily, so I fired at the nearest witch. The lasbolt burst against the old man's shield of lightning, and he cackled again, clearly no saner than the average Chaos cultist.

'This is Cain,' I voxed frantically, shifting my aim just as the girl flung another bolt of warp plasma in my general direction. I ducked, and it impacted on the bellowing lictor, making it stagger. It might have killed the thing altogether if the ethereal discharge still crackling about it hadn't absorbed some of the energy, but that's Chaos for you. Even when they're trying to co-operate, its acolytes tend to tread on one another's toes. 'The 'nids are inside the terminal! Psykers too!'

I cracked off a shot at plasma girl, and she staggered, a bloody wound opening up on her torso. I expected her to fall, but the arcane energies she was manipulating seemed to be sustaining her, and she merely smiled grimly, conjuring another of the hellish bolts out of thin air. As I ducked back into cover the boy caught my eye, our gazes locking, and a tidal wave of despair flooded through me. There was no point in fighting any more that much was obvious. Their victory was certain, so was that of Chaos, and it was only a matter of time before the forces they served swept forth from the Eye of Terror to expunge

the Imperium from the stars as though it had never been. Even the Emperor would fall, his soul shredded to sate the obscene appetites of daemons...

For a hideous, endless instant, I felt myself teetering on the brink of insanity, then my tenacious survival instinct kicked in, and I fought it, as hard as I'd fought for my soul on Slawkenberg. The Ruinous Powers hadn't managed to claim it then, despite their worst efforts, and they wouldn't now, damn it.

I drew in a deep breath, headily redolent of Jurgen, and snapped back to myself, suddenly aware that my aide had joined me behind the fused and melted remains of the pile of furniture that offered us the only shelter in sight, unslinging his lasgun as he did so, clearly reluctant to use the melta again with so many innocents in the way. The impossible nightmare the young psyker had somehow planted in my mind began to dwindle away, rapidly becoming as intangible and meaningless as any other dream does on waking.

'Liar!' I roared, and the youngster's eyes widened in shock, an instant before a vengeful lasbolt from my pistol spattered his brain, along with the taint of Chaos that permeated it, over both his companions. The priest went quiet too, apparently no longer under the dreamcaster's baleful influence, although whether he eventually recovered his wits I have no idea.

The other two slowed their advance, apparently no longer quite as sure as they had been of victory, and the girl staggered a little, as though beginning to feel the effect of her wound. The old man seemed a little closer to the floor now too, the eldritch energies

crackling around him not quite as potent as they had been, and I began to feel a flare of hope. Jurgen, it seemed, was disrupting their powers even at this distance. A desperate idea began to form.

'We need to close with them,' I said, and Jurgen nodded, accepting this apparently suicidal order as calmly as if I'd just asked for a bowl of tanna.

'Ready when you are, sir,' he assured me, producing what looked like an unfeasibly large bayonet from the collection of equipment he was habitually festooned with, and clipping it to the barrel of his gun with precise and economical movements.

'I never doubted it,' I assured him, and we popped off another couple of shots each to distract the witches again. Behind us the lictor staggered into the frame of the door, lashing out randomly with its rending claws and tearing a jagged lump of bronze out of it, while the surviving PDF troopers continued to pepper its immediate surroundings with badly aimed lasbolts. 'Go!'

We scrambled over the remains of the barricade, ripping the hem of my greatcoat in the process, and charged towards the astonished heretics, firing as we went. Both reeled back a pace or two under the impact of the hail of lasbolts, but their strange immunity to the full effect of them seemed to hold until we'd closed to within a handful of yards. The girl, her face panic-stricken, tried to conjure another ball of seething destruction into existence, but it fizzled and vanished in the air between us, and the old man fell suddenly to the floor as his shield of lightning abruptly disappeared. With a bellow of anger and revulsion I swiped his head from his shoulders

with my chainsword before he had a chance to react, and watched it bounce a couple of times before coming to rest, glaring back at me in posthumous indignation.

'How…?' the girl started to ask, before it apparently began to dawn on her that most of her torso was missing. Her knees buckled, an expression of stunned incomprehension flickered briefly across her face, and the light went out of her eyes. As she slumped to the floor, the grimace of baffled surprise fading into the slackness of death, most of the civilians around us made the sign of the aquila and spat on the three twitching bodies.

'Well done, Jurgen,' I said, breathing hard. But of course it wasn't over yet. The death of the psykers had released the lictor from their unnatural influence, and it lunged back into the attack, flinging aside the pile of furniture that barred its way in its eagerness to get to us.

Jurgen and I braced ourselves to meet the monster's charge, while the civilians scattered around us like gretchin and the PDF troopers hovered irresolute, apparently afraid to shoot at it again in case they hit us. Before we could fire our own weapons, though, the roar of a powerful engine echoed through the cavernous building and a Chimera appeared from nowhere, bouncing up the steps and ricocheting off the much-abused doors with a sound like a bell tower collapsing. Grifen's head and shoulders were visible, sticking through the top hatch, and she waved as she caught sight of us.

'Sorry we took so long getting here,' she voxed. 'Our driver broke his arm when a carnifex tried to

overturn us, and it took a moment to get someone else on the controls.'

'Your timing's impeccable,' I assured her, wondering how she expected to deal with the chitinous horror still limping towards us at an astonishing rate despite its wounds. The Chimera's heavy bolters would have been lethal to the civilians cluttering up the place if she'd tried to use them, and the hull-mounted lasguns were all positioned to cover its flanks. I soon had my answer, though. Instead of stopping to disembark the troopers, as I'd expected, the blocky vehicle simply roared on into the concourse, flattening the remains of the barricade as it came, and reducing the astonished lictor to a large, unpleasant stain beneath its treads before it had a chance to react. 'Nice driving, Magot.'

'You're welcome, commissar,' the familiar cheerful tones of one of my perennial disciplinary problems assured me, before taking on a faintly puzzled air. 'How did you know it was me?'

'Lucky guess,' I told her, feeling a sudden overwhelming urge to sit down. The civilians were all babbling at me, apparently taking my desperate charge at the psykers as confirmation of everything they'd ever heard about my legendary courage under fire, my head was pounding again, and nothing around me seemed to make any sense at all.

Well, almost nothing. Jurgen coughed diffidently, and produced a thermal flask from somewhere among his collection of pouches.

'Tanna, sir?' he suggested. Without thinking I nodded, then winced at the inevitable result.

'Thank you, Jurgen,' I said, once my vision had cleared again. 'I think we've earned it.'

CHAPTER TWENTY-THREE

'ARE YOU SURE about this?' I asked, masking my considerable surprise with some difficulty.

Keesh nodded. 'Absolutely. It took a bit of digging once we'd identified your rogue psykers, but we've been able to establish their movements for the last few years with a fair degree of accuracy.' He brought up the data on the hololith in the centre of the conference table, and Amberley nodded, as though it merely confirmed something she'd long suspected. 'They have a number of associates in common, of course, as you'd expect, but nothing away from their home plateau except this.'

'It could just be a coincidence,' I said, despite the tingling in the palms of my hands that insisted otherwise. 'There are still gaps in the records.'

'That's hardly surprising under the circumstances,' Amberley pointed out mildly. Although it seemed we had the tyranids on the run at last, having held on to all the major population centres and retaken a few of the ones they'd overrun, the war was still a long way from being over. The Navy had finally broken the back of the hive fleet, forcing what was left of it to withdraw in search of easier pickings, and the rain of spores had ceased almost a week ago. Nevertheless there were more than enough of the creatures left on the ground to pose a considerable problem for the Guard and what was left of the PDF for a long time to come. Even when the last of the plateaux were finally cleared, we'd still have the uncountable numbers of ravening organisms swarming in the deserts between them to deal with.

At least that problem that was diminishing by the day. Now that they'd run out of bioships to kill the Navy were doing their best to pick off the largest concentrations from orbit, paying particular attention to any digestion pools capable of spawning reinforcements. Orbital bombardment could only achieve so much against so widely dispersed an enemy, though, and the last die-hard survivors would have to be tracked down and finished off the old-fashioned way. That wouldn't be my problem though, thank the Emperor. Ordinary humans couldn't even hope to survive in that hellish environment, let alone fight in it, and the honour of finally declaring Periremunda free of the xenos taint would fall to one of the Astartes Chapters.

I nodded in agreement, still pleasantly surprised by the lack of nausea the motion produced. I hadn't

exactly been resting in the couple of weeks since my
nerve-shredding encounter in the starport terminal,
but I hadn't seen much actual combat either, dividing
the bulk of my time between the routine tasks of my
office, pursuing my request for an investigation of the
Gavarronian PDF now things had become quiet
enough to devote some attention to the matter, and
evading the local pictcasts, which were bordering on
hagiography these days, after what everyone seemed
determined to believe was my heroic single-handed
defence of a thousand civilians against a horde of
ravening tyranids and a coven of Chaos worshippers.

Keesh's request for a private meeting to discuss
some highly sensitive matters had come as something
of a surprise (as had Amberley's presence in the conference chamber, which had been an even greater,
and far more welcome, one), which I'd seized on
gratefully, hoping that decamping to Principia Mons
without warning would at least allow me to get
though the next couple of days without some idiot
shoving an imagifer in my face and asking me to comment on some momentous issue I'd never heard
about before.

'Quite true,' I said. The bulk of the records I was
looking at had been recovered from Skywest[1] by an
elite squad of justicars under Nyte's personal supervi-
sion within hours of the 'nids being driven off from
there, and had been classified so secret I wasn't
entirely sure that even Zyvan was allowed to look at
them.[2] I nodded at several names, linked to the three

---

1. *The home plateau of the three psykers Cain and Jurgen had encountered on Hoarfell.*

2. *He would have been, had I seen any reason to bring them to his attention.*

we were interested in by thin red lines. 'Are any of
these people available for questioning?'

'Not unless you want to stick your head down a
tyranid's throat and shout "anyone at home?"' Amberley said dryly.

Keesh looked mildly disapproving of the note of
levity creeping into the proceedings. 'Our best indica-
tions are that none of them survived the tyranid
assault on Skywest,' he said primly, 'but we can still
draw certain inferences from the way they appear to
have interacted.'

'A Chaos cult,' I said, recognising the signs. 'Or at
least a local cell of one.'

Amberley nodded, looking a little surprised at the
speed of my deduction, but I'd encountered such
things often enough before to realise what I was looking at almost at once.

'That would be my interpretation too,' Keesh said.
'Although it does seem rather unusual for a group that
small to have three members proficient in warpcraft.'
He directed an enquiring look at the inquisitor.

'It does,' Amberley confirmed. 'Which is why the
other lead should be followed up as quickly as possible.' She looked at me, smiling cheerfully, and I tried
to suppress a shiver of apprehension. 'Fortunately
Ciaphas has given us the perfect opportunity to do
just that.'

'I have?' I asked. I indicated the hololith. 'I grant you
that they all visited Gavarrone at least once in the past
five years, but my business there is entirely with the
PDF.' After a lot of memos, and some unashamed
trading on my reputation to get things moving, I'd
finally got the Munitorum to agree that I might as well

follow up the incident on Aceralbaterra myself in the
absence of any local commissar capable of handling
the case.[1] As nothing else had happened in the meantime to raise any questions about the local militia's
loyalty the chances were it was going to turn out to be
a complete waste of time after all, but at least it would
keep me comfortably away from the mopping up
operation for a day or two. 'I don't see how I can follow this up as well.'

'You won't have to,' Amberley assured me. 'But your
enquiry into the friendly fire incident will be the perfect cover for a bit of discreet poking around into
some other matters too.'

'Like what?' I asked, feeling less and less happy.

Amberley looked at me like one of my old schola
tutors pointing out that I'd missed something obvious. 'Well, you're assuming that if the PDF on
Gavarrone has been penetrated, it's by genestealer
hybrids. That is perfectly possible, of course, but the
Imperium has other hidden enemies too, don't forget.'

'You really think there's a Chaos cult hiding out in
the middle of an Ecclesiarchy fiefdom?' I asked,
unable to keep a note of incredulity out of my voice.

---

1. *Though the Gavarronian PDF would, in theory, be under the jurisdiction of a commissar specifically attached to them, in practice the
luckless individual in question had been given the task of overseeing
morale and disciplinary matters for the PDF of the entire system, along
with those of another thirty-seven equally sparsely settled Imperial
worlds within the sector. As a result, Commissar Banning spent almost
all his time in his cabin aboard one starship after another, drinking
heavily, leaving the vast majority of the troopers nominally under his
care in blissful ignorance of his existence.*

Amberley shrugged. 'Why not?' she asked.

I felt my jaw working spasmodically for a moment before I could articulate a coherent reply. 'Well for one thing, Eglantine and her singing harpies would have burned the lot of them for heretics years ago,' I pointed out reasonably.

Amberley merely shrugged again. 'If they'd even noticed,' she said, completely unperturbed by my manifest incredulity. 'In my experience people like her tend to take an awful lot for granted.'

'Well, I'll let you know if I find anything,' I said, hoping to move the conversation on to safer ground. Amberley's smile stretched, and I felt the shiver of apprehension grow stronger.

'There won't be any need for that,' she assured me happily. 'I'll be coming along too.' Then she smiled coquettishly. 'I've always thought I look good in a uniform.'

WELL, SHE WAS right about that anyway, which was something of a consolation. She grinned at me happily from beneath a standard issue Valhallan uniform cap, its dark fur contrasting well with her pale complexion and blonde hair. The greatcoat that went with it was unfastened, revealing well-filled fatigues beneath, but an absence of body armour that had surprised me at first. Then again, this wasn't supposed to be a combat assignment. Nevertheless, I had no doubt that she'd be as discreetly protected as she had been on Gravalax, despite the absence of any visible precautions.

'How do I look?' she asked, taking a sip of amasec from the crystal goblet in her hand.

We were sitting in the forward compartment of her Aquila, which had been repainted for the occasion in the drab livery of the Munitorum, and which now looked, from the outside at least, like a utility cargo hauler that hadn't seen the inside of a maintenance bay since the Gothic Wars. Precisely the kind of thing, in other words, that I might have requisitioned to transport me on a low priority administrative errand. (But it would have been considerably less comfortable, of course, not to mention lacking in cunningly concealed firepower.)

'Very fetching,' I assured her, accurately enough. 'You ought to pass for a soldier, if no one looks too closely.' That was more or less true of the rest of them as well, I supposed. After all, next to Jurgen, even Simeon looked like a storm trooper. With his implants hidden beneath the traditional Valhallan greatcoat and hat he looked more human than I'd ever seen him, a massive dose of some tranquiliser or other stilling the usual range of twitches and tics. Pelton looked the part too, his years in the Arbites no doubt contributing to the air of disciplined efficiency the uniform lent him.

The weak link, of course, was Zemelda, who, try as she might, would never look like anything other than a civilian in borrowed clothes to anyone familiar with the Imperial Guard. She'd done her best, though, even returning her hair to its natural colour for the occasion, which turned out to be a rather pleasant shade of brown. Faced with Amberley's implacable determination to bring her along I'd bowed to the inevitable, merely suggesting that we add a bandage or two to give the impression that she'd recently suffered a head wound in action. Anyone noticing some oddity of

posture or behaviour might just ascribe it to the kind
of disorientation I'd become all too familiar with
myself in the last couple of weeks. The hope was a
faint one, admittedly, but since we were going to be
dealing with PDF personnel, who were barely a step
up from civilians in uniform themselves, we might
just get away with it.

Needless to say Zemelda was just as thrilled at this
chance to dress up and play act as she had been when
asked to impersonate a lady's maid, and had to be
prevailed upon in no uncertain terms not to wince
and limp like a mummer in a mystery play.[1] At least,
to my intense relief, Rakel and Yanbel had both been
left behind, since even Amberley's relentless optimism
had baulked at the prospect of successfully disguising
either of them as soldiers.

I sipped my own amasec, trying to still the flutter of
apprehension in my stomach. She knew what she was
doing, of course, I took that for granted; the trouble
was, I had no idea of what that might be. The theory
certainly seemed sound enough: infiltrate her people
in the guise of my escort, which ought to raise few
eyebrows, since taking one was well within the
bounds of established protocol for the kind of investigation I was pursuing. After all, if the Gavarronians
did turn out to be riddled with hybrids, I could hardly
rely on their own comrades to back me up in a physical confrontation.

---

1. *A common custom on many of the worlds around the Damocles Gulf,
in which citizens celebrate holy festivals with amateur theatrical perfor-
mances drawn from the lives of the saints or the Emperor, in which
devotional material is inextricably linked with the most vulgar of knock-
about comedy.*

With that grim possibility in mind I'd intended bringing Lustig or Grifen's squad with me, until Amberley had proposed this imposture, and truth to tell I would still have preferred to do so. I had no doubt of her people's fighting ability if push came to shove, but I hadn't been in action with them as often as I had with the Valhallans, and I couldn't rely on them to cover my back in quite the same way. Their primary loyalty would be to Amberley, the Inquisition, and whatever mission she was on. I had no doubt at all that if a conflict of interest arose they'd hang me out to dry without a second's hesitation. Not only that, I still had no more than the vaguest idea of what they might be doing once we'd arrived at our destination, and I have to admit that it was probably just as well. If I had realised what they were hoping to find, you can be sure I'd have been even more apprehensive than I already was.

At least I knew I could trust Jurgen implicitly, and I resolved to stick as closely to him as I could, despite the obvious disadvantages of doing so. He'd accepted the necessity of leaving his favourite toy behind, a melta hardly being the kind of thing a commissar's aide carries around routinely on a fact-finding mission, but had been manifestly unhappy about ditching it, no doubt anticipating the possibility of further trouble. (Which, given the way things had gone since we'd arrived on this Emperor-forsaken joke of nature, I could hardly fault him for.) Denied the solace of some serious firepower he remained slumped in his seat, his las-gun cradled on his knees, obsessively checking the

functioning of every component and reciting the appropriate litany from the *Book of Armaments* repeatedly under his breath. At least it kept his mind off his usual airsickness, so I thanked the Emperor for small mercies, and tried to get a picture of the fiefdom of Gavarrone as Pontius circled widely around it, preparing to bring the shuttle in to land on the pad in the main PDF compound.

My first impression was one of neatness, in marked contrast to the other plateaux I'd flown into since my arrival on Periremunda, the usual disorderly sprawl of human habitation or untrammelled nature tidied to within an inch of its life. Broad, straight avenues cut through well-tended fields in which any weeds or wildflowers with the temerity to stick their heads above the soil would be expunged as ruthlessly as heretics, bordered by squared-off hedges whose corners seemed to form perfect right angles. The town we passed over was laid out with an equal degree of geometric precision, its streets forming a precise grid, leading naturally to the vast square in its centre where the temple of the Emperor soared majestically skyward in a positive effusion of buttresses, crenelations, and superfluous statuary.

'It's like a toy town,' Zemelda said, a note of disapproval in her voice, no doubt comparing it unfavourably to the cosy human confusion of Principia Mons, and I nodded in agreement. The relentless perfection of it all, no doubt intended to display devotion to Him on Earth in the little details of everyday life, struck me as sterile, as alien to the cluttered human psyche as the smooth functionality of a tau sept.[1] She craned her neck for a better view of

something in the distance. 'Is that where we're going?'

'No.' Amberley shook her head. 'That's the convent. We're putting down on the PDF landing field.'

Despite myself I was unable to resist turning my gaze in the direction they were looking. The Order of the White Rose, it seemed, was not exactly constrained by vows of poverty. The convent looked more like the country estate of some provincial nobleman on an agriworld somewhere, long white buildings rising no more than three storeys from the ground forming a complex series of interlocking quadrangles in which fountains played and flowers nodded gently in the breeze. Other, larger squares clearly had more utilitarian purposes, Sisters in power armour drilling or practising combat techniques with a precision Sergeant Lermie[2] would have nodded grudging approval of, or full of glossy black Rhinos ornamented with votive iconography that made them look more like self-propelled chapels than practical AFVs. The amount of detail I could make out was astonishing, given that our destination was supposed to be several kilometres from the place, and I felt a familiar tingling sensation beneath my gloves.

'Aren't we getting a bit close to their airspace?' I asked, and Amberley nodded.

---

1. *At the time of which he's writing Cain had yet to visit one of the tau's own worlds, but he was certainly familiar with their architectural style from his time on Gravalax, so the analogy might indeed have struck him then, rather than being the product of several decades' hindsight as might otherwise be inferred.*

2. *The 597th's senior drill instructor.*

'We are,' she agreed, sounding more intrigued than alarmed by this development, and voxed the cockpit. 'Pontius, what's going on?'

'Inquisitor?' Our pilot sounded genuinely baffled by the question. 'I'm following the co-ordinates the local traffic controller gave me. Do you want me to break off our approach?'

'No, not yet.' Amberley nodded thoughtfully, as if something she strongly suspected had just been con- firmed. 'Let's play this one out, and see what happens.' She looked at me, and grinned. 'I think he's just made his first mistake,' she said, a palpable tone of satisfaction in her voice. 'You must really have got him rattled.'

'Who?' I asked. 'Metheius?' Amberley nodded again.

'Him too, probably,' she agreed. That old, and pro- foundly disagreeable, sensation of not being told everything that was going on began to grow in me again, but there was no sense in letting my disquiet show, so I merely glanced across to where Jurgen was sitting. He seemed satisfied with the condition of his lasgun at last, and snapped the power cell into place with a finality that no doubt comforted us both.

'We're on the final approach, ma'am,' Pontius voxed a moment or two later, and I glanced outside again, trying to orientate myself. The wide, close-clipped lawns surrounding the convent suddenly vanished, along with everything else except a panorama of desert impossibly far below, and I suddenly realised that they bordered the sheer drop of the plateau edge. Unlike the starport on Hoarfell, however, there was no fence to prevent an incautious misstep pitching an

unfortunate stroller into infinity, and not for the first
time I found myself wondering if the blessed Sisters
were a couple of beads short of a rosary.[1] I just had
time to notice a brief, actinic flicker in the lowering
clouds to our south-west, like the largest bolt of
lightning imaginable, before the smooth green grass
was back below us, much closer this time. We passed
low over a grove of fruit trees, whose branches waved
lazily in the breeze from our passing, and skimmed a
couple of red-tiled roofs, in which repeating motifs of
aquilae and *fleur de lys* had been picked out in
contrasting hues.

'We're on final approach,' Pontius told us, a
moment before arresting our forward motion
entirely, and the familiar hollow sensation in the pit
of my stomach combined with Jurgen's audible discomfiture to inform me that we were dropping
vertically towards the landing field. White walls rose
past the viewports, to enclose us on all sides, and a
moment later a faint bump echoed through the fuse-
lage as our landing gear made contact with the surface
of the pad. Pontius powered down the engines.

'Right,' Amberley said, standing decisively, 'let's go
and see what all this is about.' I nodded, following
suit.

'Jurgen,' I said, and waited for my aide to take up his
usual position at my shoulder, before savouring my
small moment of self-assertion. I raised a hand to
forestall Amberley from leading the way out of the
passenger compartment. 'Carry on, corporal,' I
instructed.

---

1. More likely they trusted the Emperor to protect them from harm; quite
ironically, as things turned out.

'Commissar.' She saluted briskly, falling into the role she'd assumed at once with barely a hint of amusement, and formed the others up into a passable impersonation of a short team,[1] which followed me down the ramp, their lasguns at the port. Jurgen had slung his own weapon, as was his habit on these occasions, leaving his hands free to respond more readily to any request I might make of him.

We emerged onto a wide landing pad, surrounded by the white buildings of the convent, and a gaggle of power-armoured Sisters strode forward to meet us, bolters at the ready. Stilling the growing sense of apprehension knotting my stomach I nodded an affable greeting, and waited for them to move within earshot.

As our feet hit the rockcrete Pontius powered up his engines again, and the Aquila rose gently into the air behind us. The immediate departure of our transport shuttle would be perfectly normal if we were all who we purported to be, and the last thing we wanted to do was give our unseen adversaries (if they even existed) the smallest hint that there was anything out of the ordinary about my errand. Instead of returning to Principia Mons, however, Pontius would loiter in the immediate vicinity of Gavarrone, safely below the rim of the plateau, in the blind spot of any local auspex systems that might reveal his whereabouts.

---

1. *A fireteam reduced in number by the loss of casualties, but still able to be deployed effectively. Short squads, known to the troopers as 'remnants', are a common feature of many Guard platoons, and are often little more than independent fireteams themselves in all but name.*

As the roar of his engines faded I became aware of a faint rumbling in the distance, like far off artillery, and remembered the flash of light I'd seen from the air.

'Thunder?' Jurgen asked, glancing suspiciously up at the sky.

Amberley shook her head. 'The Navy,' she said. 'There must be a large concentration of 'nids around here somewhere.'

'Lovely,' I muttered under my breath, eliciting a brief, unmilitary grin from the disguised inquisitor, before her cover reasserted itself. Assuming an air of easy confidence I strode forward, addressing the Sister Superior of the Battle Sisters approaching us, and raised my hand in formal greeting.

'Commissar.' The woman returned the gesture curtly, her ash blonde fringe bobbing as she did so, and I noticed that the *fleur de lys* tattoo on her right cheek was bisected by a thin white line of healed scar tissue. This, as much as her manner, marked her out as a veteran warrior, and someone not to be trifled with. Well, fair enough, so was I. 'Welcome to the Convent of the White Rose.' Her eyes flickered past me to Amberley and her entourage, evaluating any potential threat they might have posed, and clearly coming to the conclusion that they didn't present much of one. 'I wasn't informed that there would be others in your party.'

'My aide, Gunner Jurgen,' I said, indicating him with an offhand wave. 'He always accompanies me on official business.' I glanced at Amberley, as though barely aware of who she was. 'This is Corporal Vail, commanding my escort detail.'

'Ma'am,' Amberley said, saluting, and, to my faint surprise, falling into a perfect parade rest as though waiting for further orders. The others all remained at the port, their guns ready, but not yet aimed, which was just as well considering we were outnumbered by two to one and the Sisters had power armour and bolters.

'This is something of an unexpected pleasure,' I said, determined to retain the initiative. 'I was given to understand that we would be landing at the PDF garrison.'

'The decision to divert you here was taken at the highest level,' the Battle Sister assured me, with a faintly reverential air that stirred the hackles on the back of my neck. Zyvan and Keesh were certainly both under the impression that we were sticking to the original plan, and, apart from Amberley, I wasn't aware of any higher authority on the planet. But then the Ecclesiarchy tended to play entirely by their own rules, and I began to wonder if barging into one of their pocket kingdoms uninvited had been quite such a good idea after all. The armoured woman turned, gesturing to us all to follow, and surrounded as we were by heavily armed fanatics I was understandably disinclined to argue the point. 'If you'll come with me, the inquisitor will explain everything.'

CHAPTER TWENTY-FOUR

'THE INQUISITOR?' I echoed, glancing briefly in Amberley's direction in spite of myself, but she continued to play the part of the stolid Valhallan non-com without missing a beat, and no one else seemed to notice my momentary lapse. The Sister Superior nodded as I fell into step beside her, the rest of her squad forming up around our little group in a manner that, despite the appearance of an honour guard, I had no doubt at all would erupt in a hail of bolter fire the moment we did anything they construed as untoward, and we set off across the landing field towards a wide doorway in one of the buildings surrounding us.

The air seemed remarkably fresh, I recall, no doubt because of our proximity to the brink of the plateau, scented with the fragrances of newly clipped grass

and fruit blossom, which were quite readily discernible even over the earthier aroma of Jurgen. At
this altitude the sun was clear and bright, with a
residue of warmth, although the breeze carried a chill
that quite justified my greatcoat and those of my
companions. Real Valhallans would have disdained
the heavy garments of course, preferring shirtsleeves
until there was at least a decent coating of frost over
everything, but the Sisters seemed mercifully ignorant of the fact.

'His presence here is a secret,' she explained, as
though that was obvious. 'I'm sure you understand
the need for discretion in these matters.'

'Indeed I do,' I said, nodding gravely, despite the
vortex of confusion into which my mind had just
been plunged. Amberley didn't seem overly surprised
at this development, which led me to suspect, quite
correctly as it turned out, that she'd been aware of
this other inquisitor's presence all along. I'd gathered
the impression from some of the remarks she'd made
since our association began that not everyone in the
inquisition was necessarily quoting from the same
sermon, so to speak, but it had never occurred to me
until then that her real target on Periremunda might
be one of her own colleagues. If that was indeed the
case, of course. Suppressing my confusion as best I
could, I tried to sound as calm and matter-of-fact as
my hostess. 'Battles have been won or lost before
now thanks to a careless word.'

'Well said,' a new voice chimed in, as we entered a
large marble atrium festooned with icons of the
Emperor, and the inevitable *fleur de lys*, the sight of
which I was beginning to feel heartily sick of. The

speaker was a well-muscled man with brown hair and eyes, who appeared to be in early middle age, although I'd seen too many centenarians who looked half that thanks to an over-enthusiasm for juvenat treatments to take his physical appearance as a reliable indicator of how old he might actually have been. As our little cavalcade entered the building he rose from a bench next to a trellis choked with sweet-smelling roses the colour of fresh fallen snow to greet us, smiling affably, and stuck out a hand for me to shake. 'I can see your reputation is hardly exaggerated.'

'Rather more than you might think,' I replied, taking it with confidence, as my augmetic fingers would be more than adequate to counter any subtle attempts to disconcert me by applying excess pressure. His handshake was firm and decisive, but no more than that. Evidently our peculiar host felt he had no need to resort to childish games to establish his status. To my surprise he chuckled as he let go, as though I'd just said something inordinately witty.

'Which is precisely what I would have expected a man like you to say.' He smoothed the front of his neat black tabard, which had become slightly crumpled, and nodded to the Sister Superior. 'Sister Caritas, could you see to it that the commissar's friends are taken care of? There must be something acceptable to the soldierly palate in the refectory, I would have thought.'

'Most considerate,' I said, determined not to seem in the slightest bit disconcerted by anything that happened here, even though I was understandably reluctant to be parted from Amberley at this juncture.

After all, she knew a great deal more about what was going on than I did. 'But don't take them too far. We have business at the PDF garrison, and I'll need them when I get there.'

'They'll be waiting when you're ready to leave,' the strange inquisitor assured me. I nodded.

'Dismissed,' I told Amberley, and she saluted again.

'Commissar.' She turned to the others, adopting the tone of a junior NCO admonishing her subordinates as accurately as if she'd been one since the First Founding. 'Right, we're all guests in a house of the Emperor, so I expect you to act like it. Show respect to the Sisters, mind your manners, and watch your frakking language.'

'Yes, corporal,' Pelton said seriously, and the others nodded, still playing their parts to the hilt. As they formed up to file out, I gestured to Jurgen to remain.

'This way,' Sister Caritas said, her lips compressed into a thin line of disapproval, and led the little group of pseudo-Valhallans away, the rest of her squad, to my unspoken relief, going with them. The inquisitor glanced at Jurgen, and raised an eyebrow.

'Jurgen's my personal aide,' I explained blandly. 'His security clearance is as high as my own.'

After a moment the black-clad man nodded, a hint of amusement in his eyes. 'Of course, keep him to hand by all means. I'd probably want a little backup myself in your position.' He inclined his head towards an archway leading deeper inside the complex. 'Perhaps you'd appreciate some lunch while we talk.'

'I'd certainly appreciate an explanation or two,' I said, keeping my cards as close to my chest as possible. I had no doubt that, despite his affable

demeanour, this fellow was extremely dangerous. Without Amberley to provide me with a lead, my best course of action would be to encourage him to talk, and hope to the Golden Throne that I'd be able to make some sense of the situation without giving away just how little I really knew about what was going on. 'Who you are and why you've diverted me here would be a reasonable place to start.'

'My dear fellow, how very remiss of me. Inquisitor Killian, of the Ordo Hereticus.' We continued to walk as we spoke, navigating a labyrinth of corridors wide enough to have driven a Salamander down with little difficulty. Now my peculiar host ushered me through a doorway into what was evidently a suite of guest rooms, surprisingly well appointed for so austere an institution. Large sliding doors at one end of the lounge gave on to a lawn fringed with more rose bushes, and he gestured towards it a trifle hastily as Jurgen followed us into the room, preceded as always by his personal aroma. 'Perhaps you'd care to dine *al fresco*?'

'As you wish,' I said blandly, following him into the garden. As I did so something hurtled past my head, a servo skull with a silver soup tureen slung incongruously beneath it, and I turned to follow it suspiciously as it settled over a wrought iron table in the middle of a sweet-scented arbour to deposit its burden. Someone was already sitting there, a blank-visaged techpriest, who stood slowly as we approached. Killian noted my reaction with a wry smile.

'These ones are completely harmless,' he assured me. He gestured towards the techpriest. 'Since you

insist on being accompanied by your associate, I'm sure you won't mind extending me the same courtesy.'

'Of course not,' I told him. I extended my hand, which to my quiet relief the techpriest shook with his own, rather than one of the mechadendrites wavering gently over his shoulders. 'The elusive magister Metheius, I presume.' The guess was evidently a good one, as the techpriest flinched back as I spoke, and shot a startled look at Killian from under the cowl of his robe. There wasn't enough flesh left on his face to form a surprised expression, but then he hardly needed to after a reaction like that.

'You've been talking to Lazurus, I take it,' Killian said, settling into one of the vacant chairs around the table, and motioning for me to sit. Still playing out the charade of good manners I did so, taking the opportunity of making sure my chainsword was loose in its scabbard as I moved it out of the way. Killian noticed the tiny movement, but chose to ignore it, gesturing instead to the selection of viands laid out between us. 'Can I offer you a slice of cottleston pie?'

'We've exchanged a few words,' I admitted blandly, declining the platter he held out towards me. 'At the briefing your assassin disrupted. I take it he was one of yours?' It was a reasonable guess, the Ordo Hereticus dealing with witches and rogue psykers as a matter of course, and far more likely than most other Imperial institutions to have access to their sanctioned counterparts.

'He was,' Killian admitted, without a moment's embarrassment. He took the lid off the tureen, and

ladled out a bowlful of groxtail soup, which he proceeded to sip at appreciatively. 'Are you sure you won't try some of this? It's rather good. They add some local herb to it, grows wild on a few of the lower plateaux. Might as well enjoy it while we can, I don't suppose there's much left of it now the tyranids have been through there.'

'At the risk of seeming a little discourteous,' I said carefully, 'I'm not entirely sanguine about eating anything offered to me by a man who's already made several attempts on my life.'

'No offence taken,' Killian assured me. 'But if I still wanted you dead, I would just have ordered the Sisters to take care of it as soon as you stepped off the shuttle. I doubt that even a man of your formidable fighting prowess could have subdued the entire convent.'

Well, that sounded reasonable enough, and I was getting pretty hungry by that point, so I put my doubts aside and began to dig in, finding the meal just as pleasant as my strange host had promised. To my surprise Jurgen refused almost everything other than some cold meat in bread, standing close enough behind my back to decorate it with a steady drizzle of crumbs, his lasgun hanging loose across his shoulder where he could seize the grip and swing it around to fire from the hip in an instant, a party trick that had taken more than one foe by fatal surprise before now. Metheius, of course, didn't eat a thing.

'I'm glad to hear you've changed your mind,' I said, slipping a slice of the pie onto my plate. By this point he'd eaten some himself, which wasn't an infallible

indication that it was harmless of course, but it definitely seemed safer than anything I hadn't seen him touch yet. 'Although I'm still rather vague about why you wanted to kill me in the first place.' Killian waved expansively, and swallowed a mouthful of soup.

'My dear Cain, we're both men of the galaxy. There's no need to pretend ignorance, although I'm sure Lazurus would be delighted to hear how diligently you're sticking to your cover story. He sought your aid as soon as he realised you were on Periremunda, didn't he?'

'He spoke to me at the earliest possible opportunity,' I said carefully, sticking as close to the truth as I could. I was as sure as I could be that the affable lunatic across the table wasn't a psyker himself, or he would undoubtedly have reacted as violently to Jurgen's presence as Rakel usually did, so I had no fear that he'd be able to pull the information he wanted directly from my own mind. But he was undoubtedly as skilled as Amberley at reading body language, and there was no telling what biometric monitoring systems Metheius might have been enhanced with, so there was no point in pushing my luck by telling outright lies unless I really had to. Killian nodded pensively. 'He seemed rather anxious to establish the whereabouts of your friend here.'

'I thought so,' he said, clearly believing, as I'd intended, that I'd been in contact with Lazurus for some time before our first meeting in the Arbites building, which in itself was significant. Equally clearly he had no idea of Amberley's presence on Periremunda. 'He knew you'd been on Perlia, so he must have thought he could trust you with the secret.'

'I know a little more than I used to about what I found in the Valley of Daemons,' I admitted. I gave Metheius a hard look. 'And who was evidently responsible.' I redirected my gaze to Killian. 'Although I must admit I'm surprised to find you giving sanctuary to a traitor. I thought the Inquisition and the Adeptus Mechanicus were supposed to be partners in the project.'

'Part of the Inquisition,' Killian explained, spreading ackenberry preserve on a freshly toasted florn cake. He took a bite, and regarded me sombrely as he chewed and swallowed, evidently marshalling his thoughts. 'It's rather hard to explain to an outsider, but, despite what you might have been led to believe, the Inquisition is far from united in its battle against the malign forces threatening the Imperium.' This much I already knew from Amberley, of course, but I contrived to look vaguely surprised, which, as I'd intended, encouraged him to go on. 'The artefact recovered on Perlia was given into the custody of the Ordo Xenos, which was the right and proper course of action at the time, but after Metheius discovered its most striking property, clearly it became a matter for the Ordo Hereticus.'

'I imagine there was some debate over the matter,' I said, prompting him to continue, and wondering what in the name of the Emperor he was talking about.

Metheius nodded. 'There was. Several of the tech-priests agreed with me, that the Ordo Hereticus should be informed at once, although the majority favoured retaining the backing of the Ordo Xenos, unwilling to risk a confrontation over the issue.' His

voice took on a timbre of agitation quite at odds with
the measured tones I normally associated with one
of his calling. 'I could scarcely believe their stupidity!
The key to eradicating the scourge of Chaos from the
galaxy was in our hands at last, and still they pro-
crastinated! I took it upon myself to inform
Inquisitor Killian of what we'd discovered, certain
from what I knew of him that he'd make use of this
devastating weapon against the Great Enemy at the
earliest opportunity.'

'You'd met before, then, I take it,' I said, wondering
what in the warp he was babbling about. If he really
had discovered what this *shadowlight* thing did, and it
was as dangerous as it sounded, using it seemed like
a very bad idea indeed to me.

'We had,' Killian confirmed. 'Metheius had helped
me eradicate a heretical cult among the techpriests of
a minor astropathic waystation some years before,
and was aware of my commitment to using every
weapon to hand in our struggle for survival.'

'I see,' I said, the pieces beginning to fall into place
at last. 'So you tried to poke your oar in, and the
Ordo Xenos told you to go frot yourself.' That might
have seemed an incautious thing to say, but I've
found time and again that pricking someone's pride
with an unexpectedly blunt remark can often get
them to reveal more than they intended to.

'Something like that,' Killian admitted. He
shrugged. 'Unfortunately all my intervention
achieved was tipping them off to the fact that something was going on in the Valley of Daemons that the
techpriests there were too scared to pass on. No
doubt they would have dispatched an inspection

team to resolve the matter, if the orks hadn't already invaded the place.'

'I remember,' I said grimly. Even after all these years, and all the other horrors I'd seen since, the desperate struggle to survive what I'd experienced on that unhappy world still surfaced in my dreams from time to time.

'It was like a sign from the Emperor,' Killian said, the light of something not entirely sane flickering at the back of his eyes. 'I couldn't let the artefact fall into orkish hands, and with it in my possession I knew I could cleanse the galaxy in a way the purblind fainthearts of the Ordo Xenos would never dare to even imagine.'

'So you went in and took it,' I said. Killan nodded, spraying florn cake crumbs in his earnestness with almost as much abandon as my aide.

'It was the Emperor's will,' he said simply. 'I had the means, and the determination. We stormed the place before the cowards and traitors even knew we were coming, and struck them down in His holy name.'

'You used the Sisters,' I said, remembering the bolter wounds I'd seen in the bodies of the slain, and the surgical precision of the strike. Despite the calmness of my outer demeanour, my blood ran colder than a Valhallan shower at the sudden realisation. There must have been hundreds of warriors in the convent, all of them unquestioningly loyal to this maniac. If we didn't tread very carefully indeed, our chances of getting out alive were about as great as teaching an ork to tap-dance.

Killian nodded. 'The Order of the White Rose has been a loyal ally in our purges and wars of faith for

millennia,' he said. 'They did all that was asked of them in His glorious name.'

'Nothing very glorious about gunning down unarmed cogboys if you ask me,' I said, and Metheius sighed.

'It was necessary. All traces of my work had to be expunged, if we were to continue it successfully in secret.'

'In Hell's Edge,' I said, and Killian nodded, looking as absurdly pleased as if I'd just performed some minor conjuring trick.

'So you found our old bolthole. That was remark-ably resourceful of you.'

'Unfortunately,' I said, 'by the time I got there the 'nids had found it first.'

'They had,' Killian admitted. 'The Sisters were barely able to extract us in time.'

'And the miners?' I asked, already knowing the answer.

Killian shook his head regretfully.

'We only had room for Metheius and his team. Most unfortunate. We had to shoot a few of the civil-ians who tried to get their children aboard, and the rest got quite abusive.'

'How very distressing for you,' I said dryly. Emperor knows, far better men than me have fallen on the field of battle while I looked after my own miserable skin, on more occasions than I care to count, but the sheer callousness of the man raised my hackles, I don't mind admitting it. Fortunately he took my remark at face value, seeming as impervious to irony as my aide.

'"The path of duty is often a stony one",' he quoted blithely, as though that excused everything,

apparently forgetting the rest of the sentence.[1] I
nodded, pouring some fresh recaf into a delicate
porcelain cup that held barely a mouthful, grateful
for the distraction. Tempting as it was just to draw
my chainsword and swipe his misbegotten head
from his shoulders, giving into the impulse would be
unwise in the extreme. He was an inquisitor, after all,
and I would hardly have been the first man to try it.
And even if I did succeed it would certainly annoy
the sisters, who were bound to react with some
petulance, probably involving copious amounts of
incoming fire.

'How did you persuade them to let you set up there
in the first place?' I asked instead. It was becoming
more and more clear to me that Killian was one of
those megalomaniacs who are absolutely desperate
for an audience, so consumed by the delusion of
their own cleverness that they need someone else to
appreciate it, and I might as well indulge him for as
long as possible. The more I let him ramble, the
more I'd be able to tell Amberley when I caught up
with her again, and at least while we were chatting he
was unlikely to make another attempt at killing me.

'I didn't have to,' he said simply. 'Hell's Edge was a
Gavarronian colony, and the settlers were delighted
to have friends of the convent working there.'

'I see.' I nodded thoughtfully, sipping recaf, and
wishing it was in a proper sized mug. That explained
the surprising amount of devotional literature left
lying around the place. I wondered how many of the

---

1. *The full quotation, from* The Precepts of Saint Emelia, *a work
Cain displays a surprising fondness for in several passages of his memoirs, runs* "The path of duty is often a stony one, made smoother by
thought for others."

unfortunate colonists had regretted their choice of friends when the holy Sisters had left them to the 'nids. I felt my jaw begin to tighten again at the thought, and threw out another conversational fishing line. 'I take it you've found somewhere to continue your researches?'

'Most certainly.' Metheius's voice was taking on the familiar timbre of someone fanatical about his work, and eager to discuss it. I was beginning to see why he got on so well with Killian. 'The Sisters have been most accommodating.'

'I'm sure they have,' I said, trying to project an air of outward calm. If his words really meant what I thought they did, the key to the whole affair was right here, somewhere in the Convent of the White Rose. The question was, could I find my way to it? The place was vast, and the *shadowlight* could have been anywhere. Metheius nodded eagerly.

'Would you care to see for yourself?' he asked.

CHAPTER TWENTY-FIVE

'BY ALL MEANS,' I replied, as calmly as I could, unable to believe this sudden stroke of good fortune. Mindful of the civilised façade we were trying to maintain, I glanced at Killian, who was still stuffing his face. 'If you have no objection, of course.'

He shook his head, smiling, which as you'll no doubt appreciate did little to reassure me. 'None at all,' he declared, pushing his chair back from the table at last. 'Quite the reverse, in fact.' An aura of smug pomposity hung around him like Jurgen's body odour.

I rose to my feet. As I did so, the faint rumble of the orbital bombardment rolled over us again, like the first presentiment of summer rain, and I glanced at Jurgen, exchanging a brief moment of uneasy understanding. We'd begun our long and inglorious

careers together in an artillery unit, and if those years of experience were anything to go by, that barrage was a little closer than the last one had been. That, in turn, implied that a tyranid swarm large enough to attract the attention of the orbiting starships, even in spite of the sandstorms blocking their sensors, was moving in our general direction. There was no reason to believe that we were their target, though. Gavarrone was a lot higher than any of the plateaux the roving scout swarms had scaled before the main bulk of the hive fleet had arrived, so I forced my disquiet to the back of my mind and returned my attention to the immediate problem.

'Lazurus is a fool,' Killian said, leading the way across an immaculate lawn shaded by rustling trees, 'and no threat to anyone, but a man of your well-known sagacity was a challenge of an entirely different order. The moment it was revealed that you were heading the search for hidden enemies, I realised that it would only be a matter of time before you found us. After Lazurus enlisted your aid, and you knew what you were looking for, there was never even the slightest chance that the Covenant of the Blessed would simply be dismissed as another subversive group of little significance.'

'The Chaos cult,' I guessed aloud, as though I'd always been aware of the fact, and Killian nodded, leading us through a sacristy cluttered with icons, in the centre of which stood a severely chewed-up suit of power armour. Judging by the number of votive candles surrounding it this was clearly one of the order's most venerated relics, and I began to take more notice of our surroundings, realising that we

were now deep in the convent's inner sanctum, further than most visitors would ever have been allowed to go.

'Indeed,' Killian agreed. 'Crude tools at best, but easily duped, and the ideal subjects for our work.' I still had no idea what he was talking about, of course, but nodded as if I did, acutely conscious that only the knowledge he seemed to believe I possessed was keeping me alive.

'That must have gone against the grain, though,' I hazarded. Killian looked up from yet another of the *fleur de lys* motifs decorating the barrel vaulted chamber, doing something to it that I couldn't see, concealed as it was behind his torso. A section of stonework swung away from the wall, revealing a brightly lit space beyond, and the inquisitor stood aside to usher us through the gap. 'I thought it was your duty to eliminate heresy wherever you found it.'

'Blunt and to the point,' Killian said, the indulgent chuckle back in his voice. 'Great virtues I'm sure in the military mind, but in the twilight wars we inquisitors must fight, things are rarely so simple.' He looked at me narrowly, his mood switching instantly to one of intense seriousness. 'You're afraid of Chaos, aren't you? In so far as you fear anything at all, of course. Your valour is far too well known to be in any doubt.' This last he delivered in a curiously placating tone, as though he might be afraid that he'd hurt my feelings.

The palms of my hands tingled, as I considered the question. Far more hung on it than a simple matter of courage in the face of the enemy, of that I was certain. Somehow, I knew, the answer I gave would

either convince Killian he'd been right to change his mind about killing me, or persuade him I was still a potent threat, best eliminated at the earliest opportunity. Mentally cursing the pictcasts for having given him the impression that I was a danger to his deranged plans in the first place, and trying to ignore the growing suspicion that this was precisely why Amberley had drawn their attention to me to begin with,[1] I tried to formulate a safe response.

'It's not a simple matter of courage or cowardice,' I temporised, drawing on all the diplomatic skills I'd acquired over the years. 'I've faced the forces of Chaos too often, and in too many different guises, to underestimate them. If you want to equate caution with fear, then you're perfectly at liberty to do so, but I've seen too many overconfident idiots die on the battlefield to make that mistake.' I shrugged, pretending a casual confidence I didn't feel. 'Emperor knows, I've killed enough of them myself.'

I waited, ready to go for my weapons if I had to, but Killian was nodding thoughtfully, a quiet smile on his face, as though my answer was exactly what he'd been hoping to hear.

'I can see I was right about you,' he said, as the stone wall slid back into place behind us, and Metheius took the lead, almost trotting down the brightly lit corridor in his eagerness to show off his toys. The stonework here was smooth, uncluttered by icons, statues, or those blasted three-leaved weeds,

---

1. *At the time, I just thought having a celebrated hero in the vicinity would draw attention away from my own activities. The effect this had on Killian, luring him into showing his hand openly, was merely a welcome bonus. (Though not to Cain, obviously.)*

and Jurgen looked around us with his habitual expression of vague bafflement. (Which, had I not been controlling my features with the ease of the long-practiced dissembler, would undoubtedly have been reflected on my own face.)

'Where are we?' he asked, not unreasonably, and Killian gestured around us, taking in a number of closed doors, and the electrosconces between them that illuminated our path more than adequately.

'The heart of the Order of the White Rose,' he explained, no doubt delighted to have something else to pontificate about. 'Prepared as a hidden repository for their holiest reliquaries should an enemy ever be on the verge of taking the convent, in order to preserve them from desecration. Only the canoness and the palatine know of its existence, or have the necessary codes for access.' He coughed modestly. 'And the Inquisition, of course. Several representatives of the Ordo Hereticus have found these chambers useful over the millennia.'

'I can imagine,' I said. 'So why bother with Hell's Edge at all?' Killian laughed.

'The military mind at work again, I see. I could hardly bring members of the Covenant here for our research, could I?' He stood aside to usher us through a doorway, no different to my eyes than any of the others, which Metheius had entered a moment or two before. As I stepped across the threshold I was assailed by a momentary twinge of vertigo, and stumbled, until Jurgen reached out a hand to support me. The feeling subsided again, and I sub-vocalised a curse. Of all the times for my concussion to make an unexpected return, this was about the worst one

possible. Killian looked at me, with unexpected solicitude. 'It takes a lot of people like that when they first get close to it,' he said sympathetically. 'The feeling will soon pass.' He laughed. 'Or if not, you may be more blessed than either of us have bargained for.'

In truth I barely heard this last remark, let alone had the leisure to try puzzling it out, as I'd just got my first good look at the room we were standing in. It was undoubtedly Metheius's domain, at least in theory, displaying all the usual appurtenances of a techpriest's workspace: whirring and clicking cogitator banks, piles of equipment that had no discernible function that I could see, but which were clearly drawing power from somewhere, and a scattering of data-lecterns, several of which seemed to be connected to pict screens or hololiths. The usual snakepit of cabling connected it all, with the techpriests' traditional disregard for the possibility of snagging an unwary ankle, the majority of it appearing to emanate from a metal plinth, supporting something about the size of a data-slate on which I found it difficult to focus.

An icon of the Omnissiah stood on a small polished steel shrine away to one side, making me wonder just how Eglantine would react if it ever came to her attention that one small corner of her holy of holies had been given over to the clockwork Emperor of the techpriests. Rather badly, I suspected.

Although I'd never seen the place before, something about the layout of it sparked a vague sense of formless recognition, which didn't quite come into focus until Jurgen spoke.

'It's like the shrine we found on Perlia,' he said, and I nodded. There were differences, of course, but most of the equipment looked the same, apart from the absence of bolter holes. The other major difference was the peculiar object on the plinth, and I took a few steps towards it, picking my way carefully through the tangle of cables as I did so, hoping for a better look. Close to, it didn't seem all that impressive, just a smooth slab of stone about three times as high as it was wide, so black that the light from the electrosconces on the walls seemed to fall gently into it.

'Careful,' Metheius said, and I became aware that I'd got a lot closer to the thing than I'd intended. 'There's a field of warp energy around it.' He glanced at his instruments, sounding puzzled for a moment. 'That's odd, it seems to be diminishing. No, it's right back to its usual level.' He thumped the lectern, and shrugged, while I noticed Jurgen taking a step backwards out of the corner of my eye as I moved cautiously away. 'Loose connection somewhere, probably. That's the trouble with these temporary systems.'

'Temporary?' I asked, and Killian nodded.

'Periremunda's no longer suitable for our purposes. We need a reasonably sized population, with an organised Chaos cult we can infiltrate and control, to provide us with a steady supply of experimental subjects. How else are we going to find latent psykers in sufficient quantities?'

I felt a chill running down my spine as he spoke, finally getting an inkling of what this was all about. I fought to keep an expression of dumbstruck horror

from my face. If I was right, and this maniac guessed my true feelings about his monstrous design, I'd be dead in a second, or worse. Instead I nodded thoughtfully.

'Quite. The 'nids have made quite a dent in them here.' I nodded at Metheius, hoping that by addressing my next remark to him I'd be able to keep Killian from reading me too easily. 'You don't seem to be having much luck with aliens, all in all. First the orks on Perlia, and now this.'

'Oh, quite the contrary,' Metheius said happily. 'It was the arrival of the orks that put us on the right track at last. The artefact was completely inert until the burst of warp energy that accompanied the arrival of their space hulk activated it.' I nodded, remembering how the dormant necron portal on Simia Orichalcae had been triggered by a similar phenomenon. 'Unfortunately they were rather too numerous to be easily discouraged.'

'I'd noticed,' I said. In spite of myself I looked at the object that just had to be the *shadowlight* again, the featureless black slab exerting a horrid fascination. 'Did you ever find out what it was supposed to do?'

'Its actual function?' Metheius shook his head. 'That still eludes us, but it's the side effect, so to speak, that we're most interested in, obviously.'

'Obviously,' I echoed, hoping that the side effect in question wasn't the one I'd just deduced. 'The implications of that alone are quite staggering.'

Killian nodded eagerly, an unhealthy enthusiasm burning behind his eyes again, renewing my already considerable doubts about his sanity. 'More than just staggering,' he said. 'Galaxy shaking! Think about it,

Cain, think of the possibilities! If we can reliably enhance the latent psychic powers of hundreds, perhaps thousands, of individuals on every world in the Imperium, what a weapon that would give us against the hordes of Chaos! We could crush them with their own weapons, cleanse the Eye of Terror itself of their foul taint! And once the Ruinous Powers lie prostrate and broken before the Golden Throne, we can sweep the xenos breeds from the stars, until the galaxy belongs to its rightful masters alone: pure, unsullied humankind!'

'It's a heady vision,' I said carefully, certain that he was at least as barmy as the Chaos worshippers he was supposed to hunt down. 'But there are rather a lot of worlds in the Imperium, and you've only got one of those rocks.'

'At the moment, yes.' The madman nodded, as though I'd just scored a reasonable debating point. 'That's why Metheius's research is so vital, you see. If he can determine the precise nature and frequency of the warp energy that triggers the transformation from latent to true psyker, we can build devices of our own to do the same thing.'

'We also have to refine the technique,' Metheius added, a little diffidently. 'At the moment it only works on a very small percentage of the latents exposed to it. The rest find it as fatal to the touch as an ordinary untainted human.'

'I see.' I nodded again. 'Must be rather difficult to find volunteers, then.'

'That's why we subverted the Covenant of the Blessed,' Methius explained. 'They're insane enough to take the risk, and the ones who survive, and

develop useable talents, become tools of the
Emperor without even realising who it is they now
serve.'

'Rather a delicious irony, don't you think?' Killian
was getting carried away again. 'The foot soldiers of
the enemy, duped into defending the very Imperium
they sought to destroy.'

'I can see why you find it so amusing,' I said, 'and
why you're so keen to carry on the good work.' I used
the phrase in its colloquial sense, of course, with a
fair amount of sarcasm if I'm honest, but Killian
pounced on it eagerly.

'Then you do understand!' He glanced at Metheius.
'What did I tell you? It was worth the risk of bringing
him here!'

As you'll no doubt appreciate, astonishment barely
begins to express how I felt at that moment. Feeling
as though I was inching my way along a narrow ledge
above a bottomless abyss of insanity, I nodded
slowly.

'You're hoping I can take a message to Lazurus for
you. Get him to back off.'

'Precisely!' Killian said. 'For our work to succeed,
we must be free of outside interference. Our shuttle
will be leaving within the hour, and if you were to
report back that we'd been killed, along with everyone else on the plateau, no one could possibly doubt
it, not the word of a man of your reputation.' A solid
knot of ice seemed to gather itself in the pit of my
stomach, and I glanced uneasily at Jurgen.

'I'm not entirely sure I follow,' I said, the memory
of the massacre in the Valley of Daemons rising up to
haunt me again. Killing everyone in a remote

Mechanicus shrine was one thing, but there must have been thousands of people on Gavarrone, and hundreds of Sororitas warriors in this convent alone. Quite how Killian proposed to eliminate them all unaided was beyond me. An expression of deranged cunning flitted across his face.

'The Sisters here are loyal, there's no doubt about that, but too many of them know of our presence. So I've taken certain precautions.' Beckoning to me to follow he left the laboratory, and I complied, Jurgen at my heels as always. Metheius remained, making whatever preparations seemed necessary for their imminent departure. 'If you refuse to help us, which I'm bound to say would hardly surprise me, I'm sorry to say that they'll suffice to ensure your silence too.'

'What precautions?' I asked, a little breathlessly, as I finally caught up with him. Killian paused next to another of the doors lining the corridor.

'This,' he said simply, swinging it open. I reeled back, reaching for my chainsword by reflex, and Jurgen raised his lasgun, emptying the power pack over my shoulder on full auto. The tyranid lictor inside the chamber reeled back, shrieking, and crashed to the floor, with an impact that shook dust from the crevices in the stonework. I stepped forward cautiously, keeping it covered with my laspistol as Jurgen reloaded, only then noticing that it had already been grievously wounded, and had been firmly secured to the wall by chains that looked strong enough to have held a dreadnought in check.

'Oh, bravo.' Killian clapped his hands, looking at Jurgen with something approaching interest for a moment, before returning his attention to me. 'I can

see why you insisted on keeping this fellow around. There's obviously far more to him than meets the eye.'

'What the hell's this thing doing here?' I asked, incredulous, too startled to carry on pretending we were all reasonable people. Killian looked at me blankly, as though that were obvious.

'Attracting the swarm,' he said. 'These creatures exude pheromones that–'

'I know what it is!' I practically shouted. I activated my comm-bead. 'Amberley! This lunatic's got a pet lictor stashed in the catacombs! The whole bloody swarm's on its way!'

'Traitor!' Killian screamed, almost drowning out Amberley's startled acknowledgement, drawing a plasma pistol from beneath his tabard. I already had my gun in my hand, though, and squeezed the trigger before he could bring it to bear. Instead of falling, as I'd expected, however, he suddenly vanished, with a *crack!* of imploding air.

'Frak!' I said angrily, recognising the work of a displacer field. Amberley had used one on Gravalax, and I knew the little teleportation device couldn't have taken him far. Time we got out of here, before he crawled out of whichever niche the displacer had dumped him in, and caught up with us again. Somehow I doubted that he'd still want to use me as a messenger boy.

'Ciaphas! What's happening?' Amberley asked, her voice sounding unexpectedly concerned. I filled her in as best I could while sprinting for the entrance to this bizarre hidden labyrinth, blessing the innate sense of direction that generally allowed me to

remain orientated in underground environments.[1] 'And find Eglantine,' I concluded. 'That wretched woman's the only one apart from Killian who knows how to get down here.'

'That wretched woman is already aware of the situation,' the canoness informed me coldly, apparently having overheard the entire exchange. 'Inquisitor Vail revealed her identity to Sister Caritas the moment she was out of earshot of Killian, demanded a meeting, and has convinced me of his true nature.'

'Well that was a neat trick,' I said, wondering just how she'd managed that,[2] but I had little time to speculate. A burst of light in the corridor ahead of us dazzled my eyes, and a bolt of plasma burst against the stonework, vaporising a chunk of it about the size of my head. By the worst piece of bad luck imaginable, the displacer field had dropped Killian right between us and safety.

---

1. *A talent he displayed on many occasions, and which he attributed to his upbringing on a hive world.*

2. *An Inquisitorial mandate tends to impress people; probably something to do with all those seals.*

CHAPTER TWENTY-SIX

'BACK!' I SHOUTED to Jurgen, aiming a fusillade of las-bolts in the general direction of the renegade inquisitor, which forced him to duck into the recess by one of the doorways.[1] With precious little cover to be had in the stark stone corridor I began to retreat towards the nearest cross passage, from which my aide was now spitting some covering fire of his own, having reached this welcome sanctuary a few seconds before. I smiled ruefully as I joined him. 'Never thought I'd miss those hideous statues,' I said, and Jurgen frowned in confusion.

'Which ones were they?' he asked.

'Never mind,' I told him, as another plasma bolt burst close enough for the heat of it to sear our faces. 'Back to

---

1. *Displacer fields are never completely reliable, so it's always advisable to present the lowest possible target profile even if you're carrying an active one.*

the laboratory. We have to get that *shadowlight* thing before Metheius manages to escape with it again.' The thought of something like that loose in the galaxy was enough to give me the howling gribblies, and I'd rather take on an unarmed techpriest than a psychotic inquisitor in any case. With a bit of luck we'd be able to barricade ourselves in there just long enough for Amberley to finish him off for us, and emerge in time to take the credit for recovering the all-important artefact.

'Might be a bit tricky, sir,' Jurgen pointed out. 'He's got us pinned down nicely. If we try to pull back he'll toast us for sure before we reached the next junction.' A faint hint of reproach entered his voice. 'If I had my melta I could take him out easily from here.'

'Not while he's still got the displacer,' I pointed out. With those words a possible strategy suggested itself, and I steadied my aim, bracing my laspistol across my folded arm. 'Run for it. Make a lot of noise.'

'Sir?' Jurgen looked even more baffled than usual, but as always he followed my orders to the letter, sprinting down the cross corridor we'd taken refuge in. The sound of his bootsoles echoed back in the confined space, and, as I'd expected, Killian took the bait. Clearly believing we'd both fled, he appeared a moment later in the mouth of the corridor we'd hidden in, an expression of murderous malice on his face.

'Enjoy your trip,' I told him, planting a lasbolt squarely in the middle of his chest. He just had time to look surprised before he vanished again, with another muted thunderclap of imploding air. There was no telling how far he might have gone this time,

of course, so I hurried after Jurgen as quickly as I could, catching up with him just as he reached the laboratory.

'That was quick…' Metheius began, before glancing in our direction and apparently beginning to realise that something had gone seriously wrong. 'What's happening? Where's the inquisitor?'

'Emperor alone knows,' I said, aiming my laspistol squarely at his head. He was probably mostly augmetic there, of course, so it might not do all that much damage if I fired at him, but a shot or two would certainly spoil his day. 'Step away from the *shadowlight* and keep your hands where I can see them. The mechadendrites too.'

'I'll get the stone thing,' Jurgen said, slinging his lasgun and reaching out to grab it with a grubby hand.

Metheius watched with an air of smug vindictiveness as his nail-bitten fingers closed around it, which rapidly changed to one of surprise and alarm.

'You've deactivated it!' His head swung round to examine his instruments, his voice quivering with shock. 'That shouldn't be possible!' He turned back towards me. 'What have you done?'

'Perhaps Lazurus isn't quite the fool you take him for,' I said, reaching into the pocket of my greatcoat and allowing the bulge of the perfectly innocuous data-slate I was carrying there to become visible for a moment. Clearly believing that I'd come equipped with some piece of techno-sorcery provided by his former associate (which of course was precisely what I'd intended, as Jurgen's peculiar abilities were something neither of us wanted to draw any further

attention to), the renegade techpriest edged towards me, his curiosity evidently stronger than his fear of getting shot.

'He's found some way of dampening the warp field?' Methius's voice was both avid and incredulous. 'You must let me see. This could open up a whole new line of enquiry.'

'Which we'll discuss as soon we're aboard the starship, and on our way out of the system,' Killian cut in, appearing at the door, his plasma weapon levelled. He glared at me, the stubby barrel pointed right at the centre of my chest. 'Bring it out slowly, and hand it to Metheius. You can hardly expect me to miss at this range.'

'Probably not,' I said, projecting as much calm assurance as I could, which I'm sure you'll appreciate wasn't all that easy under the circumstances. Luckily Killian had apparently bought into my fictitious reputation in a big way, which meant that his own expectation of being unable to intimidate me would help to maintain the façade. 'But those things make rather a mess. You'll probably vaporise the nullifier along with my torso.' I shrugged, keeping my laspistol pointed at the centre of Metheius's forehead, with all the steadiness my augmetic fingers could impart. 'And you must have killed enough people by now to know my finger will tighten on the trigger by reflex before I fall. If you shoot me, you'll be killing Methius too.' I risked a quick glance at Jurgen, but he still had the *shadowlight* in his right hand, and couldn't reach for his lasgun.

Killian nodded thoughtfully, as though accepting the inevitable. 'I can always get another techpriest,' he

said slowly, 'but there's only one psychic enhancer.' His finger began to tighten on the trigger, and I've faced enough madmen in my time to know he wasn't bluffing. An instant before he could fire, I lowered my arm.

'All right,' I said, holstering my weapon. He could still have shot me, of course, out of sheer vindictiveness, but if I'd read my man right he wouldn't, not for a minute or two anyway. His kind always likes to gloat first, especially if they think they've beaten you. I pulled the data-slate out of my pocket, and held it out towards him. 'You win. Here, take it.'

'I'm not that big a fool,' Killian told me. 'Hand it to Metheius. I'm sure you have some idea of jumping me the moment I lower the gun.' Well of course I've got far more sense than to start wrestling a lunatic for something that can quite easily barbeque us both if it goes off, but it never hurts to keep an enemy off balance, so I simply shrugged.

'Can't blame a man for trying,' I said. I handed the slate, in its anonymous military field casing, to the techpriest, who started fumbling with the catch, no doubt eager to see what the miraculous device his rival had apparently created looked like. 'You just press it to open the case,' I added helpfully.

Metheius froze, looking at the dull green box in his hand as if it had suddenly started ticking. 'Of course, it'll be booby-trapped,' he said, glaring at me as if I'd almost succeeded in tricking him, which was exactly what I'd been hoping for, of course. If he'd realised what the box actually contained, things would have got very unpleasant. 'Genetically coded to you, I suppose?'

'You're the expert,' I told him, letting his paranoia do the work for me, and trying not to let my relief at the sight of him stowing the thing in the recesses of his robe without any further attempt to examine it show on my face. 'Now I suppose you expect us to just hand the *shadowlight* over?' I asked Killian.

The deranged inquisitor shook his head. 'No, I expect to kill you both and take it from your corpses,' he replied, clearly relishing the prospect.

Wondering just how much longer Amberley was going to be, I shook my head pityingly. 'Well, if you're sure it can take a plasma discharge at point blank range, go right ahead,' I replied casually, keeping my hand as close as I dared to the butt of my laspistol. 'Of course, if you shoot Jurgen first, I'll have the chance to see if the nullifier works on your displacement field too. You must be standing well within its radius of effect.' I glanced at my aide. 'On the other hand, if you shoot me first, he'll have time to drop the rock and open up with his lasgun.' One of the chief advantages of a completely unmerited reputation for unwavering integrity, I've often found, is that the more outrageous the lie, the more likely it is to be believed, and Killian, don't forget, was away with the cherubs to begin with. An element of doubt began to creep into his belligerent expression.

'You.' He switched his gaze to Jurgen, but kept the plasma pistol pointing unwaveringly at my chest. 'Hand the artefact to Methius, and place your gun on the floor, slowly. If I see even a hint of treachery, I'll vaporise the commissar.' Jurgen, as always, glanced at me for confirmation, and I nodded.

'Do as he says,' I said levelly. 'We can always recover it later.'

Killian laughed. 'There won't be a later,' he reminded me. 'The tyranids are going to pick this plateau clean, and you along with it.' That had hardly escaped my notice, of course, but as usual in that sort of situation I'd found it best to concentrate on the immediate problem, on the entirely reasonable grounds that if I didn't I'd be comfortably dead by the time the next one rolled along.

'Then you'd better get moving,' I suggested, as Metheius reached out a tentative mechadendrite to take the *shadowlight* from Jurgen. As the mysterious artefact left his fingers my aide un-slung his lasgun with a truculent expression, clearly sorely tempted to use it, but, as always, he followed my orders to the letter, allowing the weapon to fall to the floor. Metheius scooped it up with his other mechanical tentacle, and trotted over to join Killian, looking absurdly pleased with himself. 'In my experience the 'nids aren't all that likely to stick to someone else's timetable.'

'Drop your weapons too,' Killian ordered, returning his attention to me. I unbuckled my weapon belt, feeling oddly disconcerted as the familiar weight fell away, and stepped out of the loop of leather as my pistol and chainsword clattered to the flagstones at my feet. Metheius hesitated for a moment, then, as I'd hardly dared to hope, handed the *shadowlight* to Killian in order to pluck my weapons from the floor without approaching me too closely.

'Thank you.' The deranged inquisitor tucked the small slab of stone under his free arm, and took a

step towards the doorway. 'I don't suppose we'll be meeting again.'

'I sincerely hope not,' I told him, hearing the clatter of bootsoles in the corridor outside at last. Before Killian even realised reinforcements had arrived Amberley was inside the room, her entourage at her heels, nodding a casual greeting to me while Pelton, Simeon and Zemelda aimed their lasguns at him. Jurgen strode forwards at once with a furious expression, to pluck his lasgun and my weapon belt from the mechadendrites of the stunned-looking techpriest.

'Ernst Stavros Killian,' Amberley said loudly and clearly, holding up her hand to display the Inquisitorial electoo that flashed into visibility as she spoke. 'You have been declared *Excommunicate Diabolus* by the Consilium Ravus of the triune ordos, and by their authority are ordered to surrender your person to answer to the charges of treason and heresy there laid against you.' She pulled a roll of parchment that would have choked a grox from inside her greatcoat, and brandished it in his general direction.

'Just what I might have expected from a pusillanimous puritan,' Killian sneered. 'Precisely the sort of tunnel-visioned weakling the Consilium would choose to send after me.'

'A tunnel-visioned weakling with rather more guns than you've got,' Amberley pointed out cheerfully, as I buckled my weapon belt and drew my laspistol to emphasise the point. Looking uncommonly pleased with himself Jurgen joined the ring of lasguns pointing at the cornered inquisitor, apparently unaware of the way Zemelda and Pelton widened the cordon a

little as he stepped up to reinforce it. 'And my Inquisitorial mandate does allow me the discretionary power of summary execution if you refuse to co-operate.'

'Then you leave me with no other option,' Killian said resignedly, lowering his plasma pistol at last. I barely had time for a sigh of relief before he pulled the trigger, blowing a hole through the floor at his feet, and sending us all reeling with the bright flash of combustion.

'Down there!' Amberley shouted, as I blinked my eyes clear of the dancing after-images. Without hesitation she leapt through the hole after Killian, Pelton and Simeon following almost at once.

I held out a hand to forestall Zemelda as she teetered on the brink. 'Wait,' I said. I pointed to Metheius, who was still staggering, disorientated and noticeably singed from his proximity to the detonation, but who would undoubtedly recover soon enough thanks to his augmetic components. 'Detain him if you can, shoot him if you can't. Jurgen, with me.'

Reasoning from the lack of any gunfire that Amberley and her friends hadn't run into anything inimical in the chamber below, which appeared to be identical in size and shape to this one from what I could see of it, though completely empty, I leapt through the hole, which proved to be a trapdoor of noticeably thinner stone than that forming the rest of the floor. I landed with a jolt that I absorbed instinctively, reflexes honed on the assault courses of the schola progenium having been augmented by years of experience on the battlefield, rolling clear just in time to avoid Jurgen landing

on top of me. He glanced around, levelling his lasgun, peering into the shadowed gloom that surrounded us. It seemed Killian hadn't bothered kindling the luminators down here, presumably because he didn't think he'd need to, but I trusted my old hiver's instincts in a place like this, and listened carefully, disentangling the sound of running feet from the echoes overlapping them with little difficulty.

'Which way, sir?' Jurgen asked, just as the distant patter of footsteps was drowned out by an agonised scream that seemed to go on forever, before finally trailing away into reverberating silence.

I pointed towards the source. 'That way, at a guess,' I said, leading the way at a rapid trot. As I'd surmised, the layout of the corridors here was identical to that of the floor above, and my knack of orientation in an environment like this didn't let me down. Within moments we'd caught up with Amberley and the others, who were staring at what was left of Killian in the light of the portable luminators they'd evidently had tucked away somewhere in their Guard-issue equipment pouches.

'What happened?' Pelton asked, his face almost as pale as a genuine Valhallan's. 'He was running ahead of us, and then he just stopped. It was like his whole body was twisting.' He broke off, unable or unwilling to continue, but he really had no need to. Killian's corpse was as deformed as the vilest of mutants, bone and muscle apparently having flowed like melting candle wax, until his soul had been wrenched from his body.

'It was the *shadowlight*,' I said, addressing Amberley directly, my words tumbling over one another in my

desperate haste to convey the danger the thing represented. 'It's marinated in warp energy. They thought we'd deactivated it somehow because they saw us carrying it, but as soon as Killian got out of range of whatever Jurgen does to psychic phenomena, he became exposed to the full power of the thing.'

'I see.' Amberley nodded, understanding at once. 'We'll need proper shielding to carry it safely.'

'Metheius was getting ready to pack it up for transit,' I said. 'There must be something in the laboratory that'll do the job.'

'Then we'd better get back there,' Amberley said. She gestured towards the sinister black stone. 'Jurgen, if you wouldn't mind carrying it for me?'

'Of course not, miss.' My aide smiled broadly, and trotted off to retrieve the cursed artefact. I was just beginning to heave a heartfelt sigh of relief, when Eglantine's voice crackled in my comm-bead.

'Inquisitor Vail,' she said. 'The tyranids are attacking.'

CHAPTER TWENTY-SEVEN

THE CANONESS WAS waiting for us in the chamber we'd
entered the labyrinth by, standing next to the mangled power armour on its display pedestal,
surrounded by a bodyguard of Celestians. The Sister
Superior in charge of them looked vaguely familiar,
but it was only when she spoke to me that I recognised her as the leader of the little troop that had got
hacked to pieces on Aceralbaterra, and whose gung-
ho imbecility had almost cost us the plateau. I
returned her greeting cordially enough, however, as
for some reason she seemed pleased to see me, and
from what I could gather of the tactical situation
through my comm-bead I'd need every well-disposed
person in power armour I could find between me
and the 'nids if I was going to get out of here in one
piece.

'I owe you a great debt, commissar,' she told me, looking oddly embarrassed. 'You recalled me to my duty, when I was so carried away by vainglorious zeal I would have neglected it.'

'Well, that's my job,' I said modestly, but the woman just nodded seriously, taking the words at face value.

'The Emperor sent you, of that I've no doubt. To have left his temple undefended while it was beset with xeno-spawned filth…' She sighed. 'It would have been a grave thing indeed to have had to confess before the Golden Throne.'

'Well, let's hope you don't have to check in there for a long time to come,' I said.

Eglantine, who until now had been pointedly ignoring me, glanced up from a huddled conversation with Amberley, her expression grave. 'None of us expect to survive this battle,' she said, as calmly as if she'd simply been commenting on the weather. 'Nor do we deserve to. Our order has been the instrument of the vilest blasphemy. All we can do is seek to atone for that sin, and pray to the Emperor that our deeds will prove worthy of his forgiveness.'

'Killian lied to a lot of people,' I told her, wondering for a moment if the late and unlamented inquisitor's insanity had been somehow contagious. 'You followed his orders in good faith.'

'That merely compounds our guilt,' Eglantine said heavily. 'We were so sure of our path, and so proud of doing His will, that we never thought to pray for the divine guidance that would have opened our eyes and hearts to the truth. Our arrogance was the seed of our own destruction.' All of which sounded like the kind of sermon that was guaranteed to bore me into a

stupor whenever we were herded into the chapel at
the schola, and which has kept me out of temples
ever since, except for those occasions on which
protocol and my position within the Commissariat
have combined to make my presence at some service
or other unavoidable.

There was clearly no reasoning with her, so I wasn't
going to waste any more breath trying. Instead I simply nodded. 'The Emperor protects,' I said, falling
back on the familiar infantryman's platitude, and the
canoness nodded too, apparently taking heart from
the well-worn formula.

'He'll need to,' Amberley interjected grimly.

Recalled to the matter at hand, Eglantine nodded.
'The swarm is already overrunning the outer walls,'
she said. 'Sister Bonica and her Celestians will escort
you back to your shuttle. After that, all our fates are in
the hands of Him on Earth.' She glanced at the plain
black carrying case hanging from Jurgen's left hand,
his right hefting his lasgun, which he'd slung from his
shoulder so that he could shoot it from the hip with
some semblance of accuracy. 'Is that the abomination
that so profaned our citadel?'

'It is,' Amberley confirmed.

Eglantine sighed. 'It seems a very small thing to
have done so much harm.'

'Killian did the harm,' I said, unable to resist glaring
at Metheius, who was tagging along as good as gold,
assisted by the occasional prod from the barrel of
Zemelda's lasgun. 'With a little help. The important
thing now is to undo it.'

'Quite.' The canoness returned her attention to
Amberley. 'As soon as you're airborne we'll regroup,

and try to keep the swarm away from the town. We'll delay it as long as we can.'

'Emperor willing, that should be enough,' Amberley said.

'I pray so.' Eglantine began to lead the way back through the wide corridors we'd traversed no more than an hour or so before, exchanging brisk messages with her subordinates, who were apparently fighting on several fronts. I listened in on my commbead as best I could, but little of what I heard made sense to me. I was unfamiliar with the layout of the convent, and the sisters used their own protocols and battle language. I was able to gather enough to infer that things weren't going at all well, though.

After a while we deviated from the route I remembered, bypassing Killian's guest quarters, and I began to see the first signs of damage: flamer burns on the frescoes, bolter holes in the statues and hangings, and the occasional body, left where it had fallen as the tide of battle ebbed and flowed. The deep gashes left in the ceramite of the first shredded Sister we chanced upon looked uncomfortably familiar to me, and I wasn't surprised to find the remains of several genestealers piled up at the next junction. It seemed the hive mind was sticking to its traditional tactics, infiltrating scout organisms ahead of the bulk of the swarm to disrupt the defences it faced, and I gripped my laspistol and chainsword a little tighter as we jogged along, surrounded by the comforting bulk of silver and black power armour.

'That way,' Eglantine said at last, pointing down a cross corridor we'd just come to. She turned and

faced the Celestian sister, making the sign of the aquila. 'Emperor be with you, Bonica.'

'And with you,' Bonica responded, 'until we meet again before the Golden Throne.' My last sight of Eglantine was a blur of motion, sprinting with all the speed her armour-enhanced muscles were capable of towards the distant tumult of battle, and the briefly glimpsed mayhem in the courtyard beyond her hurrying form. The wide corridor we stood in led to what, a short while before, had been an elegant formal garden, its wide lawns and flowering borders crushed to mud beneath a heaving sea of chitin, mandible, and doggedly resisting Sororitas, falling back slowly as that irresistible tidal wave of malign bio-forms broke against the shore of their bolter fire and expertly wielded sarissae.[1]

'Pontius,' Amberley voxed. 'We're going to need pickup fast.'

'I'm on it, ma'am,' our pilot's voice reassured us, calm as always, and I began to feel a faint flare of hope. 'There's a courtyard about six hundred metres from your present position the 'nids haven't reached yet. Big mosaic of one of the saints on the wall.'

'I know it,' Bonica assured him, and we began double-timing it away from the battle behind us, although several of the sisters looked distinctly disappointed not to be following their canoness into the jaws of death (quite literally in this case, probably).

'Good.' Amberley voxed our pilot again. 'Keep scanning for us, in case we have to deviate.' She

---

1. *A form of bayonet, much favoured by the Adepta Sororitas.*

hurdled another fallen Battle Sister, who seemed to be missing most of her head. 'There are signs of infiltration in the building already.'

'I've got you on auspex,' Pontius assured her, which sounded good to me.

We were passing through another atrium when the 'stealers jumped us, a whole pack of them flowing silently out of the shadows where statues stood in niches and ornately gilded doorways led off to silent chapels. That alone would have been intimidating enough, but towering over them all was the baleful silhouette of a brood lord, its scything talons and rending claws extended as it bounded forward at the head of its grotesquely twisted progeny.

'Run,' Bonica snapped, as the Sisters opened up with their bolters, scything down the front rank as they closed. I didn't need urging twice, breaking into a sprint for the only clear exit I could see, Jurgen at my heels. 'We'll hold them here.'

Not for long, I thought, there were too many of them, and Amberley evidently shared my opinion, running just as hard as I was for the open door and the rectangle of blue sky beyond. Zemelda hesitated, cracking off a shot at the onrushing horde, and Pelton dropped back to seize her arm, dragging her into motion again. While her attention was momentarily distracted Metheius made a break for it, sprinting away at quite an astonishing turn of speed. I assume he must have had augmetic legs, as he even managed to overtake me, which is something not easily done when I'm fleeing for my life.

'*In nomine Imperator!*' Bonica yelled, brandishing her chainsword and leaping forward to meet the

patriarch head-on. To my astonishment she sent it reeling back wounded before the thing rallied and knocked her sideways with a vicious swipe that laid her armour open. Before it could finish her off another of the Sisters hosed it down with a flamer, which cut a swathe through its smaller brethren and made it flinch away from its intended victim.

I never got to see the rest of the one-sided encounter, because at last I was through the doorway, into the courtyard with the mosaic that Pontius had spotted from the air, and Emperor be praised, there was our Aquila. It hovered gently a few metres above the ground, and began to settle, the screaming of its engines drowning out the shrieks of the Celestians dying messily behind us. So intent was I on the prospect of rescue held out by the slowly descending ramp that I never even noticed the new threat facing us, until a gargoyle swooped down from nowhere to pluck Metheius from the ground.

The techpriest rose slowly, twisting desperately in the thing's grasp, until it ripped his head from his shoulders, spattering the flagstones beneath them both with blood and lubricant. Leaving the body to fall across a delicately filigreed bench plastered with enough wrought iron *fleur de lys* to be hideously uncomfortable for anyone unfortunate enough to sit on it, the winged obscenity wheeled around in search of fresh prey, and to my horror I was able to discern a whole flock of the vile things gliding in over the wall towards us.

Had they been carrying fleshborers, I've no doubt that it would all have been over in seconds, but these, it seemed, had been bred for close combat, relying

on talon and jaw to dispatch their enemies. I took
out the one that had done for Methius with a single
shot from my laspistol, and Amberley opened up
with her lasgun, potting another as it swooped down
towards us shrieking like a daemon.

'Pelton! Get Jurgen aboard!' she ordered, the full
authority of her Inquisitorial rank in the tone of her
voice. 'We'll cover you.' My aide turned towards me
nevertheless, and I nodded confirmation.

'We'll be right behind you,' I assured him, with as
much conviction as I could muster. Arguing with
Amberley was pointless at the best of times, and under
the circumstances would be downright suicidal. I just
had to trust that she knew what she was doing, and
that once the artefact was safe we'd be able to follow
it. Guns blazing, Jurgen, Pelton and Zemelda forged
their way towards the ramp, bringing down at least a
dozen of the airborne horrors as they did so, while
Amberley, Simeon and I must have accounted for a
score or more of the remainder between us.[1]

The former commissar was darting rapidly back and
forth, tracking targets and dispatching them with the
speed and efficiency of a Hydra battery, and I hardly
needed to glimpse the distended veins in his face and
hands to realise he was benefiting from a massive dose
of 'slaught. Reflexes and aggression boosted far
beyond what the human frame was normally capable
of, he resembled nothing so much as a Khornate
berserker, an impression enhanced as the power pack
of his lasgun finally ran dry.

---

1. *Cain may be exaggerating here, but my own recollections of that*
engagement are too fragmentary to be sure.

Rather than snapping a fresh one into place, as any trained soldier ought to have done, he simply gave a howl of frustrated rage and began using the weapon as a club, battering one of the gargoyles to the ground as it swooped towards his head, its talons extended. Inevitably, so intent was he on reducing the creature to bloody mush, he completely forgot the presence of all the others. Apparently maddened by the grisly fate of their compatriot[1] the others mobbed him, tearing him into scraps of flesh and bone in a single whirling cloud of slashing death.

'Come on!' Whatever she may have felt about the gruesome death of her henchman Amberley was certainly pragmatic enough to take advantage of the distraction it afforded. While the flock's attention was diverted we sprinted for the boarding ramp, not even bothering to shoot anything on the way.

'Genestealers, closing fast,' Pelton called, and he and Jurgen began firing their lasguns from the top of the ramp, my aide having finally divested himself of the *shadowlight* in its anonymous carrying case. (In theory, I suppose, any of us could have taken the thing now that it was properly insulated, but no one seemed particularly keen to try.) After a moment Zemelda joined in too, her face grimmer than I'd ever seen it. I suspected her game of inquisitors and heretics had finally stopped being fun.

I risked a glance behind us, and wished I hadn't. The 'stealer swarm was boiling out of the building we'd left mere moments before, having apparently run out of Sororitas to kill, and was closing fast, although the

---

1. Or, rather more plausibly, the hive mind singled him out as the greatest threat among us.

brood lord at least seemed to have been taken out of the fight. On the downside, though, there wasn't enough left of Simeon to keep the surviving gargoyles interested, and they were beginning to take to the air again, rising with great slow beats of their leathery wings. Galvanised by a fresh shot of adrenaline I picked up my pace towards the belly of the Aquila, and the safe haven it offered, trying to shake off the chill certainty that I wasn't going to make it.

'No problem,' Pontius said casually, opening up with the nose-mounted lascannons at last, and the onrushing horde of 'stealers scattered in confusion, ragged holes blasted through their ranks, those behind stumbling over the smouldering corpses of their less fortunate brood mates. One of the gargoyles was clipped by the barrage of heavy weapons fire too and fell heavily, its left wing shredded, to thrash around in the viscid puddle of Simeon's mortal remains, although the others were sufficiently agile to avoid the deadly beams.

Fleeting as the respite had been, it was enough. My boot soles rang on the steel plating of the ramp at last, and the Aquila began rising from the ground, while everyone except Amberley wasted lasbolts in a final gesture of farewell. She was talking urgently to someone on her comm-bead, and after a moment of retuning I was able to catch the final fragments of conversation.

'Standing by,' an unfamiliar voice said, and then hesitated. 'Can you confirm those co-ordinates?'

'Confirmed,' Amberley snapped, in the tone that intimidated planetary governors, and returned her attention to the battlefield below.

Looking down through the gap around the rapidly closing ramp, I felt the breath catch in my throat. The entire convent was overrun by a scuttling tide of chitin, walls and buildings coated by a moving slick of bioengineered killing machines, and there seemed no end to them. Most terrifying of all, as we banked away I could see that the vast bulk of the swarm was still making its way up the side of the plateau, a heaving mass of armour, claw and talon, which stretched down into the depths farther than the eye could see.

'The sisters will never be able to hold them,' I said grimly, and Amberley shook her head.

'No, they won't,' she agreed, as the closing ramp thudded into place, cutting us off from the grisly sight. Her expression grave, she led the way back to the passenger compartment. I followed, my eyes drawn irresistibly to the panorama of destruction beyond the viewports, but my nose soon informed me that I'd been joined by Jurgen, who placed the case containing the *shadowlight* on the table.

To my surprise, it seemed, a few of the Sororitas still survived, small pockets of resistance within the convent flaring briefly before being overrun and swamped, while a pitiful handful were attempting to follow Eglantine's battle plan, forming up alongside the Rhinos that had borne them to temporary safety in a last-ditch attempt to stem the tide. My eyes were drawn briefly to a convoy of fast-moving dots approaching from the direction of the town, which proved, as our widening spiral took us over them, to be a dozen trucks packed with PDF troopers from the garrison we'd intended to visit that morning, apparently as intent as ever on following the Sisters' lead.

They'd be far too late to reinforce them, though, of that I had no doubt.

I was right. As we passed over the remains of the convent for the last time the few remaining Battle Sisters were finally overwhelmed, falling to the jaws and talons of the tyranids, holding the last scraps of ground they could to the very end. No doubt the PDF, and Emperor alone knew how many other innocent bystanders, were about to share their fate.

'On my mark,' Amberley said calmly, and the voice she'd been speaking to before crackled confidently in my comm-bead.

'Still standing by, inquisitor. You appear to be clear.'

Amberley shrugged. 'Then fire,' she said simply. I tensed, wondering what new danger she'd perceived, and waited for Pontius to trigger the lascannons again, but for several seconds nothing seemed to happen.

Suddenly, without warning, ravening shafts of energy blasted down from the sky above our heads, slamming into the ground just ahead of the tyranid advance. A plume of vaporised rock and chitin rose into the air, and our sturdy little shuttle shuddered as the shockwaves from the disrupted atmosphere battered against it. Jurgen swallowed hard.

'They've missed!' I said, in stunned disappointment, and indeed for a moment or two it seemed that the lance batteries of the starships in orbit had done just that, merely clipping the leading edge of the swarm instead of blasting straight into its centre as I would have expected. Amberley grinned at me.

'You think so?' she asked, an edge of amusement in her voice. A second later the rest of the flotilla's

firepower opened up too, dazzling my eyes as their heavy beams struck the site of the convent, evaporating buildings, and scouring the entire location down to the bedrock beneath. The remainder of the swarm began to mill around uncertainly, the directing intelligence severely disrupted by the holes being punched in it.

'Briskly prepped!' Zemelda said in awestruck tones, which I took to indicate approval. Amberley nodded, as a complete slice of the plateau sheared away and began to fall into the depths, disintegrating as it went, so that after a moment it was hard to tell which spinning fragments were boulder, and which were wildly flailing tyranids. A moment later the barrage ended, and I just caught a final glimpse of the PDF trucks slithering to a baffled halt on the new and still molten rim before Pontius turned us towards Principia Mons and they disappeared from sight beyond the frame of the viewport.

'Quite satisfactory,' Amberley agreed. 'We've got the *shadowlight* back, Killian's dead, and so is anyone else who knew about it.' She grinned happily at me. 'Apart from us, of course.'

'Of course,' I said, wishing the idea didn't leave me feeling quite so uncomfortable. Amberley smiled again, and handed me a goblet of amasec, which I downed rather more rapidly than such a fine example of the distiller's art deserved.

'It would have been nice if we'd had the chance to interrogate Metheius properly, but at least we got copies of his research data,' she added. She looked speculatively at the ominous black case, lying in the centre of the table between us. 'Now we've found a

few more artefacts on Perlia, perhaps we'll get a better idea of what this thing's supposed to do.'

'Perhaps you will,' I agreed, thinking with some relief that I'd never set eyes on the infernal thing again. (Something I was completely wrong about, of course, but at the time I was still blissfully ignorant of the galaxy-shaking events lurking in wait for us all at the turn of the millennium.)

Amberley nodded thoughtfully. 'So what are you going to do now?' she asked.

I shrugged. 'Go back to the regiment I suppose. We'll be here for a while mopping up, and wherever there are troopers there's bound to be work for a commissar.' A fresh thought suddenly occurred to me, and I sighed with irritation. 'Jurgen,' I added, 'make a note to contact the PDF on Gavarrone, and reschedule our visit of inspection.'

There was no real point to the errand now, of course, as I already knew I didn't have to worry about any further assassination attempts, and their willingness to engage the tyranids alongside the battle sisters had resolved any lingering doubts about hybrid infiltration, but cancelling it without an obvious reason would only lead to questions, something I was sure Amberley would be less than pleased about. I contemplated the mountain of paperwork that would ensue from this unexpected delay, and sighed again. A familiar odour manifested at my shoulder.

'Very good, sir,' Jurgen said, holding out the decanter. 'Would you care for another drink?'

I smiled lazily. 'You just read my mind,' I told him.

'I hope not,' Amberley said, with an uneasy glance at the *shadowlight*.

[Which isn't quite true, as anyone less likely than Jurgen to develop psychic abilities probably doesn't exist, and I was well aware of the fact at the time. Nevertheless, on that note of somewhat strained levity, this extract from the Cain Archive comes to a natural conclusion.]

ABOUT THE AUTHOR

Sandy Mitchell is a pseudonym of Alex Stewart, who has been working as a freelance writer for the last couple of decades. He has written science fiction and fantasy in both personae, as well as television scripts, magazine articles, comics, and gaming material. Apart from both miniatures and roleplaying gaming his hobbies include the martial arts of Aikido and Iaido, and pottering about on the family allotment.